BRUTAL KUNNIN

BRUTAL KUNNIN

AN EPIC WAAAGH! NOVEL

MIKE BROOKS

BLACK LIBRARY

A BLACK LIBRARY PUBLICATION

First published in 2020.
This edition published in Great Britain in 2022 by
Black Library,
Games Workshop Ltd.,
Willow Road,
Nottingham, NG7 2WS, UK.

Represented by: Games Workshop Limited – Irish branch,
Unit 3, Lower Liffey Street, Dublin 1,
D01 K199, Ireland.

10 9 8 7 6

Produced by Games Workshop in Nottingham.
Cover illustration by Grzegorz Przybyś.

See Black Library on the internet at

blacklibrary.com

Find out more about Games Workshop
and the world of Warhammer 40,000 at

games-workshop.com

Printed and bound by CPI Group (UK) Ltd, Croydon, CR0 4YY

For the LEPinoreans.

You know why.

For more than a hundred centuries the Emperor has sat immobile on the Golden Throne of Earth. He is the Master of Mankind. By the might of His inexhaustible armies a million worlds stand against the dark.

Yet, He is a rotting carcass, the Carrion Lord of the Imperium held in life by marvels from the Dark Age of Technology and the thousand souls sacrificed each day so that His may continue to burn.

To be a man in such times is to be one amongst untold billions. It is to live in the cruellest and most bloody regime imaginable. It is to suffer an eternity of carnage and slaughter. It is to have cries of anguish and sorrow drowned by the thirsting laughter of dark gods.

This is a dark and terrible era where you will find little comfort or hope. Forget the power of technology and science. Forget the promise of progress and advancement. Forget any notion of common humanity or compassion.

There is no peace amongst the stars, for in the grim darkness of the far future, there is only war.

'Sing the song of the Machine-God.
None may stay our march.

Let the merciless logic of the Machine-God invest thee.
None may stay our march.

Praise and glory be to the Machine-God.
None may stay our march.'

Translation of binharic static chorus
Litany of Praise

"Ere we go, 'Ere we go, 'Ere we go!'

Ork war song

A Temp'ry Alliance

It had been a weird trip through the warp.

Ufthak Blackhawk knew full well that there wasn't such a thing as a normal trip through the warp, because Gork and Mork had their own senses of humour and liked to mess with the boyz every now and then. He still remembered that time he'd ended up seeing out of his own kneecaps for a while. Then there were all the interesting things you might encounter on a space hulk, like those bugeye wotsits with different numbers of arms that moved like a cyboar on nitrous. That was the great thing about space hulks – never a dull moment. Even when you thought you'd killed everything on board, you'd probably still missed a bit. And even if you hadn't, odds were you'd still have some ladz with you to have a punch-up with if everything got too boring.

This journey, though, hadn't been on a space hulk; it had been on a humie vessel, one that Ufthak and his boyz had boarded and taken, and on which Da Boffin had installed and then activated a device he'd called Da Warp Dekapitator. This had caused a katastroffic warp implosion – which was apparently a good thing, although Ufthak thought that 'catastrophic' sounded like something that should be happening to someone else – and it had dragged not only the humie ship but also all the ork ships around it into the warp and along the path of its last jump, to arrive back where it had come from.

(There was also the part where most of the bodies of the dead humie crew had merged together into a reanimated mass of flesh and steel that hungered for ork blood, and also the screaming humie faces that ran around on varying numbers of insectoid legs and spat poison, but the boyz had needed something to keep their spirits up on the way.)

Now they'd reached their destination, and had emerged from the warp again with nothing more than the sudden but quickly fading sensation that Ufthak's skeleton wasn't where it was supposed to be. And what a destination it was.

'Dat planet,' Mogrot Redtoof said, looking out of a viewport, 'is made of metal.'

Ufthak nodded sagely. Back before they'd boarded the humie ship, he and Mogrot had been rivals – two warriors jockeying for position under the command of Badgit Snazzhammer. Thanks to a series of events involving a large robot, several fatalities and a head transplant courtesy of Dok Drozfang, Ufthak's undamaged head had ended up on the decapitated Snazzhammer's undamaged and significantly larger body. After a brief meeting of the minds via a headbutt, Mogrot had settled back into a role as Ufthak's right-hand ork. That didn't mean that Ufthak trusted him, of course, but at least he was fairly certain Mogrot wouldn't try to shank him unless he was already wounded.

'Looks like a humie mekboy place,' Ufthak said. 'Humie mekboy ship, coming from a humie mekboy planet. Makes sense to me.'

'Why do dey do dat, anyway?' Mogrot asked. 'Make dere planets all shiny so ya know dey've got flashy stuff ya might want, and den when ya go to get it, dey get all annoyed an' try to kill ya?'

'Dat's da problem wiv humies,' Ufthak opined knowingly. 'Dey ain't logickal.'

'Boss!'

The shout came from the other side of the bridge, where Ufthak and his ladz had taken up residence after they'd tossed out the corpses of the crew formerly stationed there. Ufthak clumped across the deck, absent-mindedly twirling the Snazzhammer as he went. It had been Badgit's weapon, a two-handed affair as tall as a humie with its legs still attached, with an electrified hammer on one side of the head and a choppa blade on the other. He was starting to get used to the feel of it now, and couldn't wait to krump a few more enemies with it.

'Wot?' he demanded, coming up alongside Deffrow. The other ork pointed with the few fingers that remained on his right hand, having blown most of them off by hitting a humie with a stikkbomb.

'Look at dat, boss! Dat ain't one of ours!'

Ufthak sucked his breath in through his teef as a jagged piece of darkness eclipsed the stars. The ships that made up the Waaagh! fleet of Da Meklord – Da Biggest Big Mek, and a warboss in his own right – were many and varied, but Ufthak was familiar with them, and Deffrow was correct: that wasn't one of theirs. Impressive though Da Meklord's flotilla was, none of them looked quite that... killy.

'Dat's *Da Blacktoof*,' Ufthak said in something close to wonder, as the shape of it became clear. It was a monstrous kill krooizer, bristling with guns and ordnance. And there, leering down at them from under the prow, was a single, huge glyph: a monstrous, one-eyed ork skull, with crossed bones behind it. 'Dat's Kaptin Badrukk's ship.'

The rest of his mob made suitably impressed noises. Badrukk was a legend across the galaxy, a freebooter of infamy and renown, and his presence here surely meant that Da Meklord's own star was in the ascendancy.

Assuming, of course, that Badrukk was here because Da Meklord had arranged for him to be. If not...

'Message from da boss!' Da Boffin shouted, bursting into the bridge in a gust of fumes. At some point in the past, Da Meklord's favourite spanner had, either due to injury or simple curiosity, replaced his legs with a gyro-stabilised monowheel, and as a result he was now both much faster than a normal boy, and spectacularly poor at navigating stairs. 'All nobs are to get over to *Mork's Hammer* right now!'

Mork's Hammer was Da Meklord's flagship, and Da Meklord only called his nobs and bosses together if he had something very important to say... or, alternatively, if he wanted to yell at them all. As a new nob, Ufthak had never attended one of these Waaagh! meets before. His chest swelled with new-found pride, and he slung the Snazzhammer over his shoulder as he turned on the spot.

'Right den!' He frowned, as a thought struck him. 'Wait a minute. Do da 'Ullbreakers go backwards?' He and his mob had arrived via boarding pods, which were still locked into the side of the humie ship after they'd broken through its ferrous hide.

Da Boffin shook his head. 'Nah. Dey got just one gear – go.'

'So how're we s'posed to get back over dere, den?' Ufthak demanded. What was the good in being a nob if you couldn't go listen to your boss telling you what he wanted you to go and stomp?

Da Boffin shrugged. 'Da humies have shuttles on dis fing. We'll nick one.'

Ufthak frowned at him suspiciously. 'You know how to fly one?'

'Can't be hard,' Da Boffin grinned. 'After all, humies can do it.'

The Waaagh! room of *Mork's Hammer* was crowded with orks mashed in shoulder to shoulder. Ufthak saw many faces he recognised and many more that he didn't, because every single ork of any authority under Da Meklord's command was here. Surly, black-clad Goffs glowered at camouflaged Blood Axes and blue-painted Deathskulls, while the stench of fuel from the Evil Sunz was almost overpowered, but instead just sickeningly offset, by the smell of squig dung that accompanied the Snakebites. However, most numerous by far were the yellow and black colours of the Bad Moons, which wasn't only Ufthak's clan, but also that of Da Meklord himself. They were smartest, the richest and the flashest clan of all, and the reason why the Tekwaaagh! had risen so quickly and so unstoppably. Sure, the Evil Sunz might drive a bit faster, and the Blood Axes might be a bit sneakier, but if you wanted the ladz with the best guns, you wanted Bad Moons.

This many orks in such close proximity was a pretty good recipe for a massive fight, especially given the egos involved. Ufthak could see the huge, horned helm and multiple back banners of Drak Bigfang, the Goff warboss; the collection of junk and scavenged armour plates under which was Gurnak

Six-Gunz, the self-proclaimed SupaLoota of the Deathskulls; and the fur-clad bulk of Da Viper, the Snakebite Overboss, whose gargantuan squiggoth was so large it allegedly had a hold all to itself in his kroozer. Any of these orks were capable of leading a Waaagh! in their own right, but no one was starting any trouble worse than jostling their neighbour a bit. No one wanted to end up like Oldfang Krumpthunda, who'd taken Da Meklord on one on one and had been… Well, no one was quite sure *what* he had been, other than it involved getting hit with Da Meklord's shokkhammer and then ending up in lots of very small pieces in very different places. Some of the boyz said they were still finding bits of him in the stew, now and then.

Horns blared, a brassy note of challenge and conquest, and everyone shut their gobs and snapped their heads around to look at the dais built at the far end. Part of the wall behind it had been turned into a massive effigy of the face of Mork – or possibly Gork, but Ufthak reckoned it was Mork – and this was now yawning wider and wider as the mighty lower jaw dropped away. Steam and smoke gushed forth, obscuring the dais but accentuating the piercing red glare of the eyes lurking near the ceiling.

Then, first as a looming shadow in the murk, and then as a mighty figure resplendent in his yellow-and-black mega armour, Da Meklord emerged from the mouth of a god.

He was a titanic figure, and that wasn't just down to the size of his armour. Ufthak's new body was large enough that he was a head taller than most of the mob under his command, but Da Meklord would have towered over him had they stood next to each other. He made ordinary orks look like grots. His mega armour made him nearly as wide as he was tall, and the bosspole rising up above his head and carrying his personal glyphs and banners added another dimension of awe to his appearance. Half of the overlarge skull that housed his enormous brain was plated in metal; in his left hand he held the shokkhammer, and his right hand disappeared somewhere into the gigantic mess of barrels, ammo feeds and coolant pipes that formed his kustom supa-shoota.

'ALRIGHT, LISSEN UP!'

The assembled nobs quietened down a bit more, each one intimidated into silence by his stentorian bellow. Ufthak stood as straight and tall as he could, to try and make sure his face was visible, even though he was standing quite far back and there were other, bigger orks with more impressive weapons and armour between him and his warboss. There was something intangible about Da Meklord that grabbed a lad by the throat, focused his attention and drove it home to him that this ork, *this* ork, was one who knew where he was going, and on whom glory and renown would be showered.

'Da humies call dis world "Hephaesto",' Da Meklord rumbled. 'Dere's a lot of 'em down dere. Da red-robe types, da ones what look like Evil Sunz, but squishier.'

A bubble of laughter ran through the assembled nobs, save for the Evil Sunz present, who were doing their best to look like they weren't glowering.

'Dey've prob'ly got a lot of interestin' tek, cos dose humies tend to,' Da Meklord continued. 'An' normally, I'd be sendin' all you down dere to get it, and kill 'em all. But dere's a little snag.'

Ufthak glanced sideways, and saw his own confusion mirrored on the other green-skinned faces around him. What could possibly be a snag to a Waaagh! as mighty as this one? Unless...

'See, some uvver gitz got 'ere first,' Da Meklord said. 'An' we could fight dem too, dat could be a good larf, but while we woz doing dat, da humies might get away, an' dat would just be a *waste*.'

Heads nodded. Humies weren't exactly a scarce resource, but you couldn't always rely on some being about when you wanted a scrap, so it made sense to use the ones that were here.

'I talked to–'

The temperature in the Waaagh! room plummeted. Ufthak could see his breath in front of his face, and faint tendrils of frost began to creep along the walls. Orks readied their weapons, unsure what was going on but ready to fight it, or, if no better options presented themselves, each other.

The air pressure increased rapidly, from unnoticeable to the point where Ufthak felt like something was pressing in on his eardrums. He shook his head and growled, trying to clear the sensation, but it persisted until–

Vorp!

A bubble of energy washed out from the other end of the dais to where Da Meklord was standing, sending the smoke of his entrance billowing, and incidentally knocking the fumes aside to give every ork in the room a clear view of...

Kaptin Badrukk.

The mightiest freebooter kaptin who'd ever lived. The hero of the War of Dakka, the Breaker of the Grand Guard, and the Plunderer of Tanhotep. He stood resplendent in his lead-lined greatcoat, his bald head crowned by his mighty bicorn, which was as tall as a well-fed grot and dripping with medals taken from the corpses of humie commanders. He was leaning casually on his longblade choppa, and had Da Rippa, a gun so radioactive its simple presence in a room practically constituted an aggressive act, tucked under his arm. He was flanked by three more Flash Gitz, each one imitating him so far as possible in their mode of dress and armament, but not coming close to rivalling his sheer ostentatiousness and utter gaudy magnificence. Lurking behind them all was an ork that had to be Badmek Mogrok, another Bad Moons big mek, who fought under Badrukk's banner and was undoubtedly the source of his teknologickal advances.

For the first time in his life, Ufthak Blackhawk laid eyes on an ork who might just be as impressive as Da Meklord.

'Ta-daaa!' Badrukk bellowed, as though he hadn't just tellyported into the middle of his rival's command structure, on his rival's warship. The sheer guts of the git was jaw-dropping.

Da Meklord turned towards Badrukk with a clank of metal and a hiss of pistons. He looked thoroughly unimpressed, but he hadn't powered up his supa-shoota or sent the triple heads of his shokkhammer whirling around each other, so violence wasn't imminent.

'Kaptin,' Da Meklord growled. 'I woz just telling da ladz about how we woz going to be havin'… a friendly kompetition.'

'Dat's right!' Badrukk beamed, showing more teef than it should have been possible to fit into one gob. 'Plenty of loot to go round down dere, I reckon. Of course, my ladz've had a bit of a head start, but dat should just help ya out! Cleared a few obstacles out da way, dat sort of fing.'

'So we're all gonna stomp da humies, an' take dere tek,' Da Meklord said. 'An' your boyz ain't gonna be shootin' mine in da back, right?'

'So long as yours don't shoot mine first,' Badrukk leered back at him. 'Dat would be a shame, when dere's so many humies to go round.'

'My forts exactly,' Da Meklord agreed. 'So we got a deal, den?'

'We got a deal,' Kaptin Badrukk said, nodding. 'Last one to da gubbinz mucks out da squiggoffs!' He clicked his fingers, and Mogrok did something. A moment later the temperature dropped again, crackling energy surrounded the freebooterz for a second, and then they were gone once more, as abruptly as they'd arrived.

Da Meklord turned towards his assembled nobs.

'Get down dere, and wotever ya do, don't let dat git's boyz get to da good stuff before ya!' His face broke into a grin every bit as toofy and menacing as the one that had graced the freebooter kaptin's. 'I fink dere's gonna be a few "accidents" before we're done 'ere, so make sure yer aiming at Badrukk's ladz whenever ya fink yer gun might go off by mistake, like when dey'z between you and da best loot. Got it?'

Ufthak joined his voice to the others in a roar of assent to assure their warboss that they had indeed got it.

'Good!' Da Meklord drew himself up to his full, magnificent height, and filled his lungs.

'Now get down dere, an' get fightin'!'

+++002+++

*…00011101011 HOSTILE by%? abb. 01100 orbit trajectory
66.88.345/99.34.236 then a_start=678ren 011011011 HOS-
TILE >40000 9r1Nt if orkoid 101 begin gggg!// 1101101110000000
110100 redo from start?…*

<Lexico arcanus?>
Zaefa Varaz acknowledged the blinking communication
icon that was flashing her identifier, with a twist to the data
code indicating that her attention was being attracted with
the desire of a response. She hastily replayed the last 23.57
seconds of noospheric communication between the members
of Hephaesto's High Council to ascertain exactly what it was
that she was required to give input on, and sighed internally.

<My apologies, tech-priest dominus,> she replied. <Clarifi-
cation: there is still no indication of planetary bombardment
from the orkoid vessels in orbit.>

<The xenos continue to demonstrate that their grasp of

warfare is primitive in the extreme,> Tech-Priest Dominus Ronrul Illutar declared. He could communicate smugness through code better than anyone else Zaefa had ever met, and was currently exercising that ability to the utmost. It was not, she had to admit, a trait she considered particularly admirable, and yet it was the one with which her mind associated him the most closely. Far more so than, say, a ferociously competent grasp of military tactics and strategy.

Hephaesto, as a forge world of the Adeptus Mechanicus, was of course military-minded to a degree. It had its own skitarii legions, its own machines of war, and enjoyed allegiance with the Knights of House Nansus. However, Hephaesto saw war as the means to an end – a way to procure raw materials or archeotech; to protect itself, its assets, or its allies; or to send its red-and-midnight warriors to reinforce its bonds with other parts of the Imperium or the Adeptus Mechanicus. The forge world's primary focus was on the rediscovery of ancient technology, on deciphering those relics, and on attempting to complete damaged or corroded plans.

Perhaps it was no surprise, then, that when war had come to Hephaesto, it was Ronrul Illutar, Prime Hermeticon of the planet's Node Primus, who had assumed the mantle of tech-priest dominus. He was, indisputably, the most senior tech-priest on the planet. He'd pierced the Veiled Region with an expeditionary fleet and returned with three different ancient STC databases, one of which had been constructed and was even now regulating the volcanic nature of the planet beneath them, converting the limitless power of the magma core into energy for the forges more efficiently than ever before. He'd negotiated peace between the Knightly Houses of Nansus and Coneale, when their conflicting honour-oaths could have torn the sector apart. When the previous Prime

Hermeticon's systems had finally failed and she'd become one with the Omnissiah, Ronrul Illutar was unanimously acclaimed as her successor.

But he had made no name for himself as a warrior, or a commander. A diplomat, perhaps. A manipulator – and here Zaefa guarded her thoughts most carefully behind firewalls of obstructive code – quite possibly. Even, perhaps, a visionary... of sorts. But for Ronrul Illutar, the actual business of war was something that happened to someone else.

<I find the lack of orbital bombardment concerning,> Zaefa said, two-thirds of a millisecond before Illutar's next utterance.

The other three members of the High Council turned their heads to look at her, their ocular implants zooming and focusing as though to get some reading on her other than that which their owners were capable of via the noosphere. Various of their aides did the same, and Zaefa forced herself not to rise to this physical expression of surprise and doubt. She had doubts herself, may the Omnissiah forgive her, and she would not regret it if she could successfully transmit them so that others might give them their full attention.

<Interrogative: why do you find this concerning?> Illutar demanded. <Such a sentiment, if honestly expressed, would suggest a desire for the xenos to prevail in this combat.>

<Clarification: I have no such wish,> Zaefa replied firmly. <I find the lack of orbital bombardment concerning because all of the data available indicates that at least some of their ships would have the capacity for such an action.>

<I fail to see why the xenos not acting on this capacity gives cause for concern,> put in Kapothenis Ull, Node Primus' forge lord. He was a hulking creature, with massively outsized shoulders lurking beneath his robes, and Zaefa

had seen him carrying items that had weighed in excess of one-quarter tonne. An entire forest of gently waving mecha-dendrites sprouted from his spinal column, topped off by a servo-arm that currently sat folded and at rest. Zaefa trusted him the most out of her colleagues on the High Council, and had considered before now whether he might not have been a better fit for the position of dominus than Illutar. Ull's primary interests were in the weapons of war that his forges created, and she knew that he would harbour a fervent desire to test them upon the enemy.

<I have assembled all available data on the orkoid threat,> Zaefa elaborated. <Although the information covers a wide variance of locations, combats and opponents, and there are some definite outliers, the overall picture is remarkably clear: an ork force, upon making contact with an inhabited world, will in ninety-seven point three two per cent of cases proceed to cause the maximum destruction that it is able to accomplish, with little apparent attention paid to the strategic relevance of its targets. That these xenos have neglected to open fire upon us from orbit suggests an agenda or strategy of which we are not aware, and have not predicted.>

<It is possible that they have forgotten how to use their own weapons,> Ull suggested, edging his code with humour denotations.

<The possibility is so low as to be negligible,> Grand Genetor Viker Yavannos declared, with her usual glacial calm. In line with her area of interest and expertise, she was less enhanced in the ways of the Omnissiah than the rest of them, although her optics were particularly fine examples of Martian DeVoss IVs. These allowed her to perceive the flow of information around her in a manner that would be impossible to a being still reliant on vitreous jelly and

corneas, but much of the rest of her body remained flesh, albeit gene-modded, and she had been known to use her vocal cords out of choice from time to time. <All the studies Magos Addenbrow and I have made of the orkoid indicate that they are able to operate virtually any ballistic or energy weaponry with what appears to be an instinctive understanding, even though their own weaponry is often unusable when in the possession of–>

<It was not a serious suggestion, magos,> Ull said, with only the faintest hint of his impatience leaking through into the noosphere. He returned his attention to Zaefa, and his presentation sobered. <Could we be seeing the results of damage inflicted by our fleet, or perhaps the result of ammunition expenditure on the behalf of the xenos?>

Illutar leaned forward, his datapresence taking on a hungry edge. <If so, it could be an opportune moment to strike back.>

Zaefa shook her head, making the physical movement to express quite how thoroughly she disagreed with the techpriest dominus' suggestion. Hephaesto's fleet had been battered by the abrupt and unexpected arrival of the orkoid horde, and forced to withdraw from the planet in order to avoid total destruction. Its voidships now sat in the asteroid belt, ostensibly to protect the mining facilities there, but in reality because that was the only option for them. They'd sparred with and destroyed a couple of smaller ork craft that had ventured towards them, but were in no position to launch – or at least, to survive launching – an all-out offensive. They only had a couple of viable uses, at this point: to coordinate with reinforcements, should any arrive; or to sacrifice themselves in a distraction gambit, if it became necessary to draw the attention of the greenskin fleet for a short while in the service of some other, greater purpose.

<There is nothing to suggest that there have been widespread malfunctions within the ork fleet's ordnance, or that they ceased fire before they intended to,> Zaefa said, running the data again, and picking out the pertinent parts as terabytes of it scrolled past in fractions of a second. <All information suggests that the orks are, against their usually displayed nature, deliberately holding their fire upon us.>

<Xenos overconfidence,> Illutar said dismissively. <We shall make them rue it, for the glory of the Omnissiah! How does the campaign progress against their landed forces?>

Zaefa interjected some urgency into her binharic cant. <Tech-priest dominus, I am not convinced that this anomalous behaviour can be reliably attributed to overconfidence. The orks are–>

<Animals, lexico arcanus,> Illutar cut in, with a snap of data that severed her communication in mid-flow. <Advanced animals, tool-using animals, but animals nonetheless. The matchless work of the biologis has determined that the orkoid xenos lacks any ability to invent or create – they merely imitate that which has already come before them, and the only possible route for their society, such as it is, is to backslide into states of increasing primitivity.>

Zaefa bowed her head slightly. To further question the tech-priest dominus would be to undermine the hierarchy of Node Primus, and indeed Hephaesto itself, just when unity of vision and purpose was of paramount importance. She had made her beliefs – or more accurately, her interpretations of the available data – known, and Illutar had decided that they were erroneous. That was his right, as tech-priest dominus.

The faintest of flickers in the green glows that denoted Forge Lord Ull's three ocular receptors suggested to Zaefa that he had glanced over at her. Such a physical action was

BRUTAL KUNNIN

unrepresented in the sea of data swimming in front of them all, and there was no change in his noospheric presence that indicated concern at Illutar's words, or support for her position. Nonetheless, she felt vaguely reassured. Illutar carried the casting vote on the High Council, but Ull's support might be critical at some point in the future.

<Repeated request: the campaign update?> Illutar said, his coding brisk, bordering on terse. Zaefa refocused herself and splayed out her fourteen fingers, the haptic implants on them manipulating the data and sending it spiralling up and outwards into full view of her colleagues.

It made for grim viewing.

Whatever other anomalous behaviour the orks were displaying, a lack of aggression wasn't one of them. They'd enacted an invasion plan typical of most armed forces in the galaxy, from the heretical reavers of the Traitor Legions and their ilk, to the ravening hordes of the tyranid menace: aim for the highest population density and cause maximum carnage. The orks had struck hard and fast, dropping wave after wave of their bestial troops onto the planet from orbit, accompanied by their many, varied, and utterly bizarre machines of war.

Hephaesto's defenders were well drilled, and had resisted the initial onslaught, but as the combat had progressed the balance had started to shift in the favour of the aggressors. Repulsor-rail links ferrying battalions of skitarii from their garrisons to the front line at Node Tertius had been disabled with explosive charges – it was hard to envisage these acts of sabotage being carried out in accordance with an orkoid strategy that understood the nature of supply and reinforcement, and they could well have simply been the work of advance parties delighting in destruction, but the impact had been devastating nonetheless. Skitarii troops could and would march tirelessly, and had begun to do just that in an attempt to fulfil their orders and join the fight, but no skitarii could march as fast as a repulsor-rail could carry them, and Node Tertius was even now being overrun as the expected reinforcements failed to arrive. Even more concerning, reports were coming in that those skitarii – three entire maniples – marching across the open salt flats of the Tiras Ocean were now being run down by ramshackle yet fast-moving ork vehicles, against which the Hephaestan troops had little defence.

Across the Continent Primus, the story was repeated. The Tyrium mines had been largely levelled by ork artillery, with the defenders forced to take shelter in the workings beneath. That was currently providing a defensible position, but not one designed to accommodate large amounts of respirating life forms for an extended period of time – and nor was it one from which there were other exits. Tech-Priest Avanis, the ranking magos present, also reported that the entrance blast doors were coming under sustained attack, and could be breached in as few as three point five two hours.

Node Quintus was surrounded and cut off. Cybersmith Za'Kul had indicated their willingness to blow the volcanic plugs and bury the ork horde with them under a flood of lava, but Zaefa had surreptitiously requested them to wait for further confirmation before taking such drastic action. Node Quintus held several important pieces of archeotech, the secrets of which had still not been unlocked, and as the planet's foremost data-smith she could not condone their loss until it became clear that all other options for their retrieval had been exhausted.

And then there was the battle around Node Primus.

<The xenos have made very few advances since our last

review of this situation,> Illutar declared with satisfaction, zooming in on the morass of green that surrounded their position. <Our defences hold them at bay. Has the astropathic choir reported any communications regarding forces being sent to our aid?>

<They have received nothing as yet,> Zaefa replied, examining the data again. She lacked the tech-priest dominus' confidence. It was true that the lines indicating the ork positions had barely advanced since their last check, and the red-and-midnight icons indicating the defending forces reflected only minimal losses, but the greenskin horde was growing in number. To Zaefa's perception, the orks were massing in preparation for an assault far greater than that which the node had, so far, been able to stave off.

<It appears the xenos are bringing more forces to bear on our position,> Ull commented. His statement lacked emphasis; instead his code was delivered with carefully judged neutrality that avoided any hint of criticism of Illutar's words. It was merely a description of the facts as he saw them, for those who received it to interpret as they wished.

<They will be thrown back or destroyed in their droves,> Illutar said. <I personally supervised the defence plans. We have trapped causeways and kill-zones–>

<Which the orks are ignoring,> Zaefa said, her agitation causing her to interrupt the tech-priest dominus. She gestured, highlighting concentrations of the greenskins' warriors. <They are not preparing for pushes into the routes we've left for them, where our elites lie in wait and where the traps have been set – they are not taking the bait! Instead they mass opposite where we feign strength, or hold high ground.>

<They seek to make us show our hand,> Illutar scoffed dismissively.

<Or they have somehow perceived it already,> Zaefa argued. <Or perhaps they have no need to – we know the orks are a warlike race. Perhaps they will deliberately attack what they see as our strongpoints, simply in order to experience violence?>

<Either interpretation could be the correct one,> Ull broke in, before Illutar could reply. <Perhaps I can offer an alternative to waiting to see which is?>

Zaefa looked at him quizzically. Yavannos and Illutar did the same.

<A fierce, pre-emptive strike into the heart of their forces,> Ull suggested, highlighting the thickest mass of orkoid green. <A blow to break the back of the monster, leaving it easy pickings for our troops.>

<The Legio is not to be deployed at this stage,> Illutar stated flatly. <We must be completely certain of what the enemy possesses before we commit the Titans to the field.>

Zaefa did her best to mask her annoyance. Illutar was confident enough in telling her that the orks posed no meaningful threat, but urged caution when confronted with Ull's suggestions? Thankfully the tech-priest dominus' attention was focused on Ull, and so he appeared to miss any alteration in her noospheric presence.

<I do not speak of the Titans,> Ull replied calmly.

<Then what is it of which you speak?> Yavannos asked. <To gamble our other elite units on such a push could leave us relatively defenceless, unless it was anything less than an overwhelming success.>

<You are aware of the broad scope of my work, but not the specifics of my greatest project,> Ull informed them all, a hint of bombastic grandiosity creeping into his code. <War remains the purest expression of our devotion to the Omnissiah. I have in my possession a prototype – something that

will, once activated with your blessings, turn the tide of this conflict comprehensively in our favour. When the success of my innovation becomes known–>

<'Prototype'? 'Innovation'?> Illutar cut him off, his code dripping with scorn. <To stray too far from the sacred texts of the Omnissiah is to blaspheme, as well you know! To what template does this construct conform?>

Ull responded with schematics, loosing them into the noosphere that hung between them all, but Zaefa could tell immediately that they were not the full picture. There were recognisable components, certainly – Imperial Standard hydraulics XXVI here, an Armiger autocannon there, a Hephaesto-pattern ventilation unit – but there was nothing to suggest how they would come together to make a construct capable of what Ull was claiming. In fact, Zaefa got the distinct impression that there was a lot missing from the information they'd been given.

It seemed that Illutar agreed. The tech-priest dominus placed all four of his fists on the table, and somehow managed to indicate through the visible waveforms of his optics that he was glowering at the forge lord.

<This is not a schema! This is disorder!> Illutar barked. <I would expect more coherence from the lowliest adept!>

The background noospheric chatter of the various aides and adepts stationed behind each of the high councillors abruptly quietened in the wake of such a serious rebuke. Zaefa would have held her breath, had her oxygen intake not been mechanically regulated to maximum efficiency for the past thirty-seven Terran years.

<I am working from ancient designs that have only recently come into my possession. If you were to see the completed creation at my forge…> Ull began, his code surprisingly calm in

the face of Illutar's scorn. It was an astonishingly open gesture, to invite his peers into the very heart of his domain. Zaefa gave as much credence as any of her colleagues to the importance of information and the necessity of it being shared for the greater good of the Omnissiah, but there were still *some* limits. Even Ronrul Illutar would not enter her forge without her express invitation, and there were definitely some... items... that she would conceal before she allowed such a thing to take place.

<This appears to require an inordinately large flow of energy,> Yavannos stated, examining the projections in detail.

<An initial output only,> Ull said, pouncing on the apparent interest. <Once activated, the war machine–>

<It will not be activated,> Illutar said decisively. <This council would need to see far more comprehensive plans before we could begin to consider giving authorisation to such an endeavour. We must first deal with the xenos threat. Accordingly, I–>

Zaefa's heart rate rose as a warning chime rang, and her body responded by distributing low amounts of threat-alert stimms to heighten her perception and reaction time. She collapsed the tactical display they'd been perusing, and pushed aside Ull's half-formed plans, then brought up the orbital readouts.

Zaefa Varaz might not have been fully human any longer, not as most of the Imperium might have reckoned it, but she was still human enough for her body to produce an involuntary fear response. It did so now, as a succession of new, ugly, jagged contacts flared into existence on Hephaesto's sensors.

<Interrogative: what is occurring?> Illutar demanded. He could have interpreted the data himself, but even Illutar knew that Zaefa's analysis would be just that little bit sharper. There was a reason she was lexico arcanus, after all.

<Further ork ships have arrived in orbit,> Zaefa replied. <They…> She paused, focused on a different icon, double-checked its readout to make sure that she had identified it correctly. <They are accompanied by the *Resolute Spirit*.>

<That is impossible,> Yavannos said, shaken so much by the news that she uttered a provable falsehood. And it should have been impossible, and yet there the ship was: the *Resolute Spirit*, which had been commanded to flee the war in orbit as soon as it had begun, to get clear of the ork blockade and seek assistance. The orks had somehow dragged it back to Hephaesto with them, in defiance of all known principles of warp navigation, let alone the haphazard method of it that the orks were understood to use.

<Assessment?> Illutar snapped at Zaefa.

<There are many variables,> Zaefa said uneasily, mercilessly interrogating the data she had for whatever she could glean from it. Ship dimensions, likely displacement, likely armaments and capacities… but whatever variables she ran, the numbers were never good. It was just a case of exactly how bad.

<Your estimate, lexico arcanus?> Illutar said coldly, as though this were somehow her fault.

She looked up at him, and fixed her optical implants on his.

<All available data suggests that there is an eighty-four point five six per cent probability that the forces available to the orks… have just doubled.>

You Call Dat a Landin'?

The landa screamed down through the clouds, rocking in the air from the shock waves of explosions as the humies' gun batteries spat flak up at them. Ufthak peered out of a viewport and, for the first time, got a proper close-up look at the world they were going to conquer.

There was, as Mogrot had pointed out from orbit, a whole lot of metal down there – most of what Ufthak could see seemed to be glinting here and there as the system's star peeked intermittently through the patchy cloud cover. A web of roads criss-crossed the red-brown rock, linking up huge clusters of buildings that looked pretty much the same as a lot of other humie buildings Ufthak had seen – and often blown up or otherwise contributed to the destruction of – in his time around the galaxy. Humies were so *unoriginal*: they didn't have any of the pizzazz or flair of a mekboy, and you could put most things they built next to something else they'd made and you wouldn't be able to tell the difference.

It wasn't like that with orks. Ufthak would be able to pick his shoota out of a pile of others – at least, unless there was another one there he liked the look of better, and he reckoned he could thump the former owner around the head to make him let go of it.

Uniform though the humies tended to be, not everything down there was the same. The landscape, for one thing: in the distance rose a smoking peak, a cone of rock hinting at volcanic forces in play beneath. Around that, up to about two-thirds of the way up its sides, were clustered what looked to be bigger and flashier humie buildings, the sort of place you might find their bosses.

'Why ain't we landin' dere?' Ufthak bellowed over the noise of the landa's thrust engine, and pointed at the volcano. 'Dat's where da good stuff'll be!'

'Dere's a force field!' Da Boffin replied, rocking back and forth on his wheel and maintaining his balance with little apparent difficulty. 'All over it! A few landas tried to put down on it, but dey just broke into bitz, and den da bitz caught fire. We gotta land further out, den get dere on foot!'

Ufthak shook his head in despair. 'If Mork wanted us to get places usin' our feet, he'd have made us Goffs! Dey're da ones who like dere boots so zoggin' mu–'

The landa's right wing exploded.

The force of the impact knocked everyone staggering – not just Ufthak's mob, but the half a dozen or so other mobs packed in with them. Even the warbikes that were revving their engines impatiently at the front of the craft began to tip over, amidst angry shouts from their riders.

'Everyone grab on ta somefing!' Ufthak bellowed, scrambling back up to his feet and wrapping his fist round a nearby support strut. 'Dis is gonna get bumpy!'

His ladz did their best to imitate him, but the deck was steadily tilting beneath their feet as the landa began to dip on one side. Then, as the unevenness of its drag in the air began to affect its progress, it started to spin.

'Oh, zoggin' hell,' Ufthak muttered, as the sky outside the viewports began to whirl. This was no way to get to a fight! He'd happily charge down the landa's front ramp and take a shot to the face if that was what Gork and Mork had in store for him, because you couldn't ask for a better fate than death in battle – except killing the other git in battle – but getting squished up inside an out-of-control landa was just naff. How could his soul go back to Gork and Mork and look 'em in the eye with that as the reason why he'd ended up in front of them again? That was no end for an ork.

A grot tumbled past his boot and ended up spreadeagled against the wall, upside down and shrieking in terror. Ufthak recognised the sawbonez patches on its overalls and looked up to see Dok Drozfang grabbing his disorderlies and allowing them to cling to various parts of his body, which the grots clearly took some comfort from. Ufthak sniggered: all it meant was that if the Dok got thrown about too much by the landing, he'd have something squishy between him and the wall, or floor, or ceiling.

Something large and dark flashed by out of the viewport. Ufthak looked around, fighting to keep his position against the centrifugal force threatening to rip him loose from his handhold. As the landa spun around once more, he caught sight of it better: huge, dirty-looking mounds of spoil looming up, getting closer and closer. There were specks of red on it, like humie blood on dark soil, and Ufthak grinned even as he swatted aside a staggering boy unable to keep his balance. He'd fought and killed the red-robe fighters on the ship the Tekwaaagh! had hijacked to come here. They hadn't been very good, but they hadn't run away as soon as the boyz had appeared, which was something. Maybe he'd actually get a decent fight out of them when they were on their own ground.

'Brace yerselves!' he roared. 'We'z about ta–'

WHUMP!

The landa hit hard enough to knock practically everyone off their feet, and jolted every toof in Ufthak's head. They'd come down with a decent bit of forward momentum, so it hadn't been a vertical drop; instead the landa was thrown into an extended skid, still spinning slowly as it ground along with a shriek of tortured metal, jolting every now and then when it hit a particularly large rock. Ufthak gritted his teef and held on. He'd experienced worse suspension on some of the trukks he'd ridden in, to be fair.

'On yer feet!' he bellowed, hauling the nearest ork upright. 'I want all of ya out dat door da moment dis fing stops, got it?'

'*Yes, boss!*' his mob chorused, and Ufthak grinned again. It was good to see that they'd taken his new authority to heart. Ufthak definitely owed Drozfang a few fungus beers for his quick thinking with that head transplant.

There was one final, terminal jolt, and the landa came to a halt. The huge loading door at the front of the craft blew outwards with a flash and bang of charges – no self-respecting ork wanted to wait for hydraulics when an explosion could get it open quicker – and the warbikes roared out in a cloud of stinking black fumes, the whoops of their riders carrying back obnoxiously to those still in the landa's hold.

'C'mon, ladz!' Ufthak yelled. 'Last one out's a grot!'

'*WAAAGH!*'

The boyz surged into motion, and Ufthak felt himself caught up in the fierce thrill of it all once more. He never got tired of the feeling of charging into combat, choppa in one hand and slugga in the other. The only difference was that now his strides were longer, his body was stronger, and instead of slugga and choppa he had a shoota worthy of a nob in his right hand, with two barrels and a skorcha underneath it, and the mighty Snazzhammer in his left.

He had his boots on a planet again, boyz around him, weapons in hand, and enemies in front of him. Life was good.

They burst out into the bright light of a Hephaesto day, and onto the dark, crusted mass of the spoil heaps Ufthak had seen from inside the landa. His nose picked up the sharp, mineral smell of them, even above the petrochemical fug in the air that spoke of the humies' industry, and their dark mass crunched under his boots.

The spoil heaps stretched away on each side of him for as far as he could easily see, and reared up above to at least twice the height of a stompa, retreating in steep slopes and rough plateaus away to the summit. There were already ladz plugging their way up them: the flashily dressed, multicoloured boyz of Badrukk's freebooter warband, who'd already been on the ground when the landa had arrived – squashing a couple of the stragglers, by the looks of the mangled arm Ufthak could see poking out from under it. They didn't seem to be making good progress though, partially due to the shifting, unsteady ground beneath them, and partly because of the resistance.

Blue-white blasts rained down from higher up on the spoil heaps, delivered by humie figures clad in red robes set off with midnight-blue trim. Ufthak knew those guns had a kick to them, but the humies carrying them didn't like it when you got up close and personal. The trick was going to be managing that, on terrain like this.

The warbikes accelerated uphill… or at least, tried to. They'd have made it, had the ground been firmer, but their spiked tyres and trak-links just kicked up huge amounts of loose spoil that doused Ufthak and his ladz, while making no real headway at all.

'Get out da way, ya bloody idjits!' Ufthak bawled at them, spitting to clear his mouth out. The bikers couldn't have heard him, but they seemed to get the idea, as after a few more seconds of frustrating revving they slewed off towards the west, bouncing and roaring down the dirty dunes towards more solid ground, in search of a way around.

And still the fire came down from above, accompanied by a slack-jawed freebooter body as one took a bolt right between the eyes. Ufthak eyed the route the warbikes had taken, wondering if that was a better option, but he quickly decided against it. There was no telling how long it would take to find a decent fight by going that way; and besides, no humie took potshots at Ufthak Blackhawk and got away with it.

'Into 'em, ladz!' he roared, and surged up towards the humies. His decisiveness was infectious, and the other mobs, who'd been milling around uncertainly as they tried to work out how to put one boot in front of the other without falling on their faces, swung into line behind him. Ufthak heard a few angry shouts at first from the other nobs at the fact their ladz were following him instead of them, but their voices quickly joined with the others as they got caught up in the excitement as well.

By Mork, but the footing was bad! Ufthak could see why the red-robes had picked this spot to defend: humies were cowards at heart, and never really wanted to get into a fist fight. He raised his shoota and pulled the trigger as he powered on upwards, and was delighted to see one of the figures crouching on the skyline dissolve into red mist as the shells struck home. That'd teach 'em!

The other humies dropped too, and for a moment Ufthak thought they'd all lost the plot, like the bugeyes with the claws did when you killed one of their finkin' beasts, but then the gunfire started up again and he realised they'd simply lain down to make themselves more difficult to shoot at.

One of the freebooterz ahead of him got hit by a shot that detonated one of the stikkbombs dangling from his belt, and the resulting explosion knocked him and his mate next to him flying in opposite directions. That gave Ufthak an idea. The slugga shots of the boyz around him were just kicking up dirt where the humies were sheltering behind the spoil like bloody cowards, so what they needed was something that could *curve*…

'Stikkbombs!' he shouted, and tucked his shoota under his left arm for long enough to pull one off his belt, rip the pin out with his teef, and hurl it. It soared up, tumbling end over end, then dropped down almost delicately behind a bank of spoil. A moment later there was an eruption of flame and shrapnel, and the sound of metallic-tinged screaming.

Ufthak grinned. That was the great thing about stikkbombs. They could kill things you couldn't even see!

The ladz with him followed his lead, and the air was abruptly full of high explosives powered by good old ork muscle. Ufthak would be the first to admit that ork accuracy wasn't exactly brilliant, as a rule, but that was because aiming was for cowards. Any true ork just let rip, and let Gork and Mork decide what went where and who died as a result. It was even better with stikkbombs though, because you just lobbed them sort of near where the gitz were, and then laughed when their arms and legs came off at funny angles. A couple of well-placed stikkbombs could really liven up a fight.

A ragged line of explosions ripped across the side of the spoil mound, and sent a veritable shower of red-robed bodies pinwheeling through the air, like they were a bunch of grots who'd fallen into a bull squig pen. Ufthak got hit in the head by a surprisingly hard leg, and glowered down at it as it landed, glinting, in the dirt by his boots. Metal! You go to all the trouble of blowing up some humies, and then you couldn't even eat the bits they left behind!

The remaining red-robes were trying to fall back, but Ufthak wasn't having any of it. He'd come down to this planet to get a fight, and by Gork's Green Grin, that was what he was going to get! He broke into a full-on charge, the sort of pace even an ork's legs couldn't keep up for very long, but in pursuit of a broken, confused enemy attempting to retreat over treacherous terrain, it was enough. He crested a rise, hurdled a dismembered corpse, and fell on the first of them.

The humie turned and raised its rifle two-handed in an attempt to protect itself, but the Snazzhammer smashed the weapon apart and carried on to drive straight into the hooded head, flattening it atop the humie's shoulders and driving it to its knees before it fell bonelessly backwards. Ufthak shot up the next one, riddling its body with shells, then casually backhanded a third aside with the Snazzhammer and sent it sailing off to his left with a *thwump* of electricity. One, with a face more machine than flesh, lunged at him with a blade affixed to the end of its rifle. The point lodged in Ufthak's shoulder, but he headbutted the humie so hard he felt its metal face cave in.

Then the ladz behind him arrived, and flowed over the rest of the humies like green lava devouring a few scraps of red-leaved forest.

+++004+++

<For Hephaesto! For the glory of the Omnissiah!>

Secutor Haphax Mitranda, field commander of the Node Primus defenders, fired their volkite charger as the chanted devotional rang through the air, and a piercing energy blast lashed out to catch an onrushing greenskin square in the chest. The shot stripped away its armour and flesh, flash-boiled its dark blood, and the resulting fireball caught two more of its kind and set them aflame. However, the xenos filth continued to storm forwards uttering guttural war cries, even while beating themselves in an attempt to put the flames out. They were stubborn, aggressive beasts, Mitranda would give them that.

<Bring them down!> they commanded forcefully, firing again. The galvanic rifles of the skitarii rangers of the Fifth Maniple barked and cracked all around them, and orks fell, but not enough. The green tide surged on towards the ramparts of the Second Wall, ignoring the South-South-Eastern Gate, zero point seven seven miles to the south-west. The

gate had been thoroughly mined, of course, with four units of Kataphron Destroyers deployed to annihilate attackers that might make it through once the explosives had been detonated, but the orks hadn't made even a cursory attack on it to test its defences. Instead they'd massed here, and struck here: a segment of the wall that was loosely garrisoned, on the basis that the troops were needed elsewhere to reinforce the weak points.

The Second Wall was entirely in line with Adeptus Mechanicus defensive engineering protocols, and had been appropriately maintained, but it was occurring to Haphax Mitranda that with the application of enough orks, pretty much anywhere had the potential to be a weak point.

<Maintain fire discipline!> they barked, not that the skitarii needed the encouragement. They aimed, fired, re-aimed, fired again, in a regular rhythm that would have surely pleased the Omnissiah on any other day. Today, however, the nature and number of their enemy meant the weapons fire was having a suboptimal impact on the conflict. Even a direct hit only rendered an ork immobile or otherwise ineffective forty-eight point two five per cent of the time, and there were many more of the enemy than could be brought down before they reached the base of the wall. The Adeptus Mechanicus usually scorned such imprecise tools of war as grenades, but Mitranda would have currently welcomed the indiscriminate nature of their destructive power.

Mitranda parsed the data streams, assessing the tactical situation even as they blasted another ork into green paste. This section of the Second Wall protected the thermic ventors, a vital part of the regulation processes for the sector's magma turbines. If they were damaged, the power grid of Node Primus could be compromised. There was certainly little chance that the xenos would fail to damage them, judging by the wanton destruction they'd wreaked so far having breached the First Wall.

<Cybernetica Datasmith Gades,> Mitranda broadcast into the combat noosphere. <Detach the Third Maniple of the Blessed Kastelans and commence at full speed to my position, prepare Conqueror Protocol.>

<*Acknowledged, secutor,*> the datasmith responded. <*For the glory of the Omnissiah.*>

<*Datasmith Gades, belay that order.*>

Secutor Mitranda recognised the datapresence of the tech-priest dominus, and apprehension gripped them. The orks had reached the bottom of the wall, and although its sheer surface was foiling their attempts to climb it, Mitranda didn't like the look of some of the more powerful weapons they were bringing up.

<Tech-priest dominus, request: re-evaluate your interjection. Battle data demonstrates that the Third Maniple's position is currently not engaged in combat, whereas the units at this sector of the wall are under attack by greatly superior numbers of xenos warriors.>

There was a momentary pause, in which time one of the skitarii next to Mitranda pitched backwards off the ramparts with a crackling scream as a shot more accurate than the orkoid norm caught them in the chest. Their fellow squad members closed ranks and continued firing, but as more orks poured forwards the greater concentration of fire was surely going to start to tell, no matter how haphazard the greenskins' aim was.

<*Kastelan Third Maniple is required to hold at the present position to counter the impending xenos offensive.*>

Mitranda scanned the data streams again, wondering what

they'd missed, but could make out nothing. <Interrogative: to what impending offensive do you refer?>

<Clarification: logic demonstrates that the invaders will shortly launch a major offensive on a perceived defensive weakness and fall into our trap, whereupon they shall be crushed.>

Mitranda spat a binharic swear word that drew a startled glance from the skitarii trooper next to them, but which they carefully filtered out of their noospheric communication. <Clarification: the current position of Kastelan Third Maniple may become vulnerable at a future point if they are not present. However, my current position is under a sustained offensive and is vulnerable at the present time. I officially request a review of this stratagem, and for the Kastelan Third Maniple to be redeployed to this location.>

<Clarification: skitarii Second Cohort, Fifth Maniple will hold position and repel the attackers. The successful defence of Node Primus is of the utmost importance. Glory to the Omnissiah!>

<Glory to the Omnissiah,> Mitranda repeated. <However, without reinforcement, this position will fall.>

<Further clarification: please refer to my most recent noospheric upload. Glory to the Omnissiah!>

<Glory to the Omnissiah,> Mitranda repeated once more, since it wasn't the Omnissiah's fault that the defence of Hephaesto had fallen to Ronrul Illutar. It was perplexing in the extreme that the tech-priest dominus was so insistent that the orks would follow certain patterns of behaviour, when those patterns had not been played out thus far. At what point, Mitranda wondered, would the evidence collected from the field begin to carry weight enough to command a change in strategies?

The omnispex on their belt beeped a warning, and their optics were drawn to the threat the alert matrix had pinpointed:

one specific ork in the crowd of green-skinned bodies below. The creature raised a crude ballistic weapon, little more than a bracing rod to direct what looked like a self-propelled explosive missile, but Mitranda had faced the greenskins before in the course of their service to Hephaesto's forces, and was well aware that the primitive nature of the orkoid weapons belied their effectiveness. The odds of the alien picking out any of the defenders between the fortification's crenellations was minuscule, but that didn't look to be its target.

<Evade!> Mitranda barked, as the rocket launched and the ork staggered backwards from the force of it. The projectile streaked towards the wall as the skitarii threw themselves away from the point of impact, and detonated with enough force to crack and shatter even the hardened ferrocrete of its structure. Two more skitarii were knocked flying by the force of the explosion, and for a moment Mitranda thought that was the worst of it.

Then, with a crunching roar that was rivalled by the bellows of triumph from greenskin throats, a ten-foot wide, six-and-a-half-foot deep section of wall and parapet crumbled outwards and downwards.

<Up! Up!> Mitranda urged their troops, but the orks weren't waiting for them to ready themselves. Shadows fell across the ruined section of the breach a moment before the first greenskin clambered into view, roaring with bloodlust as it cast around for an enemy. Mitranda's volkite charger felled it, and the one that followed, and galvanic rifles did for the two after that, but still the xenos kept coming, clawing and hacking their way over and through the bodies of their fallen in their eagerness to get to grips with the defenders. The orks still had to climb to reach the breach, but they were now climbing a ramp made of rubble and their own

dead, and it was becoming easier and easier for them to make the assault.

Mitranda switched the volkite charger to their third arm and took up their Omnissian axe in their two primary limbs, then stepped forward to face the oncoming foe. Their first swing separated an ork's head from its shoulders; the second took off an arm wielding a crude, bladed weapon nearly the width of Mitranda's body; the third bit deep into the surprised ork's body and sent it stumbling backwards, mortally wounded, into those following, but it was merely ripped apart by its fellows in their bid to break through.

Mitranda hastily scanned the data streams once more, assessing the situation as best they could. Their remaining skitarii were still firing down into the oncoming horde while Mitranda held the breach, but this segment of the wall was lost: was it best to resist here for as long as possible, to delay the enemy, or to attempt a fighting withdrawal?

Or should the skitarii withdraw, while Mitranda held the breach alone?

Heroism was not the way of the Adeptus Mechanicus. Not for them the glory-seeking exploits of the Adeptus Astartes, the martyrdom of the Adepta Sororitas, or the emotionally charged illogicism of the Astra Militarum; nor even the honour-bound charges of the Knightly Houses. What other branches of the Imperium might call heroism, the Adeptus Mechanicus simply recognised as an individual or individuals fulfilling a role to achieve a specific goal or improve the overall fighting efficiency of the force to which they were attached. In some cases, the supposedly heroic act was notable simply because the individual's peers had failed to fulfil those duties, which would have been equally expected of them.

Mitranda's choice was not based on a desire to achieve a

heroic end, versus a desire to continue existing. It simply came down to statistics: which course of action would serve the forge world better? Would a level of resistance here, where a single warrior might delay the foe for a short time nearly as effectively as a far larger force might, whilst also allowing an ordered retreat for the majority of the defenders, be more efficient? What impact did the identity of the lone, doomed defender as the field commander of the defence have? Especially in light of the tech-priest dominus monitoring the combat noosphere and overruling their orders?

They swung their Omnissian axe and cleaved another ork nearly in two, revealing yet another greenskin. This one bore a large-calibre weapon similar in size and composition to a heavy stubber, and from which trailed a belt of ammunition. Mitranda raised their axe–

'WAAAGH!'

–and the ork pulled the trigger a split second before the axe could bite into its flesh, spewing out a volley of shots from the weapon's cordite-blackened muzzle. Not even an ork could miss at this point-blank range, and the projectiles thundered into Mitranda's chest. Their artificer-crafted breastplate held under the barrage, and ricochets caromed off into the parapet, but the sheer kinetic force drove them backwards despite that. Internal gyroscopes attempted to counterbalance, to find a way to hold position, but it was to no avail. Mitranda's flailing left foot found nothing beneath it except empty air, and they fell backwards with a binharic curse.

The thirteen-foot drop allowed them to twist in mid-air, bringing their legs under them and landing in a crouch that put only minimal stress onto their bionics. Mitranda's aural sensors detected the crack of galvanic rifle fire redirecting, and a moment later the ork whose firepower had sent them over the edge crashed down next to them, dead from at least three visible electrified traumas. However, the position was clearly untenable.

<Fall back,> Mitranda instructed, retreating to get a line of sight to the ramparts. <Fall back and–>

Something huge, metallic and ugly roared overhead, several hundred feet up but descending rapidly. Mitranda turned their head to follow it, but its velocity was too much even for their reactions, and it was gone behind the towering chimneys of the thermic ventors before they could properly assess its nature.

<Interrogative: what just overflew my position?> they asked.

<*An ork landing craft, secutor,*> came the dead-voiced reply from one of the auspex servitors.

<Request: update on the status of the Icarus arrays at gun point 43H,> Mitranda demanded, firing their volkite charger again, but the ork they were targeting lunged sideways at a skitarii at the last moment, and the shot crackled harmlessly against the parapet.

<*Gun crews were engaged in melee within the last thirty seconds,*> the servitor responded. <*Position will be overrun within one minute, twelve seconds.*>

That was it. With the Icarus arrays out, the orks could begin landing their troop carrier-equivalents behind the Second Wall – as, indeed, they had clearly started doing. Mitranda didn't suspect there'd been any tactical nuance employed, it was simply that the orks had been throwing landing craft down at them and they were no longer being blown out of the sky. Intentional or not, it didn't matter. The result was the same.

All of Ronrul Illutar's carefully laid traps had been for

nothing. The orks had changed the nature of the engagement by swarming their defences with brute force and weight of numbers, and could now bypass the mined gateways, Kataphron kill points and everything else the tech-priest dominus had meticulously plotted out.

<Full retreat,> Mitranda ordered the skitarii of the Fifth Maniple, even as more orks burst through the breach, and some actually began appearing over the top of the crenellations, having managed to scale it while the defenders' attention had been drawn elsewhere. The noosphere was swelling with calls for aid, now: the orks' offensive had swept down the battle lines, rippling away from this point like waves in a vat of sacred oil.

Mitranda waited for three seconds, but the tech-priest dominus made no communication.

<...hostiles increasing, request immediate...>

<...position overrun, falling back...>

<...enemy reinforcements are–>

<All units, fall back to defence emplacements Delta,> Mitranda broadcast, as more and more reports flooded in. It wasn't just their section of the wall that had been breached; the greenskins' overwhelming ferocity had punctured the defensive line in multiple locations. Four of their skitarii took the instruction literally and jumped off the ramparts to flee the orks; the others were now being pulled down by the barbarous brutes, their superior firepower and accuracy no match for the xenos' sheer power and ferocity once within arm's reach. <K-164B Ruststalkers, reinforce Dyrg-VI's Rangers, delay the enemy advance as long as you can. Datasmith Gades, pull back zero point three miles, then engage Conqueror Protocol for ninety seconds, repeat. Noble Knights of House Nansus, secure Storage Sector 32P.>

Another skitarii was brought down by massed ork fire as they fled, but the other three converged on Mitranda's position and they began to run together, falling back towards the next defensive positions faster than the greenskin brutes could pursue.

Mitranda cast a glance up at the towering thermic ventors, and an idea struck them as they ran. It was decidedly non-standard – some might say blasphemous – but against the magnitude of the threat they faced, perhaps a non-standard approach was called for.

<Isolate power grid in Sector 47B1,> they broadcast. <Shut down thermic ventors in this area.>

It wasn't a servitor's voice that answered them this time, but that of an adept. <*Request: please clarify your last order, secutor. If enacted as requested, that will cause a catastrophic magma vent.*>

<Clarification:> Mitranda told them firmly, jinking around an area of exposed pipework as ork gunfire peppered the wall beside them. <I know.>

Red Wunz Go Faster

The first thing Ufthak knew about the new humies was when orkish yells of pain split the air.

They'd come along the ridge of the spoil mounds, only five of them, moving startlingly fast on slender bionik legs. By the time Ufthak realised they were there, they were already into the ladz on his right, laying about themselves with long, thin blades – one in each metallic hand. In fact they looked more like tinboyz than humies, with seemingly only their torsos still made of flesh. As the mob on that flank closed in around them like a gulpa squig engulfing its next meal, Ufthak wondered briefly what it was about this world that made so many of the humies here lose all their limbs. Unless they were all like Da Boffin, and chopped bits of themselves off because they thought the bioniks were better?

Mekboyz. Human or ork, they were all downright odd, and that was an end to it.

Ufthak blinked as an ork head sailed over his own, its

features bearing an expression of definite and now quite permanent surprise. A few other green-skinned limbs were flying here and there as well, and since he hadn't heard any stikk-bombs going off, it seemed reasonable to assume that the humies were actually giving a good account of themselves. There'd only been five of them! Ufthak was quite good at counting, and although he got a bit lost above five, he was rock solid up to that point.

A nasty humming sound was reaching his ears now. It seemed to seesaw back and forth across frequencies, and did strange things as it went. Ufthak could almost feel his armour vibrating, which was an even stranger sensation than that time he'd been next to a weirdboy when they'd started turning the air purple.

Well, if whoever's ladz it was on that side couldn't keep their arms and heads attached when they were fighting, he supposed he'd have to sort this mess out himself.

Uttering wordless bellows of aggression, Ufthak barged his way through the press of bodies that had closed in around the new hostiles. He saw the back of one of the other nobs – Snagit Uzdek, he thought – and was about to club him aside when twin blades swept across themselves, neatly carving poor old Snagit into three large chunks of ork that flopped obscenely to the ground and began coating the spoil beneath them with dark ichor. Ufthak levelled his kustom shoota at the humie revealed by his fellow nob's death – a gleaming, almost insec-toid creature crouched on double-bent legs, its clothes blood red with highlights of dark blue – and fired the skorcha.

Dirty-yellow flame roared out and engulfed the humie, as well as a couple of boyz that had pressed in too enthu-siastically. Ufthak hooted with laughter. You couldn't beat a skorcha for fun.

The humie barrelled out of the fire, seemingly unbothered by the fact its robes were ablaze, and one of its twin blades sliced his shoota in half.

'Oi!' Ufthak bellowed, outraged and already swinging the Snazzhammer in a thunderous underhanded arc. 'I liked dat gun!'

The crackling weapon caught the humie, although it twisted aside at the last minute to make it only a glancing blow. Even that still threw it backwards, however, and it spun through the air twice before landing heavily on its left side with an audible clatter of bioniks. Ufthak lashed out backhanded at a second, even as it killed another lad, and the Snazzhammer's thunderous discharge knocked the humie off its feet and onto its front, whereupon the mass of boyz who up until that moment had been largely kept at bay by its whirling blades fell on it with vicious glee. Mogrot Redtoof barrelled into a third, his slugga blasting and his choppa whirling in a deadly circle, driving it back step by step with a ferocity only Mogrot could manage. The humie was parrying his blows and dodging his shots for the moment, but only just. Ufthak grinned ferociously and looked around for his next victim.

Something blurred out of his peripheral vision and sank talons of agony into his left-hand side.

They punched right through the metal he'd armoured himself with and drove into his flesh, while grating disharmonies ran through his very bones. Ufthak gasped in pain and staggered sideways, but his attacker moved with him. It was too close to strike at with the Snazzhammer, but Ufthak didn't need to be able to swing his weapon to kill something with it.

He brought the Snazzhammer up with his left hand and caught it behind the head with his right, crushing the humie into his chest and pinning it there. It growled at him in a voice more electrical than biological, and he felt its talon fingers working in his side, but although the pain was shocking, they couldn't seem to reach anything vital; he was just too big.

Ufthak bared his fangs, and tightened his grip. What he could see of the humie he was struggling with made it look like the nob of this group: its robes were more finely marked, and the bionik eyes staring hatefully up at him – insofar as metal could stare hatefully, which apparently it could do pretty zogging well – looked fancier than those of its companions. It didn't matter. He'd crush the life out of it, then stomp its carcass into the dirt.

However, the humie's breathing didn't seem to be troubled by the incredible pressure he was exerting. Did it have some sort of bionik lungs as well? Ufthak wrestled with a moment of unfamiliar doubt. He could knock it free far enough to get a good swing at it, but what if it was quicker than him? These humies knew how to fight, that was for certain; it would surely know to go for his head next time, and a few of those talon-fingers in his brain would be a whole different matter to them being lodged in his side.

The humie's left arm was moving, inching awkwardly upwards, and Ufthak caught sight of a slugga of some sort gripped in its hand. He wasn't that familiar with humie designs, but anything that had that sort of glowing blue coil housed in it was probably bad news. At the moment the barrel was pointing past his body, but if the humie could get its arm up far enough to aim it at the side of his head…

Desperate times, desperate measures. Ufthak opened his mouth as wide as he could, leaned forwards, and closed his jaws around the humie's head.

It was like chomping on a jar of buzzer squigs, the way his teef rattled as the humie screamed in alarm, but Ufthak had no intention of letting go. He bit down as hard as he could until he felt a *crunch*, then reared back with all the strength in his neck. There was a snapping noise, a gush of warm wetness that sprayed over his chest, and then the body crushed against him abruptly lapsed into stillness.

He let the humie's body drop, wincing as the claws slid back out of his flesh, then spat the head out and gave it a good old boot. It sailed away, trailing drops of blood as it did so, and landed beyond the humie whom Ufthak had knocked flying with the Snazzhammer mere moments before.

It was the only one left now; Mogrot had finally landed a blow on his opponent that had cleaved it nearly in two, and it was burbling something in static as he hacked at it, while the other two had finally been mobbed and overwhelmed by the rest of the ladz. The last humie picked itself up, its left arm hanging uselessly and the blade that had been held in that hand lying in the dirt at its feet, then turned and ran.

Ufthak heaved the Snazzhammer after it. The enormous weapon tumbled end over end through the air, crackling with energy, before colliding with the back of the fleeing humie's head and blowing the skull apart with a flash of power. The mob around him broke out into whoops of raucous congratulation and approval, but Ufthak had other things on his mind.

'Dok!' he roared, looking around. Dok Drozfang emerged from the press of bodies, moving through them with the ease of an ork whom no one wanted to annoy, just in case he ended up performing serjury on them at some point. Ufthak had had that experience, and felt he'd done pretty well out of it given that dying was the other option open to him at the time, but not everyone who went under a painboy's knife – or cleaver, or welding torch – got quite as lucky.

'Yes, boss?' Drozfang asked, as his disorderlies scampered past him.

'Glue dis,' Ufthak barked, pointing at his side. 'I ain't got time to be leakin'. Den check if any of da boyz need patchin' up, but only da wunz what're gonna be good to go right after, got it? Anyone else stays 'ere. An' if any of you gitz touches dat zoggin' hammer, I'll rip yer guts out!' he added, raising his voice for the benefit of a couple of the ladz who were already casting covetous glances at the still-crackling Snazz-hammer where it lay in a pool of humie brain matter, skull fragments and shattered metal.

'What's da plan now, boss?' Mogrot Redtoof asked, licking the humie blood off his choppa.

Ufthak turned and pointed down at a row of warehouses, glinting in the sun at the base of the other side of the huge spoil heap they'd crested.

'Dat. If dere ain't somefing worth havin' in dere, den I'm a Snakebite.'

The spoil heap beneath his steel-capped boots shuddered, and parts of it began to trickle downslope as the looser bits were shaken into the grip of gravity. Ufthak looked around, searching for whatever humie trickery had caused this, but he could see nothing out of the ordinary. It was a good view from up here, actually; he could see whole hordes of boyz pressing forwards as the humies fled in front of them, and not just boyz: there were battlewagons and trukks, a few Deff Dreads, an entire mob of the Kult of Speed racing around on his left in a flanking motion and heading for a big hole knocked in the defensive wall by a stompa, and on his right…

'Dat's Drak Bigfang's lot, innit?' Wazzock asked, pulling his goggles up to see better. He wore them just in case his burna exploded when he was using it, although Ufthak didn't really see how goggles were going to help him much if the rest of his face was gone.

'Dey can't be,' Mogrot said earnestly. 'Dey're too small!'

'Dey're just far away,' Ufthak corrected him. 'Dat's def'nitly Bigfang's lot. Big-headed git,' he added, after a moment's contemplation. In Ufthak's opinion Drak Bigfang, like most Goffs, took himself far too seriously. He owed his allegiance to Da Meklord, of course, but a lot of boyz answered direct to him, and Ufthak reckoned that Bigfang would like to challenge Da Meklord if he could only muster the guts for it. That looked like his personal gunwagon down there, rolling forward amidst a whole horde of black-clad boyz and firing its killkannon at anything it could see. One of the humie buildings caught a shell square on, and bits of it began toppling down while the tiny ork figures waved their arms delightedly, and minuscule sparks of light spoke to them firing their shootas and sluggas in celebration.

But still, Ufthak couldn't see what had caused the ground to shake like that. It couldn't just be the killkannon...

One after another, great plumes of virulent red rose out of the ground and into the air, amongst and around Drak Bigfang's boyz. They were so bright they put even the flashiest Evil Sunz warbike to shame, and seemed almost sluggish in their movement skywards, but when they came down again boyz screamed and died, and when they began spreading out over the ground the boyz broke and ran. Only a few of Bigfang's stormboyz made it out, lifted to – relative – safety by the power of their back rokkits. Ufthak grinned: he'd been a stormboy briefly when he was young, until he'd realised what an idiot the uniform made him look, and he still sometimes missed the rush of wind in his face and the dead flies on his teef.

'Red rock!' Deffrow said, a touch of awe colouring his voice as another plume erupted and then spewed down onto Big-fang's gunwagon, causing it to slew to a halt and begin to melt. 'Dat's bad luck, being dere just when dat happened.'

'Dat ain't bad luck,' Ufthak said, shaking his head. 'All da humies pulled back before dat happened. I reckon dey did it somehow.'

'You serious?' Deffrow asked incredulously. 'Dat's gotta take some doin'.'

'Humies ain't stupid,' Ufthak told him firmly. 'Dey're squishy cowards wot *look* stupid, but dey ain't stupid. Not all of 'em, anyway.'

'We can't fight red rock,' Wazzock pointed out. 'Wot're we gonna do?'

Ufthak began counting off on his fingers. 'Well, one, if it's da humies doin' it, dey can't do it if dere's no humies left to do it. Two, dey ran away before doin' it dere, so'z as long as we'z close to 'em, dey ain't gonna do it.' He paused for a second, concentrating. 'Free…? Free, we'z supposed to be gettin' on wiv nabbin' flashy stuff for da boss anyway, *so get down dat zoggin' hillside and smash dose doors in, and I mean right zoggin' now!*'

The ladz took that as answer enough, and they turned and began pounding down the spoil heap towards the ware-houses that sat awaiting them. Ufthak grinned as he strolled over to pick up the Snazzhammer.

'Now dat's wot I call "inspirashunul".'

Underbelly

Gavrak Daelin skulked.

He'd skulked since he'd first come to this miserable planet, borne ignominiously within a cargo shipment, in a container that had been separated out from its fellows and ushered away into the darkness in line with manipulated shipping manifests. It hadn't been a glorious arrival – far from it. Many of his kin would have balked at such a notion. None of the others with whom he was aligned, at least theoretically, would have even entertained it.

But that was because they put emotion before logic, and glory before responsibility. Gavrak Daelin did neither. He had a purpose, and a plan, and he had been patiently working at both.

All the same, he had to concede that the arrival of the orks had been useful, and most fortuitously timed. There was nothing like a threat to make sentient beings aware of what they had to lose, and consider exactly what they would risk in order to protect what they viewed as theirs. There was also nothing like a threat to make sentient beings within a society's structure think hard on the competence of others within it. The concealed roots of ambition drank deep of the water of fear, and patience was abandoned. A slow creep towards securing one's position was catalysed by the searing uncertainty of whether there would still be a position to claim unless action was taken to destabilise the status quo *now, now, now…* and the clawing hands of uncertainty could, in their desperation, be encouraged to grasp the tendrils of another's schemes.

Gavrak Daelin had revealed himself to his chosen quarry as soon as the ork threat had materialised. He'd taken all appropriate safety measures, of course; his minions had long since prepared the way, he'd circumvented the security systems and deleted all records of his presence up to that point, and he was ready to eliminate his quarry should they prove resistant to his message. Even so, the level of risk was not minimal. It was always possible that the data he'd been given was inaccurate. It was even possible that the data was accurate, but that the conclusions he'd drawn from it were erroneous.

Then there was the nature of the quarry itself. It was certainly not going to be amenable to being eliminated, should that prove necessary. Gavrak Daelin bore the scars of thousands of years of combat, and was one of the mightiest of his kind, but even with his minions, he was still vastly outnumbered within the hive of his enemy's strength. Weak and blind though most of the so-called priests here were, his quarry was not defenceless, and Daelin had learned long ago not to underestimate an enemy. Blind, dogmatic thinking could be predicted, but to assume that your enemy would always hold to those principles, and to stake your entire strategy and existence on it, was no less blind or dogmatic.

You could not predict everything your enemy might do, but you could at least predict that they would not always react in the way you expected them to.

In the end, his countermeasures, secondary and tertiary plans had been unnecessary, at least for the moment. His quarry was not so close-minded as to be dangerously useless, but neither were they aware enough to perceive the full scope of the threat that Daelin posed. Now each thought to use the other for their own gain, but of the two of them, only Daelin fully understood the nature of their joint endeavour.

He ran one hand over the mighty flank of his creation, and felt a smile twist his ancient lips as he stared up at its towering shape. For now, it was a mere shell of metal, albeit one that radiated glorious malice and divine bloodlust. When the time was right, however, it would stride forth and wreak havoc on all that stood before it: another of his creations given life and purpose.

But only if everything was correct.

He picked up his tools and went to work once more, muttering incantations as he tightened nuts, added new rivets and lubricated gears more thoroughly, and ensured none of the lines carved into his creation's surface were disturbed or damaged. His minions mirrored his actions, working to his directives and ensuring that their master's vision was perfectly rendered.

When the time came, the triumph here would belong not to the orks, or to the Adeptus Mechanicus and their backward ways, but to Gavrak Daelin.

+++007+++

<The xenos have breached the Second Wall,> Zaefa declared.

<Your communication is unnecessary,> Ronrul Illutar replied, his noospheric presence radiating disapproval. <The data is plain.>

And yet, Zaefa didn't think it was unnecessary. Three point seven six seconds had elapsed since the percentage possibility of the assault in its current form being repelled had reached zero, and none of the council had said anything. Yavannos was studying the entire tactical display with obvious fascination, her lenses focusing on different areas simultaneously, and the faintly audible whirr of her databank memory drives suggested that she was either recording everything, comparing it with information she already had, or both. Ull was brooding, clearly unhappy but also apparently unwilling to offer suggestions since his experimental war engine had been so roundly denied. And Illutar...

Well, he just hadn't reacted. Almost as though he were

clinging to some illogical belief that if he didn't acknowledge events, they wouldn't turn out to be real. Zaefa had stated the seemingly obvious to force the tech-priest dominus to respond, to drag them onto the next step.

I could have said 'have breached the Second Wall with contemptuous ease'. That would have been no less unnecessary, but also no less true.

<Learned colleagues,> Zaefa began, interweaving respectful algorithms through her code to ensure so far as she could that her communications weren't interpreted as sarcastic. <I believe we must consider the possibility that Node Primus' defences may be inadequate to rebuff the threat we face. I would suggest that we make immediate preparations to evacuate–>

A squeal of static cut her off: an interjection of the most peremptory nature from Ronrul Illutar.

<Evacuate?> he thundered. <You would have us abandon the forges, the manufactoria, the Shrine of the Omnissiah? You would see us leave our learning, and that of our forefathers, to these beasts?>

<No, I would not!> Zaefa snapped back at him. <These would be terrible losses, it is true, but should we be able to withdraw in an efficient manner and establish a new forge world elsewhere, we can rebuild them. Our learning, however, *must* be saved! Without it, we are lost. That is why I am proposing that we commence extraction of all research onto physical data storage modules, and they, along with all unique, prototype or otherwise non-standard schema, and all archeotech and relics, are prepared for planetary evacuation.>

<Evacuation to where?> Ull demanded. <The xenos have achieved orbital superiority – our remaining ships would

not be able to approach in order for any evacuation shuttles to dock.>

<The orkoid mindset lacks subtlety, or an appreciation for fine detail,> Yavannos put in. <The lexico arcanus' suggestion has considerable merit. Based on previous engagements for which we have data, if our ground forces were still holding the xenos' collective attention to a sufficient level, any individual small shuttle would have a seventy-two point zero five per cent chance of successful launch and retreat without being engaged by either orkoid atmospheric flyers or their fighter-equivalent void craft. Once away from the planet they could make for the remnants of our fleet in the asteroid belt with only a limited chance of being followed.>

<Seventy-two point zero five per cent is not the best of odds for survival for the sum total of Hephaesto's knowledge, and the record and purpose of our very existence,> Ull argued.

<It is better odds than the current situation,> Zaefa retorted, gesturing to the tactical holo. Mitranda was doing their best – a detachment of Skorpius Duneriders were engaging heavily armoured orkoid infantry around Water Purification Facility 21 to the east, while in the west a lance of three Knights were moving to intercept infantry units and a fast-moving rabble of vehicles that were converging on Storage Sector 32P – but over an extended timeframe, she could see little chance of these achieving much more than delaying the xenos advance.

<The odds are irrelevant,> Illutar declared firmly. <The evacuation is not required: Node Primus will not fall.>

<Node Primus is falling,> Zaefa said bluntly, without bothering to feather respectful code into her message this time. <The data–>

<The data shows an unanticipated failure on the part of our ground troops to carry out their orders!> Illutar barked,

the jagged edges of his code causing Zaefa to start backwards in alarm. <The orks should have been held at the Second Wall! The fact that they were not is a logical impossibility!>

A logical impossibility. A statement, delivered by the being in overall command of Hephaesto's defence, that was utterly and obviously untrue. Virtually nothing was a logical impossibility in combat situations; the Imperium's battle records certainly teemed with conflicts in which the expected outcome had indeed occurred, but also numerous events where a particular unit, or in some cases individual, had wildly defied the odds to tilt a battle one way or the other... or, conversely, had spectacularly underperformed and caused a critical collapse in an otherwise-sound battle plan.

The worst part was that, so far as Zaefa had assessed matters, the failure of the Second Wall hadn't even been a logical *improbability*, let alone an impossibility. Their troops had been reinforcing the wrong places, and had been too slow to react to enemy movements. Tech-Priest Dominus Illutar had placed too much confidence in his own assumptions about strategy, and paid too little attention to the reality unfolding in front of them all.

And that in itself was allowable. War was a science, not an art form. Trial and error, and the testing of hypotheses, was an essential part of the scientific process. What was inexcusable was Ronrul Illutar not adjusting his hypotheses appropriately after seeing the initial results.

A warbled alarm attracted Zaefa's attention, and she expanded a portion of the holographic tactical display with a gesture. It was flashing red, and virtually every high-priority alert possible to be activated had been.

<Critical overload in Sector 47B1,> she breathed, watching helplessly as temperature gauges spiked, and then failed

as they were consumed by the molten magma rising to the surface.

<Interrogative: was this caused by orkoid activity?> Illutar demanded. <Is this another incident of sabotage, similar to the repulsor-rail damage near Node Tertius?>

<Clarification: negative,> Zaefa replied, sifting through the communications and orders that had occurred during the last few minutes, while they'd been embroiled in debate. <This was the result of a direct instruction from Secutor Mitranda.>

<The secutor ordered the destruction of Sector 47B1?> Yavannos queried, some of her optics extending almost comically from her face as they focused on the holo. <What failure in coding caused this?>

<It appears to have been a considered ploy,> Zaefa said, double- and triple-checking her facts to ensure her assessment was as accurate as possible. <They were being overrun and had commenced withdrawal. The magma vented by the critical overload annihilated a significant portion of the ork ground forces in that area. The xenos would have almost certainly destroyed the buildings themselves, since that is their nature. However, our safety overrides would likely have been unaffected, and so the vent would have been contained. By deliberately overriding the safety measures, the secutor was able to turn their withdrawal into a highly effective weapon.>

<Such a withdrawal would not have been necessary, had the secutor obeyed their orders to hold the orks at the Second Wall!> Illutar snapped. <Their resistance should have been strong enough to encourage the xenos to explore other avenues of attack, which would have led them into the traps that had been laid for them!>

<The Second Wall is lost to us,> Zaefa said, as firmly as she thought she could get away with. Illutar was visibly bristling,

his mechadendrites stirring as though they were the tails of a whole nest of agitated serpents: not angry enough to strike, not yet, but it might not be far off. <The existing traps have been ignored or evaded, and the forces charged with springing them have had to fall back, lest they be outflanked and destroyed. We need to employ the next stage of our strategy.> *Assuming you have one*, she added in the privacy of her own head, horrified both by her own impertinence and by the non-zero possibility of her critique being valid.

<Could the secutor's gambit be repeated?> Yavannos queried. <If similar areas could be exposed to magma vents in such a manner then we might not only inflict further casualties on the xenos, but also give them no option but to take a route or routes of our choosing: ones which could then be heavily fortified, mined and defended to cause maximum attrition to attacking forces, in a manner such as the tech-priest dominus attempted at the Second Wall.>

Zaefa knew that the suggestion would be dismissed as soon as the grand genetor mentioned Illutar, even by his title. Attributing the previous plan to him directly also attributed the blame of its failure to him, and that was not something Illutar was prepared to accept.

<Out of the question,> Illutar retorted. <Such sabotage merely achieves the greenskins' objectives for them! Our purpose is to protect this planet in the name of the Omnissiah, not to deliberately destroy it, or allow it to come to harm!>

<Perhaps the council would like to reconsider my proposal?> Forge Lord Ull said. <If you wish to examine my prototype, my forge is–>

<Please direct your attention to my previous noospheric upload on this matter,> Illutar cut him off. He flexed his fingers as Ull subsided again, with the forge lord not bothering

to hide his anger. <Very well, the orks have breached the Second Wall,> Illutar continued. <They are now too close for them to flee effectively. We will unleash the full fury of the god-machines on them.

<Let the Titans walk.>

Da Bigger Dey Are...

The boyz were halfway down the spoil heap towards the buildings where the humies were probably keeping their loot, and everyone was whooping and hollering and firing their guns in the air, when a trio of brassy challenges rang out. They vibrated the air, low and throbbing and powerful, yet with an edge to them that spoke of belligerent pride.

'What in da name of Gork's Green Grin was dat?' Deffrow asked, as the boyz stumbled to an uncertain halt. They weren't scared, of course they weren't – orks didn't get scared. It was just sometimes good to know exactly what and where the enemy was, before you charged at them.

None of them had to wait long to find out.

They came out of the setting sun, three massive mechanical shapes silhouetted against the reddening sky, striding with deceptive quickness along one of the many bridges the humies had built to raise one transport route above another – since humies always had to follow lines laid down by other humies, instead of just driving where they pleased like the boyz did. They were massive things, bipedal and probably four times as tall as Ufthak. The huge domes of their shoulders spoke of devastating power, and each bore a shield-shaped device beneath their right shoulder armour that blazed with actual fire, which appeared to be a deliberate decoration rather than accidental damage. However, as one stepped down from the viaduct with a fluid grace that belied its size and weight, Ufthak's gaze was mostly drawn to the truly enormous gun hanging where the right arm would normally go.

'Now *dat*,' Mogrot said from behind him, 'is–'

'Zoggin' trouble,' Ufthak finished for him, as the huge kannon tracked towards them. 'Scatta!' He pounded downhill as hard as he could, straight towards the gigantic machine, on the basis that he certainly couldn't out-shoot it, but he might just be able to climb up it and whack whatever git was presumably piloting it…

He became abruptly aware that the ladz had, as one, followed him. Instead of being a lone ork amongst many other lone orks, he was now an ork at the head of a mob of orks charging the thing with the massive gun.

'I said to scatta!' he bellowed, trying his best to get ahead of the rest of them.

'We did!' Mogrot replied from somewhere behind his left ear. 'An' we followed you!'

'Well, now try scatterin' in *different* direc–'

The gun spoke.

An explosion chewed up the ground ahead of him, throwing up dark spoil in an eruption of gouting flame and blasting it into fine powder that hung in the air like black fog, but this was not a single shot. More explosions marched towards Ufthak and his mob, as the mighty kannon spewed out projectiles at a truly astonishing speed.

Now the ladz scattered.

Not quickly enough, in some cases: assorted body parts flew past Ufthak, too torn and mangled to be of use to even the most desperate painboy. He actually tripped on a hand that someone had carelessly dropped, and went head over heels, landing on his back in the spoil and sliding gracelessly further down the slope as the filthy stuff shifted beneath his weight. Mork continued to smile on him to some extent, though: a secondary weapon on the huge humie machine, some sort of big shoota, began rattling as well, but the line of fire it stitched out went right over him and into a couple of the ladz who'd been behind him instead.

A second massive walker dropped off the viaduct and steadied itself as it landed, the magazine of its own huge kannon beginning to rotate as it cycled up, ready to fire. The first gun was still booming rapidly and blowing bits out of the spoil heap, chasing down the largest concentrations of boyz as they fled hither and thither in an attempt to avoid its deadly ministrations.

Ufthak picked himself up, cautiously watching both machines to try to get a moment's warning if their guns turned his way, but his eyes weren't for them alone. It looked like they were here to guard the humies' storage buildings, but the first one had taken up position next to a large, shiny metal cylinder. Ufthak had picked up a limited grasp of humie glyphs and language, since it was sort of useful for working out what was where when you started shooting up one of their planets, and for getting information out of captured humies while you were twisting their arms off.

He was pretty sure that cylinder was the sort of place

humies kept their fuel, and if there was one thing hanging around the Kult of Speed ladz taught you, it was that fuel made a zoggin' big bang...

'Wazsmak!' Ufthak bellowed at an ork pulling himself back to his feet after being knocked off them by one of the explosions, and pointed a claw at the shiny fuel store. 'Rokkit dat fing!'

'Yes, boss!' Wazsmak replied eagerly, grabbing his rokkit launcher from where he'd dropped it and pointing it at the walker. Ufthak frowned as realisation dawned.

'Wait, no, not da–'

Wazsmak fired, and the rokkit whistled through the air. By some miracle of intervention from Gork – or possibly Mork – it flew true, and impacted on the left shoulder of the first walker with a cheerful blossom of flame that left a small dent, a notably blackened patch of paintwork, and no other appreciable damage.

'Got it, boss!' Wazsmak beamed, turning his grinning face towards Ufthak.

Half a second later, the main weapon of the second walker blew him up.

'Zoggin' cowards!' Ufthak roared at the two machines. 'Get down 'ere an' fight like an ork! I'll wreck ya! Swear on me 'ammer!'

The third machine dropped off the viaduct and stomped ahead of its companions. Like the first two, its left hand held a titanic tooth-edged choppa that must have been, all told, twice as long as Ufthak was tall. However, instead of an enormous kannon, the new arrival's right arm bore something more akin to an absolutely stupendous skorcha. The air around its barrels was already shimmering with heat haze, and as it angled towards him so he could see the glow within building from a deep cherry red up to white-hot, and the machine bellowed one of its brassy challenges, Ufthak began to wonder whether it was possible to be burned up so thoroughly that not even your soul would make it back to Gork and Mork.

He never found out, because the Kult of Speed arrived.

The first sign of their arrival was the thunder of badly tuned engines, audible even over the war-horn of the humie walker aiming at him. Then, as the first warbikers roared into view, a hail of dakkagun shots smashed into it at knee height.

The humie machines reacted to the new threat with a speed that impressed even Ufthak, swivelling on the spot and bracing their enormous feet to lay down a carpet of fire. The big kannons thundered, blowing holes out of the ground, and the enormous skorcha focused ferocious energies onto a warbike to turn it into nothing more than a white-hot mess that came apart under its own momentum to become a smear of slag.

The problem for the humies was, it was like trying to swat buzzer squigs. Sure, their guns took out a warbike here and there, but although the Kult's vehicles were larger than an individual ork, they also moved far, far quicker. Ufthak caught sight of a shokkjump dragsta, which engaged its shokk drive just as the first of the humie walkers fired at it: there was a flash of purplish light, and then the dragsta was fifty yards away from where a new crater had been blown in the ground, and its shokk rifle took off the front half of the walker's massive choppa.

'C'mon, ladz!' Ufthak bellowed, trying to rally the remainder of the mobs that had been with him, now the walkers were focused on something else. He couldn't see any other nobs left alive, which meant he was in charge of everyone.

'Everyone' was now a ragtag mismatch of Bad Moons probably only roughly equivalent to his own mob's starting size when they'd set foot out of the landa, but that was the way of things in war. They'd be enough to get the job done, anyhow.

One by one, the orks who'd scattered across the side of the spoil heap mobbed up on him – or at least, the ones who'd scattered in one piece. The one's who'd *been* scattered courtesy of humie high explosives stayed where they were, which was generally here and there, and sometimes a different there as well.

'Right!' he shouted, as they gathered around. 'Da speed freeks are doin' dere fing, so we'z gonna do ours, right? Get down dere, grab da loot, den–'

Something screamed over their heads with a noise like the very sky being torn in two. Ufthak caught a glimpse of gold-painted wings and the leering Jolly Ork banner of Kaptin Badrukk, and heard a thunder of high-calibre weaponry. He turned to watch, but Badrukk's personal wazbom blastajet was already gone, disappearing into the distance. In its wake it left the staggering, burning wreck of a humie walker, which toppled sideways and collapsed.

It also left, appearing on the ground at the base of the spoil heap in a shimmering bubble of tellyport energy, Kaptin Badrukk and a whole host of Flash Gitz.

The two remaining humie walkers, now surrounded by a swirling mass of fast-moving ork vehicles against which their guns could make only limited headway, and reeling from the sudden loss of their companion to the blastajet's flyover, didn't pay much attention to the newly arrived orks, even if they did have big guns. It was an oversight they'd pay for.

'Let 'em 'ave it, ladz!' Kaptin Badrukk boomed, his voice audible even from further up the slope than Ufthak was. As one, the twenty or so Flash Gitz raised their snazzguns and opened fire.

The cacophony was unspeakable, and the combined light of the muzzle flares threatened to rival the light of the setting sun. The nearest walker spasmed and jerked as the concentrated barrage of exotic firepower punched through its armour, severing joints, smashing support struts and destroying circuits. After five seconds of bombardment, the walker collapsed onto its front with a crash that shook the ground.

The last humie walker realised too late that its companion had been fatally damaged, but its kannon was now hanging off and trailing sparks anyway, courtesy of something explosive lobbed by one of the speed freeks. It took two lumbering steps forwards towards Badrukk's boyz, revving its enormous choppa up to killing speed as it did so.

'An' again!' Badrukk roared, and his ladz opened fire once more. Badrukk himself aimed for the machine's head, hunched low between its massive shoulders, and the high-pitched whine of Da Rippa rang out as its shells punched through the adamantium shielding protecting the pilot. This walker collapsed too, as its legs no longer kept up with its forward momentum, and it crashed down, crushing beneath it a kustom boosta-blasta that had decided to race a warbike through the shadow of the falling war machine. The top of the walker came to rest just in front of Badrukk, who stood unruffled as the dust of its landing billowed up around him. Ufthak watched in awe as the freebooter kaptin strode up onto the back of the mighty machine, placed one boot upon the back of its head and raised Da Rippa in the air triumphantly.

'When we're done 'ere, I want dis fing's 'ead cut off,' Badrukk instructed the grot lurking by his boot. 'It's gonna look great on da front of *Da Blacktoof*.'

'Dat's an ork,' Wazzock said, with feeling.

'Well, obviously dat's an ork,' Mogrot replied. 'He ain't a zoggin' squiggoth, is 'e?'

'Nah, I mean *dat* is an ork,' Wazzock said. 'Dat's an ork wot knows where 'e's goin'.'

'An' 'e's goin' to *get da zoggin' loot!*' Ufthak barked in sudden realisation, as Badrukk hopped down from the back of his kill, and the freebooter and his Flash Gitz piled off towards the humie buildings. Ufthak broke into a run with his own ladz at his back, but they were too far away having been knocked into disarray by the humie walkers and their kannons. Even when they got to the bottom of the spoil heap, they still had to make it across the strip of ground that the Kult of Speed had now turned into part of a giant circular racetrack encompassing the three smouldering walker wrecks, the warehouses and the fuel cylinder – although a couple of the brighter warbikers had recognised this last for what it was, and were starting to siphon it off into their tanks.

Ufthak was an old hand at avoiding the barrelling, ramshackle vehicles of speed freeks, and he made it across the rapidly eroding track with no incident, although a scream and a loud splattering noise behind him suggested that at least one of his boyz hadn't been so skilled. He dodged in front of the last one, the shokkjump dragsta – and getting in front of them was always a bit of a risk, no matter how far away they seemed to be – then came to an abrupt halt as he found the barrel of Da Rippa levelled at him.

'Where d'ya fink yer goin', laddie?' Kaptin Badrukk demanded, chewing on what Ufthak at first glance thought was a cigar, but then realised was a grot's finger. The freebooter kaptin leered at him, showing off a mouth full of a quite ludicrous amount of teef, while behind him his ladz broke down the doors that stood between them and the promised riches of the humie mekboyz.

'Gettin' da loot,' Ufthak replied, but he couldn't quite summon his usual swagger when faced with this avatar of ork opulence.

'Nah, ya ain't,' Badrukk said dismissively. 'Ya ain't any of my ladz – yer not kitted out well enuff, fer starters.'

Ufthak bristled, and felt the boyz with him doing the same. As Bad Moons, they prided themselves on having the best gear around… but when faced with Badrukk and his ladz, there was no denying that they felt a bit like the grot last in line when the squigs were being doled out for lunch.

'Ya ain't even got a gun!' Badrukk sneered at Ufthak, and the problem was, the git was right. Ufthak hadn't picked up anyone else's shoota since his had got carved up by that humie with the swords, and all he had right now was the Snazzhammer, plus a few stikkbombs.

'What sort of warboss lets 'is ladz run around like dis?' Badrukk tutted, hefting Da Rippa as though daring any of them to take issue with his words. 'Ya look like decent boyz, but ya ain't gonna get anywhere followin' some jumped-up mek wot finks 'e's all dat! Wot you ladz would benefit from, is some *real* leadership.'

Ufthak blinked in surprise. 'You offerin' us a place?'

Badrukk shrugged, and grinned. 'Can always use more hands, right? We'd knock ya inta shape soon enuff. Ya could learn from a *proper* leader, one wot fights at da front. Not like dat so-called Meklord.' He leaned closer, and lowered his voice into a slightly more conspiratorial tone. 'Between you an' me, I reckon 'e's just jealous dat I can tellyport whereva I wants now, fanks to Mogrok. But wherizee, eh?

Da Meklord? Still stuck up dere on dat kroozer, instead of down 'ere stompin' 'eads like a proper boss?'

Ufthak stuck his little finger into his right ear and wiggled it. The air pressure was building, like what might happen before a storm on some worlds, but the skies here were clear of clouds, or at least ones that weren't formed of smoke. Even Badrukk was frowning, apparently wondering what was going on, which was when realisation dawned for Ufthak.

'Wherizee?' he echoed the kaptin's words, and grinned right back at him. 'I fink 'e's gonna be 'ere any minute now...'

Joining the Hunt

At last. Battle. At last.

Princeps Arlost Vass swam up out of the canticle-filled, binharic semi-slumber in which he'd been immersed. For a moment he was nothing more than an old, blind, broken body suspended in an amniotic sac, pierced by sensory implant coils receiving no input and an MIU jacked directly into the base of his skull that linked him to nothing. Then, like a room blurring into focus in the moments after a sleeper opens their eyes – and by the Omnissiah, how long had it been since he'd had eyes? – he felt the godlike power of *Lux Annihilatus* come alive around him as its plasma reactor ignited.

War calls. War calls, and we answer eagerly.

Lux Annihilatus was the monarch of the Legio Hephaesto. It was a venerable Mars-Alpha-pattern Warlord Titan that had stridden the battlefields of the galaxy for over eighty centuries. It had spearheaded the liberation of the Tyrem

Stars from the dark forces of heretics, and killed the mighty Traitor Warlord *Burning Hammer*; it had duelled with the spindly Wraith-Titans of the aeldari on Gavaro Secundus; it had smashed aside the battlesuits of the t'au on Jurillo, and shot their air support down in flames. However, in the aftermath of that engagement, Vass – or *Annihilatus* – had pressed forward too eagerly, into the teeth of the blueskins' last-ditch defence as they'd been withdrawing. Three heavy rail cannon-armed battlesuits had barred the way, enough to leave even the mighty Warlord crippled. The battlesuits had been destroyed, of course, but *Annihilatus* had returned to Hephaesto to lick its wounds and be made whole again in the embrace of the world that had birthed it, millennia ago.

With it had come the lesser companions of its battle group: the venerable Reaver *Telum Purgatio*, old enough to have walked the stars with the Emperor's Great Crusade, and the two Warhounds *Castus* and *Pollaxus*. Even though *Purgatio* had been the one to destroy the final t'au battlesuit that had so damaged *Annihilatus*, and had still been combat-ready in the aftermath of the campaign, there was no question of the three lesser Titans continuing to serve while their monarch was damaged. Even the two Warhounds, younger machines though they were, had served with *Lux Annihilatus* for over three thousand years. All attempts to rouse their machine-spirits to war after their master's fall had been avenged had been in vain. They would march with *Lux Annihilatus*, or they would not march at all.

And now, with Arlost Vass' mighty adamantium body repaired and awaiting redeployment elsewhere in the galaxy, and with the orks so obligingly presenting themselves on the Legio's literal threshold, they would march once more.

His crew were here, scrambling into the cockpit from the

boarding ladders that had descended from above: not that there was much room above the towering form of *Lux Annihilatus* in the hangar. Magos Ryzan was already ensconced in their alcove, and Vass could feel the tickling across his senses as Ryzan ran systems checks. Vass also felt *Annihilatus'* faint throb of resentment at having its internal workings monitored in such a manner, and he gently tamped it down. Best not to get off on the wrong foot for their first engagement after repairs.

'Permission to come aboard, princeps?' Moderati Indan said formally, from outside the boarding hatch. His predecessor, Hugin Mells, had been fatally wounded by the last shot fired by the final t'au battlesuit – Vass felt the anger and grief rising in his machine body, and soothed it back down for the moment – and Indan had been next in line for the position. He was known to be a well-adjusted young man, bold but possessed of good reason, and Vass had no qualms about his appointment.

'Permission granted, moderati,' Vass replied through his uplink cord, the speakers in the Warlord's armoured head giving voice to the words he'd subvocalised in his amniotic cocoon. 'You are one with us, now.'

'I'm honoured,' Indan replied formally, giving a smart salute before he climbed briskly down the ladder and took up his station at the weapons console. Enginseer Fewson busied themself attaching the control links into the moderati's implant jacks. The Titan's other crew members could walk free of this space under their own power, and experience sensations via their own senses… but then, they didn't know the glory of being truly bonded with one of the greatest god-machines to ever serve the Imperium. They had never felt the roar and kick of a gatling blaster as though it were their own arm; they had never crushed the chittering swarms of a hive fleet beneath their armoured feet; they had never pinpointed the heat source of one of their traitorous brethren two miles away with the natural ease of an unlinked human spotting a fire in the darkness.

'Don't go getting all honoured yet,' Moderati Kyrzgyn admonished her new colleague, arriving in the cockpit with a clang of boots on metal via a descent down the ladder that was more jump than slide. 'Let's see how *Annihilatus* takes to you in a combat setting first.' She clapped Fewson on the shoulder, and flipped Vass a salute he detected through the cockpit's internal imagers, and which delicately trod the appropriate line between camaraderie and respect.

'Moderati Indan is welcome here,' Vass declared, and everyone knew he was speaking for *Annihilatus* as much as he was for himself. The god-machine had experienced Indan's touch when they'd been testing the weapons' targeting systems after the initial rebuild, and Indan had been a good fit. Vass knew, in a way no one else could, that that wouldn't change just because they had live targets in front of them.

'Nothing to worry about, then,' Kyrzgyn said. She cracked her knuckles and settled into her own post, waited for Fewson to connect her up as well, then rolled her neck in the way she always did before they set out. 'Are we ready to hunt some ork?'

Vass scanned his systems, feeling his surroundings through the Warlord's sensors as though they were a part of his own body. The boarding ladders were withdrawing, the assembled insect-like menials of the Adeptus Mechanicus were hastily scurrying out of the way on the hangar floor, and his fellow princeps – Karla Praxis in *Telum Purgatio*, Wretham Horle in *Castus*, and Jumahid Sudi in *Pollaxus* – were signalling their readiness.

'We are ready. Let us hunt.'

He stretched, and *Lux Annihilatus* stretched with him, rearing up from the slight slouch in which it stood in its repair cradle. The two turbo-laser destructors on his carapace mounts nearly scraped the ceiling, and his war-horn rang out, echoing back off the walls, and building to a sound almost impossibly loud within the enclosed space of the Titan hangar. Vass noticed that several of the mortals on the ground fell over from the noise, as whatever aural implants their masters may have granted them were overloaded, regardless of any volume limiters that might be present.

As a statement of intent, it was clear. The mighty shield door at the far end of the hangar began to grind open, letting the orange-red light of Hephaesto's setting sun begin to flood inside.

'Right, then,' Kyrzgyn muttered to herself as the war-horn's throbbing call finally died away, only to be echoed by answering calls from their three companions. 'Let's see how well everything's working, shall we?'

Lux Annihilatus stepped forward, a single stride of sixty-five feet, and Arlost Vass sighed in satisfaction as gears turned, gyroscopes stabilised, coolant and lubrication pumped through their respective conduits, and he moved under his own power once more. The pain, frustration and rage of that last engagement on Jurillo was forgotten, and in its place rose the excitement of this new hunt. The plasma reactor quickened, burning more fiercely as the very heart of the machine responded to his own eagerness for battle.

'All systems are operational, and performing at near-optimum efficiency,' Kyrzgyn reported with satisfaction, as *Annihilatus* took another stride. 'We've even lost the slight limp on the left leg – I thought that was going to be with us forever.'

Satisfaction surged within Vass as *Annihilatus'* machine-spirit took stock of itself in motion, and found that it was strong once more.

'Weapons check,' he commanded.

'Gatling blaster hoppers are fully loaded,' Indan replied. Vass had not doubted that they would be – the enginseers of Hephaesto were never less than dutiful in their care and preparation of the god-machines – but it was a sign of the young man's commitment to thoroughness that he took nothing for granted, and didn't expect his colleagues to either. 'Ammo-cycling systems fully functional. Volcano cannon crystals are currently at maximum structural integrity. Turbo-laser destructor power packs at one hundred per cent.' The Titan's weapons pivoted and traversed as Indan completed his checks. 'We have full movement. For the glory of the Emperor and Omnissiah, may we slay many of the enemy today.'

'Well said,' replied Magos Ryzan, as Enginseer Fewson disappeared through the hatchway to take up their station monitoring the plasma reactor.

'Yes,' Vass declared with satisfaction. 'Well said.' He felt Indan's pleasure through the impulse links they all shared through the mighty machine with which they were bonded.

'I hope they hurry up with that door,' Kyrzgyn observed. 'Because we're not slowing down.'

It was a statement of fact as much as it was a statement of intent. Now it had been loosed from its bonds, *Lux Annihilatus* was in no mood to moderate its pace, and to attempt to restrain it would take considerable effort of concentration: effort that might soon be needed, for the war was nearly upon them.

'They'll have it open,' Indan said with assurance. 'They know their business.' It was good that he'd fallen so quickly into a rhythm with his fellow moderati – yet another reason why he was a suitable replacement for Mells.

Indan was correct, too: the massive shield door scraped just wide enough for *Lux Annihilatus* to exit the hangar without either having to slow, or collide with it. Then they were out, out into the sunshine, and out into the war.

'We have hostiles… well, pretty much everywhere,' Indan reported, as their next stride took them past the ranks of secutarii hoplites that had gathered to follow in their footsteps. Vass knew that tactical readouts from the Titan's sensors would be flashing up in front of the moderati's eyes via the noospheric inputs, much like they were for him, although his perception and understanding of the data would be far more intuitive than anything a hard-linked moderati could ever experience.

'You expected anything different?' Kyrzgyn asked. 'We already knew that.'

'I never trust anyone else's data completely,' Indan replied absently. 'I always prefer to see what my own machine tells me.'

'I'm going to like you,' Kyrzgyn said, with a grin Vass felt more than saw. 'Sir, I can turn us in any direction and we'll have targets. What are your orders?'

Vass scanned through everything he had available: the *Annihilatus'* sensor data, overlaid with the tactical readouts from the forge world's other units, along with the information from the rest of the battle group. It made for a sobering picture.

The orks were closing in on three sides, from the east, west and south. Node Primus' preliminary defences had been overrun, and the defenders were falling back to their next posts, but it was hard to see how the green tide could be stemmed.

'There aren't many priority targets,' he declared. 'Not much in the way of super-heavy vehicles, or enemy Titan-equivalents. We can crush the infantry and light vehicles easily – the question will be whether we can do enough, quickly enough.' A new icon flashed up, and he grunted in acknowledgement. 'Wait. There is one. A small walker, west-south-west. Moderati Indan, you have the coordinates.'

'Yes, sir,' Indan replied. He chuckled. 'A one-hit kill.'

'From your first shot fired in anger on *Annihilatus*?' Kyrzgyn retorted. 'A bottle of amasec says no.'

'Just don't jog me,' Indan told her, provoking a snort in response. Vass tolerated their bickering, for Kyrzgyn was already swinging *Lux Annihilatus* round and steadying it, and Indan was focusing the targeting matrixes.

'We're outside the node's void shield,' Kyrzgyn said, as the Titan's left foot grounded itself firmly. 'Take your shot.'

The Volcano cannon fired.

It lacked the massive recoil of the gatling blaster, for it was an energy weapon instead of a high-velocity mass projectile cannon, but they all felt the thrum of it as the huge power surge discharged, and the lights and displays flickered for a fraction of a second. Vass, checking his data, saw the beam of supercharged light hit its target, and the resulting explosion.

'Target destroyed,' he confirmed, a moment later. He barely needed to: they all felt the rush of vicious delight as *Lux Annihilatus*' machine-spirit witnessed its first kill of the battle.

'Amasec is on me,' Kyrzgyn said, without rancour. 'Good shooting, moderati.'

'Thank you, moderati,' Indan replied graciously. 'Sir, your instructions?'

'Take us forward, Kyrzgyn,' Vass instructed, assessing the situation. 'We need to drive these beasts back, and only overwhelming aggression will achieve that. Indan, I want the gatling blaster chewing up the infantry advancing directly ahead of us, and the Volcano cannon targeting the artillery in the south-east that is currently bombarding this sector of the Node's void shields.'

'Aye, sir,' both moderati responded. With snarling howls of their war-horns, *Castus* and *Pollaxus* raced ahead, slipping the leash now their monarch had made the first kill. *Telum Purgatio* advanced as well, looking to bring its close-ranged weaponry of a melta cannon and a power fist to bear.

'Sir, the raised causeways ahead of us block our best firing solutions on the infantry,' Indan reported.

'Bring them down, moderati,' Vass replied calmly. 'The Adeptus Mechanicus can rebuild, but only so long as we cleanse the filth from this world first.'

'Aye, sir.' Indan mentally triggered the Warlord's other main armament, and the gatling blaster's 150mm shells began to roar out, smashing the raised causeways of Node Primus' external transport loop into pulverised rockcrete. The barrage left jagged edges on either side where the causeways ended abruptly in mid-air, some atop arches nearly as tall as *Annihilatus* itself.

Then the gatling blaster fired again, and the distant ork infantry disappeared as the ground was wracked by one colossal explosion after another.

'I'm still not detecting anything that could feasibly be the enemy's overall commander,' Vass admitted, cycling through the data streams even as the Volcano cannon thrummed, and an enormous wheeled gun a mile away was turned into red-hot droplets of slag. 'There are individual pockets of what pass for elite troops amongst the xenos, but–'

'Princeps, I am detecting abnormal energy readings from

directly ahead of us,' Magos Ryzan broke in urgently, half a second after *Lux Annihilatus* registered the phenomenon on its sensors.

'Acknowledged, magos,' Vass responded, trying to make sense of what he was seeing. It burned him to admit his ignorance, but it wasn't lack of data that was confusing him – it was simply how to interpret it. 'What do you make of it?'

'I can draw no conclusion with a probability of higher than eight point two seven per cent,' Ryzan responded, even their largely emotionless voice sounding uneasy. 'These cover sixty-three potential causes, ranging from localised atmospheric phenomena to the imminent destruction of the planet via the opening of a catastrophic warp rift. I can list these possibilities in descending order of likelihood if you wish.'

'Wait until you have greater certainty,' Vass instructed them. 'Kyrzgyn, hold position. I want to know what is occurring before we walk into it.'

'Acknowledged, sir,' Kyrzgyn responded, bringing *Lux Annihilatus* to a reluctant, grumbling halt. The rest of the battle group followed suit, pausing for a moment.

Every meter, every sensor, every measuring device that Vass had access to went haywire at the same time, as a flash bright enough to penetrate even *Lux Annihilatus'* auto-tinting viewshields ripped outwards. For a moment, the god-machine was blind.

When his perception cleared, they were no longer alone.

There was a split second when Arlost Vass wondered how a hab-block had suddenly appeared in front of him beyond the ruined causeways when, mere moments before, he'd had a clear view through to the swarm of ork foot troops in the distance. Then the details of his readouts penetrated his confusion, and an unfamiliar sensation squeezed his chest.

Fear.

'Gargant!' Indan barked. 'Gargant!'

It was colossal. Arlost Vass had, once, as a young man, seen the Imperator Titan *Casus Belli* in person. He'd wept openly and unashamedly from the sheer magnificence of its might. Although *Lux Annihilatus* was an almighty god-machine, and he was thrice-blessed to have been joined with its spirit, he still recognised that against the might of an Imperator it was like a callow youth standing next to a battle-hardened warrior in the fullness of their strength.

This gargant, daubed in yellow and black paint and bearing the design of a leering crescent moon in front of what looked like crossed wrenches, was of a size with the mighty *Casus Belli*. Nearly cuboid, although tapering slightly towards the apex, it squatted in front of them like an ork god incarnated into metal: ugly and crude, on stubby legs, yet undeniably powerful. It bristled with weapons, although Vass couldn't hazard a guess as to the nature of most of them, other than the huge, outsized rotary saw blades that reared up on extendable arms from each of its shoulders. The others were obviously guns of some sort, although exactly what an ork gun might do was always a matter of guesswork, due to the sheer unpredictability of the xenos beasts.

He didn't want to find out.

'All units, fire!' Vass commanded, transmitting over the vox to his fellow princeps. Moderati Indan was already targeting, although in truth he could probably have fired in the gargant's general direction and still hit it, the thing was so vast. How had it got there? Where had it come from?

The Warhounds, faster and leaner as they were, reacted first. Each opened fire with their Vulcan mega-bolters, searching for a weak spot in the gargant's armour, but their shells didn't even leave a scratch on the foul machine's paintwork; instead they were deflected by a hazy, sparking force field that intercepted them before they even reached it.

Then the gargant answered.

Castus' void shields were bludgeoned down by a barrage of ballistic and energy fire from the gargant's multiple weapon systems. Then, when it was left staggered and undefended, trailing smoke, the gargant's belly gun spoke once. Wretham Horle and his crew died as their machine was blown apart under them, and Vass heard their screams for a split second over the vox before the transmission was cut off.

'Evade!' Vass bellowed to his crew and the two remaining members of his battle group. He fought against *Annihilatus'* immediate, feral response to stand and trade blows with this colossus. That was a fight they couldn't win; he knew that deep in his gut, and the truth of it sickened him, but their survival hinged on him overriding the god-machine's desire for unthinking violence in its efforts to avenge its fallen comrade. 'Evade, and pick your shots! We may have to take this abomination down foot by foot, but by the Omnissiah, that is what we will do!'

+++010+++

<What is the source of that anomaly?!> Tech-Priest Dominus Ronrul Illutar barked, staring at the wildly oscillating readouts on the tactical holo, centring on one point in front of the recently emerged Legio Hephaesto engines.

<Insufficient data,> Zaefa replied helplessly.

<There is a lot of data,> Forge Lord Ull retorted, gesturing to the readouts.

<Clarification: insufficient data that converges on a satisfactory explanation,> Zaefa snapped.

<We are aware that the xenos have employed weaponised force field technology,> Grand Genetor Yavannos cut in. <Could this be an example of such a weapon, on a hitherto-unseen scale?>

<It is possible,> Zaefa replied uneasily, but she had her doubts. What an abominable emotion was doubt! A magos could approach anything appropriately, even their own death, so long as they were certain of the facts...

The readings abruptly stabilised. Zaefa suddenly found

herself longing for the chilly uncertainty of doubt, for the facts were terrifying.

An enemy walker had materialised in the centre of what had been a swirling mass of energy anomalies. It was enormous: Zaefa's preliminary readings suggested that it stood one hundred and sixty-five feet tall, was not much less across at its widest point, and probably weighed as much as any two of the Legio Hephaesto battle group combined.

<*Fascinating,*> breathed Yavannos, leaning closer to inspect the holo, her hands and sleeves disrupting some of the tactical displays as she placed them on the tabletop.

<Fascinating?!> Zaefa repeated, aghast. <Magos, this is a disaster! The orks have just teleported their mightiest war machine into close proximity with our Titans!>

<That is impossible!> Illutar raged, cutting her off before she could speak again. <Teleportation on such a scale is impossible! This is a… a false positive sensor reading!>

In answer, Zaefa snapped her fingers. Her haptic implants interpreted the gesture, and the tactical holo was replaced by an overlay of pict-feeds from Node Primus' security systems. The light levels were low, as was the angle of the sun, and the air was filled with smoke and dust thrown up by the battle, but the image was clear enough. The ork gargant was very definitely there, as solid and real as anything else, and considerably more menacing. Zaefa quickly changed the display back again. Had anyone asked, she would have replied that the tactical display gave a better overview of the situation. In reality, seeing the machine with her optics chilled her to what remained of her natural bones.

<Clearly, it is not impossible,> Yavannos replied to Illutar, gesturing to the tactical readout with some excitement. <This is an unprecedented research opportunity! Whatever chance

combination of factors the xenos have accidentally stumbled upon for this to occur may be replicable on demand, if our adepts are able to study–>

<Warhound *Castus* has been destroyed,> Zaefa said numbly, as the Scout Titan's marker flashed red and vanished with an ominous finality.

<The machine is operational?> Yavannos asked in disbelief.

<Negative,> Zaefa replied, confused. <As I just stated, *Castus* has been destroyed.>

<Not *Castus*,> Yavannos said, with a dismissive snap of code. <The ork gargant. It is operational? It has come through this teleportation operational, with its systems and weapons functional?>

<Affirmative,> Zaefa said, trying to fight down her displeasure with the contemptuous disregard the grand genetor had displayed for the loss of one of their forge world's honoured god-machines. <As you can see, it is now engaging the other Titans of the battle group.>

<This is a marvel,> Yavannos said, her mechadendrites twitching in excitement. <For anything that size to be teleported is practically unheard of, but for it to be operational immediately afterwards…!> She turned to address Illutar directly. <We must have access to the gargant in order to understand how this was achieved. It *must* be captured unharmed!>

<Magos, the gargant has just destroyed one of our Warhounds, and there is considerable risk that it may repeat that atrocity,> Zaefa told her. The remaining three Titans were spreading out, attempting to bombard the gargant from all sides and prevent it from concentrating its fire to the devastating effect it had against *Castus*, but even so, the gigantic war machine was clearly more than a match for even the mighty *Lux Annihilatus* in a one-on-one engagement. Given

the notorious unpredictability of ork weaponry, Zaefa would not have liked to hazard an estimate on their chances of survival, but she did not feel that the percentages were high. <If it is not destroyed, the firepower it can bring to bear may be able to overwhelm that sector's void shield generator and leave the node undefended!>

<All defensive batteries are to engage that engine,> Ronrul Illutar declared. He was attempting to project an air of calm authority, but the cracks were there for any with the sensors to detect them, and Zaefa was most certainly one of those.

<Tech-priest dominus,> she began, as respectfully as she was able under the circumstances, <the void shields would have to be lowered in order for our batteries to fire, and our readings suggest that this would have to be done for a sustained period in order for our ordnance to achieve any appreciable effect, since the enemy machine appears to be protected by an energy shield of its own that at least approaches the efficiency of Imperator-grade void shields.>

<Then they will be lowered,> Illutar bit out.

<We are still being bombarded by xenos artillery,> Ull retorted, much to Zaefa's relief: she had no wish to contradict the tech-priest dominus again, alone. <*Lux Annihilatus* was only able to take out one emplacement before the gargant's appearance necessitated an alteration in its priorities. If we lower the void shields in that sector to allow the batteries to engage the ork machine, that sector will itself be devastated by incoming fire!>

<And your alternative is, I suppose, to demand that we approve the activation protocols for your 'experimental war machine'?> Illutar demanded. <This construct that you claim comes from ancient plans of which you have not previously made this council aware?>

<Yes!> Ull practically roared, his vox-emitters rumbling with bass that emphasised the power of his code as he rose to his full height. <Our world faces a threat like none other it has previously encountered. Only through bravery and faith in the Omnissiah will we survive!>

<Absolutely not!> the tech-priest dominus shouted, slamming one hand down on the table with sufficient force to send the tactical holos shivering for several seconds. <I will not be party to such ill-considered, unsupervised arrogance!>

<You do not have the sole voice at this table,> Ull snapped. <Grand genetor? Lexico arcanus?>

Zaefa's chest tightened. The High Council of Hephaesto was theoretically a democracy, except that the tech-priest dominus held the casting vote in the case of a tie. It would take her and Yavannos siding with Ull to overrule Ronrul Illutar... and if they did, what then? Would Kapothenis Ull proclaim himself as tech-priest dominus instead? Such a schism could paralyse their ability to coordinate the planet's defence even further.

<I cannot allow this,> Yavannos said, and Zaefa experienced a twin wash of first relief, and then guilt at being relieved that her decision would be irrelevant, and therefore she did not need to make it.

Illutar nodded curtly at her, in at least a brief acknowledgement of her support. <Then it is settled. We shall pursue other methods of destroying this threat–>

<No, we must not destroy it!> Yavannos broke in, her coding just as emphatic as Ull's had been moments before. <I am instructing a battalion of skitarii to board the machine and suppress it from within–>

<This council has taken leave of its senses,> Ull growled. <Play your doomed games, if you must. I remain committed

to the defence of Node Primus and this planet through the options available to us that have the greatest statistical possibility of success, and if that means that I must face battle myself, then so be it!> He turned in a whirl of robes and angry mechadendrites, and stalked away. Ronrul Illutar and Viker Yavannos, now engaged in a highly charged debate of their own over whether they should destroy or capture the ork gargant, and how best either of those aims could be achieved, did not even acknowledge his departure.

And so our resistance fractures, like a support strut placed under too much stress, Zaefa thought numbly. *We fight ourselves instead of the enemy, and in doing so, open ourselves to our doom.*

She opened a back channel in her communication output, hidden as best she could from her colleagues on the High Council, even from Ronrul Illutar. She was disobeying his direct order, but at some point her duty to the Omnissiah, as she saw it, had to supersede her loyalty to a tech-priest dominus who had lost control of his own planet.

<This is Lexico Arcanus Zaefa Varaz,> she transmitted to her personal adepts, layering her authorisation codes into the message. <Commence the immediate backup and stowage of all available records, with priority given to weapon schemata and unique artefacts. Commandeer all available shuttles for the purposes of evacuation preparation.>

She paused for a moment, weighing up her next words. This wasn't a calculation of odds or fractions, this was a search through her very spirit.

She reached a resolution.

<Should you encounter resistance to these orders from your colleagues, you are hereby authorised to use all reasonable force in order to comply...>

...Da Harder Dey Fall

The MekaGargant was Da Meklord's pride, an utter colossus of destructive power that could level a humie hab-block in a matter of seconds. He liked to tellyport it down right in front of his enemies, just to make them soil themselves a few moments before they were utterly annihilated by the truly stupendous firepower it carried. Ufthak had seen it wreck the largest humie tanks with a single shot, and shrug off one of those enormous bug things vomiting something at it before dekapitating it with its mega-killsaws. He'd cheered with the rest of the ladz when it had blown up one of the smaller humie gargants as soon as it had arrived, and Kaptin Badrukk had looked significantly annoyed.

'Zoggin' show-off,' the freebooter kaptin had muttered, clearly unhappy at being upstaged in such a fashion, as though he hadn't just posed on top of something he'd killed.

Then, however, the humies had got their act together a bit. Their three remaining gargants had split up – actually split up, not like Ufthak's ladz – and had started to pour fire into the MekaGargant from different directions. It wasn't enough to take it down, not yet, but Ufthak could see its kustom force field sparking away at a rate that suggested it might not last much longer. A mek's force fields were always a bit unpredictable, that was the nature of the beast, but even one designed by Da Meklord's genius probably wasn't going to last much longer against this sort of combined attack.

The humies were dodging, too, which was ridiculous: what was the point of being in a gargant if you were gonna dodge? Nonetheless, they kept trying to get out of the way of the MekaGargant's guns, and just about avoiding enough of what Da Meklord was sending towards them to avoid joining their mate as a pile of slag on the ground.

'Looks like 'e's bitten off more dan 'e can chew,' Kaptin Badrukk said with ill-concealed glee, chomping on the grot finger in his mouth with a crunch of small bones, then swallowing it happily. 'Fink about me offer, ladz, cos I don't reckon dat git's gonna be around fer much longer.' He whistled through his plentiful teef, and his Flash Gitz reappeared from their plundering, laden down with bizarre-looking humie gear.

'Ya can 'ave da leftovers!' Badrukk laughed, swaggering off with his boyz. Ufthak glowered at his retreating back. There wouldn't be any point going through what the Flash Gitz had left; picking up Badrukk's scraps wasn't going to impress anyone. Stupid Badrukk and his stupid tellyporting, jumping in front of orks what'd worked hard to get where they were…

Slowly, pieces started to fit together in Ufthak's brain.

He looked over at the fuel silo, where a punch-up had started between Kult of Speed members who each wanted to be the first to refuel so they could go roaring off with a full tank again.

He looked up at the titanic firefight going on between the gargants, with the MekaGargant hard-pressed and its return fire, at the moment, spattering off the shields of its biggest humie enemy without doing any appreciable damage.

He looked at the smashed causeways, where a veritable tangle of interweaving humie routes had been blown apart by their gargants' fire, to make a space for them to walk through.

He squinted down at the Snazzhammer in his hand, then over at Mogrot Redtoof, utterly deadly in combat and about as intelligent as a lobotomised grot.

'Right den,' Ufthak said. 'I've got a kunnin' plan.'

'A plan?' Deffrow echoed. 'Wot're you now den, some sorta Blood Axe?'

Ufthak nutted him, and Deffrow sat down rapidly, involuntarily, and in a state of some confusion.

'Da bloody cheek of it!' Ufthak fumed. '"Some sorta Blood Axe", indeed! Get up, ya git, and get goin' over dat way. An' da rest of you, go wiv 'im! Badrukk's ladz can't be movin' dat fast, dey're weighed down wiv loot, so get in front of 'em and get yerselves somefing wot we can show Da Meklord an' prove we're better dan dose zoggin' freebooterz!'

'You not comin' wiv us, boss?' Wazzock asked.

'Nah,' Ufthak said. 'Me an' Mogrot, we're doin' somefing a bit speshul. Helpin' out Da Meklord, like.'

As one, his ladz turned their heads to look over at the gargants.

'Dat's gonna 'ave to be a *proper* kunnin' plan, dat is,' Deffrow opined.

'It is,' Ufthak assured him. 'Now get movin'!' His ladz bolted off, heading towards whatever they thought looked most likely to offer up some interesting tek.

'So wot *are* we doin', boss?' Mogrot asked him.

'Jus' stick close to me,' Ufthak told him. 'Dis is either gonna be brilliant, or we're gonna die spektakularly.'

'Wossat mean?'

'Means wiv a big explosion an' dat.' Ufthak set off towards where the speed freeks were still brawling. 'Now follow me, an' be ready to clobber someone if dey need clobberin'.'

'Sounds good ta me,' Mogrot said, trailing him with a vicious grin on his face. If an ork was going to meet Gork and Mork, at the very least he wanted to be able to say that he'd died doing something big, loud or otherwise impressive.

The Kult of Speed had degenerated into an utter ruck of vehicles. The first couple of warbikers who'd smartened up to what was in the silo were on their way again, but then others had seen what was going off and had assumed that the fuel must be something super special, so they'd wanted some. The trouble was, other speed freeks had come to the same conclusion and, speed freeks being speed freeks, everyone had wanted to get it done as fast as possible. What this meant was that various drivers and gunners were punching each other to try and get hold of the fuelling hose, while the hose itself was in the hands of a bunch of grots who were sniffing the fumes rising from it, giggling, and falling over backwards.

Ufthak scanned the chaos quickly until he found the vehicle he was after, then ducked, dived and barged his way through the maul towards it. Behind him, he heard Mogrot swatting down anyone who'd taken exception to his method of progress.

'Oi!' Ufthak bellowed at an ork on the edge of the big fight. 'Dis yours?'

The ork looked around, somehow working out that the hail had been directed at him. Beside him, a squig consisting mainly of teeth chased a terrified grot through ork legs and over a buggy.

'Dat's right!' the ork said, grinning the manic grin of a speed freek who'd spent that bit too long chasing the horizon. He wore a narrow strip of something shiny over his eyes that wrapped around half his head and hooked behind his ears, although Ufthak was a left-handed brewboy if he could work out why.

'Looks fast,' Ufthak commented conversationally, nodding down at the buggy. It was the shokkjump dragsta he'd seen earlier: bright yellow to indicate the driver's affiliation with the Bad Moons clan, but with a paint job of red flames licking up the sides because, as everyone knew, red ones went faster.

'You bet!' the ork beamed, forgetting about the fuel brawl and coming over to stand proudly next to his machine. He slapped his hand lovingly on the roof of it. 'Dis bad boy can–'

Ufthak swatted him with the Snazzhammer so hard that his body described an arc up and down which landed him directly in the middle of the fight. Judging by the howls of pain and rage that greeted his arrival, his landing hadn't made him popular.

'Ain't yours no more,' Ufthak muttered to the air in general. The grot fleeing from the squig ran past him and he scooped it up, one hand around its neck, while its pursuer bayed up at it from the ground. Ufthak brought the grot up in front of his face, and it whimpered.

'You know how dis fing works?' Ufthak demanded, nodding down at the dragsta.

'Yes, boss,' whimpered the grot. 'I'm Nizkwik, I shoot da gun, innit?'

'Good enuff,' Ufthak told it. 'We're takin' it fer a spin. Mogrot!' he ordered his second-in-command. 'Yer drivin'.'

'Yes, boss!' Mogrot replied with glee, jumping behind the wheel. Ufthak clambered in on the other side, squeezing his hefty frame into the low-slung vehicle's passenger seat, Nizkwik still gripped in one fist in case the little git decided to make a run for it. A scrabble of claws behind him let Ufthak know that the squig had jumped up on the dragsta as well, and he turned around and glared at it. For a wonder, instead of pouncing in an attempt to get to the grot in his hand, the beast closed its enormous mouth and hunkered down, cowed.

'Hold on to yer butts!' Mogrot cackled, pressing the starter. The engine roared into life, a throaty, throbbing purr that quickly rose to a howl as Mogrot floored the pedal and they accelerated away. A scrabble of claws indicated that the squig had lost its balance, but when Ufthak looked around again he saw that it had clamped its jaws on to one of the go-faster fins and was clinging there with great determination.

'Dis woz a great plan!' Mogrot yelled over the rushing wind, and Ufthak sighed.

'Dere's more to da plan dan dis!' he bellowed back. Mogrot looked around at him, his disbelieving eyes watering from the speed they were already going at.

'Dere's more?!'

'Get on dat!' Ufthak told him, pointing at one of the humie roads that wound up off the ground and onto a raised causeway, like the ones the walkers had come down before Badrukk's crew had totalled them.

'Yes, boss!' Mogrot wrenched the wheel and the dragsta slewed around, then accelerated again. Ufthak had to admit, there was an appeal to tearing over the ground like this rather than slogging on foot. He'd still want to get out afterwards though, to break open some heads the proper way.

'Da shokkjump,' he growled at Nizkwik, who was staring over his shoulder at the squig in terror. 'How does it work?'

'Well,' the grot said, tearing its eyes off the squig for long enough to point at a large red button in the middle of the dragsta's dash. 'Dat's da shokka, right? When yoo'z goin' fast enuff, you hit da shokka, and den da shokkjump happens. Or sometimes it don't happen,' it added with as much of a shrug as it could manage with Ufthak's hand around its neck.

'Why don't it happen?' Ufthak asked.

'Dat would be a teknical matter, wot I don't know,' Nizkwik admitted.

'An' how fast is "fast enuff"?'

'Well… pretty zoggin' fast, boss,' Nizkwik said with the sickly smile of a grot who reckons it's about to get clobbered. 'But if yoo'z askin' for an *egg-zact* figure…'

'Never mind,' Ufthak muttered. He elbowed Mogrot in the shoulder as the dragsta screeched around a bend and began to climb, following the road upwards. 'Take dat turn comin' up, da one on da right!'

'Da one dat's gonna take us towards da gargants, boss?' Mogrot asked, obediently swerving onto a different concourse.

'Dat's it,' Ufthak told him. Ahead of them, the road rose up a little more and then flattened out into what had, at one point, been a high-rise highway that would have gone on to join up with other similar ones in a huge junction. Now, however, the routes that had stretched through there were abruptly truncated into jagged edges of rockcrete above a significant drop, certainly one that could splat an ork flat. Beyond, Ufthak could make out the head and shoulders of the largest humie gargant, currently battering at the

MekaGargant with some sort of rapid-fire kannon the length of a battlewagon.

'Fast as yer can!' Ufthak ordered, and Mogrot floored it again. The dragsta leaped forwards, its engine howling and its tyres greedily eating up the road.

'You shot dis, right?' Ufthak demanded of Nizkwik, jerking his head at the large, shiny-looking gun fixed in front of where he was sitting.

'Yes, boss!' Nizkwik said, happy to have found a question it could answer satisfactorily. 'Dat's da shokk rifle! It's well shooty, it–'

'It'll do,' Ufthak grunted, grabbing it with the hand that wasn't holding the grot and wrenching the shokk rifle loose with a few sparks and the *ping* of overstressed bolts. Nizkwik gasped in horror, but nothing exploded, so Ufthak judged that he'd got it right.

'Now hold on,' he told the grot. 'Or don't – not like I care.' He let go of its neck and switched the shokk rifle to that hand, and Nizkwik hastily clung on to the dash where the shokk rifle had been, before the wind could tear it out of the car.

'Boss!' Mogrot called, and he actually sounded a bit uneasy, which demonstrated a comprehension of possible future events that was more advanced than Ufthak had given him credit for. 'I fink we might be about to run out of track!'

Sure enough, the end of the causeway was looming up at them. Some way beyond, the huge humie gargant fired some sort of energy weapon at the MekaGargant with a screaming crackle that made Ufthak's ears feel like they were bleeding.

'Jus' keep it floored!' Ufthak barked at him, and Mogrot obliged. Ufthak flexed his fingers and eyed the rapidly approaching gulf, judging distances.

'We,' he added, hoping that Gork and Mork would appreciate his certainty and ensure it was well founded, 'don't need it.'

The shokkjump dragsta's front wheels left the edge of the causeway, and Ufthak hit the shokka.

A rapidly spinning vortex of purple-and-silver light erupted in front of them, which the dragsta immediately plunged into. There was a single moment when Ufthak could have sworn that he was being drawn out in length, his hands accelerating away into the riot of colour and his arms struggling to keep up, before his eyes followed.

There was another moment where everything was very loud and had a lot of teeth.

And then the real world erupted on him again, and the back of his head caught up with the rest of him, and the humie gargant was much, much closer than it had been.

Like, *really* close.

Ufthak grabbed the Snazzhammer off the floor with his free hand.

CRUNCH!

The shokkjump dragsta collided head-on with the gargant's enormous shoulder plate. Ufthak was thrown forward by the force of the impact and flew out of the cockpit, bouncing across the gargant's shoulder armour in an uncontrolled tumble, ending up against one of the huge shoulder guns it carried. The dragsta's nose crumpled and the back of it flipped up and over, coming down with an ear-splitting crash only a yard or so away from him, but then it began to slide off backwards as the gargant staggered sideways, knocked slightly off balance by the collision.

Ufthak found himself following the dragsta.

'Zog!' he bellowed, as the massive war machine lurched

beneath him again, taking another step and trying to correct itself. There was only one thing for it: he activated the Snazzhammer's power field with a flick of his thumb, spun it in his grip, and buried the axe end of it into the red-painted armour plate over which he was sliding. His blade bit deep, and his slide came to an abrupt halt with him on an approximately forty-five-degree angle to the vertical.

'Arrrgh!'

Nizkwik tumbled past him, flailing wildly. Ufthak aimed a kick at it as it fell, more for the sake of it than anything else, and was thoroughly annoyed to find that the grot was not only not knocked flying in an entertaining manner, but also managed to latch on to his boot and hold on.

'Fanks, boss!' it beamed up at him, big eyes bulging over needle teeth. 'I fort I woz a gonner!'

Ufthak glared at it, but trying to shake it loose might shake *him* loose too, and that wasn't going to do anyone any good: specifically, him. He grunted. He could always boot the little git off when he got his feet back under him, if he felt like it.

'Boss?' Mogrot's voice shouted, and he looked up to see his second-in-command's head poking over the curve of the armour plate. 'Yoo alright down dere?'

'Fine,' Ufthak replied, hefting the shokk rifle causally in his other hand, just in case Mogrot got it into his head that he could try to send his boss for an unexpected flying lesson and take over as nob.

'Good!' Mogrot beamed happily. He held up one hand, from which dangled the squig, suspended by its tail and gnashing furiously at the air beneath it. 'I caught dis before it fell off! Fort we might need some lunch!'

'Put it *down*,' Ufthak snapped. He braced himself, then hauled upwards as hard as he could on the Snazzhammer's handle. Even one-armed, he was able to get enough heft to pull himself up to a point where he could get a better grip with his boots – not dislodging Nizkwik, although it wasn't like he was making an effort not to – and get secure enough that he could pull his weapon out again.

'So wot's da plan now?' Mogrot asked, dropping the squig, which scrabbled at the smooth, gently curving armour plate beneath it with some apprehension. 'Are we gonna–'

The sky lit up a furious shade of red.

Mogrot jumped, Nizkwik screamed, the squig bayed in alarm, and even Ufthak flinched. The MekaGargant had turned its Gaze of Mork – the massive energy weapon housed in its eyes – on the humie gargant beneath their feet. For a moment Ufthak thought they were about to be burned alive, but then the blast subsided again leaving nothing but a faint shimmering in the air and a sudden stench of ozone.

'Why ain't we dead?' Mogrot asked, his voice full of wonder.

'Da shields,' Ufthak replied, gesturing to the shimmering. 'Da shokkjump took us froo dem.'

'Zoggin' 'ell,' Mogrot said. 'Dat was a bloody good plan, boss.'

'Told ya,' Ufthak smirked. He frowned as smoke began rising from one side of the MekaGargant. The mid-sized humie gargant away to their left was limping, but it looked like they were getting the best of the fight.

That couldn't be allowed.

'Right,' he said, working his finger into the trigger hole of the shokk rifle. 'Let's hit dese gits where it hurts.'

It took a bit of edging around the shoulder plate, and a lot of useless shouting when the gargant's weapons fired again and Ufthak thought his head was going to cave in from the noise, but it was less than a minute later when he, Mogrot,

Nizkwik and the squig were perched directly over the gargant's head, inside which, Ufthak was pretty sure, would be the humies crewing it.

'An' you don't fink dis fing's got a Gaze of Mork?' Mogrot asked dubiously, staring down at the front of it. 'Bein' burned up ain't anyfing to brag about.'

'Nah, dey can't have a Gaze of Mork, cos dey ain't got Mork,' Ufthak pointed out, reasonably enough, he thought. 'Dey just got dat Emprah, an' I don't fink 'e does zog all. Bloody useless god, if ya asks me.' He took a firmer grip on the Snazzhammer. 'On free. Ready?'

'Ready,' Mogrot nodded. Nizkwik made a vague noise of affirmation too, although what the little git thought it was going to do, Ufthak didn't know. Even the squig barked, as though it had some idea of what he was talking about.

'One, two, *free!*'

They leaped.

Ufthak landed on the very front edge of the humie gargant's head, planted both his feet, took a two-handed grip on the Snazzhammer, and swung it downwards. The crackling power field of the hammer's head hit the panels of lenses and spinning gears housed within the machine's eye slit, and punched through. It took two more swings before there was a hole large enough for them to fit through, but Ufthak could already hear screams and shouts of alarm from within, in those stupid, high-pitched humie voices.

He dropped forward into space, twisting as he did so to catch the upper rim of the gargant's eye slit, and swinging his boots through the hole he'd just made. The rest of his body followed neatly, barring a flare of pain down his left side as a jagged shard of metal tore at his flesh, and then he was inside the head.

It was a tight, cramped space, which suited Ufthak perfectly. One humie, bleeding red blood on its face from various small wounds inflicted by flying shards of metal, rose up out of its seat, trailing strange cables from the back of its head and its forearms. It was scrabbling at its belt, trying to get its gun out, but it was panicked and far, far too close to him.

Ufthak reached out and engulfed its tiny head in his free hand, then squeezed. The humie screamed, flailing uselessly at his hand with its own. Its companion managed to draw a slugga of some sort, but the puny beam of light it shot into Ufthak's shoulder was barely more painful than a solitary buzzer squig bite. He swatted it with the Snazzhammer, and its torso disintegrated into a red mist of pulped flesh, intermingled with a few red-slicked shards of gleaming white bone.

Something gave in the head of the humie whose skull he was squeezing, and suddenly his hand was sticky. Ufthak dropped the humie, now a limp corpse, and shook his fingers out. Zoggin' things leaked everywhere at the slightest provocation...

Something barrelled out of an alcove at the rear of the cockpit, a red-and-midnight-robed apparition of flailing arms and jabbing, serpentine metal tendrils. Ufthak was caught slightly off guard, but Mogrot, following him in, was not. He emptied his slugga into the humie mekboy, who collapsed to the floor and didn't move again.

'Well, dat was easy,' Mogrot commented, looking around. 'Wow. Dere's a lot of flashin' stuff in 'ere, ain't dere!'

'Yup,' Ufthak replied, because there certainly was. It was like the humies had decided that the interior of their gargant needed to be even brighter and flashier than whatever stars they could see from the surface of their planet. He frowned down at the controls, and wondered whether they could work out how to pilot it. There'd only been a couple of humies doing it; if he and Mogrot could control it and turn its guns on the other humie machines, that would end the fight outside pretty sharpish. And then maybe he could keep it, have his own gargant...

'Boss, wassat?' Mogrot asked, nudging him. Ufthak turned around to see where his second-in-command was pointing, and frowned.

There was a tank of fluid at the back of the cockpit. Ufthak hadn't paid any attention to it until now, since it blatantly hadn't posed any sort of threat, but now he could see that there was a humie body floating inside it. It was rather more grey than any humie he'd seen before – they generally came in variations of brown instead of a good strong green like the boyz – and it was even skinnier and more skeletal than the rest of that frail species. It also seemed to be lacking eyes, or at least it had cables going into its eye sockets, although it was definitely alive. Even as he watched, its mouth moved soundlessly.

'Well, dat is one of da weirdest fings I've seen today,' he said honestly. 'Humies. You never know wot dey're gonna do next.'

He aimed the shokk rifle at the tank, and fired.

Most of the front of the tank simply disappeared, and the fluid within – body-warm, and with a consistency somewhere between thick blood and wet mud – sloshed out across the floor. The humie drooped, now held up only by similar cables to the ones that had been attached to its companions who Ufthak had already killed. Its mouth gaped soundlessly, its chest heaved, and a faint whine emerged from somewhere within.

'Boss! Boss! 'Elp!'

Nizkwik the grot scrabbled in through the window from above, pursued by the squig. Ufthak wouldn't have thought the thing could have made it in, but its clawed feet were surprisingly dextrous, and it swung in after its intended dinner with a joyous bark that turned into a snarl as it pounced. Nizkwik dodged to one side at the last moment, and the squig hit the suspended humie teeth first.

The war machine spasmed as though it had been struck by a squiggoth, and Ufthak felt a secondary shudder as all of its guns discharged at once. Then there was an almighty clatter, the cables tore loose, and the humie collapsed backwards with the squig on top of it. Its limbs moved weakly for a moment before the squig bit deeply into its head and neck, and a flood of red blood gushed out.

'Dere's one under us, too,' Mogrot said, cocking his head to one side. He'd always had good hearing, had Mogrot, so Ufthak was prepared to believe him. Mogrot grabbed a hatch in the floor, hauled it up, then threw in a stikkbomb with a practised flick of his wrist and slammed the hatch shut again. A moment later the floor shook with the explosion, and something thudded wetly, as though collapsing onto metal.

Also, alarms started going off.

'Wassat?' Mogrot asked in confusion, as everything began flashing with considerably more purpose than before. Ufthak wondered if it was some sort of alert that all the crew were dead, but what was the point of that? If they were all dead, there'd be no one to hear the alarms.

He eyed the floor hatch suspiciously, then pulled it upwards.

Another humie, shredded by the closely contained blast of a stikkbomb, was slumped against a wall of a chamber that took up the gargant's chest cavity. In the middle of that chamber was something glowing with a blue-white glare that Ufthak found somehow disconcerting, especially since some of the blue-white parts were hazed with fractures that could have been recently caused by an explosion, such as the closely contained blast of a stikkbomb.

'Zoggin' shoddy humie work,' he muttered, closing the hatch again. 'We need to get out of 'ere before the bloody fing blows up.' He went back to the gargant's eyes and poked his head out, looking down.

It was a very long way down.

'Dere woz a bit of da plan wot covered dis, right?' Mogrot asked, sticking his head out too.

'Shut up,' Ufthak muttered absently. 'Maybe dere's a way out da back.' He walked back through the cockpit, past the cowering grot, and the squig, still happily bolting down red gobbets of humie flesh. Something caught Ufthak's eye, and he looked up at the humie glyphs worked into a bronze metal plate at the top of the tank. Most humies spoke the same language, and Ufthak had picked up enough of it to be able to interrogate prisoners, or order slaves around if there wasn't a runtherd handy. Humie glyphs were harder – they denoted sounds instead of concepts, which seemed really stupid to him – but he could make a fair guess at them.

'P...' he muttered, trying to read it. 'Pr... Prin? Pri... Princess!' He nudged the squig with his boot. There was something appealing about its consistent bloodthirstiness. 'Dis was Princess. Or maybe *a* princess. You want da name of wot yer killed? You wanna be Princess?'

The squig grunted happily, red blood running down its chin.

'It's a deal, den,' Ufthak said. 'Yer Princess.' He eyed the alcove at the back of the cockpit, where the humie mek had come from, but there was no obvious way down, no steps, ladders or anything like there would be in an ork gargant. But then again, ork gargants were huge, hollow things with plenty of room for boyz in the belly, so they could pour out and clobber stuff once they were close enough. Humie gargants didn't seem to have the same sort of space inside.

'Boss!' Mogrot called. 'I fink we got a def'nit problem now!'

Ufthak hurried back over to him and stuck his head out of the gargant's eye socket again. At first everything seemed fine: with the biggest humie machine out of the fight, the Meka-Gargant had turned all its guns onto its largest remaining enemy and, with no real distractions, blown it into smoking wreckage. Now Da Meklord looked to have snared the smallest gargant with his supa lifta-droppa, and had hoisted it off the ground. The thing was tilting to one side and its legs were kicking frantically, and quite comically, as the incredibly powerful traktor beam laughed in the face of the planet's gravity.

Then Ufthak realised in what direction the gargant was moving, and things became a bit less funny.

'Back of da head!' he bellowed, hauling Mogrot away from the window. A moment later the light of the setting sun was blocked out as the MekaGargant hurled its catch straight into Ufthak's new conquest.

Humie force fields could be something quite special, sometimes, and the ones on this gargant seemed to have been the business so far, but there were limits to what even they could handle – also, Ufthak conceded, it was possible that the cracks Mogrot's stikkbomb had left in the blue glowing things might have had some sort of effect. A small gargant, hurled by a supa lifta-droppa, was definitely beyond them.

Even so, the weight of the big humie gargant was substantial, and whatever stabilising wotsits it had must have still been active. When there was the thundering crash of impact as two metal monstrosities collided, and it took approximately four hundred tonnes of carefully engineered war machine straight in the chest, it still only wobbled. Ufthak, holding grimly on to whatever he could, thought for a moment that they were actually going to be all right.

Then the wobble tilted slightly further, just past the tipping point, and the tilt got more and more pronounced as the mightiest defender of the humie city began to topple ponderously backwards.

Anomaly

The sparks of life on this planet were so feeble and sparse, that was the problem.

Gavrak Daelin's great work, in common with all great works, required many things for it to be truly complete. He'd been able to source the vast majority of those things, either through simple ingenuity, or through the connections of his 'patron'. However, there were some things for which there were no shortcuts, no easy solutions.

Life was one of them.

Life was the key to so much. Gavrak Daelin held life in no particularly high regard – indeed, he was contemptuous of it in all but himself – but there was no doubting the essential nature of it. Life was a currency, a key that could unlock doors which would otherwise remain firmly closed. Life could be bartered and traded – although as Gavrak Daelin knew well, only the most foolish or the most desperate bartered and traded with their own – and

119

bring the savvy trader tools and opportunities most rare and exquisite.

But not all life was equal.

The spark was strong in some, beating hard and burning bright, where the spirit was vital and vibrant. In others it skulked and flickered, crushed down by the weight of misery, futility and pain. The former made excellent currency; the latter, far less so. And yet on Hephaesto, the latter greatly outweighed the former.

This was no shining jewel of the Imperium, no sheltered protectorate where at least some of the citizens of the False Emperor's slowly dying rule had a measure of security and luxury; this was no Ultramar, or Vorlese. Hephaesto was a forge world, and most of its inhabitants were servitors or tech-thralls. Servitors, mind-wiped menials obeying only the most basic of programming, were essentially useless to Gavrak Daelin's purposes. They had a pulse, and a certain form of life, but their spirit had been torn asunder by the very process that had made them what they now were.

Tech-thralls... well, they were at least still fully human, in mind if not in body. They had hopes and dreams, fears and desperate desires, and all of those gave them a spark that was lacking in their mindless fellows. Here and there amongst their number, life, and defiance against their miserable lot, burned brightly. However, this was disappointingly rare. Mostly, their spirits were worn thin by the endless drudgery of their existence, performing back-breaking menial labour in the service of those who considered them barely better than animals. Even the lowliest adept of the Adeptus Mechanicus could rise higher than a tech-thrall could ever dream of. All the labourers of Hephaesto had to look forward to was death.

Gavrak Daelin could assist with that, at least. He could

usher them into the embrace of death more quickly than they'd have otherwise reached it, and their journey there would certainly serve a greater purpose than the insignificant, unnoticed contribution they made to the schemes of their oblivious masters. They would even live on, in a fashion, albeit not a fashion they were likely to enjoy. But they would be a critical part of his great work, although it galled him to consider them as such.

The trouble was, he needed volume. The currency of their spirits was a weak one: they were paltry morsels, and so quality had to be offset with quantity. However, even on a forge world, even on a forge world under attack by orks, there was a limit to how many menial labourers could go missing before someone, somewhere, realised that there was a problem. The Imperium obsessed over accounts and numbers – an entire wing of their government was given over to it – and the Adeptus Mechanicus was no less exact and precise. There would be an acceptable loss threshold, a percentage of disappearances below which no questions would be asked, since it was assumed that natural wastage had taken its toll on a hard-worked and under-nourished worker population, with limited access to medical facilities. However, such thresholds were set with experience and expectation, and his activities might take the losses beyond them. Then there would be an investigation, and while Gavrak Daelin feared the immediate consequences of that very little, any irregularity could be the catalyst for factors moving further and further outside of his control.

He reached out and cupped a man's face with his hand, lifting it and turning it this way and that, studying the eyes. The man, an unwashed specimen with long, scraggly, brown hair that was already streaked with grey despite what Daelin supposed was his relative youth, stared back at him from pits of numbness. This man wasn't struck speechless and com-pliant by his awe at Gavrak Daelin's might, or terror at his visage. He was speechless and compliant because he had simply reached the limit of his ability to react in any mean-ingful way. His spirit was broken; he would accept whatever happened to him, whatever was demanded of him, by his nominal masters or by Gavrak Daelin, or by anyone else who presented with sufficient authority.

The man was one of a group of six humans, each equally ragged, each with the same dullness of expression, each snatched from labour or errand or bunk. None of them knew each other, for Gavrak Daelin would not have his minions risk taking groups of tech-thralls. It would be easy, in the short run, to overwhelm and snatch a work gang. It could, however, be ruinous in the long run, for even the Imperi-um's fools, who counted everything and understood nothing, would pay attention to a whole work gang disappearing. One person might die, alone and unnoticed, or wander off into the forge world's deep places to find their end in a manner that, while very likely to be brutal and unpleasant, might at least be more of their own choosing than perishing from exhaustion. A group of people who had been assigned a task together were unlikely to all fall prey to the same fate that would leave them undiscoverable, and such an occurrence would draw unwelcome eyes.

Gavrak Daelin always planned for the long run. Construct the strategy, using all available information. Pursue the strat-egy, adapting it as necessary. Sometimes events could not be predicted, and sometimes the strategy needed to be updated at very short notice and with minimal data to inform it, but the initial strategy had to be sound. To act without knowing your end point, and your route to it, was the act of a fool.

'Put them with the others,' he instructed his minions, stepping aside. Their staves crackled into life again, violent energies that could slay a human with one blow engulfing the weapons, but their use was not needed. The captured tech-thralls trudged forwards through the space Gavrak Daelin's imposing frame had been occupying, accepting their new lot in life without complaint or question. Their absence of spirit was useful in that respect, but it frustrated him how little collateral their arrival added to his available resources.

He reached out to the noosphere, sliding past the security measures with casual ease. His 'patron' had given Gavrak Daelin access codes, which he had accepted with a show of respect, and immediately disregarded. Such codes would limit his access to what his patron wished, and would undoubtedly leave a trail that his patron could follow, to see where he had been and what he had done. He had used the codes here and there, of course – it would raise suspicion not to – but for his real work, he relied on his own abilities.

He floated through oceans of code, drifting lightly, careful to leave no trace of his presence. Many of his kin would not understand such delicacy, for they dealt only in rock and metal, blood and death, the thunder of gunfire and the screams of the wounded. They would not see the noosphere as a potential battleground, filled with as many traps and perils as any mined approach, choke point or kill-zone – and indeed, he had once been as blind. It had taken the teachers of the New Mechanicum to open Gavrak Daelin's eyes to the full potential of this world, and show him how to move through and manipulate it with no one being any the wiser of his presence, at least until his schemes reached fruition. By the time he revealed himself, it was always too late.

He let his senses open out, absorbing a flood of information that would have sent a lesser mind into a state of catatonic shock. He could see the damage reports and the ticking, ever-increasing counts of the wounded and the deceased amongst the defenders. He skimmed over inventories of armouries, and productivity reports from nutrition farms. And beneath it all, he could feel the mighty, regulated heartbeat of Node Primus, fed by the constant power of the volcano upon which it was built, power that was harnessed and kept in check by an ancient wonder from the Dark Age of Technology.

An alert flashed, and Gavrak Daelin brought up the relevant readout. It was a tactical display of the battle outside, and the alert was the highest priority that the Adeptus Mechanicus had.

What he saw made him clench his fists in impotent rage.

Lux Annihilatus, the mighty Warlord Titan – and in fact all of its battle group – had been brought down by the orks. While he'd been lurking here in the bowels of Node Primus, the killer of *Burning Hammer* had been killed in turn. Not by him, not by his creation, not as he'd intended, not as he'd sworn to the gods. *Lux Annihilatus* hadn't been torn asunder in an act of brutal revenge for the death of the ancient daemon Titan whose welfare he had overseen for millennia. No, it had been – he scanned the reports, trying to make sense of something the Adeptus Mechanicus itself was struggling to comprehend – boarded by orks, the crew killed, and then… then a Warhound had been thrown into it, by some sort of tractor technology?

It was humiliating. His vengeance had been stolen from him by these green-skinned beasts, who understood nothing. They had no appreciation of the craft of warfare; they relied not on tactics and brutal efficiency, but on sheer numbers and attrition. And yet they'd somehow managed this, this act that he and his brethren had singularly failed to achieve during the campaign in the Tyrem Stars.

Gavrak Daelin pointed at the nearest of his minions, a pale-skinned human with a halo of waving dendrites.

'You,' he said. 'Come here.'

The man approached him obediently. He had been a lowly adept once, Gavrak Daelin supposed, until some moment of clarity had opened his mind to the glory of Chaos. Now he served his former masters no more, and had used knowledge that the Adeptus Mechanicus, in their folly, viewed as heretical and forbidden, to write himself out of their records. Whoever this man had been, whatever role he had held, whichever tech-priest he had served, none of it existed in Node Primus' databanks any longer, which meant that so far as anyone here was concerned, *he* didn't exist any longer. Now he moved in the shadows, serving the true gods under the very noses of those he used to obey.

Gavrak Daelin reached out and closed his powerful hands around the cultist's throat. The man's own hands flew up to grab at Gavrak Daelin's wrists, but his struggle was pathetically futile. His access to oxygen was gradually closed off, millimetre by calculated millimetre, slowly enough for true panic to set in. The dendrites waving around the man's head sparked with power, but the charge of his empathic-resonance coils flowed harmlessly over Gavrak Daelin's armour, bothering him not at all.

The cultist had no air now at all; his mouth was open, but it availed him not. Gavrak Daelin squeezed tighter, and tighter still, letting the man know that he could have ended him at any moment, but had chosen not to.

The man went limp as, despite Gavrak Daelin's precision, the compression finally reached his carotid artery and blood ceased to reach his brain. Gavrak Daelin waited a few more seconds, then hoisted the man up into the air and dashed him down again, one-handed. The metal plates attached here and there on the cultist's skull were insufficient to save him, and the contents of it spattered across the floor.

Gavrak Daelin inhaled, calming his beating hearts and pushing the red tinge back from the edges of his vision. The other cultists eyed him warily. None would dare disobey him, but equally, few would trust him now. He had come here as an outsider: a respected and venerated outsider, it was true, but still an outsider. He had guided them in glorious work, allowed them to share in his vision, and that had bought him obedience and service – for power, just as much as life, was a currency. He did not enjoy their blind devotion, though. He was no longer in his own forge on Sarum, where his word was unquestioned rule.

Vengeance was denied to him. He would accept this, and take what pleasure he could in the fact that *Burning Hammer* had been avenged, even if not by his hand. That in itself was a victory, of sorts. He still had other work to do on Hephaesto, and if he no longer needed to draw out and wreak havoc upon *Lux Annihilatus* and its fellows, his work had been simplified by a step. Adapt the strategy in line with developments. The piece of arcane technology currently siphoning energy from the volcano itself to power the entire node still required his attention.

He opened himself fully to the noosphere once more, ignoring as best he could the stabbing envy that was triggered by the desperate alerts concerning the fall of the Titan battle group. He glanced at the tactical readouts as generally as he could, and satisfied himself that the node was in no immediate danger of being overrun. If necessary, the High

Council could alter the frequency of the node's void shield generators so that even the ork infantry would be unable to penetrate it. It wasn't a tactic they could likely sustain for long – although their power supply was practically inexhaustible, running the generators like that would likely burn them out after only a few hours – but it should provide enough time for Gavrak Daelin to do what he needed to.

He was just about to close himself off again, withdraw from the noosphere before some roaming security program or overly inquisitive tech-adept chanced upon his presence, despite his precautions, when he sensed something that gave him pause.

There was another presence questing out through the Node Primus noosphere, much as Gavrak Daelin had been doing himself, but it was not behaving anything like he had, or indeed like anything else he'd encountered here. It didn't act with the purpose of the Adeptus Mechanicus, searching for the data they required. It wasn't a passive monitoring system, nor was it an active program hunting for security threats. It had no direction, no apparent purpose. It quested blindly, and so tentatively that he suspected none but him would have noticed it, with no apparent rhyme or reason to its progress.

In fact, its behaviour was somewhat... chaotic.

Gavrak Daelin extended his reach towards it warily. This was an unknown and unpredicted development. It had the potential to affect his plans, as anything unknown and unpredicted might, but more than that, he had to admit that he was curious. What was this thing, that could reach into Node Primus' noosphere, yet seemed not to know why it did so?

But he was wary, because curiosity was not worth his life, and who knew what the unknown was capable of?

It fled before him, recoiling from his approach before he could closely analyse its code-structure, before he could get a good idea of what it might be. He hesitated, then pursued, attempting to keep his touch feather-light, but always, always the presence retreated from him. Gavrak Daelin would not commit wholeheartedly, would not throw himself blindly into the midst of the code, lest it turn on him and sweep him away with unexpected ferocity, and so he could only give chase as it ravelled up tighter and tighter. He had it cornered now, down one branch of one trunk of Node Primus' noosphere, and he moved in hungrily, yet still warily. There was nowhere for it to go, no route it could take to shift its core past him, and so it might finally turn, like a beast at bay.

It disappeared.

He was dumbfounded for a moment, and scanned the sea of code around him as though it might reappear at any moment. Had he fallen into a trap? Was he about to be pounced upon by something that would infect and devour his noospheric presence, as he himself had done to others so many times?

No such thing occurred. The presence had retreated through the system as far as it was able, and had then disappeared. That could mean only one thing: it had a physical source, a single point of origin into which it had returned, that had then disconnected itself from the noosphere entirely. It was a primitive form of self-defence against what it had perceived as a threat, but an effective one.

At least, it would have been had Gavrak Daelin not been able to pinpoint the location and map it onto the Node Primus schematics. He would track this mystery down, and it would find it considerably harder to flee or hide from him in the physical world than it had in the noosphere.

He drew his scarlet-and-midnight robes about him, and threw the hood up. It would give him no real protection from any true investigation into his nature or identity, but the Adeptus Mechanicus could easily be thrown off simply by displaying the correct symbols and colours. Give the right signals once inside their walls, and most of them would assume that you belonged. It helped, of course, that senior tech-priests were so divergent in their appearances. It also helped that he could manipulate his noospheric presence and hide his very existence from sensors, or even bionics, if their owners were themselves connected to the noosphere. Gavrak Daelin could not have walked through Administratum or Munitorum halls unchallenged, no matter what robes he wore, but here...

Well, there would be risk. It was also true that this endeavour was not strictly necessary to the completion of his work. He told himself that he didn't know that, that chasing down this anomaly was important to ensure that there were no unexpected, last-minute obstacles to his plans. He told himself that it made no sense to focus all his attention on the Mechanicus' power source when there might be something else of value within his reach, something else he could seize.

But ultimately, he was curious. And it had been many millennia since Gavrak Daelin, who weighed matters to a nicety and constructed his strategies to take into account all predictable variables, had been curious.

+++013+++

The orks would pay for every yard in blood. So Secutor Mitranda had sworn at the very start of the defence of Node Primus, and they had ensured it would be true.

Unfortunately, it seemed the orks had no problem with this arrangement, and what was more had quite sufficient blood to satisfy even the thirstiest demands of the defenders. They had swarmed down from orbit in their thousands, every one of them a warrior. Hephaesto had its troops, some of the finest in the entire Adeptus Mechanicus, but the orks had numbers – or at least, numbers that would count. Hephaesto might have more actual bodies than the invaders, but Mitranda knew that to arm tech-thralls and pit them against the xenos would be a desperation tactic. Tech-thralls would die easily, panic quickly, and impede the swift disposition and manoeuvring of better-trained troops. Nor would they have the tactical awareness to respond to moments of opportunity, and it was only by seizing and capitalising on those moments that Node Primus might be saved.

Attrition and brute power would not win this war – not for the inhabitants of Hephaesto, anyway. Surgical strikes might.

Mitranda had gravitated to the worker habs of the eastern battlefront in search of the enemy's overall commander, if the orks had such a thing. It was, statistically, the most likely place to find such an adversary, since this was where the attack had been pushing most strongly since Mitranda had harnessed the fires of Hephaesto to incinerate the vanguard of the south-eastern offensive.

Or at least, it had been, until the orks had somehow managed to teleport an utterly immense war machine in amongst the sewage facilities directly to the south of Node Primus. The glorious battle group of *Lux Annihilatus* was even now engaging the machine and appeared to be gaining the upper hand, despite its formidable size and armaments, so Mitranda felt confident that their presence was not required. They had identified a priority target here, and they intended to eliminate it.

The habs had been hastily evacuated once the first bombardment of xenos artillery had begun to fall, the explosive ordnance varying wildly in its effectiveness but leaving the neatly ordered blocks as displeasingly asymmetric wrecks of smashed rockcrete, albeit with the occasional lone, untouched survivor standing proud. The ork foot troops were now heading due west along the wide thoroughfares with the setting sun directly behind them, and improvised roadblocks of junk and abandoned civilian groundcars were either smashed aside, or simply clambered over and ignored as the bloodthirsty xenos surged along in search of enemies. They wouldn't have far to go before they found them: two full units of Kataphron Destroyers waited in ambush, along with half a dozen Sydonian

Dragoons, their Ironstrider perpetual motion engines trotting back and forth as they awaited the right moment to charge into and break an ork formation – if such a word could be used for the unruly mobs of xenos – disrupted by heavy weapons fire.

Mitranda was not with them, however. They had noted that the orks seemed only to search for direct threats: a visible enemy, who could be shot at, or charged. They had a limited concept of stealth or concealment, and so they weren't systematically quartering the habs to sweep and clear them as they went along, as a well-organised force would. That left them open to entrapment.

<All units, stand ready for my signal,> Mitranda broadcast. They were lurking behind the shattered windows of a third-floor hab apartment, watching the orkoid filth flow past below at a pace that looked almost relaxed for them, but which was in fact deceptively quick. They appeared to be able to maintain it more or less indefinitely, and Mitranda had calculated that these orks would likely be able to run down an unaugmented human without unduly exerting themselves. The xenos were foul beasts, it was true, but that didn't mean their hardiness wasn't worthy of recognition. They appeared to have achieved through simple biology the sort of specialisation for role that the Adeptus Mechanicus required implants and bionics to achieve…

…and implants and bionics were symbols of devotion to the Machine-God, Mitranda hastily added to themself, simultaneously a great honour and a display of humility. They existed to remedy, improve and perfect the weakness of flesh. The worthy of the Omnissiah were superior to this xenos filth, and they were about to demonstrate as much.

They scanned the tactical noosphere one last time before they launched their attack. A priority notification flashed up from the alpha of the Gamma-22 Vanguard, notifying Hephaestan forces that in their recent engagement, two forces of orks had begun fighting each other. It appeared that the greenskins in the attacking force who were particularly garishly dressed would, with a little provocation, engage their more drably clothed kin. Alpha Seax posited a tactical update that if Hephaestan fire on one unit of orks could be directed as though it had originated from a different unit, along this newly identified binary, the attackers might be drawn into further intra-combats.

Mitranda approve-flashed the notification, and disseminated it to all unit commanders. Such an occurrence was further evidence of the inferiority of the xenos when set against the glorious harmony of the Adeptus Mechanicus, in which all played their part as cogs in the gears of a well-greased machine. They looked proudly at the full unit of ten Fulgurite electro-priests with them, each ready to serve the Omnissiah without question. Mitranda had hand-picked them for this strike, despite the protests of their Corpuscarii brethren. They couldn't have taken them both, of course; their theological divide over the Motive Force was too bitter for them to be relied upon to support each other when in close proximity.

<We will have no opportunity to work such tactics into our battle plan here,> Mitranda informed the electro-priests with them, as a direct follow-up to the tactical transmission they'd just sent. They eyed the xenos beneath them, for the Fulgurites could not: their biological eyes had long ago melted from the power they channelled, and they needed no electronic replacements since they sensed all living things as ghostly electrical presences. They wouldn't be able to see more subtle differences, however, whereas Mitranda could tell that these orks were all of a type, insofar as that was possible

to easily determine, clad as they were in dull browns and blacks. It would be martial skill that would complete the objective here, not subterfuge that led to the xenos fighting amongst themselves.

There it was: the ork Mitranda had identified as being the most likely candidate for supreme commander, using pict-feeds from surveillance servo-skulls. It was huge, substantially bigger than even the other elite-looking orks with it, and clad in metal armour that had to be six inches thick, covered with the pelt of some large animal and bedecked with the bones and skulls of either defeated enemies or old meals, or possibly both. Its left hand was engulfed in a massive powered claw that looked more like an oversized servo-arm, and its right bore a ballistic weapon with a barrel that Mitranda felt their head might fit down. Another massive, horned skull served it as a combined helmet and face guard, although presumably more for the visual effect than the genuine protective properties of bone.

Even more impressive than the ork, however, was its mount.

The creature was the largest living thing Mitranda had seen, outside of the Bio-Titans of Hive Fleet Naga. It was a quadruped, dark green in colour and scaled like a reptile. Its monstrous skull bore sharp teeth, some of which were near as long as an adult human was tall, while twin tusks curved first outwards and then inwards from its lower jaw, and a single horn erupted up from between its tiny, ferocious red eyes. Its upper body was covered in armour plate, in addition to whatever protection its own scales would give it, and its legs were the width of an Imperial grade-three standard support pillar.

The creature bore on its back a howdah that appeared to be little more than two captured Chimera hulls crudely welded together and with the roofs removed: since, after all, the monstrous ork within would have had to bend nearly double in order to fit into such a space. The side-mounted lasguns had been removed, of course – las technology appeared to be either not understood or simply shunned by the greenskins, although they did have some powerful energy weapons of their own diabolical devising – and replaced by two guns that looked to be the greenskin equivalent of heavy stubbers. Surrounding the commanding ork were eight others, each larger than the statistical average from observed specimens, and each clad in armour similar to that of their commander, albeit less ostentatiously endowed. There were also a couple of other orks who were considerably smaller, and were probably the beast's handlers: Mitranda dismissed them as low-priority targets.

This would be an endeavour that carried a great deal of risk, with the odds of success finely balanced with those of failure. However, Mitranda had cogitated the likely outcomes and concluded that the potential benefits outweighed the possible negatives. Although the maxim did not hold as true as when in combat against the tyranid menace, it was known that removing the commander – almost always the largest ork – from the battlefield would have a disruptive effect on a greenskin force. Unlike the tyranids, where the large creatures appeared to provide direct guidance for the smaller, simpler ones, the effect noted by Imperial tacticians in orks was that the commander's immediate subordinates would fight to establish dominance.

The specifics were, in this case, irrelevant. With the recently established friction between what looked to be rival ork factions, the removal of a highly placed commander could only help the Hephaestan forces.

<On my mark,> Mitranda breathed, keeping their binharic

cant barely audible out of force of habit, despite the fact there was little chance of an ork hearing it, and certainly none of it being recognised as a form of speech. The massive creature was getting closer, the howdah swaying from side to side as the orks atop it bellowed belligerently and the ones around the monster's feet scattered to get out of its way. They were laughing savagely as they did so, though, as if potentially getting crushed were in some way amusing to them. Truly, the mindset of these xenos was impossible to fathom.

<Glory to the Omnissiah, most benevolent Lord of the Motive Force,> the Fulgurites murmured as one. Around Mitranda, hands tightened on electroleech staves, and there was the faint crackle of electricity and the scent of ozone as the protective, contained lightning of their voltagheist fields powered up.

The ork beast drew level with them.

<Mark,> Mitranda said. They kicked out the remaining shards of plex-glass from the window, stepped onto the sill, and launched themself into space.

The enhanced bionics of their legs powered them across a gap that a fully fleshed human would have never managed to clear, and as their taloned metal feet landed on the edge of the howdah and mag-clamped on to it for maximum stability, their Omnissian axe came down in a silver arc that struck one of the heavily armoured orks and split its skull straight down the middle. The blessed weapon sheared through flesh, bone and metal, and came to rest halfway down the ork's chest.

Where it stuck.

The rest of the orks reacted immediately, and were already whirling to bring their weapons to bear when the Fulgurites, powered in their jumps by the Motive Force they worshipped, covered the same gap and landed amongst them with binharic war cries. Battle was joined in an instant: crushing, claustrophobic battle, as the chanting chosen of the Machine-God went toe to toe with the armoured brute might of the orks' elites.

Mitranda maintained their grip on the haft of their axe and somersaulted over the body of the ork in which it was still lodged to plunge the talons of their left foot into another ork's face. The beast howled in rage and pain, and brought its left arm up in an attempt to swat Mitranda away. The secutor clamped on to that limb with their right foot, then used their tertiary arm to repeatedly fire their volkite charger point-blank into its chest. The high-powered blasts melted through the ork's crude armour and vaporised its flesh all the way back to its spine, but amazingly the creature still refused to die.

It brought its ranged weapon up to point at where it thought Mitranda must be, despite their left foot obscuring its view, and Mitranda's finely tuned sensors detected the thrumming of a gun ready to fire as the ammunition hopper powered up. They released their foot's grip on the ork's face and clamped on to the ranged weapon instead, forcing it aside as the ork pulled the trigger and sent a spray of shells into the side of the building from whence Mitranda had just jumped. The ork's face, now revealed, was bleeding from gashes where Mitranda's talons had dug into it.

Mitranda gave their Omnissian axe one final wrench to free it from the body of the first ork behind them, anchored as they were with one foot on each of the second ork's arms. As the axe came clear, Mitranda brought it overhead in another double-handed swing, which arced down to split this ork's skull in two. This ork collapsed backwards more readily, perhaps in part due to now lacking most of its sternum, and Mitranda rode it down to the pitted, corroded old Chimera deck beneath it with the loud clatter of xenos-forged armour meeting Imperial plate. The first ork finally toppled from its upright stance, too, to land with an equally loud impact.

Mitranda, crouched atop their opponent, paused for a fraction of a second to get a reading on the combat taking place around them.

They had accounted for two of the enemy. Another had been fried in its armour as three electro-priests' voltagheist fields had conjoined on it. Of the remaining five, two were having the life energy drawn out of them by repeated strikes from the Fulgurites' electroleech staves. The other three, on the other hand, had fought back effectively: two Fulgurites had been engulfed in flame mid-jump and had fallen, screaming and burning, off the side of the huge beast on which they now all rode, only to be immediately dismembered by the horde beneath. Another one had been riddled with shells and was losing the last of her blood onto the decking, while two more had been crushed or bludgeoned by crude but highly effective ork power fists.

The ork commander, standing at the end of the howdah nearest the mount's head, had not yet engaged in the five point three seven seconds of combat that had transpired since Mitranda had initiated their attack. The secutor rose to their full height, intent on crossing the fourteen point one feet between them, but before they could do so the ork barked what sounded like a laugh, of all things, and slapped a smaller ork next to it on the back.

The ork so struck was one of the ones Mitranda had dismissed as a non-priority combatant. It would still need to be dealt with, of course – all orks were potentially dangerous, unlike all humans – but Mitranda had considered that it could wait until the commander and its elite bodyguard were dead. However, some instinct that went beyond Mitranda's highly developed combat programming, fine-tuned by over three hundred personal engagements and informed by tactical downloads from thousands more, alerted them that something was wrong. Instead of leaping at the ork commander, or raising their volkite charger to take a shot, Mitranda flung themself to their left, on top of the ork they'd first killed.

The smaller ork's mouth opened obscenely wide, and greenish-white light emanating from within its throat played around its fangs for a moment. Then the light gushed out, as the ork psyker vomited forth a wave of power that swept down the length of the howdah and washed over greenskin and Fulgurite electro-priest alike. Mitranda, shocked into immobility for a moment, saw metal, muscle and bone disintegrate as the foul energies made a mockery of the voltagheist fields. Three more devoted followers of the Motive Force were left as screaming lumps of melted flesh fused to the metal decking beneath them, although the two orks they'd been locked in combat with had fared little better.

The ork commander attacked.

It stepped forward and simply swatted one of the remaining two electro-priests away with its power claw, sending him screaming over the side of the huge beast on which they were riding – the creature was seemingly utterly unperturbed by the combat taking place on its back and had continued its steady, rolling pace. The second Fulgurite swung her electroleech stave at the enormous ork, and struck home. There was a momentary crackle as the blessed weapon drank deep of the Motive Force within the ork's armour, and indeed its body, but the huge xenos paid it little mind. Before the Machine-God's warrior could do more than siphon off the smallest portion of its power, the ork jerked its skull forwards and simply headbutted the electro-priest with sufficient force to smash her head into red ruin, kill her instantly, and send her collapsing to the metal deck. Then the beast turned its savage glare on Mitranda.

The ork's movements were not particularly fast, especially from the perspective of a secutor with enhanced optical upgrades and the most sophisticated combat analysis wet-ware available to the Adeptus Mechanicus, but it had a brutal economy of action that made up for it. There was also no question that the raw power in its form far outweighed even that of Mitranda's enhanced body.

Nonetheless, they flowed into their attack. This was why they had launched this ambush, after all. Besides which, being closer to the monster might discourage the greenskin psyker from launching another assault... although, these being orks, that was by no means certain.

Even with the other combatants dead or gone, the how-dah was still a relatively cramped environment for combat, due to the sheer size of Mitranda's opponent. The ork moved instinctively towards the centre of the two Chimera hulls, from whence Mitranda would have only three feet of clear-ance of its reach on either flank, and barely more than that to the front or rear. Those were small numbers indeed, for a smaller and faster fighter ranged against a powerful, lumber-ing opponent, since it would limit their advantage of speed and manoeuvrability. To attempt to wear their enemy down by goading them into lunging swings was too risky.

A head-on assault and a swift, clean kill was the only way. Mitranda fired their volkite charger three times as they closed, then ducked under the ork's power claw and cut at their opponent's left side with their Omnissian axe. The weapon cleaved through the ork's armour, and Mitranda sensed it biting into flesh, but it would take many more such strikes to bring down such a mighty opponent, and Mitranda dared not commit to a more powerful blow, lest–

They saw the ork's right foot swinging up and back a split second too late to avoid the impact against their chest. The force of the kick threw them backwards, colliding with the ork psyker.

Mitranda struggled to process what had just happened, even as they rammed their tertiary arm into the bellowing maw of the startled xenos beneath them and pulled the trigger of their volkite charger, blowing out the back of the ork's skull. Instead of being pulled off balance by its own blow, the ork commander had turned its momentum into a kick to target an enemy that had slipped past and behind it! That was not the move of a beast relying on power and savagery alone. Either the greenskins had a hitherto-unknown culture of warrior training, or their innate biological understanding of combat was more advanced than anyone had speculated. Or, Mitranda concluded, flowing back to their feet as the ork commander rounded on them, this particular ork had survived so many fights against smaller, faster opponents that it had learned suitable countermeasures from its own experiences.

None of those options boded well.

The ork roared, a basso note that seemed to shake the very air, and lumbered forwards in an attempt to trap Mitranda against the howdah's edge. Mitranda leaped upwards, counting on their powerful legs to take them over the xenos, and swung downwards with the Omnissian axe.

The blow to the back of the ork's head as it passed beneath would likely not be enough to kill it – it would shatter the bone helmet and knock the xenos off balance – but its impact was precisely calculated to assist with Mitranda's spin and carry them four point five feet further. From there, the secutor would turn, fire, and–

The ork ducked.

With no boost to their forward momentum, and no halt to the forwards spin that had begun with their axe blow, Mitranda turned more than a complete somersault and landed heavily on their front, four point five feet closer to the ork than they had intended. They rotated their lower half one hundred and eighty degrees, mag-clamped their feet to the deck and reared up, already beginning the spin that would bring their top half back into conjunction with their legs and deliver an axe blow at a diagonal angle down where the ork's neck met its shoulder, but the ork was out of position. It was too close, and had managed to turn.

A massive arm, crackling with power, reached out and crushed Mitranda to the ork's armoured chest before their offensive spin could move more than a few degrees, leaving them facing away from their enemy. Mitranda managed to get their axe up to block the claw, but to no avail: their weapon was crushed against them too, and the ork's power field sent painful data-spikes through Mitranda's senses as it began to warp their chestplate. The ork was bringing the cannon on its right hand around: if that was fired into Mitranda's side at point-blank range, it would cut them in half.

Mitranda aimed as best they could and fired blindly with their tertiary arm, and the ork bellowed in pain and rage as the hand carrying its gun was blown off. It lunged down-wards with its mouth open, seeking to clamp its jaws around

Mitranda's head instead. Mitranda thrust their volkite charger upwards and jammed it into the ork's mouth as they'd done with the psyker–

The ork bit down a fraction of a second before Mitranda could pull the trigger, and their tertiary arm splintered with a crack of metal. Red warning icons flashed up in Mitranda's vision, and not just due to the loss of their hand: they were only seconds away from their chest's structural integrity being terminally compromised by the continued pressure of the ork's power claw.

Every alert system activated, and even in the midst of mortal combat, even as the ork commander contemptuously spat out Mitranda's hand and volkite charger in preparation to take another bite at them, Mitranda still experienced shock for the first time in decades.

Lux Annihilatus had fallen.

Mitranda wasted a microsecond analysing the information, double-checking that it hadn't been an error. It had not. The mightiest of Node Primus' defenders had fallen – literally fallen – and the main southern element of the ork offensive now had little to stop them directly assaulting the void shields. Without a major alteration in the tactical situation, the node was essentially lost.

Mitranda threw everything into their two remaining fully functional arms, ignoring redline warnings as the stresses on their bionic joints grew to near-intolerable levels, and managed to force the haft of their axe outwards by an inch; and with it, the ork's power claw. The Omnissian axe bent immediately, the haft weakened by the destructive power field, but the space created was just enough for Mitranda to slide downwards out of the ork's grip before its jaws closed on their head.

The ork's fangs snapped shut on empty air, and it staggered

in momentary confusion at the disappearance of its enemy. Mitranda took two quick steps away as their Omnissian axe, now warped uselessly, landed with a clatter at the ork's feet, and assessed their surroundings for available replacement weapons.

The options were extremely limited. Electroleech staves would not fulfil their intended purpose unless wielded by a Fulgurite, and it would take more than one or two blunt sticks to bring down this monster. The other orks' weapons, whether power claws or ballistic, appeared to be integrated into their armour – and besides, orkoid technology was renowned as being virtually inoperable by anything other than a greenskin, for reasons on which Imperial magi still could not agree. Mitranda had made a study of the armaments of many xenos species, and the wild confusions of gears, cranks and other more esoteric parts that had little equivalent in Imperial engineering meant ork weapons were over-engineered to the point of uselessness.

Well. Most of them were.

Mitranda grabbed three cylinders that were clamped to the side of one of the orks that had been felled by the electropriests. A fraction of a second's analysis confirmed their initial suspicion had been correct, and they twisted the head of one of the crude grenades to arm it, then hurled it by the handle at the ork commander.

The ork wasn't taken unawares by the attack, and casually swatted the grenade out of the air with its power claw, but the explosive detonated upon contact with the weapon's disruptive field. Shrapnel blasted outwards, and Mitranda registered additional damage reports as shards of metal drove into their body, including their few remaining flesh parts. The ork, however, fared worse: it was knocked sideways by the force of the blast, and the crackling field around its armour's left arm sizzled and failed as the power source was damaged. Nonetheless, even unarmed, one-handed and bleeding from the stump of its right wrist, it was still a formidable opponent that could potentially crush Mitranda with sheer brute force. It roared at them as it recovered its balance, its mouth distending shockingly wide.

Mitranda armed a second grenade and threw it, tumbling end over end, to land directly between the ork's upper and lower jaws. The ork just had time to begin choking, and the red eyes visible through its skull helmet's eyeholes to narrow in what looked almost like startled comprehension, before the grenade went off.

Fire erupted from the ork's mouth, carrying huge ivory-coloured fangs with it, and its eyes exploded, leaving nothing but bloody ruins behind. However, whether because of the constraining effect of the skull helmet, or simply the unnatural toughness of its xenos form, the ork did not immediately keel over dead. It staggered, making a low moaning noise.

Mitranda charged, taking three quick paces over and around the corpses of other combatants, each step placed with precision. Their fourth step saw their left foot land on the ork's right knee and mag-clamp to its armour.

The fifth step saw their right foot come up to kick the ork so hard in its fractured lower jaw that, this time, its weakened cranium *did* explode.

The ork commander fell backwards, its mighty body no longer commanded by its brain. Mitranda unclamped their left foot and saw, to their surprise, one last ork looking at them. It was peering over the edge of the howdah nearest the head of the monstrous beast on which they all rode, and was, perhaps, the ork nominally in charge of directing the enormous mount. It was grinning widely, giving every impression of enjoying watching the fight, but now as it saw its commander fall, its expression began to change from savage glee to savage anger.

Mitranda threw the last grenade at it. The ork's eyes widened, and it scrambled to throw itself off the side of the beast. Perhaps it forgot exactly how high above the ground it was – or perhaps it didn't, given the xenos' rugged constitutions and general resilience to damage. Regardless, it escaped the force of the blast that erupted in its wake.

The beast, which had remained unperturbed by the commotion so far, took exception to such a loud detonation so close to its head. Mitranda felt its entire body reverberate with a tectonic rumble of rage and alarm, and then it lurched from its steady plodding walk into as close to a gallop as such a massive beast could manage.

Mitranda, their footing assured by mag-clamps, picked their way forwards to the front of the howdah despite the violent lurching from side to side. Orks were being crushed beneath the creature's huge feet, and with their ability to get out of the way limited by the presence of the hab-blocks on either side, the monster was leaving a trail of carnage behind it.

The only problem was that the ork beast was heading directly for the defensive line drawn up by Mitranda's troops and, despite its alarmed state, might still deliver exactly the sort of line-breaking hammer blow the orks would have intended it for in the first place.

<This is Secutor Mitranda!> they broadcast. <Concentrate all fire on the giant xenos beast!>

Affirmatives flashed up. Mitranda leaped back into the main body of the howdah and grabbed the enormous corpse of the ork commander, then hoisted it up with an effort that strained even their enhanced physique. It was a moment's more effort to stagger to the side of the howdah and tip it over the edge, letting it clatter to the ground below. Let the orks see how their commander had fallen. Let them feel fear. At the very least, let them retreat in disarray as they fought amongst themselves for command.

The roar of heavy arc rifles and torsion cannons split the air, and the massive beast under Mitranda's feet let loose a stentorian bellow as the energy beams bit into its flesh. Mitranda's olfactory sensors detected ozone, charred meat and burned fungus. The beast veered to one side as part of its body began to give out, only to collide with the wall of a hab-block. Rockcrete cracked and plex-glass shattered at the impact, and the creature rebounded off to stagger the other way. Mitranda waited, poised and tensed as the enormous mount's legs finally gave out properly, and it began to fall.

The secutor sprang off just before it hit the ground and crushed a few of the orks at the front of the xenos lines that had begun to engage the Adeptus Mechanicus troops. They landed in a roll and snatched up two edged weapons that had fallen from ork hands: simple metal blades attached to hafts, they were as nothing compared to the precise construction of an Omnissian axe, but they would serve in necessity. Two orks loomed up in the cloud of dust the monster's fall had kicked up, and Mitranda decapitated them both in under a second.

<Secutor! Interrogative: are you unharmed?>

<I remain functional,> Mitranda replied to the broadcast enquiry. <The objective has been completed.>

<Maintain your current position.>

There was a moment's audible warning, as the relentless *thud-thud-thud* of Ironstrider engines' feet rang out, and then the Sydonian Dragoons charged into the confusion left by the rampage and collapse of the monstrous ork beast. The remaining ork infantry was cut down by the Hephaestan cavalry's taser lances, and the combination of factors was too much even for the bestial belligerence of the attackers. Mitranda's sensors, relatively unimpeded by the dust, detected the vanguard turning tail and fleeing.

Mitranda felt a spurt of vicious pride as the xenos were routed, but instantly quashed such an emotional response. This victory, hard-earned though it had been, had been rendered far less significant by the events that had taken place to the south-west.

<All units fall back,> they ordered, not bothering to hide the reluctance in their floodstream. The dragoons were seeking to avenge the fall of *Lux Annihilatus*, and such an action would leave them overstretched and vulnerable. Mitranda also wished to wreak vengeance on the enemy, but that was not the primary function of the defence of Node Primus.

<All units fall back,> they repeated. <Fall back behind the void shields.>

+++014+++

Lexico Arcanus Zaefa Varaz had excused herself from the High Council, and had made her way to the Shrine of the Omnissiah.

In truth, she had more wished to get away from the arguing between Tech-Priest Dominus Illutar and Grand Genetor Yavannos than because she'd felt any pressing need for divine guidance. Neither of her colleagues seemed, to Zaefa, to have any concept of the reality of the situation they faced. The argument over the ork gargant had been all the evidence that she'd needed. Instead of a swift and thorough assessment of whether or not the node could be effectively defended, and if not, how the evacuation should commence, they had instead wrangled over whether the ork war machine should be destroyed or boarded and subdued, as though simply making the decision would be enough to see the action carried out.

Zaefa felt sure that the orks, who had been far from compliant so far, would provide vigorous resistance to attempts made to fulfil either aim.

She was still aware of the High Council's 'debate', for she was linked to it noospherically, but she found it easier to ignore when not in the same room. Forge Lord Ull, in his temper, appeared to have cut himself off from proceedings entirely. Zaefa could still sense his presence within the network, but he was not accepting incoming communications. This angered her, in her turn. What right did he think he had, to ignore even priority communications at a time such as this? He had been thrown back on a project in which he had clearly invested a great deal of time, effort and resources – anyone would be frustrated by that. However, the entire planet was in the middle of a war! If Ull had hoped his experimental machine would drive the orks from their door, and grant him the mantle of tech-priest dominus in Illutar's stead as a result, he was now demonstrating how manifestly unsuitable he would be for such a position. Illutar's communications might be less decisive or useful than Zaefa would have hoped, but at least he was making them.

She stepped off the maglev transport, one tech-priest amongst hundreds of other passengers, each going about their scheduled tasks. The work of the forge world's node would continue until such time as they fell to the enemy, or were destroyed to deny them to the enemy, or when the algorithms governing the shifts dictated that an untrained, poorly armed militia would be greater help than hindrance to the node's defenders. That moment would come near the end – when it was viewed that choking the enemy's advance with bodies could buy the necessary time for the higher-ranking tech-priests and the forge world's greatest treasures to escape.

Zaefa thought again about the order she'd given. It was technically insubordination, which in a time of war was a grave offence indeed. She re-examined her logic as she edged around a huge, robed figure cutting across the main flow of foot traffic, but she could find no fault with her own working. At worst, they would still be unable to get clear, and the few lives it might have cost for her adepts to carry out her orders would have been lost to the orks in any case. At best, it could speed up the evacuation of vital knowledge, or perhaps even allow it to occur when it might not otherwise have been possible at all.

She paused before the doorway of the Shrine of the Omnissiah. It was shaped in the cog symbol of the Adeptus Mechanicus, but on a titanic scale. The space through which she'd walk to enter was but the bottom tooth of the cog, which rose up to form a mighty circular void in an engraved adamantium wall standing close on three hundred and thirty feet high. If it lifted its feet slightly higher than was normal, the mighty *Lux Annihilatus* could step into the shrine: as indeed it had done at times in the past.

And as it was very unlikely to do again.

Zaefa gazed up at the shrine's threshold, engraved with circuit patterns of almost inconceivable complexity, and felt some of her body's anxiety responses still, just a little. Perhaps it would be good to spend some time here, and not just as sanctuary from the frustration of the High Council's deliberations. Perhaps it was wise to seek divine inspiration while the shrine still stood, and before the ever-present winking alerts informing the populace that the forge world was under attack became inescapable blaring klaxons, announcing that Node Primus' inner defences had been breached and the enemy was at large within the core.

She stepped across the threshold, and entered another world.

Audio baffles immediately muted the noise from the main concourse outside into nothing more than the faintest murmur. Augmented and unaugmented alike could find peace and reflection here, whether they meditated on the nature of the Omnissiah, searched for their true calling, or merely prayed for guidance on their next maintenance shift. The light cast from the prayer-engraved wall sconces was dim, too, although not dark, and Zaefa's bionics meant she could see perfectly as she made her way to a steel pew, onto which she sank with a faint *clank* as the metal of her legs met the metal of her seat with only her robes to intercede.

The smell of sacred incense was strong in the air. Robed and hooded initiates stood at each corner of the shrine, murmuring canticles in binharic: an unending litany intended to spread out through the entire node, and confer the Omnissiah's blessing upon everything within it. The walls here were also engraved in circuitous patterns that at first seemed complex yet, when viewed from afar, or from close up, or from a different angle, instead spoke of a peaceful simplicity. The walls were alive with code – not intrusive, nothing that would disturb the reflection of worshippers, but accessible to all. Within that code were the names and designations of all who had served Node Primus in the millennia since the Adeptus Mechanicus had claimed it, from the mightiest Fabricator General to the lowliest tech-thrall. Each was given honour according to their rank, and each was remembered for eternity by the great noospheric databanks.

Zaefa dimmed her optics, disabled her internal chrono, and withdrew from the noosphere for all but priority communications and alerts. She would have to return to the task of saving her home from the brutish invaders soon enough. In the meantime, she could seek solace and guidance from the Omnissiah.

The priority alert came through four minutes and thirty-seven point two seconds later, according to her chrono as it rebooted.

For a moment she wondered if the unthinkable had happened: if the orks had breached the node's inner defences far more quickly than even she had anticipated, and that sudden, violent death was even now descending on them all. Her second thought was that perhaps her evacuation order had been completed ahead of her predicted schedule, but she dismissed that possibility even before her cogitators had returned to full operational power and correctly identified the alert for what it was.

It was a private alarm, one that would go to no one else.

The security of her living quarters had been breached, and an intruder had entered.

Ufthak Gargantsmasha

The humie gargant fell backwards in eerie silence.

Well, it wasn't exactly *silent*, what with all the alarms going off, but the gargant itself wasn't making any noise. It felt like there should have been some sort of organic sound to it, a deep cry of pain and anguish as it was brought down. Instead the alarms just whistled incessantly, like the death rattle of a creature already doomed.

Ufthak, bracing himself as best he could by holding on to support struts, reflected that he'd spent entirely too much of today in large metal things that were about to hit the ground. This was no life for an ork who only wanted to stomp on some humie faces and nick their shiniest gubbinz.

The impact, when it came, threw him, Mogrot and Princess against the back of the gargant's head, which was now its floor, and dumped the bodies of the humie crew on top of them. The still-warm goop from the tank that had contained Princess' meal flooded down as well, providing an unpleasant and oddly sweet-smelling addition to their situation.

'Mogrot,' Ufthak grunted, after he'd managed to force some air back into his lungs. That was harder than he'd ever been hit, including by that tinboy on the humie ship where he'd lost his original body. 'You dead?'

'Nah, boss,' Mogrot replied, not sounding in much better shape, but pushing a headless corpse off himself. Princess barked angrily, its two stubby, clawed legs kicking as it tried to right itself. 'Wot now?'

'We get da zog outta here,' Ufthak muttered, forcing himself back to his feet and glaring up at Nizkwik, who'd been clinging to the back of one of the crew seats and had managed to avoid falling at all. The gargant's eyes through which they'd entered were up there now, but it wasn't going to be an easy climb for him and Mogrot, let alone Princess. 'Wot ya lookin' at, ya little git?'

'Boss, I fink dat's a door!' the grot replied, pointing one clawed finger at what had used to be the top of the gargant's head, and which now served as a wall. Ufthak followed its gesture, and grunted. Now he looked at it, he could indeed see the sort of wheel that humies often put on their doors. He'd never understood that: how could you steer a door? And for that matter, who put doors in the zogging ceiling?

Still, a door was a door, which meant it'd likely be easier to open than anywhere else, and time could be a factor given that Ufthak doubted the glowing blue-white stuff would have much enjoyed the crash they'd just suffered. He drew back the Snazzhammer, ready to batter his way through it.

'Boss! Boss! Wait!'

Nizkwik jumped from the seat it was clinging to and landed on the locking wheel, then stretched sideways and pressed a button. A chime sounded in the cockpit, a much less abrasive noise than the ongoing klaxon, and a light turned from red to green.

'Ta-daaa!' Nizkwik announced triumphantly. Then the wheel began to spin of its own accord, and the grot sailed off with a despairing wail to crash against a bulkhead.

'Mogrot!' Ufthak yelled, as the wheel finished spinning and the twin halves of the door began to separate outwards. 'Get yer arse up!'

His second-in-command joined him a couple of seconds later, still wiping gunk from his face, and together they climbed up into the door's alcove, then through it into the darkening world beyond. Behind them, a scrabbling of claws indicated Princess had decided to follow.

They were still some way above the ground, because the gargant's head had been sat low in its chest, more like an ork's than a humie's – which was, Ufthak thought, probably why it had been so shooty, even if it had been a bit on the skinny size. A properly humie-shaped gargant would probably just walk around looking stupid until something killed it, or it ran away from a fight and fell down a hole. Now the gargant was on its back, the shoulder and arm guns towered above them on four sides, like mighty obelisks of death.

The klaxons were even louder outside, easily loud enough to be heard over the ongoing thunder of war. Ufthak supposed that was probably a bad sign.

'Boss!' Nizkwik shouted. The little grot had made it out of the cockpit, and was pointing excitedly back in the general direction of the MekaGargant. 'Dere's a whole load of yer ladz comin'!'

'An' a buncha humies comin' da uvver way!' Mogrot said happily, throwing his choppa up and catching it again by the handle. Sure enough, there was a whole mob of 'em, with pointy sticks in one hand and full-blown shields in the other, like they were scared of getting hit or something. They were running for the fallen gargant at full pelt, which didn't seem to Ufthak to be the most sensible thing they could be doing, given the noises it was making. But then humies were just bloody odd at the best of times, like a whole race of madboyz, only less likely to start eating their own boots.

'We'll link up wiv da boyz,' Ufthak said. 'Den we can–'

Mogrot bounded off with a whoop, down from the gargant's head and over its shoulders, dropping to the ground in a couple of jumps and haring off towards the onrushing humies. Ufthak could just hear him bellowing his war cry over the klaxons:

'COME AN' 'AVE A GO IF YER FINK YER 'ARD ENUFF!'

'Oh, zoggin' hell,' Ufthak muttered. Joining up with the ladz and giving these humies a proper kicking was probably the best *plan*, since he was more likely to survive that, and then be able to bag himself some loot. On the other hand, he'd just killed a gargant, even if the crew inside hadn't put up much fight, and he'd take orders from a grot before he let Mogrot Redtoof run into a fight while he hung back.

'Sod it,' he muttered, activating the Snazzhammer's power field. 'I guess we'z doin' dis. *WAAAAAAGH!*'

He ran forwards and leaped, clean out into the air, not even bothering to hop down like Mogrot had. He hit the ground hard, but his legs were up to it, and if the wound in his side where that humie had stuck its claws in him stung a bit, well, what was life if you didn't get reminded how close it sometimes came to ending? He pounded off after Mogrot, waving the Snazzhammer around his head and bellowing as loud as he could.

'Boss! Boss! Wait up!'

He ignored Nizkwik's panicked cries, fading behind him as he accelerated. Mogrot had a head start, but Ufthak's body was bigger and his legs were longer, and he was catching his second-in-command up. They should hit the humies more or less at the same time.

The humies slowed and aimed their pointy sticks at them, like they were some sort of gun instead of the very obviously pointy sticks they actually were. Humies. Mad as squigs, the lot of 'em.

The pointy sticks began firing energy bolts.

'Oh, what da–?' Ufthak barked in frustration, throwing himself to one side. 'Zoggin' humies–'

An energy bolt kicked up dust in front of him.

'–can't even get–'

His right shoulder-armour shattered as a bolt struck it. Mogrot was knocked on his arse by another.

'–zoggin' *pointy sticks* right!'

He pointed the shokk rifle in the humies' general direction and pulled the trigger.

The world exploded.

The earth trembled. A thunderclap shook the air, so loud it was like someone had slapped him in each ear with a stikk-bomb. For a moment Ufthak thought he'd accidentally sent the gun onto some sort of supercharged setting, but then as a sudden gale hit him from behind, with an accompanying cloud of first dust and then metallic debris, he realised the humie gargant's power core had finally detonated.

He looked over his shoulder and saw the machine's chest had been blown up and out, leaving fingers of shredded metal reaching for the sky. Rising up where the gargant itself had once stood was a dark mushroom cloud of smoke and fumes with a crackling, blue-white heart to it.

The humies *had* stopped firing, and were simply standing stock-still. Ufthak couldn't see their faces, since they were hidden behind helmets, but he was willing to bet his best shoota – or someone's best shoota, anyway – that they were staring past him with the horrified expression of a speed freek seeing the warning light on their fuel gauge.

Well, if they were just going to stand there...

'WAAAAGH!' he bellowed again, and went for them.

The humies snapped back to reality, but a moment too late. Ufthak's first swing of the Snazzhammer collided with a shield and knocked one humie flying into two of its fellows, sending them all clattering into a tangled heap of limbs, armour and pointy sticks. Another one charged right into a face-melting blast from the shokk rifle and fell into a spasming heap at his feet.

'You see dat?' Ufthak yelled, swatting another humie away with a mechanical-sounding scream. 'You see dat cloud?' He kicked the legs out from beneath one, then stomped on its head. 'You see dat gargant? Dat's wot I killed!' He smashed a humie's pointy stick into smithereens with the Snazzhammer, then headbutted it into oblivion. 'You fink you got a chance against me? Against Ufthak Gargantsmasha?'

Two out of the three he'd knocked into a pile got back to their feet, only for Mogrot to hit them from the side in a whirlwind of choppa cuts and slugga blasts.

'Took yer bloody time!' Ufthak yelled at his fellow ork. 'Dis was your idea!' He drew back the Snazzhammer to flatten another humie, but suddenly Princess was flying through the air at head height and clamping its jaws shut on the humie's head. The humie screamed and staggered sideways, then fell over as Princess closed its jaws and severed its neck.

'Good squig,' Ufthak said absently, looking around for his

next opponent. One of the other humies fired a panicked blast at Princess. 'Oi, dat's my squig, ya git!' Ufthak fired the shokk rifle, but the humie was aggravatingly not tall enough for the blast to hit it. It and its two mates aimed their sticks at him, but then instead of firing back they turned and ran.

'Get back 'ere, ya bloody cowards!' Ufthak bellowed after them.

The rest of the ladz chose that moment to arrive, and surged past him howling war cries. Which was obviously not why the humies had run: they'd clearly just been overawed by his might. Ufthak sighed. That had barely even counted as a good scrap.

He drew his arm back, screwed up one eye, and hurled the Snazzhammer. It *whup-whup-whupped* through the ladz, and the axe side of it cleaved into one of the fleeing humies' back, dropping it like a stone.

'Dat's my hammer!' Ufthak bellowed, just in case anyone got any funny ideas about nicking it. He really needed to find some way of getting it back quicker when he did that. He looked around, trying to take stock of what was going on.

It seemed the humies had all had the same idea: run away. Ufthak couldn't see a huge amount from where he was, but everything he could see showed the red-and-blue colours of the humies falling back, with orks in hot pursuit. He wasn't quite sure what the humies were hoping to achieve, though. They were simply getting closer and closer in to the big volcano on which all their fanciest buildings were constructed, without any obvious way out.

'Zoggin' humies,' he muttered, striding off towards where the Snazzhammer still protruded from the body of its victim, crackling with power. 'Can't even run away prop'ly.'

Mogrot finished lopping the head off the last humie he'd been fighting with, then pulled its pointy stick out of his arm. 'Dese fings *smart*, boss.'

'Don't get stuck by 'em, den,' Ufthak told him, without looking around.

'Well, I weren't... Oi!'

There was the buzz of a small engine and Da Boffin rolled past Ufthak on his monowheel, holding the pointy stick he'd just snatched out of Mogrot's hands. He used it to flick another, discarded one off the ground, and caught it in mid-air with a cackle.

'Wot you gonna be doin' wiv dose?' Ufthak asked him suspiciously. He'd seen that sort of expression on Da Boffin's face before, and it usually ended painfully for someone.

'Dunno,' the spanner beamed at him, 'but it's gonna be fun findin' out!' He nodded back at the smoking gargant. 'You kill dat?'

'Yup,' Ufthak said, with justifiable pride. 'Well, Mogrot helped, I s'pose.' He reached the Snazzhammer, took hold of its haft and wrenched it loose – or tried to, at any rate. The humie's body came up with it, and he had to shake it a few times to get it loose. 'Get off! Bloody dead git...'

'Dey don't seem to wanna fight much now we'z got more numbers,' Da Boffin observed.

'See, dat's why I don't trust numbers,' Ufthak told him. 'Dey get in da way, can stop yer havin' a good scrap.' He frowned. 'Wossat?'

The air ahead of them had gone a funny colour. It had already seemed a bit hazy, but Ufthak had put that down to dust, or something similar and equally inconsequential. Now, however, it seemed almost... glossy.

'Da boyz've stopped,' Da Boffin said, shading his eyes with

one hand. He craned his neck back, looking up into the air. 'It's dat force field! Da one wot woz stoppin' da landas from landin'. Dey've done somefing to it, I reckon.'

Ufthak followed his gaze. Sure enough, the strange glossiness curved up into the sky, just perceptible as the last rays of the setting sun hit it. He sighed. Every time it looked like he was about to get a decent fight, something new happened. 'Let's have a look, den.'

They soon caught up with the milling, shouting mob of boyz clustered at the edge of the translucent barrier, and Ufthak barged his way to the front of the mob where one of the boyz was taking a run at the glossy air. As soon as he hit it he bounced back off looking rather shaken, to a general chorus of mocking laughter.

'Who's in charge 'ere?' he demanded, looking about. His own ladz were mixed in with a whole load of others that he didn't recognise, and a couple of back-mounted bosspoles spoke of nobz who'd likely have their own opinions about the answer to his question. One of them, a surly-looking Bad Moon nearly as large as Ufthak and sporting an eyepatch, stepped up, looking Ufthak up and down disdainfully.

'Me.'

Ufthak headbutted him. The nob's eyes crossed, and he fell backwards.

'I'm Ufthak Gargantsmasha, and no, ya ain't,' Ufthak told his unconscious body, and the boyz around him all whooped. 'Right, now dat's sorted – wot's goin' on?'

'Da humies all ran froo dis bit, right,' another ork spoke up. 'Den just as we woz about to follow 'em da air went all hard, an' we bounced off.'

Ufthak reached out until his fingers made contact with… something. It felt greasy, and slippery, and not-quite-solid, but when he pressed on it, it pressed back firmly enough. It felt like it was buzzing, too.

'Dat's just weird,' he said, and looked around at Da Boffin. 'Any ideas?'

Da Boffin was checking a gizmo he'd pulled out of one of his ever-present pouches. The thing clicked busily and various needles were spinning around, although Ufthak had no idea what they might mean. It was a mek thing, which meant he didn't have to worry about it unless it looked like it was about to explode, at which point it would probably be too late anyway.

'Dey've narrowed da wavelength of all da projektions,' Da Boffin said, as though imparting useful information. 'It's gonna increase field integrity, at da expense of efficiency, an' generator degradation.'

'Wossat mean?'

'Means we can't walk froo it 'til it breaks, but dat might happen soon,' Da Boffin told him. He shrugged. 'Or it might not. Ya can never tell wiv humies.'

'I didn't kill a zoggin' gargant jus' to stand here like a bleedin' grot,' Ufthak growled. 'Until it breaks, ya said?'

'Yup,' Da Boffin replied.

'Well,' Ufthak said, winding up with the Snazzhammer again. 'Let's see if we can speed dat up.'

+++016+++

Zaefa reached the outer portal of her personal chambers only to find that she was already inside.

Or at least, that was what the door's machine-spirit thought. It refused to open to her, and when she interrogated it with a blurt of code she realised it had recorded her as having entered seven minutes and thirty-two seconds previously, which coincided exactly with the alert she'd received. Whoever had entered her chambers had convinced the lock that it was the rightful occupant of these chambers.

What they hadn't predicted was that Zaefa had set up an alert to notify her whenever *anyone* entered her chambers, herself included. It was a minor annoyance whenever she walked through her own door, but anyone hoping to circumvent security systems through impersonation instead of force might underestimate her... well, 'paranoia' was a term that implied disordered thinking. And clearly, Zaefa's concerns had been justified.

She paused for point seven seconds to consider calling for assistance, but decided against it. Most available skitarii units were fighting to defend the node itself, and only the most important locations within still maintained any sizeable force of armed guards. Besides which, Zaefa's chambers were her own private sanctum, in which she had many delicate items. One did not undertake the level of research and study necessary to become lexico arcanus of a prominent forge world without picking up some curios along the way. Any breach of a high councillor's personal chambers might be enough to pull even Ronrul Illutar away from his grandstanding under the pretence of investigating a potential incursion, as though the xenos brutes were going to sneak into Node Primus in order to rifle through Zaefa's personal effects.

No, Zaefa wasn't going to sound a general alarm and give the tech-priest dominus the excuse to investigate and catalogue her private domain. She would deal with this herself. Whoever was within was likely unaware that she knew they were there. Even if they were, they would quickly find out that entering the sanctum of a senior tech-priest uninvited was a risky endeavour.

Then again, overconfidence was the enemy of reason. Zaefa hastily formed a distress message and placed it into the noosphere with a six hundred-second delay on it. If she was unable to resolve matters satisfactorily within that time and cancel the message, it would probably be necessary.

Thus satisfied, she pushed at the lock again, overriding its simple memory and convincing it that yes, the being on its outside was indeed the rightful occupant. It chimed a welcome and the bolts and bars inside unlatched, allowing the doors to swing inwards. Zaefa stepped through into her home.

And into a bubble of silence.

This wasn't like the audio baffles at the Shrine of the Omnissiah: this was a silence deeper and thicker, for it was a code-silence, and not one that she'd had any part in creating. Zaefa was four steps inside the entrance hall when her audio receptors picked up the door closing and locking itself again behind her.

Whoever the intruder was had not only managed to circumvent her door security and enter her chambers, but had also taken control of the local noosphere and shunted it aside. Zaefa could still detect it faintly, but it hovered tantalisingly out of reach, neither discernible nor influenceable – or at least, not without a considerable effort on her part, and one she was not sure would be successful, but *was* sure would be detectable by whoever had orchestrated this. It was mastery of code on a level she had rarely witnessed.

Whoever had entered her chambers would know she was here, and had absolutely no intention of allowing her to call for assistance.

That heartened Zaefa somewhat. An intruder who wished to limit her acknowledged, even unintentionally, that they could be compromised. She had heard, of course, of the dark adepts of the dataproctors, those who could rewrite the Mechanicus' history, and even its reality, through their manipulation of code. Such a being would have almost nothing to fear in the heart of Node Primus, where code was supreme and the unaugmented barely existed. Whoever her visitor was, they felt it prudent to take safety precautions around her; and they would be wise to.

'Your presence is, of course, known to me,' she announced, using her flesh voice to do so. 'May I congratulate you on your manipulation of the noosphere? It has been some time since I have witnessed such talent.'

She stood still, awaiting a response. She had carefully modulated her vocal tones to contain no implication of either threat or fear, although of course such things were so crude compared to the purity of code-based communication, and interpretations could vary depending on inaccuracies in the speaker's delivery, idiosyncrasies in the recipient's aural abilities, and variations in cultural norms. Now to see how the intruder would react.

The entrance hall in which she stood was a mere thirty-three feet long, and Zaefa had paused just under halfway along it. It was ten feet wide, and tiled in a manner reminiscent of a regicide board set at a forty-five-degree angle to the walls: an affectation Zaefa had seen in the grand foyer of the planetary governor of Ortib IV, and had decided to replicate. Through a door to her immediate left lay an ablutions closet for any visitors whose connection to the flesh was somewhat closer than Zaefa's own, and although it had been several decades since she'd received any such visitors here, it was not unheard of. The door to her immediate right was the storage cupboard for her cleaning servitors, currently powered down and idle.

Directly ahead of her was the archway that led into the globular main chamber, and it was to this that she proceeded when she did not receive an immediate reply. It was not, technically, the most efficient manner in which to store her various possessions, but Zaefa did not completely hold with the prevailing doctrine of how a tech-priest should conduct themselves. So much of what she studied and worked with came from cultures that did not follow the cold pathways of logic, so why should their secrets be discovered solely through the application of such? Information was not the same thing as knowledge, after all: knowledge was divine, and required *understanding*. Zaefa's brain was still organic, for she was not a *silica cogitatus*, an abomination; therefore, understanding might still come to her as she moved through her collection, or through a piece being set in conjunction with another apparently unconnected piece, or even through the way light fell during different times of the day.

Ronrul Illutar had dismissed her opinions on these matters with something as close to a sneer as pure code could get; but then again, Node Primus was currently suffering the gravest threat ever recorded to its existence precisely because Ronrul Illutar had expected the orkoid invaders to behave logically and predictably, instead of attempting to understand his enemy.

She entered the main chamber, halfway up one wall, and her olfactory receptors picked up the increased scent of paper and glue. Much of the curving wall was occupied by shelves on which she stored primitive, plant fibre-based knowledge stores. Some were truly ancient – a few were encased in their own private stasis chambers – while some had been gleaned from cultures in which more sophisticated forms of data storage were unknown. Others still had been status symbols, physical embodiments of knowledge used to demonstrate their owners' wealth or privilege in a way that humble data crystals could not.

The central axis of the globe was taken up by the heating spike: a porous metal cylinder, roughly the width of Zaefa's own body, which carried up heat from the volcanic activity below to keep the chamber at a suitable temperature – more for her possessions than for her, since Zaefa's body was capable of withstanding far beyond the extremes of any weather condition that would occur on Hephaesto, save perhaps a direct lightning strike. The heat from below could also be shut off, allowing excess heat from her chambers to bleed off upwards, if for some reason the temperature was in excess of what she desired. It was an elegant piece of engineering, and one that was only possible thanks to the STC construct recovered by Ronrul Illutar which allowed for the easy and permanent regulation of the volcano's power.

Zaefa made a quick check of her surroundings before she moved from the platform on which she stood. Her sleeping chambers were directly opposite, and since they too opened directly onto the main room, she could see from her current position that no intruder was present. Her observatory, where she studied the night sky through spectrally enhanced magnoscopes, was ninety degrees to her right and thirty degrees elevated from her current position. She could not see every part of it from her location, but she strongly suspected that the intruder was not there.

Below her, where the globe of the main chamber flattened out to become a floor, a panel in the wall was open to reveal a void beyond lit by the actinic glow of sodium lamps. Unlike the other parts of her collection – the books on the walls, the examples of exotic taxidermy and botanic specimens positioned on platforms throughout the main void, linked by gantries and ladders around the thermal spike, and the geology samples stored in racks up near the ceiling – the items contained within that space were not on general view. Even those visitors whom Zaefa invited into her sanctum, and they were few, did not see the items beyond that panel unless she specifically desired them to. Indeed, the panel was hidden as well as she could manage: even opening it was entirely dependent on delicate dextrous manipulation of a concealed mechanism, in order to avoid leaving any form of code signature that could be detected and activated by an intruder.

As she focused on it, she saw that a hole had been punched

in the panel by some means, and it had been physically wrenched aside. The intruder had detected the void, but had not known how to access it. They did not know everything about her; although due to their employ of brute force, they now knew more than she would have liked.

In turn, she now knew that their physical strength was not inconsiderable.

'You appear to have damaged my abode,' she declared, beginning to traverse the steps downwards towards the level of the main chamber's floor. 'I must ask you to state your intentions.'

Five more seconds passed with no response, as Zaefa continued to descend. Then a voice replied.

'How much do you know about the items you have hidden here?'

It was a deep voice, and imposing. It was resonant in the manner of a bell, but with a faint buzz at its edges that could have been the influence of machinery – or, then again, could have been something entirely different. It was not confrontational, neither aggressive nor defensive, but was laced with a confidence unusual in someone discovered intruding in another's personal domain, and with an authority that expected to be answered.

Zaefa's mental list of possibilities for the intruder's identity narrowed further. Furthermore, and to her great surprise, she experienced a sensation of creeping discomfort that she could only categorise as dread. She had not experienced such a reaction in decades, and her voice would have trembled involuntarily, had the prosthetic delivering it been able to.

'Statement: your question is too inexact to be answered without somewhat in excess of three hours of verbal explanation, not allowing for subsidiary questions,' she declared, reaching the bottom of the stairs. The private storeroom was not far away from where she now stood – too close, even given the curvature of the walls, for her to see within. However, a shadow was cast on the floor outside by the lumens within as the intruder shifted position, and the shape thus formed allowed her to further extrapolate the likely nature of her uninvited guest.

Threat response systems began to activate, increasing her pulse and respiration rates, and auto-stimms began to reduce her reaction times ready for combat or flight, as required.

'Then I will be more exact, Lexico Arcanus Zaefa Varaz,' the voice replied, and Zaefa could detect the faint underpinnings of irritation within it. 'How much do you know about the device next to which I am standing?'

The invite to approach was plain, and Zaefa fought down her annoyance at the intruder taking such a tone with her within her own domain. Whoever they were, they were clearly in search of information; this was an interaction she could use to her advantage, for now.

She reached the doorway and looked within.

Even with her deductions so far, even with her systems prepared and alert for the threat, the sight that greeted her still triggered a wave of fear and panic that only a death grip on her physical reactions allowed her to control and conceal. The great height, close to ten feet; the massive width of the body; the writhing mechatendrils that snaked out of the armour's back-mounted power pack, equipped with powerblades and fusion cutters and other, less recognisable devices; the flowing, hooded cloak in the colours of Hephaesto; and the armour itself, with its grille-like faceplate and huge shoulder pauldrons and, most telling of all, the unembellished iron skull on the breastplate, pitted and rusted but still identifiable. Zaefa had amassed an enormous amount of knowledge over her life, and the merest skimming of her databanks allowed her to put a positive identification on the intruder.

Traitor Astartes.

Iron Warrior.

Heretek.

The presence of such an enemy of the Imperium within Hephaesto's Node Primus automatically led to other logical conclusions. Firstly, that the ork invasion might have been precipitated in some way by this being or his associates, although that was by no means a given. Secondly, that there were already gaping holes in Node Primus' security systems: this wasn't an invasion of her chambers by another Mechanicus adept who otherwise had every right to be present within the node; this was the work of an enemy who could have expected to be challenged at any moment he was visible.

Thirdly, and following on from the second point, he would almost certainly have had assistance in some manner. There were other traitors, other hereteks within the walls.

'You are informed as to my identity,' Zaefa told the Iron Warrior, managing to keep her flesh-voice level in what she felt was an admirable masking of her genuine alarm. 'Courtesy would suggest that you should inform me of yours.'

The Iron Warrior's grille-faced helm tilted to one side slightly. 'What makes you expect courtesy from one such as I?'

'You are here seeking knowledge,' Zaefa told him. 'You have requested that knowledge from me, instead of attacking me upon sight. Courtesy assists in social interactions. Since we are engaging in social interaction instead of combat, the protocols of social interaction should be followed.'

The Iron Warrior snorted. 'Ah, the Mechanicus. Logical and

dogma-bound as ever. Very well, lexico arcanus – you are speaking to Warpsmith Gavrak Daelin, of the Fourth Legion.'

'I am intrigued to have met you,' Zaefa replied, which was honest enough. Let the heretek think she was so far beyond human norms that she truly did not register the threat of his presence, or view him as anything other than an interesting oddity; that was surely a better way to proceed. She resisted the urge to reach out to the noosphere, from which she was still separated by Daelin's void. She would not risk that until she had no option, for if he thought that she was attempting to summon aid then he would surely attack.

'You had questions?' she said, before he could speak again. She felt the scrutiny of his helm's eye sockets for a second before he responded, as though he was assessing whether she truly was so blasé about his identity, but then he replied as though there were no possibility of anything being amiss.

'This machine,' he said, half-turning to gesture to the device next to him. 'What do you know of its nature and origins?'

It was an odd artefact – one of the oddest in Zaefa's most private storeroom, and that was saying quite a lot. The main body of it stood nearly seven feet tall, and consisted of a fluted, stone-like structure. It was wider at the base, apparently for stability, then narrowed halfway up, before broadening again into a shape similar to that of a font or basin. It was not uniform in shape all the way around, however, and had indentations and protrusions that fitted with its flowing form, but which appeared to have been created for some purpose that Zaefa had not yet been able to define.

The opening at the top, meanwhile, was some two feet across and nearly a foot deep at its deepest point. Into the base of this depression were set shards of crystal, a purply green in colour, the base of each having been smoothed into a perfect cylinder in order to fit into a matching socket, but with the rest left in its jagged, unworked form.

This in itself would perhaps appear to be no more than an ornament, but that impression was dispelled by the rest of it. Attached to the side of the main body were five metallic arms, multijointed and with the impression of arachnid limbs, each tipped with a needle-point that was sharp to a microscopic level.

'A curio,' she replied, doing her best to sound unconcerned at the Iron Warrior's query. 'I procured it when I was part of an explorator fleet in the Segmentum Obscurus.'

'I did not ask where you found it,' Daelin said, not looking at her. 'I asked what you knew of its nature and origins.'

Zaefa decided to gamble. 'It is human-made, of course, although perhaps by a civilisation lost even before the Great Crusade–'

The Iron Warrior held up one gauntleted hand, and for a moment Zaefa wondered if she'd miscalculated tremendously by mentioning the time period in which this being's predecessors, and perhaps even this being himself, had rebelled into heresy against the Emperor of Mankind. Would violence now follow?

'Human-made?' Daelin snorted contemptuously, and Zaefa relaxed a little. 'Hardly. Come now, lexico arcanus, what about this looks "human-made" to you? This is of xenos origin.'

Some of Zaefa's threat response systems cycled up a little more, in spite of her willing them not to. She hadn't been sure! She hadn't! But even she wasn't certain if that was true. After all, to be in possession of a xenos artefact was… well, opinions ranged from 'risky' to 'heretical'. Could she have actually deceived *herself* about her true opinions on it? Had she buried her concerns behind her curiosity, telling herself that she couldn't be sure, and therefore should not act on incomplete information?

But then again, who was to say this traitor would be telling the truth? Although it was certainly true that she'd stated the artefact was human-made in order to see if she could bait the Iron Warrior into confirming that it was not. The heretek considered himself her superior, so let him correct her if he wished.

'I had considered the possibility that it was aeldari,' she admitted, and was astonished to find that she experienced a faint rush of both alarm and excitement at finally stating that out loud to someone, even someone as threatening as the Warpsmith. It was almost freeing, in a sense. What was Daelin going to do? Decry her as a heretic? The notion was laughable. 'The central column bears chemical similarities to the few samples I have managed to find of their main building material.'

'Aeldari?' Daelin grunted, bending to inspect it a little more closely. 'Perhaps. But these...' He gestured at the mechanical arms. 'I have slaughtered those miserable, wailing wretches on a dozen worlds. I have ripped the hearts out of their great spacecraft, and brought low their mightiest war machines.' He shook his head. 'Never have I seen the aeldari work with metal in this fashion. Nor have I seen them join their creations with those of other races, yet if the central element of this is aeldari, it is not theirs alone.'

'The arms do, superficially, appear to be afterthoughts,' Zaefa agreed. 'However, no matter that they jar aesthetically with the organic appearance of the main body, such investigations as I have conducted suggest that they are connected to the very core.'

'And what is in that core?' Daelin asked.

'I have been unable to determine from scans, and unwilling to damage the outer casing to inspect it more closely,' Zaefa informed him. 'It has a different density to the outer layers, that much I can say without question.' She decided to take another risk.

'What made you aware of the artefact's presence in my chambers?'

Daelin didn't answer her immediately, instead continuing to stare at the artefact. When he did reply, his voice was a touch less forceful than before, as though tainted by faint uncertainty.

'It called to me.'

'Interrogative: it communicated with you?' Zaefa asked, shocked beyond measure. 'By what means?'

'Through the datasphere,' Daelin said. 'I detected a presence, something different to the inane chatter of your kind. When I attempted to investigate, it withdrew before me, and eventually disconnected itself entirely. The origin point of the signal was unmistakeable – these chambers. I tracked it here in person, and only discovered your identity as I entered.'

A memory flashed up in Zaefa's recall: a large, robed shape pushing across her line of vision as she made her way towards the Shrine of the Omnissiah. A swift analysis demonstrated that it was of similar enough dimensions for her to be eighty-seven per cent certain it had been Gavrak Daelin. The Iron Warrior must have been employing some form of sensor-obfuscating code screen, so he was seen without being recognised for what he was.

'You are certain that it was this?' Zaefa queried, still struggling to believe that the Iron Warrior could be telling the truth. However, the notion of anything else within her chambers performing a similar feat was just as unlikely.

'Unquestionably,' Daelin replied. 'I can feel the same presence within it now. That is why I have pushed back the noosphere here – I wish it to have no option other than to engage with me. And yet it does not.' He reached out to the shards of crystal, and tapped the pointed end of one very gently with a finger. Now she looked again, Zaefa could see the Iron Warrior's left arm was in fact a bionic shaped to exactly match the size and dimensions of its corresponding right limb, which was still apparently whole and encased in the ceramite of his armour.

'What are these?' Daelin asked. 'They must have some function, rather than being decorative.'

'My analysis identified them as salludo crystals,' Zaefa informed him. 'Very rare. Judging by the lining of the sockets into which they slot, which appear to be coated in a substance that is receptive to the specific mineral make-up of these crystals, I hypothesise that they form some sort of power core.'

'A power core?' Daelin scoffed. 'There is no power here, I can see as much.'

'There is certainly no conventional energy source,' Zaefa conceded. She approached the artefact, and reached out a mechadendrite to delicately remove one of the crystals from its slot. This close to the Iron Warrior she could almost feel the *wrongness* bleeding off him: the corruption, the scrapcode, the aeons of slaughter and bloodshed. She forced herself to remain calm, and not to give off any signs of heightened anxiety. 'However, it is my belief that when activated, by a process with which I am not yet familiar, this artefact will drain power from these crystals through some form of chemical reaction. You may inspect the sheath yourself, if you wish.'

'Hmm.' Daelin reached forward with his right arm to take hold of a crystal himself.

Zaefa attacked.

Her left foot stamped on Daelin's right boot and mag-clamped to the floor around it, locking it down; both her primary arms reached out to clasp the Warpsmith's right arm, holding it extended forwards. Two of her mechadendrites flashed out to intercept the Iron Warrior's mechatendrils, while the third activated the lascutter at its tip and blasted a hole in Daelin's armour at a weak point where it covered the right armpit.

As soon as the lascutter withdrew, her fourth mechadendrite rammed the salludo shard she'd removed from the artefact into Daelin's cursed flesh.

Gavrak Daelin, Traitor Astartes, was an inhuman, gene-enhanced warrior who had further improved himself by fusing his body with heretical technology. He was, without a doubt, a lethal warrior who could slay most foes.

A senior tech-priest of the Adeptus Mechanicus, even a lexico arcanus, was not most foes. Zaefa Varaz might have devoted her existence to the collection of knowledge and the compiling of data, but with that had come the understanding that the galaxy was an extremely dangerous place that made no distinction between active combatants and interested observers. Her reaction times and physical tolerance levels were far beyond biological norms, and while nothing about her person would be classified as a weapon per se, the difference between, for example, a meltagun and a melta-torch was a purely academic one when at point-blank range.

She also knew what Gavrak Daelin apparently did not, which was that salludo shards were lethally toxic to carbon-based life forms. Whether or not the Iron Warrior still counted as one remained to be seen.

Her advantage of surprise lasted for one hundred and

thirty-two milliseconds, and then Daelin moved. He made no attempt to remove the shard, nor did he try to free his right foot. Instead he spun to his left, presenting his back to her: a strange move for most combatants, but not for one armed with mechatendrils that jutted from his spine.

Zaefa mirrored him the moment he adjusted his position, and her mechadendrites clashed with his mechatendrils, each seeking to gain the advantage. She narrowly wrenched aside a stab from a powerblade; he gripped her melta-torch to redirect its jet of super-heat over his shoulder at the last moment, blasting a four-armed sculpture of Xantian jade into smithereens.

Zaefa released his right foot, clamped both her feet to the floor, and wrenched forwards. Back to back, and tangled up as they were, Daelin was pulled completely over her head. His hands found her wrists as she drove him down to the floor, but her rising knee caught him in the faceplate with enough force to shatter his helm.

The Iron Warrior was momentarily stunned by her blow and Zaefa plunged a lascutter towards the back of his neck, but he swatted it away with a mechatendril at the last moment and surged back up to his feet with a roar of rage. His skin was pallid, his head was bald and criss-crossed with scars, and one of his eyes had been replaced by a bionic. He wrenched his arms wide, seeking to detach hers, but her enhancements telescoped out to match his reach. He spat viscous black acid, but Zaefa jerked her head aside to avoid the attack. However, the corrosive liquid splattered over one of her mechadendrite arms, and she felt the structure of it beginning to weaken.

'Mechanicus fool,' Daelin snarled, as their secondary limbs fell to duelling again. His words revealed sharpened metal teeth that had somehow remained undamaged by his acidic saliva. 'I'd have left you to your fate had you merely answered my questions!'

'I would not have extended you the same courtesy,' Zaefa replied. 'For you are an abomination.'

Daelin laughed. 'Blind, weak little dead thing.'

He unleashed a torrent of scrapcode.

It sleeted through Zaefa's defences, tearing at her operating systems. Her vision fuzzed; the strength of her limbs abruptly sapped; her mechadendrites became sluggish and her awareness of their positions faded. Even as she struggled, his powerblade-armed mechatendril dipped past her compromised defences and plunged into her shoulder, making her gasp as pain receptors activated. Daelin was seeking to destroy everything about her.

But he overreached himself, for he sought a complete victory too quickly.

'Ave Deus Mechanicus!' Zaefa hissed, marshalling all her code-lore, and struck back. Unlike Daelin's blizzard-like attack, seeking to abrade her into nothingness, Zaefa's strike was a lance of code directed at the heart of the machine-spirit that guided the Iron Warrior's armour. The backwash of the contact engulfed Zaefa in nausea she hadn't felt for two centuries, for Daelin's armour was a corrupt and malign entity that was a far cry from either of the suits of loyalist power armour Zaefa had managed to gain access to during her life. Nonetheless, her blow struck home: her code-lance, charged with all the purity of her belief in the Creator, the Scion and the Motive Force, pierced the rotten heart of the machine to which Daelin had grafted himself.

'What...!?' Daelin gasped, as systems upon which he had relied for millennia abruptly failed or outright rebelled. He slewed to one side, and his scrapcode assault ceased as he redirected all his concentration on regaining control of his armour, and therefore his body.

Zaefa drove her lascutter directly at his face.

Daelin was too quick: he'd had a moment to recover himself, and that was all he needed. Now his combat instincts took over again and he disengaged, backflipping away with an agility that belied his huge size and ponderous form. He landed on two feet.

He staggered, and an expression of consternation crossed his face as black blood leaked from beneath his right arm.

'Do stay,' Zaefa implored him, advancing as menacingly as she could. 'I am intrigued to learn how the toxins of a salludo shard interact with the tainted flesh of a fallen Astartes.'

Gavrak Daelin wrenched the shard out with a mechatendril and flung it away; it shattered against the wall with a crash. He bared his teeth defiantly, but Zaefa could tell that the Iron Warrior knew something was wrong with him. It was too much to hope for that the toxins would kill him, or even disable him for long – even a regular Space Marine would likely be able to fight off its effects given time – but it might provide her with enough of an advantage to finish him.

Maybe.

The emergency klaxons began to sound. The noosphere crashed back in as Daelin released his hold on it, but unlike him, Zaefa didn't need it to know what was happening. Far ahead of even the most pessimistic schedule, the orks had breached the node's void shields. Xenos beasts were loose in the main node.

They were out of time.

Daelin turned and ran. Zaefa could, perhaps, have caught him. She could, perhaps, have fought him for control of the door to her sanctum to prevent him from leaving. She made no effort to do either of those things. To do so was to invite further combat when she was by no means certain that she could win. Let Daelin go. She needed to complete her work: she had to salvage her most valuable personal possessions, and complete the evacuation of the node's datastacks and prototypes.

Her assessment of the noosphere's information brought her to a halt. She scanned it again to double-check that she had interpreted the information correctly, that she hadn't been confounded by some form of after-effect of Daelin's scrap-code attack. But no, it remained clear.

The void shields hadn't failed. One segment, in the southern sector, had been deliberately *lowered*. It was even now being reinstated, but a force of orkoid infantry and minor war machines had penetrated into the node. The authorisation signature on the shield's deactivation was clear to someone of Zaefa's rank: Grand Genetor Yavannos.

Which would explain why the standing orders to the defence forces were for the xenos to be 'captured intact for study' instead of exterminated.

Zaefa clenched her fists with rage. Yavannos' academic interests had always outweighed her sense of self-preservation, but this was a new level of idiocy even for her. Zaefa could almost see the logic of allowing the xenos in piecemeal, to try to chew them up bit by bit instead of waiting for the fields to fail and then be overwhelmed, but to order the troops to capture them? She snorted. The disaster such an order would surely cause might even convince Illutar to approve Kapothenis Ull's prototype war machine as a desperate last gambit...

A prototype war machine.

A prototype war machine that contained some elements of recognised Mechanicus technology, but whose schematics seemed ill-defined in a manner out of character for the forge lord. A prototype war machine that Illutar himself had described as potentially heretical, and when there was an Iron Warriors Warpsmith present in the node.

'Kapothenis,' Zaefa muttered to herself in horror, reaching through the noosphere to try to contact Secutor Mitranda. 'Kapothenis, what have you done?'

Up Close An' Pers'nal

Ufthak wound up and swung.

The Snazzhammer crackled through the air and impacted on the strange, glossy, buzzing air where Da Boffin said the humies' force field was. The impact gave off a strangely dull, flat sound, and there was spitting and sizzling as the weapon's power field interacted momentarily with the strange force that the humies were using to keep Ufthak and his ladz out of their city, but the humie tech held firm. Ufthak glowered at it.

'Yeah, we tried dat,' someone said from behind him. Ufthak didn't dignify the comment with a response. Instead, he turned the Snazzhammer around and had a go with the axe head.

There wasn't a noticeable difference in result, although Princess apparently liked the momentary light show, and grunted in what might have been appreciation.

'Maybe we should see if dere's a way round?' a different voice suggested helpfully. 'Go in anuvver way, like?'

'Give over, Gorrukk. Yoo fink da humies are just gonna leave a hole fer us to find?'

'Humies put backdoors in everyfing, right? Cos dey always wants a way to get away from a fight...'

Ufthak ground his teef together. He'd never yet been so vexed by a bit of zogging air, and he'd had about enough of its cheek.

'Hold dis,' he told Mogrot, handing him the shokk rifle.

'Okay, boss, but–'

Ufthak spat on his palms, gripped the Snazzhammer two-handed, and took three steps back and one to the side. He inhaled deeply through his nose, exhaled through his mouth, then ran at the force field and swung the Snazzhammer with all the considerable might of his two arms.

He saw the first spark fly, felt the beginning of the impact travelling up the Snazzhammer's haft, through his hands, up his arms...

...and then the force field gave way.

There was no explosion, and no crackle of failing technology, but between one moment and the next the strange glossiness that formed the nearly transparent barrier between Ufthak's ladz and the main part of the humies' city disappeared. Ufthak staggered forwards as the expected resistance to his swing vanished before it could properly kill his momentum, and his metal-shod boots took him over the faint line that the bottom edge of the field had marked in the dust.

He was through.

'Didja see that, ladz?' Mogrot bellowed. 'Da boss just smashed dat force field!'

Ufthak turned around and grinned at the assembled mass of Bad Moons boyz, whose open-mouthed staring quickly resolved into raucous cheering and waving of their shootas.

Behind them, Ufthak could see more orks closing in on him, boyz and warbikers and even a Deff Dread or two, all gravitating to the destruction of the fallen humie Titan and looking for the ork who'd managed it. Which was definitely him, even if Mogrot had dropped the stikkbomb that had shattered its power wotsits, because Mogrot would never have got there if it hadn't been for Ufthak's brilliant plan. Besides, Mogrot wasn't looking to argue.

And beyond them, its thudding footsteps bringing it closer and closer, was the MekaGargant. Ufthak grinned wider, imagining Da Meklord peering through a make-bigger device and seeing Ufthak appearing on the head of the humie gargant, then climbing into it and it suddenly stopping fighting, and then climbing out of it again when it fell over, just before it exploded, and *then* smashing a hole through the force field.

Things might be looking up.

'Mogrot, gimme dat gun back!' he yelled, and his second-in-command obediently tossed him the shokk rifle. Ufthak caught it, and never mind that he accidentally pressed the firing stud in doing so and blew one boy's leg off. Everyone laughed, and even the lad who'd ended up unexpectedly on the floor would see the funny side of it once he'd had a replacement fitted, Ufthak was certain of it.

He didn't need to issue any further instructions. The boyz surged forwards – those with the requisite number of legs, anyway – and they piled into the heart of the humies' domain together.

Farther away from the volcano, the humies' buildings had been smaller, and lower, and more spaced-out. There'd been plenty of room for them to move stuff from one place to another, as humies loved to do, and then dump it somewhere for a while – like that slag heap Ufthak's landa had come to rest against – before maybe moving it somewhere else, when they got round to it. The MekaGargant was stomping through great, stinking, shallow pools of water and humie filth that Ufthak could smell even from here. From what he'd seen of them, they'd all been about the same size and shape, so presumably the humies had made them that way on purpose.

Here, however, there was no space, no piles of spoil or waste, no open ground or pools of water. The buildings had closed in and reared up, and these were massive edifices supported by buttresses and topped by spires, or big metal statues of humies, or other, less comprehensible stuff. Unusually, the two-headed bird Ufthak had come to associate with humies over the years wasn't particularly visible. Instead there was a different symbol repeated over and over, looming out of walls and inscribed into doors: half a humie skull, half a cogwheel. Ufthak supposed it was the clan badge of these humie meks, or something.

'Where're we even gonna find any loot worth havin' in dis place?' Mogrot asked as they pounded down one of the gaps between buildings, cutting through from one humie road to another, through which ran a series of large pipes. 'It could be anywhere!'

'Look for da humies,' Ufthak said sagely. 'Dis is where dey live, right? So dey're gonna be guardin' da best stuff. An' if dat fails,' he pointed up to where the peak of the volcano would be, if it weren't currently obscured by a humie building, 'we go higher up. Boss humies like to see over da top of everyfing, innit? S'like bein' in da head of a gargant, when yer bigger dan everyone else. An' boss humies'll have da good tek.'

'Boss!' someone shouted. 'Yoo hear dat?'

Ufthak slowed and held up one hand, and the mob came

to a somewhat unsteady halt behind him, while Princess bounced around his feet. He listened hard, concentrating. Sure enough, there was a wheezy whine coming from ahead, and slightly to the right, if he was any judge.

'Wossat, den?' he asked, annoyed that he couldn't recognise it.

'Sounds like one of dem floatin' tanks,' an ork with a particularly large choppa put in. 'We 'ad to deal wiv a few of 'em when we landed.'

'Floatin' tanks?!' Ufthak shook his head. 'Wot's wrong wiv traks, or some wheels? Floatin' tanks. Dese humies, I ask ya.' He worked his shoulder, limbering it up ready to swing the Snazzhammer again. 'Right, let's get down da end dere an' see wot dey got.'

Ufthak and his mob reached the end of the pipeway just as the whining grew louder and a red-and-midnight humie vehicle hove into view. It was a strange thing indeed, hovering along at about waist height, as though there were anything beneath it except empty air. These humies seemed to be able to make air do a bunch of things it didn't normally, and Ufthak was having no truck with it. He didn't even slow; he was already moving, so it seemed a waste of time to stop and try to take a shot with the shokk rifle when he had a perfectly good hammer in his hand.

He burst into the thoroughfare and lashed out with the Snazzhammer, clipping the thing's near back end. It erupted into flame and smoke, and the tank began to spin away from him. Ufthak noticed two things at more or less the same time. Firstly, the tank wasn't an enclosed vehicle; it was open-topped, and packed with humie troops.

Secondly, there were three more of the zogging things coming right up behind the first one.

Ufthak threw himself to one side to avoid the second. He could have theoretically just ducked down and let it go over him, but something told him that it had to keep itself off the ground *somehow*, and he wasn't sure he wanted to be between the tank and the ground when whatever-it-was was doing its thing. The rest of his mob were piling out now, guns blazing and choppas swinging, and shots were *spanging* off the floaty-tanks' armoured sides as they slewed to a halt through some means other than standard friction.

The boarding ramps at the front came down, and Ufthak was expecting the zip and whine of bullets, or the blue-white crackle of those lightning guns some of the humies had – maybe even the incandescent, roaring blast of a plasma weapon. Instead, one of the humies pointed something bulky and matt-black at him, and a moment later a large, amorphous and dark shape flew through the air and ensnared him. He staggered for a moment, more through surprise than anything else. This wasn't like anything that humies had shot at him with before, and he thought he'd seen just about everything they had...

It was a zogging *net*.

His fury at their bloody cheek was just getting going when the strands of the net crackled into life, and his entire body was wracked with spasms as electrical discharge forced him into violent muscle cramps. His stagger turned into a stumble, and then into a fall as his right leg treacherously disobeyed him and toppled him over onto the rough, red road surface beneath him. He caught sight of other nets flying through the air, landing on boyz in twos and threes, and then activating. Orkish cries of pain and rage filled the air, and other humies stalked forward on metal legs, holding batons over which played more subtle strands of stunning power.

Ufthak managed to get the tips of his fingers through the thick mesh of the net and, fighting through the muscle spasms, tore it wide apart. The crackling power died as the strands gave way before his fearsome strength, and he shrugged it off to surge up to his feet and into the three humies advancing on him.

He wielded the Snazzhammer one-handed, swatting it backwards and forwards, sending his enemies flying sideways, their torsos crushed and spraying blood, before they were able to respond. Most humies barely came up to his chest now, and they just seemed so *slow...*

The rest of his ladz were having none of it, either. If the humies had fired the nets and then used regular guns they might have got a few of the boyz, it was true; but they hadn't, and so they didn't. Whatever game the nets had been designed for, it wasn't orks; the mob's charge, which had faltered in the face of the unconventional humie offence, began again as they fought their way free. The humies piled in gamely enough, perhaps realising that they were doomed now anyway, but it was never going to be anything like a fair contest when all their sticks did was make an ork jump a bit. The humies were shot to pieces, cut into chunks, and generally stomped into reddish paste within a matter of seconds.

The floaty-tank drivers didn't seem to fancy sticking around now their mates had been pulped, but they didn't have a choice in the matter either. Ufthak didn't even have to lift a finger; his ladz swarmed up the boarding ramps and swiftly overran the pair of crew on each of the four tanks, killing their momentum, apart from the one Ufthak had first hit with his hammer. That one proceeded to veer around in a very tight circle, while the orks on board whooped at the novelty of it.

'Are dey wantin' a fight, or not?' Mogrot asked him, kicking what was left of a humie corpse. 'Why're dey usin' dese stikk fings?'

'Beats me,' Ufthak confessed, looking around. He could hear the shouts and war cries of other groups of boyz, and plenty of dakka, from various other directions in this maze of buildings. He couldn't hear any humie weapons though, so it sounded as if the humies were, for reasons only known to themselves, trying the same trick elsewhere. He also heard the distinctive roar of warbikes, accelerating away somewhere to his left, and by the sounds of it they were heading further up into the city, towards the top where he reckoned the humie nobs would be. He clenched his fist angrily. If they reached the good stuff before him…

He looked around, and was rewarded with the sight of Da Boffin picking his way between a buttress and where the last pipe curved down into the ground. The spanner could leave a regular ork in the dust on the flat, but his wheel meant he was rather more limited when it came to rough terrain and obstacles. Behind him came Princess and, Ufthak was considerably less pleased to see, the scrawny shape of Nizkwik, hanging back and still eyeing the squig warily.

'Oi, Boffin!' Ufthak bellowed, jerking a thumb at the humie floaty-tank. 'Can ya drive one of dese?'

Da Boffin squig-hopped over a body and landed on a humie skull, crushing it with an entertaining splintering sound, then looked over the nearest tank with the practised eye of an ork who'd been asked to fix vehicles considerably less conventional than this by one speed freek or another, at some point in the past.

'Yeah, shouldn't be too 'ard. All ya need is "go", and left or right.' He motored straight up the ramp, through the boyz, who pressed themselves against the side of the vehicle to make way for him, and began fussing with the controls.

'Whoo'za good squig?' Ufthak asked Princess, as the squig bounded up to him. 'Izzit yoo?' Apparently it was, because Princess squealed raucously, so Ufthak tossed it a humie arm that seemed mostly meat, and it crunched it down gleefully.

'Got it, boss!' Da Boffin called, as the tank lurched around drunkenly. 'What's da plan?'

'Up dere!' Ufthak told him, pointing one clawed finger towards the highest bit of the humie city. 'Sod all dis scrabblin' around. I wanna be right up dere, where it's all shiny an' dat!' He jumped up onto the boarding ramp as Da Boffin brought it round again, and Princess followed. Nizkwik did too, wailing in alarm as it nearly flew off, but to Ufthak's vague disappointment the grot managed to hold on. There were half a dozen or so orks already packed into the tank, armed and eager.

'What about us, boss?' one of the others asked forlornly, from a tank that was gently spinning in a circle.

'Ya got yer own ride dere, you work it out!' Ufthak told him. He climbed up beside Da Boffin, to where a couple of humie big shootas rested, and tracked them up and down, and then side to side. 'Let's go. Bet dey won't even notice us when we're in dere tank.'

'Like da tinboy on dat humie ship didn't know yer woz orks cos yer woz holdin' up dead humies in front of ya?' Da Boffin asked him.

Ufthak shrugged. 'More or less.'

'Boss, it noticed real quick, an' den yer had to hit it wiv da hammer, an' *den* it blew up an' killed ya.'

'Got close enuff to hit it wiv da hammer, tho,' Ufthak pointed out smugly. 'Dat's da point. We ain't gotta get all da way. Just close enuff. Den we can start hittin' fings.'

The Binding

The journey back to Kapothenis Ull's forge was far harder and more dangerous than the one Gavrak Daelin had made away from it. The alarms were singing their song of danger and combat, and the vigilance of the Adeptus Mechanicus had increased as a result. Even the codeshroud that kept his true nature hidden as he walked beneath the noses of his enemies was tested with increasing frequency and urgency, as the node's security systems responded to the full battle alert by repeatedly checking on the identity of all beings within their sphere of influence. Daelin could no longer rely on his background shrouding casually sliding him past the notice of those around him, while he used swift stabs of code here and there to deflect the occasional, more direct enquiries of surveillance programs in the same manner as a master of unarmed combat might bat aside the clumsy swing of an aggressive but unskilled pugilist. Now he was forced to devote all his resources to persuading the security systems that he had every right to go where he pleased, while simultaneously remaining completely unremarkable to them.

He was sure he could feel the presence of that tech-priest, Varaz, as well. She was somewhere in the noosphere, hunting him – not like a predator hunted prey, for he would never be prey, but in the manner of a predator seeking a rival who had invaded their territory. Daelin had fled their combat because he had underestimated her abilities and would need to devise a new approach if they were to fight again. He'd also been weakened by that accursed poisoned crystal, the salludo shard; his metabolism was fighting the effects off now, but it was a potent toxin indeed. If they were to clash again, one on one, he would be unaffected by it and, now knowing her capabilities as he did, he was confident he could overwhelm her in short order.

However, he wouldn't be facing her one on one. When they'd been in her chambers, Varaz had been isolated and unable to summon assistance. If she were to locate him here, in the hub of her kind's power, she would be able to call allies to help bring him down. Even if he could completely shut down her noospheric communication, Gavrak Daelin would struggle to override the auditory sensoral input of every member of the Mechanicus within earshot of his adversary's physical voice. No, he had to keep moving.

In that sense, at least, the penetration of the node's defence fields by the ork invaders would assist him. Node Primus was already operating at its highest possible alert level. Even if Varaz were to disseminate information about his presence into the system, it would be one top-priority security alert amongst many, many others. However, in other respects the orks' arrival could not have been more poorly timed. They

were brutish savages, but they were efficient and effective warriors and killers, and at close quarters they were very likely
to overwhelm the Mechanicus' last defences. Gavrak Daelin
needed to ensure his work was completed before they reached
it. The consequences otherwise did not bear contemplating.

He took a chance, and let himself through an access hatch
out of the main corridor down which he'd been hurrying.
His parsing of the node's data feeds had alerted him to a
maniple of skitarii approaching, their bionic legs hastening
them forwards in metronomic lockstep, and although the
likelihood of them noticing him was low, the potential risk
if they did was too high. He wasn't far from Ull's forge, now;
better to trust to access ways and service corridors instead of
the general thoroughfares.

This wasn't to say that his new route was risk-free, of course.
He descended a ladder from brightly lit, sterile corridors into
a world of semi-darkness, dank air and rusted pipes carrying
water, power and clean air. Cleaning servitors were virtually
unknown here, and the transition encapsulated the essential
dichotomy of the modern Mechanicus: a gleaming surface,
underpinned by a little-understood mess of slow degradation
and vermin. It wasn't the giant rats watching him suspiciously
from the shadows that concerned Gavrak Daelin, however.
Since it was less frequently used, his access to this corridor would be all the more notable to the security systems,
and at times of battle alert, entry to such places would be
closely monitored in case enemies sought to gain access to
them. He could scrub the record of his entry, but only a fool
placed total confidence in their ability to outwit an enemy.
He hurried onwards beneath flickering lumens, reaching out
into the noosphere to ensure no combat-servitors on exter-
mination protocols had been dispatched to his location,

while the ceramite of his soles rang out on the metal grilles beneath his feet.

He'd just rounded a corner when the orks attacked.

He was caught totally unaware: he'd been so fixated on avoiding notice from the Mechanicus that he hadn't considered the possibility that the orks could have infiltrated so far into the node already. Besides which, Gavrak Daelin knew orks as bellowing slabs of muscle and belligerence, powerful and crude. You heard them before you saw them, and there was a fair chance of smelling them before that, too. These flowed out of the darkness like murderous shadows, their clothes patterned in imitation of Imperial camouflage and their blades blackened to minimise the chance of them glinting in the light and giving away their owners' positions.

There were seven of them, each a deadly foe in its own right, but even when taken by surprise, Daelin was not about to easily fall victim to this xenos filth. He drew his bolt pistol and stitched a row of shots up the first ork's chest, culminating in a final shell between the alien's deep-set red eyes that blew its skull apart. Then its fellows were on him.

Daelin lashed out with fists and feet and his mechatendrils, his every thought now focused on combat and survival. He shattered an ork's ribcage with a punch, lopped off an axe-wielding hand with his powerblade, grabbed a green-skinned wrist and pointed it at another ork even as the first one pulled the trigger of its firearm. He jerked his head backwards to avoid snapping, fang-strewn jaws, and ducked a decapitating swing, but there were too many blows to avoid altogether. He felt a shell carom off his left pauldron, and two strong hands seized one of his mechatendrils and hauled him sideways, directly into the path of a huge axe. The weapon, razor-edged and powered by the ork's brute strength, sheared through Daelin's ceramite breastplate and buried itself into his torso.

Daelin roared in pain and anger: anger at the greenskin's temerity, and anger at his own flesh's weakness in registering the wound. His powerblade buried itself in the skull of the ork who had hold of his mechatendril and it dropped like a stone. He lashed out sideways with a boot, ignoring the screaming agony in his chest as he did so, and sent another ork crashing into the one whose ribs he'd broken, even while seizing the throat of the axe-wielder in front of him. The ork snarled in anger and released its weapon to grab at his wrist, looking to prise it loose. Daelin brought his bolt pistol up to put a shell through its head, but the ork let go of his left wrist with one hand and grabbed at the bolt pistol as well. They struggled for a moment, xenos muscle against warp-infused, genetically engineered might, before one of Daelin's mechatendrils snaked up to pluck the bolt pistol from his hand and fire it before the ork could react. It fell backwards, now missing half of its head.

Daelin's backplate shivered as it turned a blow from another ork blade, but one of his mechatendrils extended a foot-long steel spike and rammed it into the ork's eye socket. Daelin wrenched the axe out of his chest, releasing a gout of black blood as he did so. *Iron within, iron without.* The weapon's edge had been dulled by his blood's corrosive properties, but it was still keen enough to sever at the elbow the other arm of the ork from whom he'd already taken a hand. The ork howled in pain and rage, and flung itself at him bodily: Daelin swatted it aside, and into one of its fellows. It was the ork whose ribs he'd broken, and the xenos showed almost admirable fortitude in rolling the handless ork off itself and staggering up to continue the fight, but it was alone and injured. Daelin emptied the rest of his bolt pistol's clip into it to put it down, then advanced on the last member of the infiltrating party, which was trying to struggle up while leaking blood from two stump-ended limbs.

'I can use you,' Daelin told it viciously, as his mechatendrils wrapped around its thick neck and began to squeeze.

He emerged from the access tunnels into Kapothenis Ull's forge a short while later, to find the imposing, robed figure of the forge lord waiting for him. Ull was stalking up and down with the *click-click-click* of his metal feet ringing out on the floor, and rounded on Daelin with a swirl of red and midnight-blue fabric as the supposedly secret access hatch slid open.

'You abuse my hospitality, my lord,' Ull snapped, his tone not clipped and peremptory simply because of his mechanical voice. 'We agreed that you would remain concealed here, to avoid unnecessary que–' He cut off, then raised a digit to point past Daelin. 'Interrogative: please explain that.'

'It is an ork,' Daelin told him through gritted teeth, as his mechatendrils wrenched the alien's unconscious body into the forge after him. 'There was an advance party of them in the access tunnels.'

'I am familiar with orks,' Ull said, although Daelin would have been surprised if that statement was as true as the forge lord probably thought it was. 'Why have you chosen to bring this corpse here?'

'It isn't a corpse,' Daelin said. 'The ork lives.' Only just, since Daelin's mechatendrils were restricting the flow of blood to its brain sufficient to keep it unconscious: a considerably more difficult feat with an ork than a human, who were rather less hardy. 'It will be of use in the binding.' He started forward, unwilling to let Ull's presence pen him in any longer. Ull stepped aside to let him past rather than stand in his way, but Daelin could almost feel the waves of displeasure coming off the forge lord. Caution and wisdom might suggest that he should still be playing the role of arcane counsellor and mystic, the mummery that had convinced Ull to give into his hunger for knowledge, but Daelin was hurt and angry, and his patience for fools was near its end.

He must still exercise some caution, however. Although looks could be deceiving, if Lexico Arcanus Varaz could near match him in combat when he was fresh, Forge Lord Ull could almost certainly defeat him, wounded as he now was.

'We are out of time,' Ull said, matching his stride to Daelin's, and staying very slightly closer to him than Daelin would have preferred. 'The ork offensive has reached the main node. If there are already infiltrators in the tunnels–'

'Have you convinced your council to give the project its approval?' Daelin interrupted him. May the True Powers save him from the Mechanicus' interminable bureaucracy! Ull would happily expand his work beyond that which was approved by his close-minded dogma, but had remained stubbornly insistent on receiving proper approval for it, even though any such approval would be granted on the basis of falsehoods and part-truths. That was the problem with Ull as a tool: he didn't just crave success, he also craved recognition of his supposed genius *before* he'd even done anything.

'No,' Ull replied scornfully. 'They are blind, wilfully blind, and divided. The time has come to act independently of them. My authorisation will suffice to draw the necessary power, especially in the current state of emergency when attention will be directed elsewhere.'

At last. 'Then let us begin,' Daelin said, not bothering to hide his satisfaction. He made his way over to the machine, dragging the ork with him. A handful of his minions approached, and he let the xenos fall to the floor. 'Connect it,' he told the cultists, who obediently hastened to carry the alien into a locking pod before it could regain consciousness.

'You would include a xenos in this work?' Ull demanded, with some distaste.

'The spark of life is necessary to lure the ethereal,' Daelin told him. 'The origin of it is virtually immaterial. The ork is strong and vital – when combined with the others we have gathered, it will suffice.' He ran through the calculations in his head again, but he was certain of their accuracy. These were equations that no mortal mind could even comprehend without twisting in upon itself in madness, let alone perform, but Gavrak Daelin had studied these arts for millennia. 'Do what you need to in order to ensure the power supply.'

Ull uttered a blast of tightly focused binharic – although not tightly focused enough for Daelin not to detect, analyse and memorise it – and then nodded curtly. 'It is done. We have full access to the Node Primus grid. Only a direct countermand from the tech-priest dominus will override it, and even that will take time.'

'As you stated, we are out of time,' Daelin told him. 'The main ork offensive approaches – if we are to throw it back, we must act now.' He strode across the floor to where his chest sat. It was an oblong of blood-red wood nearly as long as he was tall, carved from the corrupted trees of Tandarr IV and bound in star-iron from the Helicon System, where the faces of the True Gods could be seen in the flames of its green sun by those who knew how to look.

'Interrogative.'

Daelin stopped, and turned. Kapothenis Ull had not moved,

but the forge lord seemed to have grown in stature somehow, and the shadows within his robe had deepened.

'Lexico Arcanus Zaefa Varaz has sent me a communique flagged with the highest-priority alert available to her. In it, she speaks of a Traitor Astartes by the name of Gavrak Daelin who invaded her personal chambers and who, she fears, is leading me down the path of the heretek. How is it that my colleague on the High Council not only knows about your presence here, but also is aware of your identity?'

Daelin cursed inwardly. He never should have indulged that wretched tech-priest! He'd intended to get the information he'd desired, then kill her: as a result, sharing his name with her would have meant nothing. As it was he'd underestimated her, and although Zaefa would struggle to make her voice heard above the general alerts within the node, she was certainly capable of haranguing an individual such as the forge lord.

'I spoke with her,' Daelin acknowledged. There was too much potential evidence to the contrary to dispute Zaefa's claims. 'I had discovered evidence of a fascinating piece of technology within her chambers, hidden from her colleagues, which I sought to procure. I was unsuccessful.'

'And in doing so, you drew attention to your presence here, and potentially brought down ruin on my head!' Ull snarled. The *click-click-clack* of a largely mechanical body altering its configuration emerged from within his robes: an overt threat, to someone who understood the ability of the senior Mechanicus to store weapon components within their frames and reassemble them for use at will. It was a pale simulacrum of the Obliterator virus, a limited technological equivalent of the warp-spawned biological powers granted by the disease of Chaos, but it could still be dangerous enough.

All around, the noise of the forge quietened as Ull's adepts ceased their seemingly endless menial tasks and froze in attention. Daelin's minions did likewise. His Negavolt cultists and Ull's lackeys were natural enemies, each regarding the other as weak-minded fools enslaved by a heretical dogma. Had they encountered each other under normal circumstances, they would have attempted to annihilate each other and, in the case of the Mechanicus, reveal their enemies to the wider node to expose and destroy them. It was only the combined force of their masters' wills instructing them to cooperate in the interests of their great project that had held the conflict at bay so far.

Now that uneasy truce balanced on a razor's edge.

'You are an intelligent being, forge lord,' Daelin said, schooling his face and his noospheric presence to hide even the faintest suggestion of anger or impatience. It wasn't a difficult task: Iron Warriors largely lacked the emotional weaknesses of their brethren – only the stoic Death Guard came close – and knew well that any form of emotion could be exploited and capitalised on by an enemy, in the same manner as they themselves would seek out the chinks in a foe's defences. On the surface, Daelin would appear as nothing more than a rational warrior. His withering contempt for the tech-priest was buried beneath layers of glacial calm.

'You knew the possibility of discovery, and you accepted it as a risk,' he continued. 'Now, as our work draws to a close, it is far too late for such exposure to damage your standing here. Your glory will hinge on the success of your creation, as is correct and proper. If it works – and it will – then none will be able to deny the power that you have wielded, and naysayers will rightly be exposed as jealous pretenders, unable to approach your triumphs.'

Ull still didn't move. 'The work is ready to be completed?'

'The ethereal binding is all that remains,' Daelin told him. 'I require my tools, and then we can finish what we started. When the engine is suffused with ethereal energy, you can direct its power as you see fit.'

There was a faint flexing and contracting within Ull's robes, and whatever changes he'd made to his body were apparently reversed. The forge lord nodded stiffly once, with an accompanying noospheric bleat of approval.

'Then let us finish this.'

'Take up your position in the command throne,' Daelin directed him, turning back to his warp chest once more. He ran his fingers, ceramite-encased flesh and metal prosthetics, over the locks of which only he knew the combinations, and muttered the rites necessary to unfasten them. The bolts slid back and the wards around the chest dropped away, allowing him to raise the lid to reveal his tools: the ritual *kri* blade, into which was carved spells of summoning, and the mighty forge hammer that would seal the bindings. He drew them forth, and was bathed in the power that emanated from them. Even a being as sober and humourless as Gavrak Daelin could not help but take a moment to contemplate the stark beauty of these tools. They would help him reshape the galaxy.

'You have no time to waste in idle contemplation,' Ull stated from above. He was scaling the external chassis of the engine, his fingers, feet and mechadendrites apparently effortlessly finding sufficient purchase to support his body. Daelin watched him clamber the remaining distance to the control throne, which he then lowered his body into. It had been crafted specifically for Ull's measurements: none other than the forge lord of Hephaesto would control this instrument of destruction.

MIKE BROOKS

Or so the forge lord thought.

'Remember, I cannot communicate with you once the rite has commenced,' Daelin said, ignoring Ull's temerity. There was no point in risking things at this late stage simply to snap at a fool's sharp words. 'To interrupt the incantation would mean that at best we lose the etheric power I am attempting to harness, and at worst it will be directed in an uncontrolled and destructive manner.'

'I have perfect recall of all of our previous communications,' Ull informed him. 'The Mechanicus deletes nothing. Perform your role.'

'Very well,' Daelin replied. He approached the machine, placed his splayed fingers on its left forelimb, and began to chant.

It was an ancient language that he uttered, one that had never been intended for mortal voices to speak. Even Daelin, far beyond human and now, by the glory of Chaos, far beyond even the feeble nature of the Imperial fools who liked to think themselves his equal, struggled to form the syllables. It was as though the language had a will of its own, and was trying to twist his tongue to its own ends. He was not entirely sure that was not the case, for even these rites that he'd used many times before still clung to some of their mysteries, but Daelin hardened his will and forged on. *Iron within, iron without.*

He reached the first marking point: without breaking the rhythm of his incantation, he withdrew his hand and struck the point where it had been with his forge hammer. Sickly, bloody light bloomed on the surface of the metal and crawled over it like dry lightning across a cloud-wracked sky. The first part of the binding was complete. Still chanting, he moved to the left hindlimb and began the process again.

'If your ritual can be quickened, it should,' Ull stated from above. Daelin forced himself not to react to the tech-priest's words, not to falter or lose focus. The 'ethereal' to which he'd referred was nothing more than a sop to Ull's sensibilities, of course – an archaic term which even the Imperium's own scholars would never have used. He'd lured Ull in with tales of the ether, a power harnessable by those with the knowledge and the will, and with which tasks of almost unimaginable complexity could be accomplished. But the ether was the warp, and the warp was no storehouse of benign power just waiting to be tapped, but the realm of the gods themselves, as well as many other, more minor beings. However, even those more minor beings still wielded power that would be considered colossal by any mortal.

And none of them were benign.

Daelin reached the second marking point, and smote the war machine once more, sending another crackle of light across its surface as the binding auras sank into the very metal. Already, Ull would find it a struggle to remove himself from his command throne, but he had no intention of doing so, and so would not notice until it was too late. And besides, the bindings were not, strictly speaking, intended for him.

'Lexico Arcanus Varaz approaches, accompanied by Secutor Mitranda and a small infantry force,' Ull declared, as Daelin moved on to begin his chanting over the right hindlimb. He stumbled over his words slightly as the import of Ull's statement registered with him, and he felt the language he was attempting to manipulate twist in his mouth, seeking to control his vocal cords. He fought back and mastered it once more, but it had come close to escaping him and ruining his work. Why was the forge lord telling him these things? Why was he not dealing with it himself? Daelin risked loosing a quick instruction into his floodstream, ordering his cultists to arm themselves and prepare for battle.

The third marking point. He struck the limb with his forge hammer, and pressed on.

He could feel the subtle thrumming of the machine now. It wasn't under power yet, of course, because he hadn't initiated the final activation; this was a more subtle resonance, one detectable only to a being such as him, with his enhanced senses and experience.

'They are at the main door,' Ull said. 'I shall delay them for as long as I can, but Varaz is a gifted cryptographer and my ability to keep her locked out of the entrance systems may be limited.'

Daelin was aware that all around him, menials were snatching up tools and weapons and moving into defensive positions, ready to give their lives in defence of their master's work. And give their lives they undoubtedly would, for these were no mighty tech-priests, armed with the finest weaponry they had plundered from armouries or explorations. These were simply sprocket-tighteners and incense-lighters, more familiar with wrenches and las-welders than with autoguns or power staves. As for the Negavolt cultists, they were devoted to the Inverted Motive Force and would fight fiercely, but they were a rabid mob, not the sort of well-organised fighting force Daelin would choose to put between himself and a Mechanicus secutor, accompanied by whatever troops they had brought.

'Hurry!' Ull urged. 'It is illogical and wasteful for the forces of this planet to engage in combat with each other when the xenos are so close at hand. Conclude this rite, so that I may demonstrate the wisdom of our path!'

Daelin struck the final mark of binding, and watched the

power crawl over the engine's structure. The vessel was ready. Now he needed to call forth the being that would fill it.

The engine was pockmarked with cavities, into which had been inserted those luckless individuals who had been marked for service. Most of them were broken-spirited tech-thralls, held in place by segmented metal binders and isolated from their surroundings by a crystalflex screen that served to silence any pleas or entreaties they might make as they waited for their fate. However, the most recently filled recess held the ork Daelin had overcome in the access tunnels, and it was to this that he now moved with the athame glinting in his hand.

The ork had recovered consciousness and was straining against its bonds, although it did not look to be in any danger of breaking them. Its grotesque mouth was opening and shutting as it bellowed and raged silently at its imprisonment, and Daelin found himself slightly impressed at the beast's hardiness. Most humans, finding themselves newly without hands, would have fallen into a state of catatonic and agonised despair, even assuming they hadn't bled to death from the wounds. The ork's dark blood had clotted quickly, preventing any further loss, and it fought to get at Daelin with no apparent thought given to the fact that it not only lacked weapons, but also any ability to wield one.

He began the second incantation, this one in a different tongue, and felt the spell begin to pull at the very essence of his being. He was enacting a summoning, but a summoning exerted a force both ways. Even with the spiritual anchors he had cast about himself, even with all of his experience, there was still the danger that his spirit could be sucked howling into the warp.

The injuries he'd taken in battle began to throb as the warp sought out his weaknesses. The wound in his chest flared up like a spike of ice, and his own black blood started to drip again. The spell was searching for life force on which to feed, and as the caster, he was the most obvious and available source.

This was where the craft and skill of a Warpsmith lay. Not in the working of the engine, although that was important. What made Gavrak Daelin mighty was his ability to stand before the denizens of the warp armed only with his own being, and bargain.

The spell caught, and the crushing weight of a monstrous presence manifested. It had no physical form, but all those around felt its might. Cultists fell to their knees. Tech-adepts began to wail, and some simply collapsed as consciousness was blasted from their minds. Frost began to creep over the war engine's limbs.

Who calls Te'Kannaroth? spoke a voice inside Daelin's skull. It was as deep as the night, older than the stars, and shot through with shards of malice. It echoed around his head in maddening fractals of splintering sound, but these were no physical sound waves, merely his consciousness struggling to cope with the true nature of the communication that had been thrust into it.

'Gavrak Daelin, Warpsmith of the Fourth Legion,' Daelin replied through teeth gritted with effort and pain. Above him, he heard Kapothenis Ull make a wordless noise of alarm and distress. The forge lord, bound to the engine as he now was, would have heard the daemon's voice inside his head as clearly as Daelin had.

The daemon spoke again, and its tone shifted to one of amusement. *You do not seek to bind me against my will, servant of the Undivided Star?*

'No,' Daelin said. 'I would not insult you so. I offer a

compact. This vessel, with which to make sport in the material world.'

And in return?

Until today, Daelin would have bargained first for the destruction of *Lux Annihilatus*. With the Warlord Titan already brought down by the orks, and his vengeance thus snatched from him, he could concentrate on other priorities.

'Beneath the skin of this city lies an artefact I desire,' he replied, weaving power into his words so that they might hold the daemon to its purpose. Gavrak Daelin might offer his creation without deception, but he was not so great a fool as to call forth a daemon without ensuring that its first act would not be to crush him. 'The Mechanicus use it to siphon power from the volcano on which we stand. For me to seize it, I require the Mechanicus and ork forces present to be... removed.'

He felt the daemon's intelligence pry into his knowledge and understanding, seeping in like water into a lock, then freezing to burst it open. There was no defence against a being so powerful, and Daelin had long ago learned not to try. When dealing with a Greater Daemon, you attempted to deceive them at your gravest peril.

If this artefact is removed from its current location, the full power of the volcano will be unleashed?

'It will,' Daelin acknowledged. The daemon would not have understood such a concept on its own, for although its mind was a mighty and powerful thing, it did not easily comprehend such matters of technology. With access to his knowledge, things were different.

Then we have an accord. Proceed with your rite, Warpsmith.

Gavrak Daelin reached out with a trembling hand and fumbled for the release catch of the crystalflex door behind which the ork still raged. The strain of maintaining the spell and communicating with the daemon was ravaging his body, for he had used his own life force to begin the summoning, and was holding himself from being drawn into the warp through sheer force of will. He would recover, given time, but now he needed to transfer the anchoring point of his sorcery from his own life force to that of another.

Or in this case, many others, for the daemon was a mighty one and would not be lightly brought forth from the warp, even with its consent.

He managed to get the casket open. The ork's bellow filled his ears.

'Engage power!' Daelin roared. Two of his cultists who had remained at their post hauled down the mighty lever that, subject to appropriate clearance, connected the forge directly to Hephaesto's primary power grid. Millions of volts of energy flowed into the engine's circuits, priming it for its holy baptism, the sacred moment when the power of the warp would be joined with the power of what the Mechanicus thought of as the Motive Force.

Daelin plunged the kri, flickering with corposant, into the ork's chest.

The ork immediately went rigid, and its raging ceased. Pale light burst forth from its eyes and mouth as the power of the spell tore through it, stripping its life force from its body and casting it out into the warp. Daelin nearly collapsed as the burning tension of the spell left him and flowed out into the engine, jumping from living body to living body incarcerated in the cavities set across it. Each one flared with pale, dead light as the sacrifices were drained and their souls offered up, and the temperature in Ull's forge plummeted.

Atop the engine, in the prison that he had believed would

be his command throne, Kapothenis Ull screamed as the spell reached him. His soul would be bound to the engine as well, available to assist the daemon in the operation of its living metal armour, and should it be destroyed then he would be cast forth into the endless torment of the warp, there to know an eternity of suffering as the price for his vanity and ambition. His soul's connection with his physical body, however, was instantly and violently severed.

Without Ull's countermeasures to Varaz's attacks, the sequence of access doors that separated the forge from the communal areas of the node slammed open, one after another. Daelin grinned savagely. Too late. They were far too late.

Above him, the largest daemon engine constructed outside the Eye of Terror for seven millennia took its first breath.

+++019+++

<Interrogative: what is causing the delay?> Secutor Mitranda demanded, and Zaefa suppressed an entirely organic noise of frustration.

<Clarification: Forge Lord Ull is resisting my attempts to override his security measures,> she replied. Kapothenis was throwing up flashwalls and codetraps nearly as fast as she could negotiate them, and although she was making some headway, it was like attempting to drive a watercraft upstream against a river in spate.

<Are you certain the forge lord is not merely attempting to preserve the sanctity of his personal workshop?> Mitranda asked, and Zaefa could detect the slightest hint of uncertainty in the secutor's floodstream. It was certainly a gross breach of protocol to attempt to force entry into a high council-lor's private forge, and it wasn't a measure Zaefa had settled on lightly.

<He has ignored my communiques regarding my concerns,>

she told Mitranda. <I know Kapothenis. He could not hide deception from me if he replied, and he in turn knows this. The only satisfactory explanation for why he has not denied collaborating with a traitor and heretic is that he knows he cannot do so without confirming my suspicions, and thus he has only confirmed them anyway. Besides which,> she added, defusing a particularly obstructive piece of code, <the node is under attack. There is no reason for the forge lord to be cowering within his domain when he should be taking up his role in the defensive structure.>

<A structure from which we are absent,> Mitranda rejoined, somewhat uneasily. They had requisitioned two units of skitarii infantry, who stood at parade-ground readiness in the corridor behind them. <The xenos attack is chaotic and unpredictable, even to me. Confounding variables abound. We should prosecute this operation as swiftly as possible in order to return to the defence of the node and ensure maximum efficiency of that primary directive.>

<I have already taken steps to preserve our knowledge and data,> Zaefa replied. <If the node is lost, our learning will endure.> *Most of it. Assuming the orks do not have further surprises in store that will drastically affect the ability of our shuttles to escape, which is by no means certain.* <And orks are orks, here and everywhere – even killing all of the invaders would have no impact on their proliferation as a species. But behind this door there lurks a being who rebelled against the Omnissiah Himself, who perverts the form and function of the blessed machine-spirits for his own diabolical ends. Eliminating him is the greatest service we can perform at this juncture.>

<I still wish to prosecute this operation as swiftly as possible,> Mitranda said stubbornly. They eyed the door in front

of them, and hefted the Omnissian axe in their primary hands. They'd apparently lost their favoured weapon in an attempt to assassinate the orks' leader, but had managed to procure another from their private armoury. <If subtlety avails us not, perhaps force of arms may gain us entry?>

<Bearing in mind the structure of the doors, the design of your weapon and the maximum force you can bring to bear, there is a ninety-five point three two per cent chance that my method will be quicker,> Zaefa told Mitranda, attempting to keep any hint of smugness out of her delivery. <There is also a thirty-seven point one seven recurring per cent probability that any such attempt from you would in fact hinder the doors' operation, thereby negating my own–>

Kapothenis Ull flatlined.

It was the only way Zaefa could describe it. One moment he was actively fighting her, albeit through a communication silence that could only be deliberate, and the next moment all of his defences spasmed wildly, then went inert. At the same time, Zaefa thought she heard screams. Even more worryingly, she thought she somehow recognised Kapothenis' voice amongst them.

<Did you sense that?> she asked, appalled. In front of her, the series of doors separating them from Ull's private forge unlocked, one after another. <The screams?>

<I have reviewed my audio sensorial data, and I detected nothing,> Mitranda replied.

<Nor did I,> Zaefa said. <But I still heard them.>

<As did I,> Mitranda admitted after a moment. They let out an angry blurt of binharic. <Units, forward on me. Let us proceed with all speed.>

<And appropriate caution,> Zaefa added, but the secutor and their troops were already moving, flowing through

the first door and into the private spaces beyond. Zaefa followed them, pulling her gamma pistol out from her robes.

She'd been into some of Ull's chambers before, of course, although not for a little while. She performed quick visual scans of them as she moved through after Mitranda and the skitarii, then compared the data to her memories. It was very rude to record images of another tech-priest's private quarters without their express permission, but Zaefa's hunger for knowledge of all kinds usually overcame her social mores in such a situation. What she noticed disturbed her.

There were virtually no observable differences between the nature of Ull's quarters now and her records of them. To all outward appearances, even in the privacy of his own rooms to which he need not admit anyone against his wishes, there were no telltale texts, fanes or other indication of heretical beliefs. Whatever had driven Kapothenis Ull down this dark path, he had not been recently overcome by a drastic change of mentality.

Could he have always harboured such beliefs, and no one had noticed? Although there was an even more worrying possibility: was Zaefa the only one who *hadn't* noticed? What of Illutar and Yavannos? Had all of the High Council fallen to the darkness, and Zaefa was the sole member left who still honoured the Omnissiah as she should? Had Illutar's opposition to Ull's war machine not been due to his concerns over its viability and deviation from Mechanicus standards, but originated from simple envy and rivalry? If her colleagues had indeed fallen, Illutar's apparent indecisiveness and Yavannos' insistence on taking non-lethal measures against the orks could be reframed as deliberate sabotage of Hephaesto, the Imperium and the Mechanicus. Surely that was a far more likely explanation than her colleagues, high-ranking members of the Adeptus Mechanicus that they were, being short-sighted, protectionist and incompetent?

Zaefa was dragged back to the events unfolding in her immediate vicinity as gunfire erupted from in front of her. The bark and roar of galvanic rifles mixed with screams of pain and binharic cursing, and unpleasant buzzing, crackling noises that made Zaefa feel like something was reaching into the back of her brain and putting pressure on the circuits within it. She hurried forwards, following the skitarii as they moved through the final door with crisp military precision, their weapons discharging as they eliminated the resistance that Ull had apparently prepared for them. Then more screams came, louder this time, and the last skitarii was knocked back through the doorway and sprawled out across the floor, writhing in agony as their joints sparked with overloads. Their attacker followed them through, and Zaefa got a look at the forces with which the forge lord of Hephaesto had aligned himself.

Pale skin, pockmarked with interface sockets and lined with scarification in the shape of corrupted circuits; hands holding twin staves, crackling with the unfamiliar energies that had so overloaded the systems of the luckless skitarii on the floor; head surrounded by thrashing mechatendrils; and attached to their back, a contraption that must have served as some sort of battery or reservoir for the power they wielded. From behind their corroded breath-mask they screamed a wordless challenge of hate and pain, and surged towards her.

Zaefa raised her gamma pistol and shot them in the head, and they dropped to the floor as a smoking corpse.

'Lexico arcanus!' Mitranda shouted, both with their flesh voice and as an urgent data stream. 'Attend to the forge lord!'

Zaefa hurried past the still-spasming skitarii and emerged

from the final door onto a gantry that clung to the wall perhaps halfway up the towering space that made up Kapothenis Ull's personal forge. To her right and her left, skitarii led by Secutor Mitranda were shooting their way down and up stairways as they fought to drive back the ragtag mix of heretics that opposed them, some of which still wore the robes of Hephaesto, but despite the gunfire ringing out around her, it was not this that arrested Zaefa's attention.

Above even where she now stood, sitting ramrod-straight upon what looked like an approximation of the Throne Mechanicum that one would find in a Knight, was a motionless body she recognised as Kapothenis Ull. She reached out all her senses towards him, but detected no signs of life. Brain activity, heart functions, respiration – all were at zero. Ull was dead, and despite his revelation as a heretek and the sheer illogic of such an emotional reaction, Zaefa felt a knife of grief enter her heart.

Two hundred and thirty-seven milliseconds later, she realised what Ull was sitting on. Forty-three milliseconds after that, she registered the readings that were coming from it.

It was terrifying.

It was not as tall as a Warlord Titan, not quite, but in terms of sheer mass it must have been greater. This behemoth stood on six legs rather than two, and it took up fully half the horizontal length of Ull's forge, which was itself one of the largest single spaces in Node Primus. All of the internal bracketing and subdivisions had been removed at some point since the one and only time Zaefa had been allowed in, leaving only the external walls and the construction gantries around the monstrosity that had taken shape in the centre. And what a monstrosity it was.

Its shell was multifaceted and jointed like some giant

crustacean. Its shape was bestial, almost as though a noble Warhound Titan had been devolved by some dark arts into a more primitive, savage form. And indeed, the thing's head bore some resemblance to the feral snout of a Warhound, but twisted and warped into something that was vaguely reptilian, though far more reminiscent of the deep-ocean predators that Yavannos had shown Zaefa once.

Instead of hunkering low between its shoulders, the head was situated at the end of an extended neck that thickened to where it joined the machine's body. Here the thing's torso stood on two massive, powerful front legs: giant, simian-esque limbs terminating in knuckle-down fists that looked capable of ripping a super-heavy battle tank apart. From its shoulders, on either side of where Kapothenis Ull's body sat, there protruded giant gatling blasters such as that which *Lux Annihilatus* had wielded, while enormous mechatendrils erupted from further back along its sloping spine, until the thing's body tapered down to two pairs of squat but power-ful hindlegs, considerably shorter than the destructive pillars at the front.

And it was alive.

Not alive in the sense of active and functioning, like a Kastelan robot; nor alive in the sense of a human mind joined with a machine-spirit, like a Titan; nor even alive in the sense of a heretical thinking machine. This machine was *alive*, in a way that moved beyond concepts of technology and biology, and fused them into something mighty and infer-nal and utterly, utterly terrifying. Even as Zaefa watched, the structure of it seemed to change: the gatling blasters swelled subtly, the ornamentation around their muzzles melted from cherubs and eagles into leering, razor-toothed faces topped with spiralling horns, and the tendrils on its back formed barbs along their lengths. Even its colouration altered, as the red and midnight of Hephaesto sloughed away to reveal stark, steel-grey armour plate bordered by angry, jagged brass.

She raised her gamma pistol and sighted down its barrel at the distant head of Kapothenis Ull. Her friend might be dead, but there surely was a reason he had been bonded to this monstrosity in the first place. If his form were destroyed, might it not hamper the processes of this unholy war engine?

Or was she just trying to cling to the notion that she might be able to influence events, when confronted by a creation far beyond her ability to fight?

The moment of hesitation and introspection cost her, for a metallic blur erupted up from the gantry below and slammed bodily into her from the side, bellowing in wrath. The Iron Warrior was here, and he sought revenge.

Zaefa had not come unprepared for battle. She rolled away from the impact of Gavrak Daelin's initial attack and came up to her feet with enough space and time to equip herself. She drew a power sword from beneath her robes, holding it in the off hand to her gamma pistol, and her mechadendrites armed themselves as well: phosphor blaster, lascutter, melta-torch and a robust hypodermic of a particularly virulent nerve toxin which, it was rumoured, might be enough to overload even the nervous system of a Space Marine. Zaefa had acquired a vial of what was supposedly the same recipe as that an Imperial assassin had used to great effect on Space Wolves bodyguards during an attempt on the life of the Celestarch of Navigator House Belisarius, and now seemed like as good a time as any to find out whether her sources had been accurate.

The Warpsmith came at her. In one hand he wielded a mighty hammer that would have taken two normal humans to even lift, yet which he moved as though it weighed virtually nothing, and in the other he held his bolt pistol, which he fired as he advanced. Even moving at superhuman speeds, his accuracy was near perfect, and the bolts struck at Zaefa's centre mass.

They detonated on her refractor field, with which she'd also equipped herself before she'd left her chambers.

Zaefa fired back with her gamma pistol, but Daelin's reflexes were astounding; he ducked and rolled under the blast before her finger had tightened on the trigger, and she merely melted a section of gantry railing beyond him. Then he was up again, his hammer swinging for her head.

She brought her power sword up to parry his blow, and the arcane force that wrapped itself around his weapon clashed with the power field of hers. The sheer physical strength of his blow nearly knocked her weapon from her hand, despite her bionic enhancements. She stumbled to one side, whirled and struck back, sweeping the blade at his thighs, but the heretic knocked her sword aside contemptuously with the haft of his hammer, then fired his bolt pistol at her head. She managed to duck aside before the shell left his gun, and her refractor field deflected it away to impact on the forge wall somewhere beyond her right shoulder, but he seemed even faster and stronger than when they'd clashed in her chambers. She could see further injuries to him, including a rent in the chestplate of his armour and tracks of black blood below it, so he had to have seen other combat since they'd fought, and yet he was still able to fight in this manner. She could only assume that it was some form of manic fervour, brought on by the apparent completion of his purpose here.

They lunged at each other again, feinting and ducking, swaying and rolling – sword against hammer, reflexes and refractor field against bolt pistol, mechatendrils against mechadendrites, and reflexes and power armour against gamma pistol. Zaefa's dermal sensors could tell that her gamma pistol was starting to heat up from its repeated firing, but she was yet to catch her enemy squarely, as was attested to by the various holes in the gantry and its surrounding railings. Meanwhile, she had dodged or her refractor field had turned all but one of the bolts Daelin had fired at her, and that had impacted on one of her body's armour plates, leaving it twisted and buckled, but the joints and circuits beneath unharmed.

Her gamma pistol reached critical temperature at the same time as Daelin's bolt pistol ran out of ammunition. The Iron Warrior mag-clamped it to his thigh with a practised motion too swift for her to take advantage of, then swept out an engraved blade with that hand instead. Zaefa's optical sensors told her that it fulfilled the five criteria necessary for it to be considered a ritual object by the standards of Imperial anthropologists, and also that it was lethally sharp.

The first stab was turned by the refractor field, but even such advanced technology was always going to struggle in prolonged, close-quarters combat, and it overloaded with a jolt that she felt, and which Daelin noticed. He thrust again, this time at her face; she swayed backwards, and slashed up at his wrist with her lascutter while she parried his power-blade mechatendril with her power sword, but he'd already pulled his blow back and was lashing out with a kick at her legs. She was too slow to adjust and he swept her legs out from under her, but she braced her landing with her mechadendrites, then rolled aside as his hammer slammed down onto the gantry where she'd been a moment before. The force of Daelin's blow was so great that the head of his hammer punched through the panelling beneath their feet, and the moment it took for him to free it again allowed Zaefa to spin on her mechadendrites, mag-clamp her right foot to the floor as an anchor, and lash out with her own kick at the back of his knees.

A normal human seeking to sweep a Traitor Space Marine's legs out from under him would likely end up with nothing more than a broken tibia for their troubles, but Zaefa's bionics and skeletal enhancements took her far beyond baseline human. The force of the impact registered redly on her internal damage monitoring systems, but it was within tolerable parameters, and it also succeeded in its aim. Gavrak Daelin toppled backwards like a felled tree… and caught himself on his mechatendrils.

From her back, Zaefa lashed out with her power sword, and severed the nearest two halfway down their length.

Daelin collapsed onto his right side, the side nearest her, but he turned into the roll and brought his left arm over, and with it came his hammer. This time, Zaefa wasn't fast enough to avoid it: the massive weapon slammed down into her chest, crushing her against the metal panelling of the floor.

Damage alerts flashed up and she dismissed them with a desperate blink. She barely needed their input: pain wracked her torso, too severe even for her to ignore, and her augmented lungs could barely draw in air. Not only had they been damaged by the blow, but Daelin kept the hammer pressed in place, pinning her down and restricting her breathing further as he regained his feet, slightly unsteadily due to the now-uneven weight distribution of his mechatendrils. Zaefa could survive without oxygen for far longer than a normal human could, of course, but as Daelin hefted his ritual knife, she suspected that was going to be academic. She aimed her gamma pistol at him, willing to take the risk as to whether or not it had cooled sufficiently, but Daelin kicked it out of her hand before she could pull the trigger. She hacked at the hammer's haft with her power sword, but the strange field around it still turned her weapon's molecular-disrupting field, and she couldn't reach his hand to try to sever his digits. Even her mechadendrites were useless, flattened as they were beneath her body by the Iron Warrior's weight and strength.

'I hope you haven't moved that device,' Gavrak Daelin said, his face twisted in hateful triumph. 'It would be a shame if the orks destroyed it before I could get my hands on it.'

He reversed the grip on his knife, spinning it expertly in his hand, so the blade pointed downwards. Zaefa could see how the next few moments were going to unfold: he would drop to one knee and plunge his weapon into some critical part of her body, such as her head, or neck, or chest. Her only hope was that her enhancements would allow her to survive the first blow, so that she might have a chance to strike back and, perhaps, escape.

The gantry moved.

It lurched to one side with a screaming shriek of metal as though caught in an earth tremor, but there was no seismic activity taking place. It wasn't until Zaefa heard the snap and pop of rivets and securing bolts giving way, and metal being torn asunder as though it were nothing more than parchment, that she realised the horrifying truth.

The war engine was moving, and destroying the construction gantries as it did so.

The initial jolt didn't shake Daelin loose, but the Warpsmith stayed his blow as he looked up in apparent delight as his construction shifted. Then, as the supporting poles beneath their level of the gantry were wrenched loose, the floor beneath them began to tilt downwards into the hole left by the shifting war engine.

Now Daelin stumbled a couple of steps – only until he activated the mag-clamps that still functioned within his ancient armour, but it was enough to free Zaefa. Her own mag-clamps allowed her to stand even as the gantry veered downwards, although the pain in her torso nearly bent her double anyway. She caught a glimpse of the massive war machine beginning to turn, saw one enormous foreleg lash out to sweep aside the remaining gantries that still clung to the beast's front end…

Gavrak Daelin, standing upright in relation to the gantry but now, as she was, almost at ninety degrees from the vertical, had resheathed his knife and reloaded his bolt pistol in the moments while she'd been distracted. He raised the weapon in a single, fluid motion. With her refractor field non-functional, her mobility limited by the necessity to use mag-clamps, and her chest already damaged to the point that moving was painful, Zaefa calculated that, based on the Iron Warrior's combat efficiency so far, she had less than a thirteen per cent chance of evading his first shot, with subsequent shots dropping the likelihood of her survival into realms so small they could be effectively discounted.

An Omnissian axe tumbled end over end past her shoulder, gravity adding to the already considerable force behind it. The same factors that limited Zaefa's mobility applied equally to Gavrak Daelin, hanging horizontally from the soles of his ceramite boots as he was. He managed nothing more than an aborted jerk of his torso before the axe struck him dead centre in his chestplate.

Had it struck the armour in its pristine condition then the wound might not have been so grievous, but Secutor

Mitranda had succeeded in hurling their axe's sanctified edge into the breach already carved into the traitor's plate by a previous, unknown assailant. The Omnissian axe drove into the weak point and penetrated still further, the huge curved blade cutting so far into Daelin's chest that the top edge cleaved through his jawbone, and spilled dark blood backwards down his cheeks.

The Iron Warrior spasmed. A choking gurgle emerged from his mouth, and his bolt pistol and hammer both fell from his hands. He lifted one foot from the metal and reached above his head as though to try to catch them, but the power left his limbs as he did so. His body bent backwards as far as the constraints of his armour would allow, and for a moment his face gazed, unseeing and upside down, at the fruits of his labour.

Then the weight of his body became too much for his single boot still attached to the gantry, and he fell.

<You have my gratitude,> Zaefa said, retreating further up the gantry to a point where the angle of the floor beneath her was less steep, and wincing in pain as she did so.

<You gratitude is unnecessary,> Mitranda replied shortly. They seized Zaefa's arm as though to secure her against a similar fall to that which had claimed Daelin, and pointed towards the war engine. <Lexico arcanus, what do we do about *that*?>

Zaefa wearily ran through all her databanks that might in any way be relevant to their current situation. Heretekal abominations of this type were not completely unknown, but this one exceeded the size and apparent capabilities of any of which she'd heard, and they themselves were utterly terrifying in their own right.

The daemon engine roared. It went beyond mere sound;

it was a physical sensation, one with the power to vibrate the very atoms of the body, the power to reach into the soul and tear at it with claws of infernal fury. Zaefa doubled over in pain and panic, and beside her, she felt Mitranda tremble with a similar affliction.

The daemon engine lumbered into a run, a terrifying sight for an entity that massive. After only a few paces it reached the forge's main door, a massive slab of metal some two hundred and sixty feet high and nearly that across, through which even the mightiest of war machines Kapothenis Ull had created could pass.

The daemon engine reared up and struck them a titanic, double-fisted blow. The doors crumpled outwards with a thunderous boom that caused Zaefa's audio receptors to momentarily enter a protective shutdown, and the huge sheets of metal were knocked skidding across the ground outside. The daemon engine turned its head to the sky and bellowed in rage and triumph, its mouth and eyes now lit internally by fires Zaefa knew not the origin of, then thundered away into the night.

<We can do nothing about that,> Zaefa panted miserably. <The Legio Hephaesto is no more. Even if they were, I fear they would have met their match. All we can do now is to evacuate as fast as we may, and pray to the Omnissiah that the divine knowledge of this node can be saved.>

<And that the orks and that thing tear each other to shreds before they turn on us,> Mitranda added bitterly.

Sport of the True Gods

Te'Kannaroth, the Scythe Of Mourning, the Ruinstar, breathed deeply of the air and felt it rush in past the metal teeth of its new body, down its multi-segmented neck, and into the mighty drum of its chest. It had been aeons since it had experienced this realm, since it had tasted the corpses of stars that formed the gases of the air. It felt once again the strange, falling sensation of time that passed under its own rules, steady and inexorable, time that was not subservient to the whim of whatever power controlled the realm in which it existed. Such pervasive order, such permeating regimentation, was like a splinter in the mind to a being birthed in the warp when the mortal stars were young, but Te'Kannaroth was no minor power cast adrift in the materium with a weak anchor.

Te'Kannaroth was armoured in a body of fire and metal, and it was mighty.

It had emerged from the structure in which its body had been created onto a plaza that interrupted a wide processional, which, it had gleaned from its connection with the mind of the Warpsmith, was how the humans here moved the products of the forge to wherever they were needed. The processional cut through the other structures around and linked up with others, winding away down the slopes of the mountain of fire on which the mortals' settlement was built, and away to their network of transport routes. Te'Kannaroth's keen vision penetrated the darkness of the night, cut through the glare of the humans' illuminations and down to where the abhorrence clustered.

The abhorrence. Living, thinking beings over which the True Powers could hold little influence. Resistant to the hated Changer, resistant to the Grandfather of Disease, and resistant to the snares of excess cast by the Dark Prince. Even the Blood God, mightiest of the Ruinous Powers, could not offer them any outlet for their warlike nature that was not provided by their worship of their own brutish gods. The abhorrence proliferated, vermin with an infuriating inability to acknowledge the power of Chaos.

The wretched aeldari understood that power all too well, for it had broken the civilisation they'd once been so proud of. Now the miserable survivors shied away from the glory of the eight-pointed star like the snivelling, broken whelps they were. They were the last remnants of a dying breed, and even their greatest minds – such as Essenyl Greymoon, the farseer who had banished Te'Kannaroth's last physical form – were just intelligent enough to know their peril, but lacked the wit to realise that their damnation and destruction had merely been delayed. The metal-skinned husks that had once been the necrontyr also knew of the True Powers, but they were soulless, mindless automata now, worthless to the gods. Even humans, those fleetingly brief sparks of petty malice, could appreciate a small sliver of the majesty of Chaos when it stood before them, as their souls were flayed from their bodies and their minds peeled back from sanity.

Yet the abhorrence would see only another enemy to fight. Even those amongst them who could bend and shape reality to their will drew that power mainly from the massed latent psychic ability of their kin, not from the raging tempest of the warp. It was as though the glory of Chaos were simply irrelevant to them.

Te'Kannaroth's gaze picked out an enormous effigy of the abhorrence's gods, a gigantic, squat, yellow-and-black walking fortress that had now approached to the foot of the mountain. However, it was held at bay by a shimmering curtain in the air, an energy field projected by the humans that, for the moment at least, kept most of the abhorrence from prosecuting their attack.

Te'Kannaroth's attention was momentarily diverted by human shouts of alarm, and the sparkle of energy weapon fire. A group of these metal-limbed mortals had assembled not far from it, and had turned their guns on it. The impacts of their shots were as drops of gentle rain upon a mortal's skin, and Te'Kannaroth chuckled in amusement at their futile hubris. It turned to face them fully, letting them drink in its might, then returned fire.

The spinning barrels of its shoulder cannons whirred into a blur of motion, hosing them with high-velocity rounds and filling the night air with the concussion of ballistic fire that sounded like the laughter of the thirsting gods. The uniformly level surface of the plaza was chewed up into shards as Te'Kannaroth walked its fire up to the humans, delighting at the psychic taste of their morale shattering along with the paved slabs on which they stood, until the shots reached them and their bodies were likewise broken, releasing their souls to the tender mercies of the warp. Three fled in an attempt to escape the horror, and Te'Kannaroth chose not to gun them down from behind. It lurched into a run instead, its energy effortlessly powering the metal pistons and gears of this strange, delightful body. The clenched fists of its mighty forelimbs crushed the first two into wet red smears decorating the shallow craters it had left, but it snatched up the third between two digits, delicately turning it this way and that as the human screamed in utter terror. Then Te'Kannaroth activated the power field that it could summon around its fists, and watched in fascinated delight as the human's flesh burned away and its metal prosthetics melted.

Truly, the Warpsmith had performed his task well. This body was all Te'Kannaroth could have hoped for.

Te'Kannaroth's senses were not wholly of its daemonic origin. Its fusion with this metal form allowed it to access the sensors built into the frame by the being whose corpse still sat rigidly between its shoulders, and the wailing spirit of that human was trapped in this shell along with it, mixed with the other spirits whose sacrifice had given the Warpsmith's summoning the power it needed. Te'Kannaroth turned its gaze inwards, hunting down the shade of the human known as Kapothenis Ull, and pursuing it into the darkest corner where it had hidden itself away. Then Te'Kannaroth reached out a psychic claw and snared its quarry, hauling it out for examination.

The soul that squirmed in agony upon its talon had been a proud man, who had considered himself more than a man by dint of how much of his body he had replaced with mechanical parts. Now, however, his soul was naked and unadorned, and radiated terror like a beacon in the darkest night.

Come to me, Te'Kannaroth purred, *and serve Khorne.*

Kapothenis Ull screamed. Te'Kannaroth drank him in.

New understanding flowed through the daemon's consciousness, as the dregs of the human's soul provided context to the sensations Te'Kannaroth was experiencing. Weapons targeting systems sprang into action and brought crosshairs to bear on identified threats, as well as throwing up blizzards of information about range, elevation, crosswind speed and other minutiae. Te'Kannaroth suddenly knew its exact location in Hephaesto's Node Primus, and could access schematics for the entire city including power grids, water mains, sewage outlets and defence systems.

And in and amongst the various defence systems were the generators for the void shields that held the abhorrence at bay.

Savage glee surged through Te'Kannaroth. It could stalk this city and terrorise the humans; it could lay their manufactoria and shrines low, break open their shelters and feast upon their mortal forms and immortal souls, but such pastimes would be pale amusement at best. Most of the humans' forces were mustered near the border of the void shields, ready to bring the abhorrence to battle when the fields finally failed; there were some greenskins in the city already, according to panicked vox messages, but not the main force. That still lurked beyond the void shields, hammering futilely at them.

Te'Kannaroth looked down the mountain again, picking out what it now knew the humans termed a mega-gargant, a mighty war machine. The daemon knew that the mega-gargant was more than just a war machine, however, in the same way as Te'Kannaroth itself was. The mega-gargant was an idol to the gods of the abhorrence, and although it would have been dangerous in any case, it was further imbued with might by the belief of the greenskins that followed and worshipped it. To them, it was the very symbol of their gods given form in metal, and which now bestrode this planet as a walking altar of death and destruction.

For Te'Kannaroth, it was a challenge that could not be left unanswered, and an enemy that would test the capabilities of its new body to its limits.

It moved again, following the buzzing scent of the generators as much as it was the plans of the city. The Mechanicus had become properly aware of its presence now, and they were scrambling reserves intended to fight a last-ditch defence against the abhorrence to meet it, but they were a mere annoyance. Te'Kannaroth could hear their communications and knew from whence they would be coming, and that the forces sent against it were paltry opponents. Three Chimeras rounded a corner and opened fire, but the daemon engine lumbered through multi-laser blasts to hammer both its fists into one of the transport vehicles, buckling its shell and crushing those within, then heaved up the wreckage to hurl it at the next. The third began to reverse, but Te'Kannaroth opened its mouth and, instead of a roar of rage, vomited forth a blast of witchflame that engulfed the Chimera and melted it in a conflagration of green-white fire.

The void shield generator was close. Te'Kannaroth turned its muzzle upwards, sniffing out the source, then drove its right forelimb into the wall of the nearest building. It punched through rockcrete, but the shell of the construction was firm enough for it to raise itself up and drive its other forelimb in, as high as it could reach. Then, pulling itself upwards with the infernal power of its daemonically enhanced metal body, Te'Kannaroth began to climb.

Half a minute later, it levered itself over the edge of the building's flat roof, its rear legs kicking away crumbling masonry in the process, and approached the thick antennae that focused and directed the southernmost of the overlapping sheaths of power that formed Node Primus' void shields. The tech-priests monitoring it fled, but Te'Kannaroth paid them no mind. It reached out and gripped the antennae array, then pulled it clean out of the building's roof.

The shimmering field in the south winked out of existence, and the immediate guttural roar of bloodthirsty approval from the throats of the abhorrence assembled beyond it rose up into the night. Their effigy briefly drowned them out with its war-horns, brazen and blaring.

Te'Kannaroth raised the antennae over its head in one fist, fired a volley of white-hot projectiles from its shoulder cannons into the sky, from whence they arced across and then fell on the city like savage rain, and screamed its own challenge back at the gargant.

It was time for the gods to go to war.

Da Loot

Ufthak was prepared to concede that these humie tanks were respectably quick, which wasn't necessarily a surprise given that they were red, and everyone knew that red ones went faster. They were pretty shooty, too: he'd had a good laugh using the big shootas on top to strafe a bunch of humies who hadn't got out of the way in time, and some of the ladz had had a go with the ones sticking out of the sides, as well. Even so, Ufthak couldn't help but feel that there was something essential missing from the experience – namely, the bumps. The zogging machine just floated straight *over* everything, that was the trouble. It was like suspension, but worse. How were you supposed to know you were in a vehicle if you didn't get a bump every other second that felt like it was going to compress your spine? It was no wonder these humies were a bit soft, they'd probably never taken a hard knock in their lives.

'Which way, boss?' Da Boffin shouted over the whip of the

MIKE BROOKS

wind, the wail of alarms and the general commotion of a
humie city that was under attack and wasn't happy about it.
'Ya wanna go inside da main complex, froo da front doors?
I bet dey keep dere best loot inside!'

Ufthak tried to think like a humie. If he had a lot of loot
that he didn't want someone else to take, what would he do?
Well, he'd knock their teef down their throat, but humies
didn't tend to think like that. This was harder than he'd
thought.

'Nizkwik!' he barked, and the grot jumped.

'Yes, boss?'

'If ya wanted to stop anuvver grot from gettin' somefing
good wot you fort was yours, wot would ya do?'

The grot rubbed its chin thoughtfully. 'Uhh... I'd probably hide it, boss!'

Ufthak nodded. It sounded like a reasonable explanation
for what sneaky humies might do, but he still wasn't quite
convinced. There were layers and layers to the tricky blight-
ers, that was the problem.

'An' wot if dey was gettin' *really close* to where ya hid it?'

Nizkwik frowned. 'I might pick it up an' run away!'

'Run away! Dat's it!' Ufthak snapped his fingers as the
answer came to him. That's what the humies would do! They
couldn't fight well enough to keep the ladz off their loot,
and they couldn't hide it now Ufthak was nearly on top of
them. The only thing left was to take their loot and scarper.
Mork's teeth, but he was smart sometimes! 'Right, lessee...
Dey can't go sideways, cos da Waaagh!'s all around dem. Dey
can't go down, cos dere's all dat melty rock down dere and
dey'd burn. Which means...'

He wracked his brain.

'Da only way is *up!* Boffin, take any road wot's headin'

242

uphill!' He looked up, scanning the humie city that clung to the mountainside like a particularly stubborn bit of dung on the side of the Drops. It was hard to see properly from where they were, only halfway up, but while a lot of the humie buildings had big pointy roofs and spiky whatnots on top, there looked to be a big flat bit with nothing on top of it at all.

'But, boss,' Wazzock spoke up, 'dey can't go up *dat* far, dere's only so much mountain.'

'Dey're gonna run away into space,' Ufthak said confidently. 'Ya see dat? S'gotta be where dere landas put down, cos humies've gotta have a speshul place for everyfing. Dey can't just go where dey please, dey ain't got da brains to make it work – dey'll get in each uvver's way, an' crash, an' start fightin'.'

'Yeah, but we do dat,' Mogrot pointed out.

'Ah, but humies die easier dan we do,' Ufthak said, tapping the side of his nose knowingly. 'If dey just fought each uvver all da time dey'd all be dead. Zoggin' useless, if ya asks me.'

Da Boffin threw the humie tank into a hard left at a junction, the weird floaty teknology somehow managing to change direction even though it had no wheels to grip the ground with. Ufthak looked around and saw another two tanks following them: the rest of his ladz had worked out how to operate the humie vehicles in fairly short order, and had caught up with Ufthak's when he'd ordered Da Boffin to slow so they could shoot up those unsuspecting defenders.

They'd only just got onto their new heading when a rattle of heavy gunfire erupted from behind them. Ufthak growled in outrage and swung around once more. Were his own bloody ladz shooting at him?

What he saw provided a slightly more understandable explanation, if a no less annoying one: half a dozen warbikers had clearly already been roaring along the road they'd just joined, had seen what they'd thought were a trio of humie vehicles pull out ahead of them, and were now looking to shoot them up. Ufthak pulled a stikkbomb from his belt, primed it, and hurled it in a high, looping arc. The two tanks following him passed underneath it while it was still in the air, and it hit the ground in front of the first warbiker. Fire bloomed and shrapnel erupted outwards, and the leading bike was blown sideways and upwards, pinwheeling across the road surface with the rider suddenly experiencing the joy of flight, at least until he hit the ground again with a very final-looking head-first impact.

His demise didn't bother the rest of them, of course. They simply swerved around the upended, smoking bike and came on, whooping.

That gave Ufthak an idea.

'Keep ya headz down, boyz!' he bellowed, with enough volume to be heard even by those of his mob who were in the other tanks. 'Headz down! Dose bikers want a race! We'll give 'em a race!' He turned to Da Boffin and leaned close enough to whisper into his ear. 'Get us up to dat landa pad before da bikes. I don't want no humies in dere to know we'z orks, just dat we'z gettin' *chased* by orks. Got it?'

'Blood Axe finkin', boss?' Da Boffin chuckled. Ufthak glowered at him.

'Fer an ork wot's meant to be smart,' he told the spanner menacingly, 'yoo'z walkin' a fine line.'

In answer, Da Boffin kicked the throttle up another notch, and the floaty-tank surged forwards that little bit faster. In terms of sheer engine power, Ufthak was willing to bet the warbikes had the edge, but they were hitting bumps and whatnot, which slowed them down a bit. The floaty-tanks had nothing to slow them down except air, and despite the fact that it was contorting Ufthak's ears into all manner of strange configurations, the air wasn't doing enough of a job to allow the bikers to catch them yet.

'Dat one!' he bellowed at Da Boffin, pointing at a turnoff that cut away uphill from their current route. Da Boffin leaned the tank into it, peeling them off from the main highway, and the rest followed: Ufthak's mob and the warbikes alike.

'Looks like dere's some uvvers goin' da same way!' Da Boffin pointed out. Sure enough, Ufthak could make out some more humie vehicles ahead of them, moving rather more slowly. These wheeled trucks didn't look like they were designed for combat; they certainly weren't armoured, and were attended by frantically waving red robes, who were seemingly trying to organise everything at once. Whatever it was they were doing, they clearly thought it was extremely important. But then again, in Ufthak's experience, that applied to all humies at all times.

'Go froo 'em,' he instructed Da Boffin, and ducked down to hang on better as the spanner threw the tank into a series of jinking turns. Ufthak heard angry humie shouts that quickly turned to panicked screams as the warbikes opened up again with their dakkaguns. A few of his ladz took potshots as well as they flew past, but they probably didn't hit anything, and anything they did hit would likely be attributed to the warbikes. So far as any humies watching knew, these three floaty-tanks were on their side, being chased by ork speed freeks.

He hoped.

Something large began to lift into the sky on a pillar of flame that lit up the night sky, and Ufthak pointed the Snazz-hammer at it triumphantly as the humie shuttle began to tilt, angling its nose up towards the beckoning blackness above. 'See! Dat's wot I'm talkin' about! Dey're tryna get away wiv da loot!'

They screamed past the last humie vehicle and flew under an archway that had apparently been carved to look like it was made out of lots of humie skulls, unless it actually *was* made out of humie skulls. You never could tell with humies. They didn't at all like it if you tried to take their skulls, but then they still went and did weird things with them anyway, like make them float around and carry guns.

Another junction loomed ahead. Humie glyphs were plastered up all over the place to tell them which way to go, those strange scratch-marks they made instead of nice clear picts, but it didn't matter that Ufthak didn't have time to read them. The shuttle had come up from their right, so that was where they needed to go. Da Boffin knew it too, and threw the tank into yet another turn.

And there it was, ahead of them.

A thick-looking wall bristling with guns, most of which were aimed upwards to clear the skies of any menace to the humie ships that would be coming and going from within. The road they were now on led up to a gate which was open, and through which were straggling a few more humie vehicles. On either side of that gate, however, were gun towers, and the quad-barrelled gun each one held was most definitely *not* pointed at the sky: it was aimed down the access road.

'Duck, or ya gonna be missin' a head!' Ufthak bellowed. He suited actions to words and threw himself down into the tank's belly alongside his ladz. Even Da Boffin was hunkering down behind the driving controls, trying to make himself as inconspicuous as possible. 'Now, when we get froo dat gate I want all da humies killed, wivvout blowin' up wotever dey've got wiv 'em, right? We ain't come dis far just to blow up da loot we'z supposed to be gettin' for Da Meklord! So choppas an' sluggas only – no stikkbombs, no burnas, no rokkits. Uvverwise–'

A throaty roar of gunfire erupted ahead of them, interrupting him. Ufthak looked upwards and was delighted to see the incandescent streaks blazing overhead. His plan had worked! The defenders hadn't taken the time to properly suss out exactly who was coming down the road, and were targeting the obviously orky warbikes instead of the cunningly disguised orks inside the humie floaty-tanks.

'Uvverwise,' he continued, hoping everyone present had noticed the results of his genius, 'we'z gonna see exactly how long ya can survive wivvout ya head, on account of me removin' it. Got dat?'

'Yes, boss!' his mob chorused agreeably. Close-in work wasn't something that any ork was going to sulk about, in any case.

'Get ready, ladz!' Da Boffin shouted, from his vantage point where he could actually see what was going on. 'We'z gonna be froo da gates in FREE!'

Ufthak gripped the Snazzhammer.

'TWO!'

He eyed the shokk rifle dubiously, then hastily attached it to a spare strap and slung it across his shoulder. It was probably a bit too shooty to risk inside the walls; he might take a chunk out of something impressively shiny.

'ONE!'

Everyone tensed.

The two gun towers sailed by, their tops just visible from his position low down in the tank, and Da Boffin did something with levers that resulted in a violent deceleration. 'Dat's it, we'z in!'

'You two, an' you two,' Ufthak said, pointing at two pairs of orks. 'I want you up da ladders an' sortin' out dose gate guns before they turn around on us.' He raised his voice to a roar. 'Da rest of ya, GET OUT DERE AN' SCRAG 'EM!'

The button to lower the ramp was agreeably large and red, and an ork hand hit it on the second try. The ladz didn't even bother to wait for it to lower fully, vaulting over it while it was still at a forty-five-degree angle. Ufthak followed, twirling the Snazzhammer absent-mindedly, and took a quick look at where they were.

It was a huge, flat area, bounded by a wall of the same height all the way around, in typically predictable humie style, and illuminated by floodlights to help the humies' weak eyes, which couldn't cope in darkness. There were five shuttle craft still on the pad, and all of them had red-robed humies scuttling around them and the huge number and variety of crates and boxes that were in the process of being loaded onto them, like insects in the wake of a predator that had broken open their nest. He reckoned that his ladz must have been outnumbered four or five to one, but based on their initial reactions, very few of the humies seemed to be up for a fight.

That was a shame, since a fight was what was coming to them.

All three tanks had made it through the gates, which had slammed closed behind them. One warbiker had made it through as well, surviving the hail of fire that had been directed his way, although judging by the pall of smoke now rising on the immediate other side of those gates, at least a couple of his mates had managed to dodge the gun towers' bullets without being quite quick enough to get through a rapidly narrowing gap, and had gone head first into the gates instead.

The warbiker was already gunning his engine and rampaging off, aiming for the largest concentration of humies, which was at the other end of the pad, and shooting his dakkaguns for all he was worth. Ufthak ignored him; if the git looked like he was going to wreck anything particularly impressive then he might have to do something about it, but otherwise it was pointless trying to rein in a speed freek.

Ufthak had taken this all in within the space of a heartbeat or two, his practised eye assessing the situation and coming to the conclusion that there was nothing here that was likely to pose his boyz any sort of real threat. Then he loped into a run, even overtaking one or two of the slower members of his mob, before they all piled into the group of panicking humie defenders who were clustered around the lowered ramp of the nearest shuttle.

It was a slaughter. There weren't really any fighters here, just humies who moved boxes and humies who counted boxes as they were moved. The quick ones, mainly in red robes, didn't want to fight, and couldn't. The strong ones, with huge bionik claws to lift and carry stuff, were too slow to realise what was going on until they were already dead. Ufthak laid about him, killing two or three at a time with the hammer. He didn't even need to pull a gun, it was over so quickly.

'Dat it?' Mogrot asked, disappointment filling his voice as he looked around. His tunic was stained so red he could have almost passed for an Evil Sunz boy, if you didn't look too closely.

Echoing steps of metal on metal rang out from within the shuttle, and the entire mob swung around as one. Two pairs of lights blazed out, swaying up and down and from side to side in time with the steps, and then two walkers emerged into the actinic glare of the floodlights. Ufthak had seen their like before – mini humie Dread-things, sort of like their version of a killa kan – hanging around with the really squishy humies with the guns that shot bits of light. They'd normally have some sizeable guns of their own strapped to them, but these just had larger versions of the bionik claws some of the humie loaders had. They were obviously just here to move some of the heavier cargo, rather than provide any form of protection. All the same, they weren't small, and they accelerated down the ramp with considerable momentum.

Ufthak unslung the shokk rifle and blew the legs off the one nearest him. The armoured body of it fell, and slid down the ramp with an ear-clenching screech.

'Waaagh!'

Mogrot had quickly scaled a pile of crates, and launched himself off the top of them onto the other walker. It veered, trying to shake off its unwanted passenger, but Mogrot went to work on its roof with his choppa, and a few moments later he'd prised off the access hatch, which he hurled away into the darkness. He emptied the clip of his slugga downwards, and the machine staggered to a gyro-stabilised halt as its pilot was turned into a broken mess of flesh and bones. The rest of the mob piled onto the stricken cockpit of the other walker. Someone shoved a stikkbomb through a view slit, and that was the end of that, although it didn't stop Nizkwik from jumping up and down on it and shrieking aggressively.

'Anyone else want some?!' Mogrot roared from his new perch, waving his slugga and choppa triumphantly. He turned on the spot, and looked out across the landing pad. 'Huh. Guess not, den.'

Ufthak peered around the nearest stack of crates and saw the rest of the humies all fleeing towards another big gate at the far end, but they were much too far away to catch now. The lone warbiker accelerated into view, dakkaguns blazing, but some desperate shots rang out from the humies and something hit him hard enough to send him and his bike sprawling into a skid that kicked up sparks like rain. The rider came to a tumbling and somewhat battered halt, while his vehicle continued on until it hit the boundary wall, whereupon it exploded. The humies didn't press their advantage and converge to clobber the rider like the ladz would have, though; instead, they hurried on to the gate, managed to get it open, and disappeared through it before the ork could do more than get unsteadily back to his feet and stagger around a few steps. Ufthak looked up and around, and saw the boyz he'd sent to take care of the gate guns descending ladders again, so it looked like there wasn't going to be any more action from that quarter, either.

'Right, ladz,' Ufthak said, trying to keep their spirits up. 'So we didn't get a good fight, but wot we *have* got, is all da zoggin' loot! Just look at dis!' He slapped one of the crates. 'If da humies were tryin' to get away wiv it, dat means it's da good stuff. Let's get 'em open, den we can show dat Badrukk who da flashest gitz are, yeah?'

The mob fell on the crates and containers with gusto, ripping or hacking them apart to get at the contents. Ufthak kept a stern eye on things, directing Da Boffin to anything that looked particularly complicated.

It was a strange mix of things that they valued, these humies. Weird devices abounded, some of them stranger-looking than even the oddest mekboy gizmo. There were a lot of small, flat oblongs of metal and glass, too, which Ufthak couldn't see any use for but which Da Boffin was utterly delighted by, for reasons he didn't even bother trying to explain. But then there were also some finds that had obvious applications.

'Boss, check dis out!' an ork – Narlob, maybe? – shouted, hauling the side off a large crate that stood higher than Ufthak to reveal the contents.

Ufthak had seen beakie armour before, many times. He'd even seen that really thick beakie armour with helmets that weren't actually beaky and instead had an expression a bit like an ork who was having real trouble doing his business at the Drops. And he'd also seen their Dreads, too: familiar, squat shapes, far more similar to an ork creation than the spindly ones the pointy-earz used. But this was something new. It was massive, pretty much as big as him, with compact guns the size of his head hanging off the underside of each fist. It also had a dramatically enlarged section behind the shoulders, with lots of air intakes, large fans and other confusing gubbinz.

'It's, like…' Narlob peered around the back of it. 'It's got a space inside! Where a beakie would stand!'

Ufthak shoved him out of the way and frowned. Sure enough, the back of the armour swung open, and inside there was space for a fully armoured beakie.

'Dat's weird,' he said flatly. 'Mork's teef, I dunno. Who needs armour on dere armour?' He flicked it with one taloned finger. 'Pretty solid, I'll give it dat.' He realised Da Boffin was eyeing him. 'Wot?'

'Reckon it'd fit ya.'

'Ya wot?'

'Yeah.' Da Boffin buzzed forwards on his wheel and produced a handheld burna. 'Needs takin' in a bit around da legs, get a bit of da surplus junk out da middle, but humie stuff is easy to hack up. Give us a few minutes an' we'll 'ave ya an armour suit any nob'd be proud of.'

Ufthak rubbed his jaw with his thumb, then nodded. Beakies were tough, no lies there, and their armour was the business. And to be honest, he'd been thinking he needed something a bit more impressive to wear now he was a nob. 'Alright, get goin'. Everyone else–'

A razor-edged cry filled the night and sent the sky to shaking. It was as though someone had infused the entire city with malice, and then given it a voice.

'Wot woz dat?' Deffrow asked, the item he'd been studying dropping from his fingers.

'Eh,' Ufthak said with a shrug, as he watched Da Boffin start working on what was about to become his new armour. 'Prob'ly nuffin' we need to worry about.'

+++022+++

Alarms rang loud through Node Primus, and they rang long,
but there was no one to respond to them.

The void shields that had been keeping the massed greenskin horde at bay had been on the verge of failing anyway,
so great had been the strain on the generators as they tried
to keep the fields modulated to a frequency that wouldn't
let infantry through, so the fact that one had winked out of
existence hadn't been surprising. Even so, Zaefa Varaz, running through the internal thoroughfares of Node Primus'
main complex, had harboured severe doubts that this was
the result of a standard generator failure, even before she'd
scanned the communications from the tech-priests who had
been attending to it, and had read their panicked-sounding
accounts. It seemed that their standard error reports contained no category for 'generator destroyed by unholy
perversion of technology created by a Traitor Astartes', and
this inability to follow protocol worried them very nearly as

much as the fact they'd nearly been killed by a rampaging blasphemy.

The problem was, there was no way to respond. She had identified the daemonic machine as a threat and made everyone with sufficient security clearance aware of it – not that she was receiving any replies from either the tech-priest dominus or the grand genetor, and she wasn't sure whether to be alarmed or relieved by this – but it had crushed the few resources available to be thrown at it. Meanwhile, the rest of the troops were still engaged in a last-ditch defence against the onrushing orks, although Zaefa's readouts showed icon after icon winking out. The Mechanicus' troops were exacting a high toll on the attackers, but the xenos seemed to neither notice nor care. There was no longer any concept that the defence was anything other than a delaying action, especially with some orks still loose after being let in by Yavannos' meddling, and now the daemon engine running amok as well.

<I should be with the troops,> Secutor Mitranda stated from beside her, as they ran.

<Illogical,> Zaefa told them firmly. <Not even your presence and direct tactical intervention could repel this attack. The numbers are incontestable. The node is lost, and the only remaining course of action is to evacuate all high-ranking personnel and research materials.>

<Despite that–>

<Secutor, do not persist in this folly,> Zaefa ordered them. <You have spoken to me before about your scorn for the Space Marines' culture of hero-worship and self-sacrifice, and how they perceive their prevalence for throwing away lives on lost causes as brave and honourable. Yet now you would engage in the same behaviour?>

<I have not previously experienced a defeat of this magnitude,>

Mitranda muttered. <It is possible that the extent of it has over-ridden my rationality in some way.>

<I consider that to be the most likely explanation,> Zaefa replied. She scanned the noosphere, which was still operational despite the damage the main complex was now taking from ork artillery. <The first shuttle is away, and the remnants of the fleet have been summoned to approach as close to the planet as is practical, bearing in mind the ork presence in orbit.>

<The tech-priest dominus did not overrule you?> Mitranda asked, surprise showing in both their voice and their floodstream.

<He did not,> Zaefa said grimly. <It appears that he has accepted the tactical reality of the situation. Although unlike you, he has expressed no desire to join the fighting as a result. He is proceeding to the evacuation point.>

She checked the itinerary. Her own most valued possessions – including the device that Gavrak Daelin had so worryingly and yet intriguingly identified as being of xenos origin – had been packed up by her servitors and were ready to be shipped out once loaded. She had already tweaked the arrangements to ensure that Illutar and Yavannos, should they appear, were on separate shuttles to her and her belongings. She had rationalised this by it being illogical for all three remaining members of Hephaesto's High Council to risk their lives together, when they would be ascending in unarmed shuttles into what might very well become a second space battle. However, in truth she conceded to herself that it was because she had no wish for them to have any opportunity to inspect the contents of her private chambers.

It was, of course, simply coincidence that some of the personal possessions that her two colleagues had identified as being a priority, once they'd accepted that evacuation was necessary, had also been allocated to the shuttle Zaefa would be travelling on. That was the way, with last-minute additions to an existing plan: things had to be fitted in wherever space could be found. If the High Council had granted Zaefa full authority to plan the evacuation from when she'd first suggested it, instead of forcing her to coordinate it behind their backs, it wouldn't have been an issue – or at least, that was what she would tell Illutar if he questioned her logistical decisions.

The hallways were emptying out now. All expendable denizens of the node had been armed with whatever weapons could be found and sent to face down the greenskins. All that remained were priority personnel and their accompanying aides, along with servitors who were either transporting the remaining valuable items to the landing pad or were still proceeding about their regular maintenance patterns, since they lacked sufficient combat ability to be worth the time and effort of reprogramming.

<Lexico arcanus! Lexico arcanus!>

The breathy shout came from Durrill Addenbrow, a senior magos biologis who had worked closely with Viker Yavannos on a number of projects. They were hurrying out of a side corridor, where it joined the main thoroughfare down which they were running, and their multitude of arms cradled a selection of specimen cases and collection jars. Behind them stomped two ogryn servitors, similarly laden down, and a piebald cyber-mastiff.

<Yes, magos?> Zaefa answered, not slowing her pace. Addenbrow fell in beside her, the whirr of the tracks with which they had replaced their legs reaching a high whine as they did so.

<I am led to believe that this disruption is your responsibility?!> Addenbrow demanded.

<If by 'disruption' you refer to the fact you are being evac­uated before the orks break into your chambers and kill you: yes,> Zaefa replied shortly.

<Orks?> There was a momentary pause, and Zaefa's data senses detected Addenbrow scanning the noosphere. <Ah. I see.>

Zaefa didn't bother to hide her irritation. <How in the name of the Omnissiah could you not have been aware the planet was under attack?>

<My normal operating procedure is to isolate myself from the datacasts,> Addenbrow replied, without any indication that they considered this to be an error on their part. <They distract me from my work, and other magi regularly seek my input on matters in which I am not an expert, have no interest, have not agreed to be consulted upon, or any combination thereof. It is a shame that I was not aware of the presence of orks in our system, however: Grand Genetor Yavannos and I have made a considerable study of their biology and culture.>

<Culture?> Zaefa scoffed. <Magos, this is a poor time to jest. 'The largest ork rules' is not the same thing as having culture.>

<I have no sense of humour,> Addenbrow retorted stiffly. <My words were completely serious. Although primitive when compared to our own society, orks when gathered in numbers do display variations which we can identify as hierarchical and, indeed, what appear to be traditions or practices specific to->

<Do you have any insights on how best to eliminate them?> Mitranda cut in grimly.

Addenbrow considered for a few moments. <Most studies to which I have access have spoken highly of lascannons.>

<How insightful,> Mitranda muttered. They had armed

themself with a power sword and a taser goad after Gavrak
Daelin had fallen backwards off the gantry with their Omnissian axe wedged in his chest, but that was a combination
which Zaefa felt required getting far too close to an ork to be
effective. It wasn't that she doubted Mitranda's combat effectiveness, but she'd feel a lot more comfortable with a means
to pick the beasts off at range, should they encounter any.

A new alert flashed up. It would barely have been note-
worthy amidst the cacophony of other alarms and warnings
that filled the air, both audible and noospheric, but its originating location was what drew it to Zaefa's attention.

<There is trouble at the landing pad,> she said, trying to
control the beginnings of a threat response inside her body.
The data was increasingly suggesting that the odds were swinging against them escaping the planet alive, but she needed
to remain calm, in order to make the best decisions. <The
orks may have->

The floor shook. The walls shook. The ceiling above them
shook, and crumbs of rockcrete hissed down as the super-
structure of the building shifted, ever so slightly.

<Something big just hit the main complex,> Mitranda
declared. Zaefa didn't need their analysis: the fact that a large
part of the building had just turned to white noise and static
in her monitoring confirmed it. It was a section more or less
at the opposite end to where they were – and therefore closest to the orks' main offensive – but if the greenskins were
now bringing weapons to bear that could do that much damage then their peril had increased once more.

The complex took another hit, just as they passed the
junction that would have led them to the primary power
generation facility, and the noosphere ceased functioning,
along with half of the lumens.

<Ashes of Mars!> Zaefa spat in rage and frustration, as the thoroughfare dropped into patchy light and shadow. The noosphere's enabling circuitry was laced throughout the walls of Node Primus' main complex, and it stood to reason that sufficient destruction would render it unusable, at least unless and until circuits could be patched and workarounds found. That would theoretically be possible, but not under current circumstances. Now, just as she was most in need of up-to-date information on the current situation, Zaefa found herself floundering in a world that was unexpectedly dark and silent. She was still receiving vox traffic and dataflows, of course, but the comprehensive picture was gone.

<There are a number of beings approaching from the direction of the landing pad,> she informed Mitranda, sifting through the available information as best she could. <I believe that they are Mechanicus who have fled from an ork advance party, but at present all I can do is track their progress through automated doors, and the length of time the doors remain open to allow them all through.>

<Acknowledged,> Mitranda replied, hefting their weapons. They all slowed, unwilling to charge headlong into an unknown situation. <Magos Addenbrow, if you have any form of personal protective equipment about your person, I suggest you equip it.>

<As you say, secutor,> Addenbrow replied. A whirring noise emanated from within their robes, and a sharp-nosed barrel emerged up from behind their right shoulder, then pivoted forwards to bring the rest of the sizeable weapon into view.

<Interrogative: what is that?> Zaefa asked in astonishment.

<It is a miniaturised lascannon,> Addenbrow replied, as a targeting device dropped over their right ocular implant. <It

lacks a little of the punch and range of the Mars Mk VII, but I find it quite adequate for most circumstances.>

<It was my understanding that you were unaware of the orkoid presence here,> Mitranda said.

<I was.>

<And yet you are equipped with the very item you declared most suitable for the current threat?>

<In my experience, there are very few hostile threats that can't be at least partially resolved by the judicious application of a lascannon,> Addenbrow said, with the faintest air of self-satisfaction. <As such, I keep one about my person whenever I may be entering into a potentially unsafe situation.>

Zaefa shot another glance at the magos, and readied her gamma pistol. <You realise, secutor, that if the access corridor to the landing pad is blocked by hostiles, we have very limited other options?>

<I do,> Mitranda replied. <Which is why we must–>

Zaefa heard the noise behind them at the same moment as Mitranda whirled, their weapons coming up. Addenbrow's cyber-mastiff barked at the section of panelling as it slid aside near silently. Mitranda lunged at the figure that burst forth from within...

...and pulled their power sword strike a hair's breadth before it bit into the robed body of Tech-Priest Dominus Ronrul Illutar.

<Secutor,> Illutar said in greeting, the machine flatness of his voice failing to completely hide his alarm.

<Tech-priest dominus,> Mitranda replied, withdrawing their weapon and returning to a relaxed position. <I was not aware of any access tunnel with an entrance at this location.>

<Indeed,> Illutar agreed, stepping forward to emerge fully. Behind him came Viker Yavannos, but the pair appeared to

be alone. <Some information is available only to the Fabricator General.>

The few remaining visible biological components of Mitranda's face were not particularly expressive, but judging by what Zaefa could see, if the secutor had retained biological eyes then their glare could have melted lead. <Interrogative: there are passages within this complex of which I am unaware?>

<Clarification: please refer to my most recent informational upload,> Illutar stated, turning to face Zaefa. <Lexico arcanus. The evacuation is proceeding according to schedule?>

According to my *schedule, you self-important circuit-licker,* Zaefa thought, then hastily double-checked that she hadn't communicated any such sentiment in her data stream. <Yes, tech-priest dominus. However, reports suggest that the landing pad has come under attack, and–>

The closest door in the direction of the landing pad opened, and Zaefa whirled around again, raising her gamma pistol. Mitranda dropped into a guard position, and Addenbrow's lascannon hummed as it rapidly reached maximum charge.

The flood of Mechanicus adepts, tech-thralls and flight personnel came to a shambling halt in the face of the weapons aimed at them. Then, after a second of assessing and recognition, every single one of them began clamouring.

<…orks came…>

<…had to tactically withdraw…>

<…guns of excessive size…>

<*Everyone cease communicating immediately!*> Illutar boomed, and for a wonder, they did. <Interrogative: have you been followed?>

There was a general consensus that no, they hadn't been.

<Secutor, logic dictates that we must retake the landing pad from the xenos before they receive reinforcements,> Illutar

declared. <Please proceed with all speed using the resources at your disposal. The grand genetor and I are fully armed, and able to assist.>

Fully armed? Zaefa felt considerably under-equipped clutching her gamma pistol, even with the armaments of her mecha-dendrites. It made sense that two senior tech-priests would pause in their flight to ensure that they were able to protect themselves in the middle of an invasion, of course it did. However, something had snagged her thoughts, and wouldn't let go completely. How could Illutar have been so foolishly confident in their troops' abilities to repel the ork attack, yet take the precaution to fully arm himself? How was it that he and Yavannos had clearly been at each other's throats over the instructions to kill or capture the greenskins, yet now had come through secret tunnels together? It would be logical for senior tech-priests to cooperate in the face of imminent death, but where had their cooperation been earlier?

It was, of course, possible that Illutar and Yavannos had updated their data and their corresponding behavioural tendencies as events had unfolded, but Zaefa still couldn't shake the image of how normal Kapothenis Ull's chambers had been. How there had been no outward sign of corruption, even in his personal environment. It was clear to her that the wiles of the Archenemy could be buried deep indeed, and she still could not completely shake the notion that perhaps she had been the only untouched member of Hephaesto's High Council. What better way for a traitorous prime hermeticon or grand genetor to sow further corruption and confusion than by conspiring to let a forge world fall, then ensuring their own safe escape in order to continue their work elsewhere?

She became aware that Mitranda had addressed her, and

refocused her attention on her immediate surroundings. <Your pardon, secutor, please repeat?>

<I require you to stay close to me, lexico arcanus,> Mitranda said. <Your knowledge of the contents of the different shuttles will be invaluable should we be unable to completely reclaim the landing pad, and therefore be forced to engage in an incomplete evacuation.>

<Of course,> Zaefa responded, but she couldn't escape the feeling that Illutar and Yavannos were both eyeing her.

Did they suspect that she suspected them?

Da Flash Git

Da Boffin was just clamping up the back of Ufthak's new armour to fix it in place when a veritable cacophony of gunfire erupted from beyond the landa pad's gates. The fusillade was accompanied by the ringing sound of abused metal, so it was fairly clear to Ufthak that it wasn't just a fight that had broken out on the outside: someone was trying to break in by shooting the gate down.

'Reckon it's da humies, boss?' Deffrow asked, readying his slugga.

'Nah,' Ufthak said. 'Dey'd know how to get froo. S'gotta be some uvver ladz wot had da same idea as us about da loot, but were too late.'

The gunfire continued. The centre of the gate was beginning to warp and buckle inwards under the sheer weight of the fire that it was taking.

'Got any idea who it might be?' Da Boffin asked. Ufthak snorted.

'Yeah, I reckon.'

He shrugged his shoulders, testing out the armour. The legs had needed taking in, as Da Boffin had said, and they'd had to lose the arms completely because Ufthak's were far longer than any humie's. That meant he'd also lost the hand-gunz, but he was happy enough with the shokk rifle, and he wouldn't have wanted to not have the Snazzhammer. Besides, the rest of him was now encased in something that would make even 'ard boyz envious. It was a shame it was still a gunmetal grey, but that just meant he could give it a proper Bad Moons paint job once they'd finished looting the place...

The centre of the landa pad gate finally blew in. There was the scream and whine of ricochets as additional shots rang out and burst through, widening the aperture even more, until finally the barrage ceased. There were a few moments of relative silence, insofar as such a thing ever existed in a warzone, and then a be-hatted figure strutted through the gap between the ravaged metal gates.

Kaptin Badrukk.

He whistled through his teef, and his Flash Gitz came piling through the gap after him, each one hefting their snazzgun. They were laden down with captured humie loot, hanging from their waists and strapped to their backs, but Ufthak grinned as his gaze took them all in. Sure, Badrukk's boyz had done well for themselves, but it was his ladz who'd hit the *real* muthalode.

'"Not kitted out well enuff", my arse,' he chuckled to himself, looking around. His ladz had done a number on the humie stashes and had cannibalised anything that had looked even remotely like a weapon, hastily strapping or welding them together on the spot until they now bristled with just as many gun barrels as any Flash Git. Even the lone warbiker, apparently known as Bogrip, had attempted to get over the disappointment of losing his bike. He'd actually picked up the two handgunz from Ufthak's armour, and he was now peering through the sights of one while cackling.

'Wot's goin' on 'ere, den?' Badrukk boomed, striding across the ground between the ruined gate and where Ufthak's mob were clustered around the humie shuttle nearest to it. 'Lookin' after da loot for us, are ya?'

Ufthak guffawed. 'Dat's good, dat's good! Shame ya couldn't get 'ere any quicker, really it is. Fing is, see, we got 'ere first, an' so all dis loot is ours, now.'

Badrukk's brows went up so fast they nearly knocked his bicorn hat backwards off his head. 'Is dat so? A buncha grot-lickin' Bad Moons like yoo fink ya gonna just take what ya like an' leave nuffin' for da rest of us?'

'Yeah, dat's about right,' Ufthak retorted, drawing himself up as tall as he could. Da Boffin had needed to do a quick hack job on the top of the armour too, since humies had their heads sticking out the top of their shoulders all ready to get knocked off, instead of low down between them for safe keeping, but he was still a bit taller than Badrukk, and the freebooter kaptin clearly didn't like it. 'And wot's a buncha squig-sniffin' gitz like *yoo* gonna do about it?'

Badrukk scoffed. 'Is dat a challenge?'

'Sounded like one to me,' Ufthak told him. All around them both, orks began to ready their weapons for a good old scrap.

Badrukk's eyes travelled down to the shokk rifle in Ufthak's right hand. 'See ya found yerself a gun, den.'

'Dat's right,' Ufthak said.

'I mean, if yer can call it a gun,' Badrukk chuckled, hefting Da Rippa. 'Now *dis*... dis is a gun.'

'I'm hearin' a lotta talkin',' Ufthak sneered, every nerve in his body tensed and ready to spring into action. 'Ain't seein' no shootin'.'

'Ya wanna see shootin'? Is dat right?'

'Got me some new armour, too,' Ufthak said. 'Ya might've noticed? Fort I might give it a bit of a test. Nuffin' too bad. Ya gun might do.'

'Boss?'

Badrukk's eyes narrowed furiously. 'Oh, I'm gettin' da feelin' yer tryin' to provoke me, yoof.'

'Boss!'

'"Yoof"?!' Ufthak snarled. 'I ain't takin' dat from some git wot's dressed like a whole mob of madboyz! I'll–'

'*Boss!*'

'WOT?' Ufthak bellowed, rounding on his mob, ready to clobber whichever idiot it was who kept shouting for him. 'Mork's teef, I'm gonna tear yer zoggin'–'

'Boss!' Snagrab shouted, pointing wildly towards the other end of the landa pad. 'Da humies are back!' And sure enough they were, a small flood of red-and-midnight robes who had clearly emerged out of the gate they'd all disappeared into earlier. They'd made a run for it towards the shuttle nearest to them, and were now clustered together while they hurried up the ramp.

'So dey are,' Ufthak muttered. He looked back at Badrukk. 'If we go an' clobber dem, yer only gonna nick da loot, ain't ya?'

Badrukk sniffed dismissively, and brought Da Rippa up to point at the humies. 'Biz'niss first, innit. We stomp dese gits, and den' we 'ave further discusshuns about whose loot dis is. Deal?'

'Deal,' Ufthak nodded. 'Alright, ladz, into 'em!'

+++024+++

The blast door, thick enough to have at least a chance of keeping out the debris from an exploding shuttle, slid aside with a faint grinding noise. Zaefa's olfactory sensors were full of the scents of unguents, oil and sweat from those around her, but she was still able to pick up the faint scent of night air from outside as a light breeze washed over them.

She also detected promethium, cordite and the stink of orks.

Secutor Mitranda stepped through the door first, their weapons extended, and Zaefa heard the faint click and hum of their targeting auspexes as they scanned the area.

<The greenskins are still here, but are clustered around the shuttle at the far end, and have not yet noticed me,> Mitranda reported, quickly and quietly. <They appear to have looted or destroyed many of the items that were gathered here, but their efforts look to have been concentrated on those nearest to them. The shuttle closest to us appears to be undamaged and its contents largely undisturbed.>

Zaefa checked the inventory again. The closest shuttle was the one on which, amongst many other things of more general use such as data cores, most of her possessions had been loaded. She breathed a quiet sigh of relief.

<It is one hundred and eighty-eight point nine feet from the blast door to the shuttle's ramp,> Mitranda continued. <I recommend speed, and–>

The sound of many high-powered ballistic weapons reached them, even louder than the other distant noises of battle. Zaefa leaned her head out and triangulated the noise to be originating from the other side of the landing pad's main road entrance, which was currently sealed off by the security gates. Somehow these orks had got past those without damaging them, but it seemed that someone or something else was applying a more direct method.

<Could it be reinforcements?> Ronrul Illutar said hopefully.

<Unquestionably,> Yavannos replied. <But for whom?>

<I do not recognise those sounds as ones made by any Munitorum-issued weapon,> Mitranda said, their head cocked to one side. <It is highly likely that those wielding them are orks.> They turned to face Zaefa and the rest. <We should move now, while the enemy is distracted and before their numbers increase.>

<Agreed,> Illutar said. <Commence evacuation!>

They ran.

Mitranda, who had the backwards-bent legs of a Sicaran Infiltrator, raced ahead and easily outpaced the rest of them. Zaefa followed as best she could, aware of their instructions that she should stay close, but the best she could do was to more or less hold her position at the head of the hurrying pack. The clatter of feet on the ground, the whirring of Durrill Addenbrow's tracks and even the gale of her breathing and the thunder of her heartbeat in her own ears all convinced her that the orks would hear them, would turn, would attack...

It didn't happen. She reached the base of the ramp without any sign of the xenos being aware of their presence. Mitranda was clinging with their tertiary arm to one of the hydraulic stanchions that extended from the ramp's end up into the body of the shuttle, while their primary limbs still held their melee weapons ready just in case an unexpected threat should emerge.

<Inside!> the secutor urged, their ocular implants focused on the orks still gathered at the far end of the pad. Zaefa paused to follow their gaze and saw that there were now two different sorts of ork there. One gathering, mainly clad in black and yellow, were interacting in some way with the second faction, whose multicoloured clothing and accoutrements made them look like an artist working with paints or powders had upset their palette over them. One ork stood out though: the largest present, wearing a suit of unadorned metal that was oddly familiar...

<That is the Centurion suit!> Zaefa breathed in horror, as a shock of recognition coursed through her. She zoomed in, and felt anger responses rising in her body when she saw the brutal, crude alterations made to its dimensions to fit its new owner... no, new *wearer*, for she could not countenance that the ork had truly taken possession of such a valuable piece of equipment. Where were the Hephaesto-pattern assault bolters, an as yet unsanctified upgrade – although it was surely only a matter of time – to the equipment usually carried by Inceptor squads? Had the orks damaged the Mk II Accipter jump pack? Had they even recognised it for what it was? The only functioning prototype for what would surely become the next advance in Adeptus Astartes battlesuits had been

stolen and was being worn by a xenos savage, and there was nothing she could do about it.

<We must retake the other shuttles,> Illutar declared firmly, stopping next to her.

<That is impossible,> Secutor Mitranda said flatly. <We need to board this shuttle and take off as soon as is practicable.>

<Absolutely unacceptable,> Illutar retorted, his voice rising in volume. <I have checked the inventories for the craft and seventy-two per cent of my personal possessions have been loaded onto the one third in line from where we stand! It is inconceivable that I should leave this planet without the vital work on which I have spent decades!>

<Similarly, my most important studies and samples are in that shuttle,> Viker Yavannos cut in, pointing at the next shuttle over. <To lose them would set back the Imperium's knowledge base by–>

<It *cannot be done!*> Mitranda snapped. <We lack the combat capacity to engage the xenos for any length of time and retain a statistical chance of survival!>

<Spoken like a warrior with no understanding of the value of learning!> sneered Illutar. <You may excel at waving sticks of varying sharpness and electrical charge, but my collected works–>

<Would not be here at all if it were not for me!> Zaefa broke in, frustrated beyond endurance. <You lacked the wit to plan for your own failure! Were it not for my foresight, your collections would still be inside the complex from which we have just fled, and even this single shuttle would not have been prepared for our use!>

Ronrul Illutar drew himself up, his data stream flickering with rage like a circuit board about to overload. <Secutor, as *tech-priest dominus*–>

<We have been seen,> Mitranda said, and Zaefa subjectively felt the temperature drop even though her instruments informed her that no such change had taken place. A quick glance confirmed the secutor's words: the orks had broken into a headlong charge, and a moment later their bellowing war cries filled the air. Despite their bow-legged gait, they were eating up the distance at an alarming rate. Then the muzzle flashes began, and projectiles of various natures began flying overhead and whistling past. None were hitting home as yet, but the sheer volume of fire meant that it could only be a matter of time.

<I order you to engage!> Illutar barked at Mitranda.

<Your order is illogical,> Mitranda retorted, <and I->

Zaefa drew her gamma pistol and fired.

She punched her first shot into Ronrul Illutar. Her second took Viker Yavannos in the torso before the grand genetor could react. Both staggered backwards and fell, wounded but still alive.

<I denounce you as traitors and hereteks!> Zaefa shouted, already retreating back up the ramp. Illutar and Yavannos were already stirring, but it seemed that their confusion and alarm at being unmasked had slowed their reflexes, and they did not immediately return fire. <Your conspiracies doomed this planet! Now you suffer the consequences!>

Secutor Mitranda stared at her for a moment in apparent disbelief. Then, as an ork round glanced off their shoulder and sent them stumbling forwards, they bounded up the ramp after her. The ramp was already starting to rise: to Zaefa's surprise, it was Durrill Addenbrow whose hand was on the activation rune.

<I was about to close it anyway, and let the four of you decide if you were boarding or not,> the magos biologis said

by way of explanation as the ramp ground shut behind Zaefa, leaving Illutar and Yavannos stranded outside. They hesitated for a moment, and Zaefa became aware of the many eyes on her. <You stated that the Fabricator General and the grand genetor were hereteks?>

Zaefa quickly scanned the faces of those gathered with her in the cargo hold. The shuttle's engines were powering up, which meant the flight crew must have already made their way to their stations: that was good. Hopefully the orks' weapons would be able to do little more than scratch the hull in the time it would take for the thrusters to come properly online. They would all be free of this planet very shortly – albeit only to take their chances with the ork fleet – but what would the situation on board the shuttle be when they got there?

Technically, she outranked every other person on board. But she'd also just shot her own technical superior, so the chain of command was not necessarily something she could rely on in present circumstances.

<Yes,> she said, with as much authority as she could muster. <Secutor Mitranda can confirm that Forge Lord Kapothenis Ull had become corrupted by hereteks and unleashed an abomination upon our world, so clearly not even members of the High Council were free from the potential influence of the Dark Mechanicum. Bearing in mind the highly questionable and contradictory orders issued by the tech-priest dominus and the grand genetor, I am forced to conclude that they were also working to bring about the downfall of Hephaesto, albeit through different means. Even just now, Illutar sought to delay our departure and throw away our only martial resource, Secutor Mitranda, in an attempt to either ensure we did not escape, or to rescue his own

corrupted possessions, which meant more to him than the lives of his subordinates.>

The thrusters fired, and the shuttle began to lift off. Those with mag-clamps or similar securing mechanisms activated them reflexively, while those without wailed as they were thrown across the deck by the sudden movement.

<Secutor Mitranda?> Addenbrow asked.

<I can confirm the treachery of Forge Lord Ull,> Mitranda replied. <I do not wish to speculate on the motives of the other High Council members.>

<Your logic is compelling,> Addenbrow said to Zaefa. <And it would appear equally logical that with our previous grand genetor now stripped of her rank due to her treachery, Hephaesto-in-Exile requires a new magos biologis to occupy the position, in the interests of continuity and consistency?>

Zaefa studied them, attempting to read their intentions, but nothing about Addenbrow's body language or floodstream gave anything away. <It would indeed. To my knowledge, you would be the best placed to fulfil this function.>

Addenbrow nodded. <I concur. Very well, that seems to be in order. I assume you will be taking on the responsibility of Fabricator General?>

Something tightened in the ghost of Zaefa Varaz's biological stomach, an old reflex with no relevance to her current situation. <I... would be honoured to serve in that capacity.>

<As you are the only surviving member of the previous High Council, the appointment seems an obvious one,> Addenbrow declared loudly. They turned on the spot, tracks whining forward and back as they rotated to look at the other refugees. <Do any of those here assembled object?>

Zaefa saw the eyes and ocular implants of Hephaesto's underclasses. Saw them focus on Addenbrow and their shoulder-mounted lascannon, on Mitranda and their power sword and taser maul, on the hulking presence of Addenbrow's servitor ogryns and the silent presence of their cyber-mastiff.

There was a chorus of unanimous consent and approval.

<Very well, it is confirmed,> Addenbrow said, with an air of satisfaction to their words. They turned again to face Zaefa, and bowed from the waist. <Fabricator General. I will proceed to the cockpit and make enquiries with the crew as to what arrangements can be made for us.>

<Thank you, grand genetor,> Zaefa said, slightly absently. She checked over the inventory in her data files and compared it to what she could see in front of her, locating the crate in which the xenos artefact from her chambers had been packed. There was the crate, labelled and stored as expected, at the base of one of the stacks. But could she be certain that the item itself was inside? <Please carry on. I wish to familiarise myself with the full nature of our incomplete cargo...>

Lords of War

Te'Kannaroth hunted.

Hephaesto was a forge world, and Node Primus was its figurative heart. Here was where the greatest and largest creations were brought forth: not just war machines, but enormous drilling rigs, giant earth-shaping machines, titanic land crawlers, and myriad other devices through which humanity still sought to settle the savage galaxy and tame it to their whims. Such creations needed suitable highways down which they could move, either under their own power or via that of transports, and it was along these colossal highways that Te'Kannaroth stalked.

The Mechanicus were in disarray, now. The failure of the southern void shield had been a breach through which the unstoppable tide of the greenskin army could pour, and the humans' resistance had been swept away. Some survivors still fought on, digging into defensive positions and giving their lives to take a few more invaders down with them in a last, futile display of unwitnessed and unremembered defiance. Others fled, their machine-like organisation and stoicism lost as fleshly concerns clawed their way back to prominence in psyches where they had long been suppressed, and sent their hosts running in desperate, selfish bids to find some way to survive a little longer.

The abhorrence cared not. Te'Kannaroth could sense this, even as it fell upon vehicles containing panicked, quivering tech-thralls, and obliterated them with repeated blows from its mighty forelimbs. Servants of Chaos delighted in the souls they took, each one a fresh new treat for their masters, and none more so than the followers of Khorne. Every life Te'Kannaroth extinguished was a hymn to its patron, an individual morsel of pain and suffering that glorified the Taker of Skulls. Yet for the orks, violence and death was not special, was not sacred. They fought and they killed for no reason except that it seemed to please their simple minds. Even the warriors of the False Emperor killed in His name. It was a strange concept, that the warriors of the modern Adeptus Astartes, mewling by-blows of greater ancestors, had more in common with the followers of Chaos than either of them did with the abhorrence.

Te'Kannaroth sniffed the air. As the city took more and more damage, the information provided to it by its sensors grew less and less reliable, for the Mechanicus' data network was no longer fully functional. There were gaps in the tactical readouts – great blotches of blank space where what remained of the node's defenders had no information on what was occurring or what troops were present – and as a result Te'Kannaroth was equally blind. However, the daemon engine was not reliant on the devices of mortals alone, for it could see and hear and smell its surroundings, and it was these senses that it now used to pinpoint its prey.

It was a trivial matter. Even in a city wracked by war, even amongst streets of half-ruined buildings, where innumerable fires now burned and the air was thick with soot and ash, and the thunder of falling masonry mingled with the clamour of weapons fire, Te'Kannaroth could sense the abhorrence. The stink of their green flesh and their crude, fume-belching vehicles. The sound of their primitive guns and their ragged, guttural war cries. Their very presence was an itch in the daemon engine's consciousness, a slowly spreading blight of psychic irritant.

It met the first tendrils of the ork advance when a cavalcade of ramshackle vehicles swung around a partially ruined building on the corner of an intersection ahead of it. They slowed for a moment, apparently astounded at the sight of the hulking monstrosity of animated metal, then gunned their engines and accelerated with belligerent whoops. Guns coughed into life, spitting out streams of explosive shells. Many flew wide, despite the size of Te'Kannaroth's body, and those that struck home did little more than dent or scratch it, but the riders came on regardless.

Te'Kannaroth set itself on its six limbs and opened fire. The spinning barrels of its shoulder cannons ripped up the rockcrete of the roadway and annihilated the front runners of the pack before they could take evasive action. Some of those following managed to swerve around the fusillade of shells and came on, but Te'Kannaroth vomited a stream of warpfire that swallowed half of them, then leaped at the three survivors. One managed to accelerate beneath its power fists, but was shredded by the daemon engine's thrashing mechatendrils as it swung by its rear. The other two each met their end as Te'Kannaroth's full weight slammed down on them, via its clenched fists.

The daemon engine paused to pick up the remnants of its victims, distend its jaws, and swallow down the wrecked metal. Within the furnace of its body, fell powers transmuted the scrap into new ammunition for its shoulder cannons. Then it stalked forth again, hunting for the walking effigy of the abhorrence's gods.

The next wave of orks were not far behind their outriders. Te'Kannaroth detected the stench of a mass of greenskin bodies as it pounded between many-storeyed manufactoria and refineries, so it was no surprise when a horde of them boiled out of a burning building and swarmed towards it. Te'Kannaroth might have admired their courage in attacking something against which they were no more than biting insects, but it knew that courage was not a concept the abhorrence understood. They advanced upon it, waving their puny weapons and bellowing impotent threats, and Te'Kannaroth let them come, then plunged into their midst to break them.

They did not break.

Individuals died, of course, smashed into smears on the rockcrete by the daemon engine's power fists, eviscerated by its mechatendrils, or simply crushed beneath its hindlimbs as it pivoted and turned. Te'Kannaroth wrote a symphony of slaughter on and with their bodies, but the accursed things kept coming, and kept fighting. Te'Kannaroth laid about it, but now the orks were clambering on it, hacking at its metal hide with their primitive blades and wedging crude grenades in between its armour plates. It shook itself and managed to dislodge some of its attackers, but several still clung on, and others were already replacing those who'd been knocked loose.

A sudden, sharp spike of pain lashed through Te'Kannaroth's body, centred on its hindmost left limb. It roared in fury and turned, crushing more orks beneath it as it did so, and found itself staring down at a small group of greenskins who were rather more heavily equipped than their fellows. One of them pointed a weapon at Te'Kannaroth and a projectile shot off it, corkscrewing through the air. It sailed through the gap between Te'Kannaroth's head and its left shoulder cannon, and exploded in the building behind it with enough force to knock a hole in the wall wide enough to drive a Rhino through.

Te'Kannaroth raised its left fist and brought it down. Most of the orks scattered, but one bellowed angrily and swung some sort of hammer up to meet its doom, in a gesture of pitiful defiance. It was only just before its fist made contact that Te'Kannaroth noticed the hammer looked to be nothing more than a stick with an explosive device strapped to the end.

The ork died as the daemon engine's fist slammed down. The ork's weapon, however, detonated on impact, and Te'Kannaroth tasted pain again. Its fist was still functional, but it was damaged, and Te'Kannaroth had forgotten these unwelcome sensations that the mortal realm could inflict upon a body. Now it began to truly understand the bargain that it had made, for although the spells anchoring it within the armoured shell that Gavrak Daelin had constructed meant it could not be banished anywhere nearly as easily as when in its natural form, where it relied on the energy of the warp to maintain its presence, the anchoring was not a voluntary arrangement. Te'Kannaroth could not leave this shell until the shell was destroyed, and although it was mighty indeed, it was not invulnerable.

The orks were taking aim again, with weapons that Te'Kannaroth now knew could damage it: perhaps not damage it greatly, but enough to cause pain, and impinge on its effectiveness. The daemon engine had no more time to waste with these distractions. It needed to seek out its true quarry.

Te'Kannaroth lumbered into a run, flattening any orks unable or unwilling to get out of its way, and shaking loose a few more in the process. It ignored the howls of rage and derision that arose behind it, because it paid no mind to the wailing of mortals. It could sense the gargant ahead of it, and knew that the war effigy would also be using the widest highways of the Mechanicus to advance as far as it could into the node.

Te'Kannaroth moved to meet it.

A series of explosions confirmed the gargant's position: the enormous war machine was using some of its smaller weaponry to shoot at and blow up promethium reserves it had encountered, apparently for no reason other than to enjoy the destruction. Te'Kannaroth zeroed in on the billowing plumes of thick, black smoke that rose up towards the even darker inkiness of the sky, underlit by the soot-tinged glow of dirty flames.

Through yellow fire and black smoke strode the yellow-and-black monstrosity that bore the orks' warlord – the walking, mechanical idol worshipped by the green-skinned hordes.

The form of Te'Kannaroth's jaws had not, of course, been constructed with speech in mind. The wisp-like vestiges of Kapothenis Ull remembered only that he'd wished to create a great war machine, and had followed the beastlike designs of Gavrak Daelin in order to strike fear into the hearts of his enemies. However, with the power of the warp, all things were possible.

'*Blood for the Blood God!*' Te'Kannaroth bellowed in challenge, and opened fire.

Twins streams of incandescent fire ripped out of its gatling blasters, a hail of shells so furious that they almost formed solid lines of light connecting the two behemoths. The force fields protecting the gargant flickered into life, and twin patches of glowing energy battled to keep the engine safe from the harm directed its way. Te'Kannaroth vomited forth a warpfire blast, aimed directly at the gargant's squat head, but the force field caught that as well, and its energies were harmlessly dissipated.

The gargant struck back. A searing beam erupted from its eyes, slicing through the air with a stench of ozone, but Te'Kannaroth veered to one side and the lance of energy simply tore a trail of ruin along the highway behind it. Sundry other smaller weapons opened up as well, the chatter of their shells nothing more than an inconsequential nuisance to the daemon engine. Te'Kannaroth belched warpfire again, and watched the force field flicker uncertainly.

Then the gargant's belly gun spoke, and the shell struck Te'Kannaroth full in the chest.

It was agony like nothing the daemon had ever experienced. Even the most exquisite tortures of the warp, even the pain of being banished by that snivelling coward Essenyl Greymoon, did not compare to this. Te'Kannaroth was knocked sprawling, its six limbs no longer answering to it, the armour of its chest cracked and shattered from the sheer force of the impact. For the first time, possibly ever in its existence, Te'Kannaroth experienced desperation. It had no fear of this armoured shell being obliterated, for it would rise from it and return to the warp, immortal and undamaged, but to be trapped in this form while the damage wreaked upon it was transmitted inescapably into its very being...

The gargant's war-horns blared, and it lumbered forwards.

Enormous, saw-edged circular blades mounted on multi-jointed hydraulic arms began to whirl faster and faster, the initial buzz rapidly modulating upwards into a whine which sounded like it would be sufficient to cut through bone on its own. The orks were looking to confirm their kill.

Te'Kannaroth would not have it.

It exerted its will, bludgeoned back the agony of its existence and forced its limbs to function once more, dragging its bulk up from the pockmarked rockcrete of the thoroughfare's surface. Targeting systems found their locks, and its gatling blasters let rip again, only to see their efforts once more turned aside by the gargant's force field.

An arcane weapon mounted on the gargant's left side sparked and flashed, and Te'Kannaroth was abruptly seized by an invisible force. The ground began to drop away beneath it as the orks' tractor technology began to raise it helplessly into the air, ready to smash it back down onto the ground. Once that happened, Te'Kannaroth would be unable to recover before the gargant was on it, gigantic kill-saws whirling.

The daemon focused all its form's considerable firepower on the gargant's left side, aimed directly at the weapon holding it aloft. Finally, *finally*, the force field gave under the pressure, and flickered out of existence. A moment later, and the tractor generator exploded as a warpfire blast washed over it and melted it into uselessness. Te'Kannaroth dropped, but although the force of its impact shattered the rockcrete beneath it, it had not fallen from high enough to damage its shell any further.

The gargant was not so lucky.

Multiple fires sprang up across the effigy's body as electrical feedback from the simultaneous force field failure and weapons malfunction coursed through it. It veered to the right as steering systems suddenly became even more uncooperative than usual, and the next thunder of its belly gun demolished a line of buildings some way to the side of where Te'Kannaroth was gathering itself.

The daemon engine struck. A quick volley from its gatling blasters stitched lines of damage across the gargant's now-unshielded flank, and nearly severed the tractor weapon from the machine's shoulder. Then Te'Kannaroth charged, crossing the ground between them faster than the orks could bring their machine around, for they were a disorganised rabble attempting to control a creation largely beyond their comprehension, whereas Te'Kannaroth was a single mind of pure malice in command of a body that, although wracked with pain, still bent to its owner's will.

The impact of its charge actually rocked the gargant, massive and solid although it was. Te'Kannaroth slammed its left fist into the gargant's chest, cracking the armour; with its right it caught the arm of a descending kill-saw and then lashed out with its mechatendrils to anchor the limb in place. With it secured, Te'Kannaroth began to bend the limb, seeking to snap it off completely.

The gargant's belly gun boomed, but Te'Kannaroth was slightly off-centre from the front of the war machine, and this shot too flew wide. The head was trying to rotate to bring its energy weapon to bear, but the electrical fires were clearly impeding its operation.

The kill-saw limb sheared off, broken in two by Te'Kannaroth's might, and the daemon engine let the still-whirring blade fall to the ground. With the gargant still anchored in place by its right hand's grip on the remnants of the kill-saw limb, Te'Kannaroth began pounding the ork war machine repeatedly with its left, over and over, deforming the crudely welded body inwards.

The daemon engine's left gatling blaster focused its fire on its enemy's right kill-saw arm, which was sweeping across perilously close to the gargant's head in its efforts to reach the monstrosity savaging it from its left. The rounds battered at the limb near where it connected to the gargant's torso; as it came back for another pass, the metal gave way with a rending shriek, and the gargant's other close-combat weapon fell to the ground.

Te'Kannaroth roared in rage and triumph, and with one final punch it penetrated the gargant's armour, plunging the crackling might of its enormous power fist deep into the heart of the ork war machine. Te'Kannaroth could sense the glowing presence of the generator that powered the gargant, and closed its fingers around it. Then, with a primal bellow, it ripped it loose.

The force of the resulting explosion nearly blew Te'Kannaroth's power fist off, but it survived well enough to withdraw the crushed wreckage of the generator from the gaping wound in the gargant's chest. Te'Kannaroth distended its jaws again, and rammed the still-warm metal down its throat, the gaps between its armour plates expanding to let it pass as though the daemon engine's neck were a vast, metallic serpent. The gargant had gone dark and motionless, its remaining weapons drooping and powerless, the only light on it now the various fires that had sprung up and gone unchecked.

Te'Kannaroth lashed out with its right fist and delivered a thunderous uppercut that tilted the enormous war machine too far back for its centre of gravity to recover. It thundered to the ground with an impact that sent a shock wave rippling out through the air, blasting aside the dust and soot that hung there, and sending the smoke clouds billowing away. Its torso, not designed to withstand the force of its own weight, warped and flattened some more. Panels were knocked loose, or fell off entirely. A few large orks stumbled out of the wreckage, having somehow survived the mighty impact, but they were beneath notice.

Te'Kannaroth laughed. It was a hideous, twisted, wheezing and metallic sound, the sound of a furnace in agony, or an earthquake in a scrapyard. Silver malice coursed through the daemon engine's body, and the ingested materials of the gargant's generator flowed into place around the wound in its chest, reinforcing the armour and making it whole once more.

The ork war effigy had been brought low, and the might of Chaos had been reaffirmed. Now Te'Kannaroth could hunt as it pleased… but first, it had a bargain to keep.

It twisted its head around to look up towards the apex of the volcano. Thanks to the information in the schematics it had been furnished with, it knew that the near-mystical device that allowed the Mechanicus to harness the raw molten power of the planet was situated there. That was what Warpsmith Daelin had desired. His desire for it – amongst other things – had been the reason he had created this body, and he had poured that desire into the bindings that allowed Te'Kannaroth to inhabit the shell.

Te'Kannaroth did not know if Gavrak Daelin still lived, for the Mechanicus had stormed Kapothenis Ull's forge just as the daemon had been bound into this form, but it hardly mattered. Without the moderating power of the archeotech device, the volcano's full power would be unleashed to devastate Node Primus, and all living things within it. And that, Te'Kannaroth thought, would most definitely be a sight worth witnessing.

Mortal Krumpin'

Ufthak's ladz hadn't really got to this last shuttle yet; they'd only smashed open a few of the crates that had still been kicking around the bottom of its ramp, and he didn't think any of them had been up inside it at all. The humies had, typically, chosen the shuttle with the most loot left and the furthest away from a possible fight to steal – and it was definitely stealing, because this landa pad was Ufthak's now – and they all piled up into it as the boyz approached, like the wimps they were. It took Ufthak a few seconds to realise that a couple of the humies looked like they were having an argument about something, and then one of them whipped out a fancy slugga and zapped two others right in the chest, before running away inside.

The ramp raised, and the shuttle's engines started up, leaving the two other humies to pick themselves up right in front of the orks.

'*Hold it!*' Kaptin Badrukk bellowed, to Ufthak's surprise.

What was even more surprising was that every boy there, Ufthak included, came to a halt instead of piling right into the two humies and giving them a good clobbering.

'Get inta dat landa!' Badrukk ordered, pointing his choppa at the shuttle. 'You an' me, laddo,' and here he pointed directly at Ufthak, 'we needz to settle somefing. Pick one of 'em.'

Ufthak pointed at the humie closest to him, which looked to have the slightly fancier robes. 'Dat one.'

'Alright den,' Badrukk grinned toothily. 'First one to kill dere humie's da betta ork.'

The two humies were getting back to their feet now, and though neither of them looked completely comfortable, and Ufthak could see where their robes had been burned away by the shot that had struck each of them, the metal beneath looked more or less intact. Clearly it was going to take more than a hit from a fancy slugga to end either one. The humies themselves seemed confused as to why the orks weren't all charging them at once – which, to be fair, was something Ufthak himself still wasn't entirely clear on – and were chattering back and forth quietly to each other in a language that made them sound like giant mechanical insects.

Still, the opportunity to prove himself as a better ork than Kaptin 'Flash Git' Badrukk, Terror of Da Stars and kommanda of *Da Blacktoof*, was not an opportunity to be passed up. Sure, Ufthak had killed a humie gargant and knocked in a humie force field, but that was all *humie* stuff. It was good, but you expected humies to be a bit squishy, unless they were beakies.

'So when we startin'?' he asked.

'Now,' Badrukk replied, raising Da Rippa.

Both the humies moved.

They were a bit larger than normal humies, kind of hunched

over and that, but Ufthak had still thought the competition would basically come down to which of he and Badrukk could land a good blow first. He hadn't expected each of the humies to produce a veritable arsenal of weapons from under their robes, held in several different bionik arms, and go on the attack.

Ufthak threw himself to one side as a blunt-nosed gun came up, and not a moment too soon: white-hot flames gushed out, so powerful he could feel the wash of heat even though the blast itself didn't get within a couple of grots' lengths of him. His new armour was bulky, but surprisingly light for what it was – say what you liked about humies, they took the business of protecting themselves very seriously, and sometimes they were even good at it – and he vaulted back up to his feet to fire his shokk rifle at the humie. The blast flew wide, which might or might not have been because the humie ducked aside, but which definitely caught one of Badrukk's gitz in the back and knocked a hole in him so big that the only way he was going to survive was if his head got stuck on someone else's body, and sharpish.

The humie returned fire with some sort of big shoota that had emerged from under their left arm, balanced by two more bioniks. It was far more accurate than Ufthak, since the rounds struck him clean in the chest, but the humie armour held firm and Ufthak ignored the juddering impacts to stride through them, while ricochets whined off all around him, and swing the Snazzhammer at the humie's head.

It ducked, annoyingly, and lashed out with a pair of crack-ing powerblades. The humie's speed was astonishing; its strikes and reaction times were far quicker than anyone or anything Ufthak had fought recently, and he had to bring the Snazzhammer around in a hasty sweep to knock his enemy's blows aside. He caught a quick glance over his opponent's shoulder of Badrukk lashing out with the long, curved blade of his choppa to beat back the various waving arms of the other humie, so at least the kaptin hadn't made short work of his.

The humie's skorcha came up again, ready to fire at point-blank range, but Ufthak swatted it with the Snazzhammer and it disintegrated in an explosion that knocked the humie sideways with the force of it. This infuriatingly took it just out of reach of Ufthak's return sweep, which would have likely taken its head off, and when he took a step forward for another go the humie lunged at him with one of its blades extended. He veered aside, but it took him in the shoulder, and the pain of it caused him to let go of the shokk rifle.

'Ow!' he bellowed. 'Zoggin' little git!' He aimed a kick at the humie, but it dodged around the blow and slipped behind him as his momentum started to carry him around. It was undoubtedly seeking to plant its knives in his back.

Sucker.

Ufthak lashed out backwards with an unsighted blow of the Snazzhammer, and was rewarded when it made contact with a loud crackling noise and a satisfying shudder of impact up his arm. He finished his pirouette to find the humie flat on its back a buggy's length away, its chest now considerably dented and with smoke rising from it.

'Sorted,' Ufthak chuckled, but the humie wasn't done yet. It pushed itself back up off the ground using the weird metal wavy things coming out of its spine, although its movements were a bit less fluid than they had been a moment before. Ufthak shrugged and charged at it, the Snazzhammer raised over his head in both hands, ready to bring it down and terminally flatten his opponent.

A split second before impact, the humie sprang to meet him, too fast for his eyes to follow. There was a flurry of movement and then he was stumbling to a halt, the humie nowhere to be seen and sudden sharp, stabbing pains beneath both his arms.

The reason for the sharp, stabbing pains was the fact that the humie had buried both of its knives up to the hilt in him, when his arms had been raised. Ufthak howled in anger as his torso was wracked by burning spasms, for the power fields of the blades were still active, and he could feel the Mork-damned things cooking his flesh. He stumbled around, reaching for one of them to try to claw it out.

Metal components were erupting down the humie's arms and forming themselves into two long-clawed gauntlets, one on each of its main arms. Energy crackled across the claws as they activated.

'Oh zoggin' 'ell...'

The humie flowed forwards, sweeping its two new weapons over and across each other in dazzling offensive arcs. Ufthak, unable to fully lower his arms because of the knives still buried in him just above his ribs, was forced to back away and make the best attempts at parrying with the Snazzhammer that he could. The humie lunged for his midsection and he just managed to step back in time, then catch the other weapon on the Snazzhammer's haft as it flashed towards his head, but he couldn't keep this up.

He stumbled back another step, off balance, and the humie bunched itself up for a moment under its robes. Ufthak, seasoned warrior as he was, could see what was going to happen next: the humie was going to launch itself into the air, powered by the very unhumie-like bionic legs it had, and drive one of those sets of lightning-wrapped claws at his face. Even though he knew it was about to happen, he wasn't going to be able to dodge that blow.

The humie straightened, its legs powering it into the jump.

And then it landed again, rather more abruptly and lopsidedly than it had undoubtedly intended, because just before it had left the ground a large mouth filled with sharp, savage teeth had latched around its left ankle. Princess growled furiously, both its clawed feet scrabbling at the ground as it touched down again following its short and somewhat unexpected flight, its teeth clinging on to shiny metal and a few scraps of cloth that had been caught in its jaws. The humie looked down and uttered a stuttering, electronic blurt that nevertheless managed to convey its anger and frustration, and its entire body abruptly became wrapped in crackling power. Princess squealed, and the force of the charge blew it backwards, sending it rolling across the ground with smoke rising from it.

Ufthak had already moved. Unable to properly lower his arms to bring the Snazzhammer down, he took another step backwards and launched into a spin with the weapon held outstretched in one hand at the humie's head height. It was an attack that, if the humie had been paying attention, would never have connected.

The momentary distraction afforded by a squig becoming unexpectedly attached to its leg, on the other hand, meant that it became properly aware of what the badly wounded ork in front of it was doing just a heartbeat too late.

The Snazzhammer connected, and the contents of the humie's red hood were flattened by a combination of a warping power field and the sheer brute force of a solid metal surface impacting at high speed on something that was, when put to the test, slightly less solid. Unidentifiable pieces of machinery flew outwards, accompanied by bits of humie that, while not exactly any more identifiable, could certainly be recognised as bits that shouldn't be scattered across a wide area if their owner was going to keep on living. The humie's trunk collapsed to the ground with a clatter, and without even a final defiant buzz.

'Oh yeah!' Ufthak bellowed triumphantly. "Ow'd ya like dat, ya fancy metal git?!' He looked over at Kaptin Badrukk, just in time to see the freebooter make a final lunge with his choppa and slam the point of it right through the other humie's body, coming clean out the back. The humie wilted, all its limbs drooping at once, and Badrukk kicked it off his blade to let it slump to the floor with just as much finality as Ufthak's had. He looked over at Ufthak, and his glower was discernible even beneath the brow of his hat.

'I fink,' Ufthak said, gritting his teeth and drawing out one of the humie's powerblades, then throwing it to the ground while his own blood crackled and dried on it, 'dat yoo woz sayin' somefing about me bein' da betta ork?'

'An' 'ow're ya workin' dat one out, den?' Badrukk retorted.

'Killed mine first,' Ufthak pointed out, removing the other blade. Mork's teeth, that felt better, although he was going to be leaking for a while.

'Yer needed a squig to help ya,' Badrukk sniffed. Ufthak wandered over to Princess and nudged the squig with his boot. It burbled and managed to roll up to its feet, although it looked rather sorry for itself and had lost a few teeth. Still those would quickly be replaced. Ufthak found himself rather pleased it had survived, and realised that he'd actually become quite fond of the stupid little bitey thing.

'Call it a draw, den,' he suggested. 'Fer now. We got uvver fings to do.'

'Yeah, like–' Badrukk turned around, wincing a bit at some injury he'd been dealt in the fight, then came to a shocked standstill. 'Wot da zog've yoo lot been playin' at? Where's dat landa gone?'

'Well, it sorta flew up a bit on dese little rokkits, and den da big rokkits on da back end went *vrrrroooom* an' it went *nyeeoooooowwww* an' sorta flew off dat way, an' den up some more,' one of Badrukk's Flash Gitz replied. 'I fink,' he added, somewhat uncertainly, as his kaptin stalked towards him.

'You *fink*?' Badrukk bellowed. 'I toldja to get in dat landa, an' yer tellin' me yer ain't even sure where da zoggin' fing *went*?!'

'Yeah, but we woz sorta watchin' you an' da Bad Moon fightin' dose humies, an' da landa kinda snuck off while we woz busy. Good fight, kaptin, ya really stomped it!' the Flash Git added hopefully. 'Yoo'z da best, everyone sez so!'

Badrukk growled. Then he brought Da Rippa up and unleashed a volley of shells at his luckless subordinate, who disintegrated under the weapon's fearsome power. Everyone else standing nearby, both Flash Git and Bad Moon, took several steps backwards. Each of them was well aware that Da Kaptin could just have easily chosen them to make an example of, and in fact might still do so.

'Boss! Boss!'

That voice was considerably higher-pitched, and Ufthak recognised the ear-bothering tones of Nizkwik the grot. He stomped around to face the little git, tempted to set Princess on it as a reward for the squig's good behaviour, but the grot's next words froze the command in his throat.

'Ya gotta come an' look at dis!' Nizkwik hollered, from where it was perched on the top of the landa pad's boundary wall. 'Dere's a big metal *fing*, an' it's headin' for da MekaGargant!'

Every ork assembled there broke into a run, inter-faction rivalries forgotten in their haste to see what in the name of Gork and Mork the little runt was on about. Ufthak barged his fellows aside, using his size and weight to clear a path and scramble up the steps to the little pathway that ran around the inside of the ramparts, where presumably humie defenders would have stood if they hadn't been too busy getting their heads kicked in somewhere else instead. Once there, he looked downwards and southwards, across the city in the direction Nizkwik's black-nailed finger was pointing. The MekaGargant was advancing up one of the humie's widest roadways – one of the few routes that would accommodate it – which ran directly south, and the landa pad was high enough and situated in just the right position to give a view straight down it to where the confrontation was occurring.

Ufthak wasn't sure exactly what he'd been expecting from the grot's description – maybe another humie gargant of some sort, or one of their enormous tanks? Certainly not the enormous metal monstrosity that, as he watched, began exchanging shots with Da Meklord's greatest creation. It was a bit like someone had taken the biggest squiggoth ever bred, then made it even bigger, then made it a bit bigger again, and *then* had put a couple of massive guns on its shoulders, beefed up the front legs, split the back legs into two pairs of smaller ones, lengthened the neck, covered the entire thing in metal, and given it some tentacles on its back for the sheer hell of it. So it wasn't really that much like a squiggoth at all, Ufthak conceded to himself, but that was the closest comparison he could get in terms of things he'd seen before.

'I din't know da humies had one of dem,' Kaptin Badrukk admitted from further down the wall, scratching his forehead.

'Don't reckon dat's da humies',' Ufthak said. 'Don't look

nuffin' like da rest of what dey'z used, plus it's da wrong colour an' all.'

'Well if it ain't da humies', 'ooz is it, an' where did it come from?' Badrukk demanded. 'Don't tell me dere's one of dem pointy-earz warpy-webby gates around 'ere, wot they pop out of, shoot yer a bit an' den pop back into.' He spat. 'Can't stand da bloody pointy-earz.'

'Nah, dat looks more like one of da spiky ladz' fings,' Ufthak opined knowingly. He laughed as the MekaGargant's belly gun smashed the whatever-it-was backwards. 'Dunno where it came from, but it ain't gonna matter much. Da boss'll sort it out.'

Sure enough the supa lifta-droppa on the MekaGargant's shoulder began to glow and spark, and the strange six-legged metal brute was lifted off the ground.

'STOMP 'IM!' Ufthak's boyz began to chant, slamming their weapons on the wall in time with each other, and with the chant.

'STOMP 'IM!'

'STOMP 'IM!'

'STOMP 'IM!'

The weird metal thing fired all of its guns at the Meka-Gargant, and suddenly the force field wasn't there any more. A moment later and the lifta-droppa was destroyed, and the six-legged beast dropped back to the ground.

'STOMP...'

It didn't break. Instead, it pounced on the MekaGargant like a gargantuan squig upon its prey.

'Oh ho ho!' Badrukk crowed, as the MekaGargant started to take a proper hammering from whatever-the-hell-it-was. '"Da boss'll sort it out", will 'e? Will 'e indeed?'

Ufthak watched in shock as Da Meklord's pride and joy

was hastily disassembled with extreme violence. First one kill-saw came off, then the other, and then the enormous yellow-and-black body was opened up like a can and the generator ripped out. The bizarre monstrosity finally delivered a monstrous uppercut that knocked the MekaGargant over backwards with a crash that was audible even where they were, albeit a couple of seconds later.

'Yoo could take 'im, kaptin!' one of the Flash Gitz piped up loyally to Badrukk, who let out a tearing laugh.

'Don't need to, do we, ladz? Da Meklord's just met somefing wiv a bigger bite dan wot 'e's got, an' I don't give two shakes of a grot about 'im.' Badrukk shook his head, still chuckling. 'Nah, dat fing don't look like it's got much loot on it, an' dat's wot we'z here for. Let it go stompin' about a bit – might be funny.' He turned to Ufthak, his mouth twisted into a sneer. 'O' course, if you wanna go an' have a go at da fing wot just stomped yer precious Meklord, be my guest. Dat *will* be funny. Might even come an find ya, afterwards. Reckon you'll be pretty flat an' spread over quite a wide area, so it shouldn't be too 'ard!'

'Might jus' do dat,' Ufthak told him, sneering right back, although he could see a couple of his ladz exchanging dubious glances.

'Well, 'ave fun!' Badrukk chortled, clearly not believing a word of it. 'Come on, ladz, back to work! Dese gitz might've cleaned up out 'ere, but dere'z a big humie building right dere what's gotta have some of dere best stuff in it!'

'...dat one gettin' shelled, kaptin?' one of the Flash Gitz spoke up, accompanied by the thunder of another explosion in the near distance, and the rumble of falling masonry.

'Yeah, so get on wiv it quick!' Badrukk barked. 'Dat's an order, ya miserable lot! Get movin'!'

There was a flurry of loose salutes and variations on 'Aye-aye, kaptin!', and then the Flash Gitz were hurrying down the steps again. The door through which the humies had re-entered the landa pad still looked firmly shut, but Ufthak didn't think it would stand up long to a concerted battering from all those snazzguns.

He looked back at the thing that had destroyed the Meka-Gargant, and saw it disappear behind a huge building. It looked like it had something definite on its mind, if it had a mind, and that didn't involve ploughing into the rest of the Tekwaaagh! forces advancing through the humie city. He leaned out over the rampart and craned his neck, trying to keep track of it as it traversed the grid of roads, interspersed as they were with pockets of muzzle flare as individual fights still raged, and plumes of smoke where some enterprising ladz had found something that burned well.

'It's headin' uphill,' he muttered to himself. It wasn't coming for them, though – not for the landa pad. He turned and looked to his left, up at where the volcano's summit rose into the night sky. 'Wot's it want up dere?'

But then again, it didn't really matter what it wanted up there. What mattered was how he was going to stomp the bloody thing flat when he didn't even have a Dread, let alone a gargant. He needed something really big, really quick, and really killy…

Inspiration struck.

'You!' he barked, pointing at Nizkwik, which jumped in fright. 'Come wiv me!' He grabbed the grot before it could protest and jumped down from the rampart to the surface of the landa pad, where Da Boffin was revving his engine in frustration, since he really didn't do well with stairs.

'Some giant metal git just did for da MekaGargant,' Ufthak

told the spanner without preamble. 'Now, I gotta plan, an even betta one dan da one wot killed da humie gargant, but first I'm gonna ask ya a question, an' ya gotta be sure yer answer's right. An *you*,' he added, holding up the squirming Nizkwik, 'needs to make sure ya listens very, very carefully...'

Reach Fer Da Skies

Kaptin Badrukk was herding his Flash Gitz towards the door that separated them from the humie building, and seemed primarily focused on wielding his choppa and bellowing orders. That might have been why it took him a few seconds to realise that there had been a faint tugging sensation in the region of his waist. Ufthak saw him reach back and absent-mindedly check the back of his coat with the hand that held his choppa, and then when it didn't encounter what he'd apparently expected it to, the freebooter whirled around searching for the thief.

By that time, of course, Nizkwik was already halfway back to Ufthak and Da Boffin, an expression of stark naked terror on its face and the pilfered gizmo clutched desperately in its two skinny arms.

'Come on!' Ufthak bellowed at it. 'Run, ya zoggin' runt!'

To give it some credit, Nizkwik was definitely running as fast as its little legs could carry it. Kaptin Badrukk roared in anger and raised Da Rippa.

'Zigzag!' Da Boffin yelled, and Nizkwik veered off to one side as a blast from Badrukk's weapon chewed up the landa pad's surface. The Flash Gitz kaptin howled in rage and tried again, but now Nizkwik jinked back the other way, and the volley of deadly shells once more missed their target.

'Here ya go, boss!' the grot squealed, lobbing the gizmo at Ufthak before disappearing behind him with the apparent intention of putting a very large ork between it and further attempts at violent reprisal. Ufthak caught the piece of tek and immediately handed it to Da Boffin.

Kaptin Badrukk raised Da Rippa, pointing it straight at Ufthak. He was pretty sure not even the fancy beakie armour was going to hold up against this.

'Here goes nuffin',' Da Boffin said, which weren't exactly the most encouraging words Ufthak had ever heard, and pushed a large red button on the gizmo's side.

The world stretched out, then snapped back into place so fast Ufthak stumbled forwards. The smell of the air around him had changed, from bang-powder and smoke and the breeze of a mountainside, to oil and orks.

Lots of orks. Really strong orky smell. Many orks had been here, all at the same time, on more than one occasion.

He wasn't on the landa pad any more. He was inside somewhere, inside something that wasn't particularly big, and which had curving metal walls, and various blinking lights and flashing wotsits, and…

…and he was standing on what he realised was a telly-port pad.

'It worked!' Da Boffin shouted triumphantly, punching the air while rocking backwards and forwards on his wheel. 'It worked! We'z in da git's flyer!

'An' not *Da Blacktoof*,' he added. 'Dat could've been... interestin'.'

Ufthak grinned as widely as he'd ever grinned before. Everyone knew that Kaptin Badrukk liked to tellyport places these days now he'd taken up with Badmek Mogrok, didn't they? And Ufthak himself had seen Badrukk and his Flash Gitz tellyport down from his kustomised flyer to wreck those humie walkers, hadn't he? But who would've been smart enough to figure out that Badrukk would've needed something to tell the tellyporting wotsit when to do it and where to send him – something he might carry with him so he could tellyport back out of somewhere when he was done? And not only that, but to grab a nearby spanner and get him to quickly work out which of the many bits of bling on Badrukk it was likely to be, and *then* send a sneaky grot to go and nick it?

Ufthak zoggin' Blackhawk, that was who.

A small, pathetic sound made him turn around. Nizkwik was hunched over on the tellyport pad, and throwing up. Ufthak rolled his eyes. He hadn't wanted the grot to come along – in fact it was supposed to have been left behind, so as to give Badrukk something to work his anger out on – but he supposed the tellyport homer must have caught it up with him and Da Boffin.

A clatter of footsteps dragged his attention away from the miserable gretchin, and towards an ork in the bright colours of Badrukk's freebooterz, who skidded into the tellyport chamber and came to an abrupt halt.

''Ere, you shouldn't–'

Ufthak zapped him with the shokk rifle. It was a close enough range that he couldn't really miss, and the ork's legs collapsed as soon as his top half flashed out of existence, pulled who knew where by the mystery that was shokka technology.

'Come on!' Ufthak bellowed, surging forwards. The growl of an engine and the squeak of a tyre told him that Da Boffin was following, and he ducked through a doorway and into the cockpit. Another ork was there, flyboy goggles over its eyes, and it gaped at him for a moment too long before it tried to react. Ufthak grabbed it by the front of its fur-lined jacket and tossed it bodily out of the cockpit's roof.

Or he would have done, had the canopy been open. Instead he simply slammed the luckless flyboy into it head first.

'One second, boss,' Da Boffin said, and hit a button. The canopy popped up and swung back, and this time when Ufthak hurled the stunned freebooter upwards he tumbled out over the side of the flyer with a strangled scream.

'Get us in da air,' Ufthak ordered Da Boffin, as the spanner hit the same button to close the canopy again, just in case any particularly enthusiastic freebooterz slowed them down by climbing up and in before they were under way. 'An' where are we, anyway?'

'Dunno, boss,' Da Boffin admitted, buzzing to the controls and proceeding to throw levers, flick switches and press buttons with a precision and confidence that Ufthak found utterly baffling. But those were the mysteries of being an ork: some orks were innately good at making things work, and other orks – like Ufthak – were innately good at punching someone's teef down their throat. 'Reckon we'll find out once we're in da air.'

He pushed up a final lever, and the engines kicked in with a roar.

The flyer sprang forward, like a squig-hound which had been straining at the leash and had now been let off it.

Ufthak grabbed at one of the flyboy seats to avoid falling backwards, then wrestled himself into it, although it was more of a perching situation given the bulkiness of his armour. There was a faint, despairing wail followed by a slight *clang* from somewhere behind them, as Nizkwik bounced off something hard.

'Dat's wot I'm talkin' about!' Da Boffin laughed, somehow managing to get himself into the other flyboy seat, although it took a bit of contorting to get his mechanised lower body to fit. It suddenly occurred to Ufthak that an ork who'd replaced his own legs with a motorised wheel was possibly quite close to being a speed freek anyway, and since there was nothing a speed freek liked better than going fast, and since nothing went faster than a flyer, Da Boffin was very likely in his element.

'Up we go!' Da Boffin cackled, slamming another lever forwards. Something changed in the vehicle, because its nose abruptly began to tilt up, and as another burst of acceleration hit, Ufthak felt the familiar dropping sensation in his stomach which told him that they'd left the ground behind them.

'Let's 'ave a look,' Ufthak muttered, levering himself up to squint out of the cockpit's sides. Now they were off the ground he could get a better idea of where they were, and even though night had come, he'd got enough of a look at the layout of the humie city when he'd been coming down in his landa – before it had been blown out of the air – to more or less remember where everything was. That was another thing he was good at: remembering the layout of a battlefield from a quick glance. Otherwise how would you know the quickest way to get to whichever gitz you were trying to stomp? Sometimes they tried to shoot your face off if you stuck it up to take a look too many times.

'Dat way!' he instructed Da Boffin, pointing out of the cockpit to the right. The flyer had been set down on a large, mostly clear area of flat ground some way to the west of the main humie city, close up against a few buildings. Said ground was now crawling with orks, along with a whole slew of vehicles laden down with squig cages, dakka crates and all the other stuff that rolled along in the wake of an ork offensive. Some of the orks were jumping up and down and waving their fists, or sometimes weapons; Ufthak waved back cheerily, then turned to face the direction in which he'd instructed Da Boffin to take them.

There were still some lights on in the humie city, although there were gaping holes of darkness, and other, larger glows where fires raged. However, the main light source visible was the smouldering red of the volcano, roiling away at its summit and spitting the occasional spark into the air. If Ufthak squinted, he was fairly sure he could make out a large, dark shape scaling the mountainside, now above even the highest line of humie buildings. It was dwarfed by the scale of the volcano, but the fact he could make it out at all from here still spoke to its sheer size.

There it was. The Gargant-Killer.

Da Boffin hauled the flysticks around, and the flyer banked in the air. There were no anti-flyer guns shooting up at them now, and even the rest of the shimmering force field dome that had covered the main city was down, so there was nothing to prevent them from taking the fastest route directly towards their quarry.

'Wot in da name of Mork's Teef is *dat?*' Da Boffin asked in utter astonishment as the volcano grew larger in front of them, and he saw what Ufthak was directing them towards.

'You neva seen nuffin' like it before?' Ufthak asked him.

A pity: he'd have liked to know who to blame for this particular annoyance.

'No, boss,' Da Boffin admitted, 'dis is a new one on me. An' wot's it doin'?'

The Gargant-Killer had reached the summit, and looked to be smashing at the rock there with its enormous forelimbs. Even as Ufthak watched, he saw it rear up and then bring both crackling fists down in a colossal hammer blow that splintered stone and sent newly made boulders tumbling away, some down the mountainside towards the city and some into the red-lit crater.

'Don't care,' he said flatly. 'Ya know where da gunz are on dis fing?'

'Yes, boss,' Da Boffin said, curling his fingers around big red triggers on the flysticks. They were coming up fast on the Gargant-Killer, which was still apparently intent on smashing a bit of the mountain into smithereens, for reasons Ufthak couldn't guess at.

'Den let it have it,' Ufthak ordered him. 'All of it!'

'Yes, boss!'

Da Boffin squeezed the triggers, but instead of the guttural roar of the flyer's entire payload being released to scream across the intervening gap and blast the Gargant-Killer into wherever it was that would be waiting for it, all that emerged from the body of the craft was a thin line of big shoota fire. It struck home, sure enough, but it didn't have the desired effect: the monster's head snapped up and around, but all they'd done was attract its attention.

'Dat's it?!' Ufthak bellowed, infuriated and astonished.

'Dat's it!' Da Boffin echoed him. 'I don't get it, dat's definitely da trigger–'

'Move!' Ufthak yelled, as the Gargant-Killer's mouth opened

and revealed a green-white glow that looked decidedly unhealthy. He grabbed one of the flysticks and shoved it, and the flyer responded by rolling sideways just as the Gargant-Killer vomited a blast of energy at them, as though it were some sort of gigantic weirdboy.

'We got anyfing else?' Ufthak demanded, as Da Boffin brought the flyer back under control again and they climbed for the sky, weaving back and forth. 'Wot about bombs? We got any bombs?'

'Don't look like it, boss,' Da Boffin reported sadly, tapping gauges. 'I dunno, maybe dey was reloading, an' dat's why it woz on da ground? Looks like dat big shoota's da only fing wiv any dakka.'

'Dere's gotta be somefing,' Ufthak muttered angrily. 'Bring us around again! I want anuvver go at it!'

'But, boss–'

'Dat's an order!' Ufthak barked. He grabbed the triggers of the flysticks in front of his seat. 'I ain't come dis far to go back wivvout killin' dat fing!'

'All right, boss, here we go,' Da Boffin said, although Ufthak was fairly sure he could hear reluctance in the spanner's voice. Da Boffin pulled the flysticks around and sent them back towards the Gargant-Killer, which was now rearing up and outlined in shadow by the glow of the volcano's fires behind it. The ripping fire of its own kannons, kannons far more power-ful than the pitiful big shoota of Badrukk's flyer, began flashing towards them, and Da Boffin dived to take them under it.

'Alright, ya ugly git,' Ufthak snarled at the Gargant-Killer. 'Time ta die!'

He squeezed the triggers on his flysticks.

The big shoota coughed out a few more rounds, then ran dry.

'Oh, zoggin' hell...'

'Boss! Boss!' Nizkwik burst into the cockpit and scrambled up onto the arm of Ufthak's chair. 'Where are we? Wot's goin' on? I–' It peered over the dash, saw the Gargant-Killer, and screamed. 'Arrrgh! Boss! It's da fing! We gotta kill it!'

The grot cast around frantically, saw a big red button on the dash, made the reasonable assumption that a big red button controlled the weapons, and tried to stamp on it as hard as it could.

'No!' Da Boffin shouted, grabbing its foot before it made contact. 'Dat's da ejecta!'

Ufthak looked at the button, looked back up at the Gargant-Killer looming larger and larger in his field of view, and came to a decision.

'Good enuff.'

He hit the button.

The canopy above them blew off, and then both seats were propelled upwards by explosive charges hidden beneath them as the ejecta activated. Ufthak's stomach dropped away as he rose up into the air, with Nizkwik still clinging to one arm of the chair and howling in utter terror. The flyer shot by underneath them, its thrustas burning as hard as they could go and leaving white spots in his retinas, on a direct collision course with the Gargant-Killer.

The Gargant-Killer's guns found the flyer, but when the fuel in the wings exploded it simply turned an enormous metal missile into an enormous, partially flaming metal missile. By the time the Gargant-Killer realised that its attacker wasn't going to be changing course, it was too late for it to move out of the way. Ufthak met the Gargant-Killer's eyes for a solitary moment just before the impact occurred, eyes that burned with an internal fire, and the strangest sensation he'd ever experienced ran through him. If he'd had the vocabulary to describe it, he might have said that it felt like a mark had been laid upon his soul.

The flyer struck the gigantic beast straight in the chest. The speed and force of its impact was so great that the flyer splintered into wreckage, but the Gargant-Killer's torso was crushed and ripped open, and one massive foreleg was torn clean off. It was knocked backwards by the impact and seemed to hang in the air for a moment, clawing at the sky with its remaining foreleg in a futile attempt to escape the grip of gravity, but to no avail. It dropped out of sight, and a moment later there was a slightly brighter flare of light, which was all the indication the volcano gave that the Gargant-Killer and the remains of Kaptin Badrukk's flyer had fallen into the lava lake.

There was the scream, though. That was high, and harsh, and titanically loud, and lasted for longer than it probably should have done. However, alarming though it was, Ufthak had other things on his mind: namely that the upwards arc of the chair he'd been sitting in had come to an end, and he was about to fall a long way towards the mountainside below, unless a building on the uppermost edge of the city happened to catch his fall first – and he was fairly certain that wouldn't necessarily be an improvement.

Also, although the chair had boosted him upwards, since flyboyz didn't believe in such things as straps it was now falling away from him, *but the bloody grot was still clinging to his arm*. Ufthak couldn't imagine a more humiliating way to die than having a grot clinging to you.

'Boss!' Da Boffin shouted, slapping himself in the chest. 'Green button! *Green button!*'

Ufthak blinked, looked down at his chest and, as gravity got its teeth into him and began to truly draw him down towards his doom, slapped the blinking green button on the right side of his chestplate.

The bulky backpack let out a roar, and suddenly he was flying again! It was a back rokkit, like what stormboyz had! Using a rokkit pack was a bit like riding a squiggoth: once you learned how, you never forgot. Or sometimes you did forget, and then you died, but no one had ever forgotten more than once.

Nizkwik shrieked again, as though flying were somehow more terrifying than falling to its death. Grots. It was like the gods had shrunk humies and made them green, for some joke only they could fathom.

Ufthak leaned forward, and grinned as the wind whipped around him. Now he plummeted downwards, faster than he would have been falling, but also faster than Da Boffin was falling, and as he approached him Ufthak reached out a hand and seized the flailing spanner by the back of his jacket, right where the leering yellow crescent of the Bad Moons was stitched on. Then he swung his feet back down, getting the blast of the rokkits under him once again and swooping low over the first streets that formed the part of the humie city that had encroached the furthest up the mountain, and killed their momentum just in time to hover three feet or so above the ground.

He dropped Da Boffin, who landed on his wheel and, through some teknologickal marvel of internal gyro-wotsits, managed not to fall over. Then Ufthak held Nizkwik up in front of him.

'Cor,' the grot said, its eyes wide. 'Fanks, boss! I fort I was–'

Ufthak dropped it, then as it fell squawking towards the ground, booted it. Nizkwik described a long, looping, wailing arc, and landed somewhere out of sight in what looked and smelled like a place where humies dumped their trash.

'Hah!' Ufthak laughed. Truly, sometimes the simple pleasures were the best. He flicked the green button again which, as he'd hoped, turned the engines off, and landed next to Da Boffin. 'Well, dat's dat. Killed da zoggin' fing. Do ya s'pose any of da ladz saw it?'

'Uft-hak!'

He looked up.

'UFT-HAK!'

The chant was going up from rooftops, and from windows, and a mob of yellow-and-black-clad shapes emerged out from behind a building, laden down with what might have been loot, and might have been junk, and dragging what was almost certainly half a dead humie behind them.

'*UFT-HAK!*'

'Yes, boss,' Da Boffin said with a grin. 'I reckon some of da ladz saw it.'

Da Fires of Hephaesto

Da Meklord wasn't dead. Ufthak had been in the middle of a group of orks chanting his name when they'd parted, and he'd looked up to see the looming presence of Da Biggest Big Mek advancing on him.

'Dat big git flattened da MekaGargant right enuff,' Da Meklord had chuckled, 'but it's gonna take more dan dat to get rid of me! Ripped da generator out in da chest, dinnit? Didn't touch da head. Obviously we got knocked about a bit when da zoggin' fing got knocked over, but if ya ain't survived one gargant wreck, ya ain't lived!'

He'd looked thoughtfully up at the volcano's summit, and rubbed his jaw. 'Yer certain ya got it, den?'

'Yes, boss,' Ufthak had said, and he'd said it with respect, but perhaps not quite the same sort of respect as he'd have said it the day before. He'd killed a gargant. He'd knocked in a force field using only the Snazzhammer. He'd outkilled Kaptin Badrukk – squigs be damned. To top it all off, he'd killed a Gargant-Killer, the Gargant-Killer that had killed Da Meklord's MekaGargant. He felt he was entitled to be bloody proud of himself. 'Def'nit. Fell into da volcano.'

'Well, I fink we'z cleaned out da city of mosta da good stuff,' Da Meklord had replied, eyeing him. 'I wanna go an' take a look up dere. See wot's wot.'

And so the assembled orks had trudged up the mountain-side, all the way to the top, to the shattered rim of the crater where the Gargant-Killer had been battering at the rock. And then Da Meklord looked over the edge, and Ufthak saw his eyes widen.

'Well, Mork bite me,' Da Meklord whistled through his teef. 'Dere's a bit of dat git Badrukk's flyer down dere.'

Ufthak stepped up beside him and peered down as well, screwing up his eyes against the fierce light of the lava that bubbled below, and saw what Da Meklord had seen: a piece of fuselage strewn on the interior slope that hadn't fallen into the crater, with just enough paint clinging on to be recognisable as Flash Git colours.

'Ya didn't fink I woz lyin', didja?' Ufthak asked. He suddenly became aware how easy it would be to push Da Meklord, or barge into him, and knock him clean off the crater's edge and send him skidding down that same steep internal crater wall towards the lava below. And he might catch himself, and he might not, but if he didn't... well, it was Ufthak whose name had been chanted not that long ago, not any other ork's.

'Course I didn't,' Da Meklord guffawed, clapping Ufthak on the shoulder with a meaty blow that almost, but not quite, made him lose his balance and topple in; that almost, but not quite, sent him skidding down that steep internal crater wall towards the lava below. And had that happened then he might have caught himself, and he might not. 'Just wanted to see fer meself, dat's all. Pity dere's none of dat big git left. I'd have liked to give it a good kickin', even if it couldn't feel it no more.'

Ufthak nodded, and took a step back from the edge. Just in case.

'Dat new armour ya got dere?' Da Meklord asked, looking Ufthak up and down. Or rather, down and more down, since he was taller... but not by as much as Ufthak remembered.

'Yes, boss,' Ufthak replied. 'Some sorta beakie fing. It ain't bad, but nuffin' an ork can't improve on. Da Boffin's already had a crack at it. An' I'll get it all painted up in proper colourz, too.'

'Get anyfing else?' Da Meklord asked, taking his own step away from the crater rim, the small stones beneath his feet crunching and crushing beneath the weight of him in his mega armour. 'Anyfing for ya boss?'

Ufthak beamed at him. 'Oh yes. Show 'im, Boffin.'

Da Boffin chugged up, carefully managing the steep and slippery terrain in a manner that Ufthak was pretty sure an ork buggy on four wheels couldn't have managed, let alone a spanner on one. Da Boffin handed over a whole fistful of those oblongs of metal and glass he'd been so excited about back at the landa pad. 'Here ya go, boss. Whole loada humie weapon plans. Dere's a partic'ly dakka one in dere, fer a big kannon what goes on da front of a kroozer...'

'Dat's wot I'm talkin' about!' Da Meklord proclaimed happily, seizing them with barely disguised greed. He raised his voice. 'Alright, you lot, lissen up! Dis 'ere's Ufthak Blackhawk, an' 'e killed da fing wot bashed in da MekaGargant! So from now on, yer callin' 'im da Big Boss, right? If 'e says ya do somefing, ya do it! Unless I sez uvverwise,' he finished, with a sidelong look at Ufthak, but Ufthak didn't care. Big

Boss! A Big Boss could tell nobz what to do! And he might have to clobber a couple, but he reckoned that shouldn't be any problem. The main thing was, Da Meklord knew who he was now. That meant he'd get into all the best fights, and get his pick of all the best loot...

'Gerrout da way, ya scurvy squigs!'

Ufthak tensed. He knew that voice.

'I said move, or yer gonna taste Da Rippa!' the bellowing voice ordered, and Bad Moons shuffled reluctantly aside to reveal the scowling, gaudily dressed and impressively hatted shape of Kaptin Badrukk.

'You!' he bawled, pointing at Ufthak. 'You stole my flyer! And den you crashed into dat fing, and *wrecked* it!'

Ufthak didn't see any point in denying it. 'Yeah.' He tightened his grip on the Snazzhammer. He was Big Boss now, and that meant he didn't back down from anyone. 'An' wot ya gonna do about it?'

A few tense moments followed, where every ork present eyed their neighbours and got ready to start breaking heads.

A broad, toothy grin spread across Badrukk's face.

'Nuffin'.'

Ufthak's forehead wrinkled in confusion. 'Nuffin'?'

'Nuffin'!' Badrukk repeated. 'Oh, I woz gonna kill ya when yer grot nicked me tellyport homer and ya disappeared, an' doubly so when I realised yer'd nicked me flyer, but den I saw ya crash it into dat fing an' I ain't gonna lie, dat was *brilliant*. I ain't even mad! Prob'ly time fer me to get an upgrade, anyhow.'

Ufthak felt utterly wrong-footed. He'd expected some sort of repercussion from nicking the Flash Git's personal flyer, and here Badrukk was, laughing and saying it was no problem? Ufthak wasn't really sure how he felt about that. After all, a fight was a fight, and a fight was good, but there were a lot of orks here, and every ork that died would be one less to go and fight things that weren't orks somewhere else, and so that would have seemed sort of a waste.

'Maybe I'll nick dat one, too,' he said, feeling something of the sort was expected of him, but Badrukk took no notice.

'What I wanna know, is wot dat fing woz doin' up 'ere,' the kaptin said. 'Couldn't make it out from where I woz.'

'It was diggin', or somefing,' Ufthak said, pointing at the mess of broken rock beneath their feet. Some orks were standing on it, but most were staying off it. 'Dunno wot for.'

'I reckon dat's worf findin' out,' Badrukk said, with a gleam in his eye. 'Come on, ladz, let's get shiftin' dis stuff!'

The Flash Gitz with him bent to it, picking up pieces of rock and throwing them away. Not wanting to be outdone, the Bad Moons joined in, and soon the night was full of smashed boulders being hurled down the mountain as far as ork muscles could propel them, with each hurler claiming victory due to either distance achieved, or weight of the rock thrown, or both.

Before long, most of the debris had been cleared away and the faint gleam of metal was revealed. It was longer and wider than several orks laid out head to boot, and it was dented, from where the Gargant-Killer had been hammering down on the rock above it, and in one place it had been punctured.

'Dat ain't much,' one of the Flash Gitz said.

'Dat ain't wot we're lookin' for,' Da Meklord replied, his own interest clearly now piqued. 'Dat's a roof, or a lid, or somefing. Wotever it is we're after will be inside.' He activated the twirling heads of his shokkhammer. 'Let's get it open!'

He brought the famous and feared weapon down. There was a bright blue flash, and a large chunk of the metal disappeared to reveal a dark gulf beneath. However, Ufthak's keen eyes could just make out a further reflection down in the gloom.

'Dere's definitely somefing in dere!' he shouted.

'You 'eard Da Meklord!' Badrukk bellowed, and the rest of the ladz set to with choppas and power klaws. It was a matter of moments before the lid – or roof – was cut open and prised apart, and they stood around looking down at…

…well, Ufthak still wasn't sure. It certainly looked very impressive, he had to give it that. It was probably about the size of a trukk, and covered with intricate vents and lots of flashing lights – humies did love flashing lights – not to mention various dials and levers. It was humming gently, but didn't seem about to explode, so that was something.

Kaptin Badrukk hopped down into the gap between the thing and the wall of the chamber it had been enclosed in, and proceeded to walk around it, prodding at it. Ufthak heard a couple of metallic *clanks* as he progressed.

'Well?' Da Meklord said. 'Wossit look like?'

Ufthak became suddenly aware that, of course, there were two warlords here, and only one of them would be able to claim this whatever-it-was. If Badrukk said it was valuable, Da Meklord would fight him for it, which meant Ufthak and the Bad Moons would be fighting the Flash Gitz. If Badrukk said it *wasn't* valuable, Da Meklord would think he was trying to pull a fast one, and they'd probably end up fighting anyway.

Clank

'Well?' Da Meklord shouted again, as Badrukk continued walking around the machine. 'Wot d'ya see?'

Kaptin Badrukk placed a small, shiny gizmo on the machine, which stuck to it with a *clank*, then looked up at Da Meklord and at Ufthak.

He grinned.

'A pair of suckas.'

He pressed a button on his cuff and four bright flashes of light lit up the hole, one from each corner of the machine, one from the site of each *clank*. When the light died down again a moment later, Badrukk was gone.

And so was the machine.

'Why, ya little–!' Da Meklord roared, turning and shaking his fist at the sky above them. Somewhere up there, Ufthak suspected, Kaptin Badrukk had just appeared back on *Da Blacktoof* with all the loot he'd collected from his rampage through the humie city, plus the mysterious piece of humie tech they'd just uncovered.

'You lot!' Da Meklord bellowed, turning his wrath on the assembled Flash Gitz who, much to their chagrin, hadn't been tellyported back up with their kaptin. Da Biggest Big Mek didn't even bother to speak again, but his kustom mega-blasta fizzed and whined as it began to power up. Seeing the way the squigs were running, the Flash Gitz thought quickly and came to the same conclusion.

'Never liked 'im much anyway...'

'...not much of a kaptin...'

'...Da Meklord, now dat's an ork wot's goin' places...'

'...come wiv our own gunz!'

Da Meklord growled deep in his throat, and so incandescent was his rage that it felt like the very ground was trembling in sympathy with it.

Actually, Ufthak realised, it was. Trembling, at any rate. He couldn't be quite sure of the cause, but that seemed rather less important right now than the fact that the red glow behind him was suddenly more marked, as though the lava creating it was beginning to rise.

'Everyone down da mountain!' he bellowed, just as Da Meklord was about to vaporise a Flash Git and start a real brawl. Orks were nothing if they weren't survivors – well, unless there was a particularly tasty brawl on offer, where the joy of a good scrap outweighed the possibility of getting killed – and so it only took a moment for the rest of them to work out what he was yelling about, and that you probably couldn't fight a volcano. Within a second, a mass stampede had begun.

Ufthak slapped the green button on his chest again, but his backpack merely coughed once and boosted him a few strides, then died. Zogging humie tech, you couldn't trust it.

Other plumes of bright, burning red were rising now, searing aside the night as they oozed forth from the earth: not fast, not truly fast, but fast enough, and completely, utterly unstoppable. Ufthak saw one new tongue of molten rock burn its way through a wall in seconds.

'Back to da landas!' Da Meklord bellowed from beside him, getting as much speed as he could out of his mega armour. 'Back to da landas, and get off da planet!'

'We're givin' da planet up?' Ufthak asked his boss in surprise. He'd thought they'd just get out of the way and let the mountain tire itself out, like they sometimes did.

'I got wot I wanted,' Da Meklord growled. 'If wot Da Boffin said is true, da humies wot woz here had some real good weapon plans, and wot a humie makes dat's good, orks can make betta. We're gonna tool up da Waaagh! fleet, and den we're gonna start wreckin' worlds so bad dat even Gork an' Mork 'emselves are gonna sit up and take notice!'

Even charging down a mountain, even running away from an erupting volcano, Da Meklord still found the time and the breath to spit.

'But before we do, we're gonna test da lot on Kaptin *zoggin'* Badrukk…'

ABOUT THE AUTHOR

Mike Brooks is a science fiction and fantasy
author who lives in Nottingham, UK. His work
for Black Library includes the Horus Heresy
Primarchs novel *Alpharius: Head of the Hydra*,
the Warhammer 40,000 novels *Rites of Passage*
and *Brutal Kunnin*, the Necromunda novel *Road
to Redemption* and the novella *Wanted: Dead*,
and various short stories. When not writing, he
plays guitar and sings in a punk band, and DJs
wherever anyone will tolerate him.

YOUR
NEXT READ

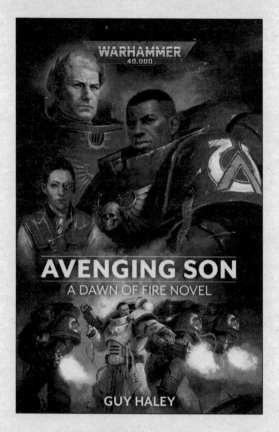

AVENGING SON
by Guy Haley

By the will of the reborn primarch Roboute Guilliman, the Indomitus Crusade spreads across the galaxy, bringing the Emperor's light back to the Dark Imperium. In the Machorta Sound, a desperate mission could determine the fate of the crusade – and battle is joined…

An extract from
Avenging Son
by Guy Haley

'I was there at the Siege of Terra,' Vitrian Messinius would
say in his later years.

'I was there…' he would add to himself, his words never
meant for ears but his own. 'I was there the day the Imperium died.'

But that was yet to come.

'To the walls! To the walls! The enemy is coming!' Captain Messinius, as he was then, led his Space Marines across
the Penitent's Square high up on the Lion's Gate. 'Another
attack! Repel them! Send them back to the warp!'

Thousands of red-skinned monsters born of fear and sin
scaled the outer ramparts, fury and murder incarnate. The
mortals they faced quailed. It took the heart of a Space
Marine to stand against them without fear, and the Angels
of Death were in short supply.

'Another attack, move, move! To the walls!'

They came in the days after the Avenging Son returned,

emerging from nothing, eight legions strong, bringing the bulk of their numbers to bear against the chief entrance to the Imperial Palace. A decapitation strike like no other, and it came perilously close to success.

Messinius' Space Marines ran to the parapet edging the Penitent's Square. On many worlds, the square would have been a plaza fit to adorn the centre of any great city. Not on Terra. On the immensity of the Lion's Gate, it was nothing, one of hundreds of similarly huge spaces. The word 'gate' did not suit the scale of the cityscape. The Lion's Gate's bulk marched up into the sky, step by titanic step, until it rose far higher than the mountains it had supplanted. The gate had been built by the Emperor Himself, they said. Myths detailed the improbable supernatural feats required to raise it. They were lies, all of them, and belittled the true effort needed to build such an edifice. Though the Lion's Gate was made to His design and by His command, the soaring monument had been constructed by mortals, with mortal hands and mortal tools. Messinius wished that had been remembered. For men to build this was far more impressive than any godly act of creation. If men could remember that, he believed, then perhaps they would remember their own strength.

The uncanny may not have built the gate, but it threatened to bring it down. Messinius looked over the rampart lip, down to the lower levels thousands of feet below and the spread of the Anterior Barbican.

Upon the stepped fortifications of the Lion's Gate was armour of every colour and the blood of every loyal primarch. Dozens of regiments stood alongside them. Aircraft filled the sky. Guns boomed from every quarter. In the churning redness on the great roads, processional ways so huge they were akin to prairies cast in rockcrete, were flashes of gold where the Emperor's Custodian Guard battled. The might of the Imperium was gathered there, in the palace where He dwelt.

There seemed moments on that day when it might not be enough.

The outer ramparts were carpeted in red bodies that writhed and heaved, obscuring the great statues adorning the defences and covering over the guns, an invasive cancer consuming reality. The enemy were legion. There were too many foes to defeat by plan and ruse. Only guns, and will, would see the day won, but the defenders were so pitifully few.

Messinius called a wordless halt, clenched fist raised, seeking the best place to deploy his mixed company, veterans all of the Terran Crusade. Gunships and fighters sped overhead, unleashing deadly light and streams of bombs into the packed daemonic masses. There were innumerable cannons crammed onto the gate, and they all fired, rippling the structure with false earthquakes. Soon the many ships and orbital defences of Terra would add their guns, targeting the very world they were meant to guard, but the attack had come so suddenly; as yet they had had no time to react.

The noise was horrendous. Messinius' audio dampers were at maximum and still the roar of ordnance stung his ears. Those humans that survived today would be rendered deaf. But he would have welcomed more guns, and louder still, for all the defensive fury of the assailed palace could not drown out the hideous noise of the daemons – their sighing hisses, a billion serpents strong, and chittering, screaming wails. It was not only heard but sensed within the soul, the realms of spirit and of matter were so intertwined. Messinius' being would be forever stained by it.

Tactical information scrolled down his helmplate, near environs only. He had little strategic overview of the situation. The vox-channels were choked with a hellish screaming that made communication impossible. The noosphere was disrupted by etheric backwash spilling from the immaterial rifts the daemons poured through. Messinius was used to operating on his own. Small-scale, surgical actions were the way of the Adeptus Astartes, but in a battle of this scale, a lack of central coordination would lead inevitably to defeat. This was not like the first Siege, where his kind had fought in Legions.

He called up a company-wide vox-cast and spoke to his warriors. They were not his Chapter-kin, but they would listen. The primarch himself had commanded that they do so.

'Reinforce the mortals,' he said. 'Their morale is wavering. Position yourselves every fifty yards. Cover the whole of the south-facing front. Let them see you.' He directed his warriors by chopping at the air with his left hand. His right, bearing an inactive power fist, hung heavily at his side. 'Assault Squad Antiocles, back forty yards, single firing line. Prepare to engage enemy breakthroughs only on my mark. Devastators, split to demi-squads and take up high ground, sergeant and sub-squad prime's discretion as to positioning and target. Remember our objective, heavy infliction of casualties. We kill as many as we can, we retreat, then hold at the Penitent's Arch until further notice. Command squad, with me.'

Command squad was too grand a title for the mismatched crew Messinius had gathered around himself. His own officers were light years away, if they still lived.

'Doveskamor, Tidominus,' he said to the two Aurora Marines with him. 'Take the left.'

'Yes, captain,' they voxed, and jogged away, their green armour glinting orange in the hell-light of the invasion.

The rest of his scratch squad was comprised of a communications specialist from the Death Spectres, an Omega Marine with a penchant for plasma weaponry, and a Raptor holding an ancient standard he'd taken from a dusty display.

'Why did you take that, Brother Kryvesh?' Messinius asked, as they moved forward.

'The palace is full of such relics,' said the Raptor. 'It seems only right to put them to use. No one else wanted it.'

Messinius stared at him.

'What? If the gate falls, we'll have more to worry about than my minor indiscretion. It'll be good for morale.'

The squads were splitting to join the standard humans. Such was the noise many of the men on the wall had not noticed their arrival, and a ripple of surprise went along the line as they appeared at their sides. Messinius was glad to see they seemed more firm when they turned their eyes back outwards.

'Anzigus,' he said to the Death Spectre. 'Hold back, facilitate communication within the company. Maximum signal gain. This interference will only get worse. See if you can get us patched in to wider theatre command. I'll take a hardline if you can find one.'

'Yes, captain,' said Anzigus. He bowed a helm that was bulbous with additional equipment. He already had the access flap of the bulky vox-unit on his arm open. He withdrew, the aerials on his power plant extending. He headed towards a systems nexus on the far wall of the plaza, where soaring buttresses pushed back against the immense weight bearing down upon them.

Messinius watched him go. He knew next to nothing about Anzigus. He spoke little, and when he did, his voice was funereal. His Chapter was mysterious, but the same lack of familiarity held true for many of these warriors, thrown together by miraculous events. Over their years lost wandering in the warp, Messinius had come to see some as friends as well as comrades, others he hardly knew, and none he knew so well as his own Chapter brothers. But they would stand together. They were Space Marines. They had fought by the returned primarch's side, and in that they shared a bond. They would not stint in their duty now.

Messinius chose a spot on the wall, directing his other veterans to left and right. Kryvesh he sent to the mortal officer's side. He looked down again, out past the enemy and over the outer palace. Spires stretched away in every direction. Smoke rose from all over the landscape. Some of it was new, the work of the daemon horde, but Terra had been burning for weeks. The Astronomican had failed. The galaxy was split in two. Behind them in the sky turned the great palace gyre, its deep eye marking out the throne room of the Emperor Himself.

'Sir!' A member of the Palatine Guard shouted over the din. He pointed downwards, to the left. Messinius followed his wavering finger. Three hundred feet below, daemons were climbing. They came upwards in a triangle tipped by a brute with a double rack of horns. It clambered hand over hand, far faster than should be possible, flying upwards, as if it touched the side of the towering gate only as a concession to reality. A Space Marine with claw locks could not have climbed that fast.

'Soldiers of the Imperium! The enemy is upon us!'

He looked to the mortals. Their faces were blanched with fear. Their weapons shook. Their bravery was commendable nonetheless. Not one of them attempted to run, though a wave of terror preceded the unnatural things clambering up towards them.

'We shall not turn away from our duty, no matter how fearful the foe, or how dire our fates may be,' he said. 'Behind us is the Sanctum of the Emperor Himself. As He has watched over you, now it is your turn to stand in guardianship over Him.'

The creatures were drawing closer. Through a sliding, magnified window on his display, Messinius looked into the yellow and cunning eyes of their leader. A long tongue lolled permanently from the thing's mouth, licking at the wall, tasting the terror of the beings it protected.

Boltgun actions clicked. His men leaned over the parapet, towering over the mortals as the Lion's Gate towered over the Ultimate Wall. A wealth of targeting data was exchanged, warrior to warrior, as each chose a unique mark. No bolt would be wasted in the opening fusillade. They could hear the creatures' individual shrieks and growls, all wordless, but their meaning was clear: blood, blood, blood. Blood and skulls.

Messinius sneered at them. He ignited his power fist with a swift jerk. He always preferred the visceral thrill of manual activation. Motors came to full life. Lightning crackled around it. He aimed downwards with his bolt pistol. A reticule danced over diabolical faces, each a copy of all the others. These things were not real. They were not alive. They were projections of a false god. The Librarian Atramo had named them maladies. A spiritual sickness wearing ersatz flesh.

He reminded himself to be wary. Contempt was as thick as any armour, but these things were deadly, for all their unreality.

He knew. He had fought the Neverborn many times before.

'While He lives,' Messinius shouted, boosting his voxmitter gain to maximal, 'we stand!'

'For He of Terra!' the humans shouted, their battle cry loud enough to be heard over the booming of guns.

'For He of Terra,' said Messinius. 'Fire!' he shouted.

The Space Marines fired first. Boltguns spoke, spitting spikes of rocket flare into the foe. Bolts slammed into daemon bodies, bursting them apart. Black viscera exploded away. Black ichor showered those coming after. The daemons' false souls screamed back whence they came, though their bones and offal tumbled down like those of any truly living foe.

Las-beams speared next, and the space between the wall top and the scaling party filled with violence. The daemons were unnaturally resilient, protected from death by the energies of the warp, and though many were felled, others weathered the fire, and clambered up still, unharmed and uncaring of their dead. Messinius no longer needed his helm's magnification to see into the daemon champion's eyes. It stared at him, its smile a promise of death. The terror that preceded them was replaced by the urge to violence, and that gripped them all, foe and friend. The baseline humans began to lose their discipline. A man turned and shot his comrade, and was shot down in turn. Kryvesh banged the foot of his borrowed banner and called them back into line. Elsewhere, his warriors sang; not their Chapter warsongs, but battle hymns known to all. Wavering human voices joined them. The feelings of violence abated, just enough.

Then the things were over the parapet and on them.